Points of Origin

By

John L. Orr

INFINITY
PUBLISHING

Copyright © 2008 by John L. Orr

ISBN 978-0-7414-4191-8

Cover Concept   *Christopher A. Master*

Printed in the United States of America

Published November 2012

INFINITY PUBLISHING

Toll-free (877) BUY BOOK
Local Phone (610) 941-9999
Fax (610) 941-9959
Info@buybooksontheweb.com
www.buybooksontheweb.com

To my brothers and sisters
in law enforcement
and the fire service.
The same, but different.
- June 1991 -

Foreword

When I outlined the manuscript of Points of Origin in 1989-1990, I had no formal fiction writing experience. The first draft sat gathering dust in a file in my home office, in my briefcase, a few notes in a firehouse locker, and a pile of "idea cards" littered the trunk of my on-duty car.

It was not until I enrolled in a Glendale Community College fiction writing course, in February 1990, that actual chapters appeared on my low-tech Hewlett Packard personal computer. The instructor of the college course, Les Roberts, a successful TV producer and published author of fiction, motivated me to produce the book. His teachings were basic, but the eight-week course fascinated me. Famous as he was, informal after-class discussions revealed the man approachable and a gifted mentor. On emergency call-out standby for half the sessions, held at a local high school campus, Les tolerated my periodic unannounced departures and jackrabbit exits from the nearby faculty parking lot when I was paged to a fire or explosion scene.

Near the end of the course, Les said, as a final exam, he would give a professional critique of three chapters of any manuscript his students produced. At that time, in May 1990, I wrote fiction in the same format as the 6-8 police/investigative supplemental reports I produced weekly for the Glendale (CA) Fire and Police Departments. What little instruction I had to that point consisted of a one-day search warrant affidavit course, but over 11 years experience producing police reports. Points of Origin started out like many of the articles I already had published in the *American Fire Journal* since 1982: pretty dry, cut-to-the-chase narrative. Still, Mister Roberts encouraged me to continue writing fiction. With a few suggested reference books and a subscription to *Writer's Digest* magazine, I launched a real effort to complete Points of Origin.

Over the next twelve months I took the basic idea of a firefighter-gone-bad plot and launched the pursuit of a fictional bad guy. Even with the reference books and Les' class, Points still came out as pretty barren reading, I thought. In the first chapter, I introduced the antagonist, Aaron-the-pyro and the fictional "evidence" I put on paper made the protagonist's chase take a natural investigative progression.

With 6-8 new real-life criminal cases assigned to me on-duty each week, Aaron stayed on my radar as just another entry on my daily-to-do list. Sneaking home on lunch hours and sitting in front of my PC on weekends and holidays, Points grew legs and moved forward, along with pipe bomber and insurance fraud arrests I made. Several of my actual cases took a year or more to lead to an arrest so Points fit nicely into my schedule.

One of Les Robert's lessons, character development, stressed making your protagonist likeable, the antagonist reprehensible, and "write-what-you-know" in your first efforts. I followed the guidelines faithfully, modeling Aaron after several of the more mysterious serial arsonists I apprehended in my 12-year law enforcement career. There was never any question my protagonist, Phil Langtry, was based on me, my assignment, investigative style, and successes. I wrote what I knew. The task was pretty simple. Until I neared completion of the manuscript.

Points started out with Aaron setting small nuisance fires, secretly sneaking around in darkened alleys, like a typically insecure firebug He gets bolder, but only to set drive-by daylight brush and grass fires.

In September 1990, I received a Be-On-the-Lookout (BOLO) flyer in my office, from the Bureau of Alcohol, Tobacco & Firearms. The warning advised West Coast law enforcement agencies to be alert for a series of arson fires occurring in open-for-business retail stores. The series started earlier in 1990, in the mid-west, and progressed to the latest series in Phoenix, Arizona. I toyed with the concept of Aaron advancing to such bolder firesetting, but his character development made him too insecure to audaciously enter an open K-Mart to do the dirty deed with others present. Not until the BOLO series seemed to reach the West Coast in late 1990. To juice up my story, I altered Aaron and made him daring. I folded reality into my fiction by using the real BATF cases.

The concept of telling outright lies was foreign to me in my day-to-day life, but fiction writing is, by definition, falsehoods. I found it difficult to alter Aaron's established personality from my own apprehension of over 40 identified series firesetters. Then I heard taking literary license was accepted practice. So I forged my story to make it more salable, re-writing about 50% of the text, and sent out queries to publishers and agents.

After passing around a few copies of the Points of Origin manuscript to colleagues for review, in early 1991, I became a suspect in a series of retail store fires occurring in California over a ten-year period.

A lone fingerprint, found in a small fire in a Bakersfield, California retail fire in 1987, was compared directly to me and 11 other "suspects" in the summer of 1989. Two latent print examiners verified the print was not mine, nor did it belong to one of the other men on their list.

Following the 1990-1991 retail store arsons in the L.A. area, the fingerprint was again examined, but with "enhancements" hand-drawn on the image. On April 17, 1991, the augmented print became mine, and started a quest to prove me as "...the most prolific serial arsonist of the 20th century..." Subsequently, I was erroneously arrested on December 4, 1991, and my Points of Origin manuscript became the cornerstone of a misguided task force investigation and trials.

Nothing in Points reveals facts about the real fires in the actual federal or state cases that only the "real" arsonist knew. However, three sentences from my 104,000-word manuscript were presented in affidavits, press releases, and in court documents and became the impetus for ensuing trials. The provocative sentences, less than forty words total, convinced two juries this manuscript was my "confession."

Read Points of Origin as the mystery novel it is. A simple police procedural, penned by a novice firefighter/writer trying to start a second career. After multiple wrongful convictions, I found a need to pen my side of the real John Orr story. Muzzled by lawyers from 1992-1999, I finally decided to tell my tale in the autobiography, Points of Truth... Revelations of "...The Most Prolific Serial Arsonist of the 20th Century."

I'll let the reader decide whether Points of Origin is evidence, or fiction.

John Orr
August 2007

1

1988

Santa Ana winds typically diminish in the late afternoon and become benign breezes into the night. This hot August evening wasn't typical.

The gusts rushed across the San Fernando Valley like a tidal wave. Dusty clouds pushed upwards against the sun's softening one hundred-degree rays as it disappeared behind the horizon. Crashing into the valley's bordering range, the flow eddied as if lost, creating whirlwinds across the ridgeline. Instead of ebbing like a wave, pressure built up behind the front and overcame the barrier of the Hollywood Hills. The flood of wind peppered commuters' windshields with dirt and leaf litter. Like salmon headed upstream, drivers battled as they fled the deteriorating city of Hollywood before darkness descended. The wind blew smells of overflowing trashcans and cooking odors around the island-like residential areas between Hollywood and Sunset Boulevards. Exhaust smells mixed with the melting pot of itinerants, residents and curb creatures hiding in the jumble of crowded buildings.

The brightest stars winked to life and overcame the glare of neon and fluorescent lighting below. Dust swirled around the illuminated HOLLYWOOD sign, casting a pinkish hue on the thirty-foot letters. From the flatlands of the glitzy city the sign appeared to be smoldering, but nobody paid any attention or cared if it was.

After the day workers flee, the streets are almost deserted. There is a lull as night falls and streetlights wink to life, as if signaling the beginning of a different side of Hollywood. Locals emerge from ancient apartments and appear on balconies, fire escapes and curbs. Shadowy figures flow down the narrow side streets toward the activity and businesses on the boulevards. Nobody uses the darkened alleys. The filthy passageways crisscross the area like loose threads of an old net.

Traffic on Sunset was brisk. Most commuters used the four-lane thoroughfare, avoiding the tourist-infested Hollywood Boulevard. Corner strip malls and a few markets are the only open businesses, with the exception of the more mobile trade of male and female prostitutes.

A light-colored '69 Chevy peeled off from the artery, eliciting angry words and causing horns to honk even though the twenty-nine-year-old driver signaled his intention to turn. Clear of the busy street, the plain looking man silently raged but didn't turn around to vent his feelings. Instead, he idled through the market parking lot hesitantly. He avoided several convenient spots near the store entrance and slithered through the rows until he found what he wanted near the center of the field of asphalt. He slipped in next to a pickup truck and a low slung Triumph just two slots away. Aaron shut off his lights and motor, then slouched down behind the wheel. The mixture of warm asphalt and oil drippings caused his nose to wrinkle as he scanned his inside and outside mirrors. Both were quickly adjusted to accommodate his new position. He peeked over the dashboard and gave the outward appearance that he was waiting for a dawdling spouse or friend still in the store. His heart thumped ponderously as he fought to keep it from racing out of control. He opened a three-day-old *Los Angeles Times* and rested it against the steering wheel. The inner pages collapsed as he reached across the seat. Feeling a cold hard object, he smiled and scanned the mirrors again and readjusted them to give himself a panorama of the front of the market. No one approached. He raised his nose, sniffing the air like a dog responding to the rustling of a food wrapper.

Dressed in a T-shirt and shorts, Aaron was lightly tanned. He and the car both blended in with the area. His close cropped dark hair was a bit too neat around the ears and collar, the car maybe a little too shiny, but no one paid any attention anyway. That's the way he wanted it.

His hand closed around a compact pair of binoculars. Ignoring the newspaper piled in his lap, he brought up the optics and focused on the entrance to a darkened alley across Sunset Boulevard. His eyes adjusted to the flashes of passing cars and their headlight, his breath a whisper on his slightly parted lips. He blinked and it flared quicker than he expected.

He waited.

He had planted the device seven minutes earlier and already the paper bag was on fire. The flames spread to a weathered cardboard box, then began eating away at the side of a discarded sofa next to it. He lowered himself even further in the driver's seat and squinted through the binoculars for a better view.

2

It was a moonless night. The flickering light from the fire looked obscenely out of place, scarring the otherwise serene August evening. Flames now totally illuminated the alley, carport and the three cars inside. He was the only one who saw the growing fire over three hundred feet away. As the fire burned through the sofa's vinyl covering, polyurethane stuffing ignited explosively. He almost expected to hear the advancing flames but knew that the fuel would burn silently, bringing no attention to its ferocity. Smiling faintly, he jumped when car lights swept the interior of his Chevy. Fighting the urge to sit up, he glanced into his outside mirror to confirm that it was just a customer parking in the lot.

He scanned his mirrors again.

A young woman approached the Triumph. She carelessly ignored him and opened her door. He held his breath, hoping she wouldn't notice him and the fire. She saw neither and simply pulled her car out and drove away. Again he smiled as he looked back at his fire. The binoculars weren't even necessary now. The flames had attacked the underside of the wooden storage lockers in the carport and thick, black smoke was banking down off the roof to darken the flames. The fire had only been burning three minutes, but the entire sofa was already belching brilliant flame. A gust of wind blew through the alley, chasing the smoke around the side of the building. His smile broadened as a warm gust hit the side of his face through his open window. The Santa Ana winds were kicking up.

Aaron lifted up his binoculars and marveled at the flames. He wanted to be closer. It was his and he needed to be near it, but fear kept him still. Again he glanced around the parking lot. Traffic on Sunset Boulevard passed by quickly but still no one saw the blaze.

Another minute passed and the wind died. The smoke began to rise straight up into the dark sky. Peering through the binoculars, he saw a young Mexican girl curiously glancing into the alley from an apartment directly above the blaze. She turned as if speaking to someone behind her. A man's face appeared and the smoke blew into the window. The window slammed shut. At the same moment, the fire found a can of spray paint in the storage lockers and exploded with a dull, thundering whoomp. Heads turned, including Aaron's. Several people in the lot were waiting for friends who were shopping, and they suddenly opened their car doors, got out and looked at the inferno.

Seconds later the man from the apartment appeared clad only in a pair of jeans. As he rounded the corner of the carport, he raised his hands up to ward off the intense heat from the fire. He disappeared and returned with two other men and a garden hose. They were driven back. The fire now engulfed the storage lockers. Flames banked down off the ceiling and licked at the convertible top of an old Buick parked in a stall next to

3

two other cars. Bits of the flaming fabric fell onto the car's seats and set them on fire, too. The smoke, belching from the tips of the flames, was now being forced straight up in a column by the 1500-degree fire at its base.

Bystanders began to collect on the edge of the market parking lot, blocking Aaron's view. He started his car and grinned sardonically. Driving to the edge of the parking lot, he let out a long breath, feeling more comfortable with a large crowd gathering but he was still tense. Moments later, sirens could be heard in the distance. Aaron thrilled to their sounds as he felt a presence on his left. Just outside the driver's side window, a man stopped within inches of him. Aaron slowly reached down to the seat and pulled the newspaper over his binoculars.

"Some fire," the disheveled man said to no one in particular.

"Yeah, wonder where the fire department is?" Aaron mumbled, irritated by the intrusion.

"Wonder how it started. Shit, where's the fire department?" the vagrant said, without looking at Aaron. Concerned the transient might draw attention, Aaron put his car in gear and backed out of his parking space. The man didn't move and Aaron saw several people watching as he talked to himself. The sirens got closer and he tried to pull onto Sunset. A line of trucks roared up the street and stopped at the nearby intersection. Bystanders shouted, pointing at the huge fire, as if the rescuers couldn't see it. The firefighters called in their report, asking for additional help on the radio as a Battalion Chief, still blocks away, ordered them to evacuate the apartments surrounding the involved building. Another engine was told to drive into the alley and start extinguishment. Obediently, the firefighters turned their rigs and drove around the block for a safer approach to the burning apartment. Aaron pulled onto Sunset and drove slowly past the alley. Out of nowhere an engine raced by, a blast of the air horn startling him. He quickly pulled to the curb and the engine turned into the alley entrance. A line of hose stretched out the back of the engine to a fire hydrant. A firefighter hooked up to supply water to the front line activities.

Aaron's view of the fire here was good, but people continued to flock around, making him extremely uncomfortable. He was in his car. A car would be remembered readily, while his face would not. Debating whether to park somewhere and walk back, Aaron saw a clean-cut man about thirty staring into his car. Cop, Aaron thought. He casually put his car in gear, found a break in the traffic and pulled out. Looking in his rear view mirror, he saw the man continuing to watch. Fearing the man was an off-duty cop, Aaron tried to act normal. He drove a block and pulled into a darkened gas station parking lot, then backed into a space next to a pay phone. Slowly he brought his binoculars back up to his face and scanned the crowd, looking for the man. He found him as he climbed into the driver's side of a red, near-new Mercedes.

"He ain't a cop," Aaron sighed out loud as he relaxed and returned his attention to the fire. Thick black smoke was now turning to steam. Where seconds before Aaron's heart had been racing and he was excited, his body now relaxed and his mood changed to disappointment. His eyes dropped and he shook his head as if he had just lost a friend. "Shit!" he mumbled while slapping his steering wheel. "Damn."

Police cars arrived and started diverting traffic around the hoses and Aaron decided to move on. He pulled back onto Sunset and felt his erection straining against his shorts. He cupped his hand over it as he drove, shuddering at the prospect of another fire. The thought made him feel better. He had cruised the area earlier in the evening and knew of several other alleys that offered opportunities for more action. He had already set two fires in Hollywood since six o'clock, but both were discovered quickly by people passing by and were extinguished without the fire department responding. He had been setting fires for almost ten years now, and he knew better than to try to get a good fire going around dusk. People were active at that time, coming home from work, jogging, kids out playing. Industrial areas at dusk he found much more productive. Manufacturing buildings, warehouses and small businesses usually had trash and miscellaneous junk accumulated next to the structures and the burning detritus readily ignited the buildings. Aaron knew that cops patrolled the deserted industrial areas frequently, so he shied away from them. They were spectacular fires, though, and he still took the risk. Having an alibi ready made him more comfortable, just in case he was stopped. If a cop pulled him over, his story was simple. He was on his way home and saw several kids playing in the area and they were flipping matches at each other. He was staying in the area in order to stop them or, at least, make sure they didn't start a fire. The story itself, to Aaron, sounded plausible, but most cops would doubt it if there were also a fire nearby. A ready suspect in the area, Aaron would most likely be detained for further investigation.

He drove slowly through the gaudy downtown Hollywood area and took out several cigarettes. He set them on the seat beside him and constructed several of his devices. His sexual excitement continued to build. He had relived his earlier fire and was further inflamed by women on the streets and in cars next to him as he drove. Hookers were everywhere, and their scantily clad bodies caused him to stroke himself. He dared not approach one for fear of an arrest. The L.A.P.D. constantly swept through the Hollywood area by fielding undercover officers posing as both male and female prostitutes.

He thought of the police and reached under his seat and found an old mechanic's rag wrapped loosely around a large .45 Colt Military automatic. He brought it up to his lap and grabbed it roughly, enjoying the weight of it in his hand and pointed it at the floorboards.

"Nobody will ever catch me," Aaron whispered as he put the gun back under the seat. He knew that if he were ever stopped while he set up one of his devices, the automatic would come out quickly and keep them away. If it was a cop, he would have to die.

It was unlikely that Aaron would ever become a suspect and he knew it. His time delay devices gave him from a couple of minutes to almost an hour before the fire actually started after placement. When the fire did start, Aaron was always some distance from it. The unlucky individual who was walking by when the fire started was the suspect, not Aaron. By distancing himself from the ignition, he felt totally safe from any involvement with how the fire started. He occasionally walked into the area where his fire was burning, but only well after it was discovered and there were other people watching. He was a loner and insecure. "His" fires gave him the much-needed attention he craved, providing him with feelings of importance and recognition. He was, after all, the only one who knew how the fire started. That, to him, made him a very important person.

Although attractive physically and athletically built, Aaron found himself insecure and unable to initiate relationships. He gravitated toward overweight and less than attractive females; too insecure to believe an attractive person would be interested in him. His conversations were inept and usually self-centered, causing normal people to avoid him. He had no regular friends. Even his co-workers found him difficult to relate to. The only time he could talk to people was around his fires after they were burning. He could then share his knowledge of firefighting and fire equipment and fit in with the scene where he could be the center of attention. Several times he had found bystanders paying too much attention to him, and their probing caused him concern they might suspect him. Still, he needed the attention and his fires gave him that. It was worth the risk.

Aaron had already killed five people in one of his fires. He rationalized the deaths as he did everything. It wasn't his fault. The people just acted stupidly and their deaths had nothing to do with the fact that he set the fire. They just reacted too slowly.

"It was too bad about the baby but, shit, it wasn't my fault."

2

The only thing disturbing the serenity of the canyon was the sound of traffic along Chase Drive. The street was nestled into the hills just north of Los Angeles and serpentined its way up the narrow canyon from the flatlands of the affluent suburban city. Chaparral, sage, dried grasses and an occasional cluster of oaks blanketed the mountain range. The smell of car exhaust was flushed out of the canyon by the gusting Santa Ana's. Scents of the fresh mown greens at the Chase Country Club and sage flowed from the warmed vegetation. Shadows filled the canyon floor as the sun set. Some of the commuters had already turned on their headlights despite the early hour. Rows of partially lighted homes lined the hillsides in a zigzag pattern that looked like a garland on a Christmas tree.

In his rented room near the ridge, Phil Langtry rolled over onto his back and looked out the large window on the east side of his bedroom. He silently cursed his forty-two year-old eyes for failing him so early in life and couldn't figure out why he didn't see the rising sun blasting in. He normally awoke refreshed but he was weary. Movement felt like he was lying in a tub of glue. He was slightly nauseated and sweaty. Phil glanced at his wristwatch and figured it out. It was early evening, not morning. His mouth felt dry and his lips chapped.

Now all he had to do was ascertain why the hell he was sleeping at seven p.m. on a Thursday.

Phil propped his head up by folding over two king-sized pillows and added the comfort of an ugly, fringed purple throw pillow on top. It just wasn't comfortable until he adjusted the purple monstrosity under his neck. Partially clothed, he realized that he had been sweating in the late afternoon August heat. He smiled to himself as he remembered the first time he saw the purple abomination. It was in his third wife Marta's

7

living room on the end of an equally ugly sofa where they had just finished making love. His smile broadened and he felt better already.

He took a deep breath and reached for his pager on the nightstand. It was on the vibrate-alert mode and would have made little or no sound if it had been activated while he slept.

"Shit," he sighed and pressed the retrieve button. No phone numbers were illuminated in the tiny window. The fire department wasn't looking for him. He hadn't missed anything. He relaxed and stared at 3,000 foot Mt. Thom across the canyon. Two deer grazed in the shade of an oak, their dark brown bodies contrasting against the grasses. Phil estimated their distance at about 350 yards. His .243 would be just perfect to bag one, he thought. His stomach tightened. The killer instinct wasn't what it had been when he was younger. In the same moment, his mind went to the .45 auto on the nightstand beside him. He turned his head automatically to ensure it was close by. A firefighter for many years, his last ten had been spent as an arson investigator. Still a smoke-eater at heart and used to helping people, he was required to wear the gun. Not everyone he came in contact with wanted his kind of help.

His duty weapon was in its light clamshell holster. The butt end was covered with a dark, sooty mass with white highlights.

Fire debris, Phil thought.

His mind went back over his activities of the past day. He had been awakened at 3:15 a.m. by the fire department dispatch center. A vehicle fire in a garage had extended to a neighboring shed and finally spread to an eight-unit apartment building. The fire ground commander called for a second alarm, needing additional units to prevent the fire from spreading. Fire investigators are automatically contacted when a second alarm or better is called; the theory being that the quicker the investigator arrives, the more likely he may catch an arsonist still in the crowd watching. Arson is the only crime where the crook is found still sticking around after doing the dirty deed.

Phil chuckled. The fire was his first nighttime call-out in weeks. His mind focused on the day's events. It was almost 5:00 a.m. after he discovered the accidental origin of the fire. Instead of returning home, he went straight to the fire station office and started typing his reports. The fire business in the city of 175,000 had been slow but the paper attack remained constant. The phones didn't ring at 5:00 a.m. anyway, making it much easier to finish reports without interruption.

At about 8:15, his partner, Ashley Nolan, showed up, justifying his tardiness by saying he went to see the fire scene on his way into work. He hadn't taken a radio home with him and surely hadn't been aware of the fire. He probably just ran into one of the firefighters who worked the blaze as he came into the station. Not being on call this week, Ash would not have been notified at home of the second-alarm fire.

Just a poor, dumb cop, thought Phil. Ash was Phil's third cop partner. Nolan's predecessors' short careers caused most of the local cops to steer clear of volunteering for the position. Phil's known aversion to uniformed cops ensured there were only two volunteers when the opening came up. Cops assigned to the fire department to assist with fire and arson investigations didn't take long to realize what a gravy train this arson job was. No roll-call, no uniforms, no sergeant looking over shoulders and a hell of a lot less paperwork. Still, Phil appreciated their backup.

Nolan, only on the job six years, was twenty-nine and had an A.A. in Administration of Justice. Married to a native of Ecuador, he spoke fluent Spanish and even looked Hispanic with jet-black hair and dark eyes. His slim build and tanned skin enabled him to pass for everything from Armenian to Yemeni. He'd been with Phil for a year but in that time had proven himself an adept investigator. Working fire-damaged scenes, he quickly learned how to spot the area of origin and already had a unique interviewing style when he came on board. Unfortunately, his typical cop libido and propensity to party, on as well as off duty, had created a rift. Ash had shown up at work with booze on his breath once already and phone calls from numerous women indicated more problems in the future. Still, Phil liked him. The younger man's influence had reawakened an interest in dating again. The ink on Phil's divorce was still wet after two years.

The rest of the day was filled with return visits to burned-out apartments to talk with owners and tenants, as well as insurance people. At 2:00 p.m., Phil felt drained and began the drive back home to Chase Canyon. He had no sooner passed Station Five when they were dispatched to a grass fire nearby. Phil heard the alert on the radio and looked over his shoulder in the direction of the reported small fire. He saw a light grey smoke column, followed seconds later by a thick black cloud pushing into the sky. It was more than a grass fire.

He turned his four-door Chevy around, flicked on the red lights and siren and headed toward the smoke. At the same time, the dispatchers came on the radio and advised the now responding engine that callers were reporting the grass fire had spread to a garage. The dispatch was upgraded to include two more engine companies, a ladder truck, Battalion Chief, and an arson investigator—him. Juveniles had been seen in the area before the fire, according to a 911 caller. The investigation took another hour and Phil drove home exhausted and dirty. By 4:00 p.m., he had collapsed into his bed.

He woke up at 7:15 p.m. with a tremendous thirst for a beer. He ascended the stairs leading to the main floor of the two-level hillside home. The smell of Mexican food greeted him. Sean, his roommate, was preparing his usual dinner of scratch-made gourmet delights. The cuisine seriously contributed to Phil's already twenty pounds overweight six-foot frame.

Sean was a former cop turned private investigator; a very successful one at that. He had recruited Phil after they both worked an arson fraud locally. They shared investigative secrets and sources of information, as well as expensive night-vision and eavesdropping equipment. Sean also taught the smoke-eater how to cook. Similar to Phil in appearance and age, Sean sported a salt and pepper beard and wore glasses most of the time. Insurance companies lined up for Sean's expertise in insurance frauds of all types—faked burglaries and robberies, phony car accidents and bogus slip-and-fall claims. Phil worked full time at his arson job for the city but always had free moments to assist Sean. The extra money was incentive enough but the pair made a great team and the former cop was a whiz at sleuthing. Sean was Sherlock and Phil was not far behind.

Their friendship was a typical cop relationship and they were both Vietnam vets. Sean had originally coped with his war experience with a bottle but, as he aged, found solace in work and the outdoors. Phil's feelings about the war were mixed since he was an R.E.M.F.—a rear echelon motherfucker. He spent his thirteen months as a crash/rescue man at Ton Son Nhut Air Base. Although exposed to mortar attacks and some firefights, Phil braved flames instead of bullets. He had a lingering guilt he didn't do enough while in Nam. Maybe that's why he continued to be a firefighter when he got out. Maybe it was just safer.

"You look like shit! Didn't you go to work today?" Sean queried.

"Yeah, it was really busy. I came home at 4:00 and just crashed. They had me up since 3:30 this morning."

"Yeah, I heard the phone ring but I didn't know if you went out or not," said Sean. "Judging by the condition of your shorts, I'd say it was a pretty good fire." Phil flushed as he realized he had stripped down to his boxers. They were soot stained and grimy.

"This has been a weird day. Good thing Beth isn't home yet," mumbled Phil, referring to Sean's wife.

"She's running late. Went by Sears for a white sale or something." Phil grabbed a Bud from the refrigerator and sat down at the dining table that overlooked the canyon. Sean was already half finished with his tumbler-sized bourbon. Maybe his second, judging by the stage of his cooking. It was almost done.

"Hungry?" Sean asked.

"Yeah, I could use something. Thanks."

As Sean made up a plate, Phil scanned the morning *Los Angeles Times* he had missed earlier in the day. A small headline caught his attention. A series of fires in Hollywood reportedly destroyed or damaged four garages and carports. The fires occurred in a two-hour time

10

frame. Phil skip-read to the end where it inevitably said, *"cause of the fires is under investigation."* He laughed out loud, thinking that any idiot would know that four accidental fires couldn't possibly happen in a ten-block radius in a two-hour time frame. It was obviously a serial arson. He explained to Sean the reason for his chuckle even before being asked.

"One of my adjusters got the assignment for the one just off Sunset," Sean replied. "You wanna go look at it for the insurance company?" He immediately said yes, knowing Saturday was only a day away. Even though he was on call, running over to Hollywood for a quick investigation outside his own jurisdiction would take only an hour or two.

"There seems to have been a lot of those serial fires lately," Sean said quizzically.

"Yeah. Usually it's just a string of brushfires that goes down during the summer, but the garage thing is happening pretty regularly around L.A. lately. Burbank had a few, too." Phil thought back to a series of small brush fires he had investigated earlier in the summer. The arsonist favored weekdays between noon and 4:00 p.m. He would use a time-delay cigarette-glue bead combination and throw it into the brush as he drove by. The time delay gave the arsonist 10-15 minutes before it went off. Thirty cars could go by before the device would set off the brush and grass. None of the witnesses could ever remember what kind of car drove by fifteen minutes before the fire. They all thought Phil was a little strange asking what kind of cars drove by before the fire. All the witnesses said that it had to be the car that was seen racing away at a high rate of speed at the time of the fire's discovery. A common mistake, thought Phil.

A city councilman was a suspect briefly when an overzealous cop pulled him over because his car was seen driving away quickly.

"Yeah, I was driving away at a high rate of speed, you asshole. I live up the canyon and went home to report the fucking fire!" explained the indignant council member.

The remains of the device were recovered about 50% of the time. Usually, fire crews would destroy the evidence during the extinguish-ment, but Phil got lucky several times. He found a "trademark" in several of the devices. The "trademark" of this particular arsonist was attaching coins to the device for additional weight. The farther it was to the grass from the moving car, the larger the coin or coins he used. Serial brush fires were common, but the structure fires occurring around the area were not. This was a peaceful community with few fire problems. Except for today, anyway.

Sean broke his concentration by enthusiastically discussing their upcoming deer hunt. Phil didn't really want to go hunting, but knew he would anyway. Work seemed to take up most of his time and he hated to leave, even for a week. Ash was competent enough to cover his absence, but working a good case was as exciting, if not more so, than deer hunting.

His thoughts were again interrupted, this time by his pager vibrating at his side. He looked down at it and found it amusing that it was hanging onto his underwear. He depressed the button and called up the return phone number. It was Marta, his ex-wife, not a dispatcher at the fire department.

"Page? Or are you playing with yourself?" asked Sean.

"Page. It's Marta, and before you say a word..." Phil feigned anger.

"I wouldn't say anything," Sean laughed and threw a dishtowel at Phil. It ended up in the enchilada remains.

Marta had a long-time hold on Phil. Though now divorced for more than two years, his normal cool demeanor was always shaken by Marta. He had tried to reconcile after their separation, but Marta wouldn't have it. They still loved each other but just weren't right together for any length of time. Except for sex. Their sex life was the only thing that held them together most of the time. It was probably the only reason she was paging him. *Okay by me*, he thought.

Sean didn't care much for Marta. She had seriously hurt Phil, and he resented her for not recognizing Phil's weakness and letting him go completely. Sean thought briefly about probing Phil's thoughts but kept quiet.

Phil reached for the kitchen phone, then stopped, not wanting Sean to hear his conversation. Phil could read Sean's face and knew the look of genuine concern.

3

The sun was setting over mountainous Griffith Park as Aaron reevaluated his plans for the evening. He hadn't planned on setting any fires tonight. He had made a date with a casual acquaintance but she provided a last-minute excuse for not being able to go out with him. He was furious at the perceived rejection, regardless of her excuse. Several quick phone calls found no one interested in going out with him, so he just drove. The setting sun illuminated the grass-covered slopes in the hills above the freeway and he was drawn to them. Traffic was heavy, and by the time he got off the Ventura Freeway, it was getting too dark to set any brush fires. Setting a brush fire required him to throw a lit cigarette out of his moving car into the dry grass. As the sun set and shadows fell on the canyons, a lit cigarette would look like a shooting star coming out of his car window. Canyon residents, terrified of brush fires, would notice his actions immediately. During the day was okay. At night—no way.

He pulled over to the side of the broad boulevard, the main thoroughfare running north to south through town. The north end, where he was, had small businesses and apartments lining the streets.

There he sat thinking.

A large cypress tree stood next to a real estate office. The tree looked like a long, thin penis, he thought. Broad at the bottom, narrow at the top. His mind quickly analyzed it for its fire potential. He knew cypress trees well. He had destroyed many of them and knew it would burn furiously when ignited.

He decided, glancing up and down the street, that he had been sitting in the car too long and might be remembered by people in the area. As he pulled out into traffic and, passed the real estate office, he saw one of its large glass window was in direct contact with the cypress. The heat from the burning tree would break the glass readily and ignite the heavy curtains on the inside. Aaron smiled and drove on about a block. He looked to his left and saw Fire Station Six and knew exactly what he would do. He remembered several vacant lots about a mile away. If he set a fire in one of the vacant lots, it would take Engine Six out of its quarters and give his fire at the real estate office time to really get going.

"This will be so fucking cool," he said to himself as he drove.

His mind raced

About a mile down the road, he found the ideal vacant lot, bordered by two apartments and an alley. As he drove through the narrow alley, he slowed where it intersected to a street. He quickly reached into a paper bag next to him and pulled out a tube of glue and a cigarette. He squeezed glue onto the cigarette about a quarter-inch from the filter. Ten to twelve minutes delay left time enough to drive back and set fire to the cypress tree. As he drove across the street and continued into the alley, he lit the cigarette with a lighter and choked on the foul taste. Not being a smoker he could have used incense sticks for time delays, and avoided the foul-tasting cigarettes, but incense sticks didn't stay lit when thrown. They had to be physically placed and also left a foreign sweet smell on his clothing that could be readily detected.

Another 300 feet down the alley and Aaron came alongside the vacant lot. He dropped the cigarette out of his window and continued driving to the end, accelerating to the boulevard. He constructed another device as he drove toward the real estate office and turned left onto Fairview Street. He found a parking space in the residential area bordering the boulevard and stopped to examine the device. This device was adjusted to give him about a ten-minute delay. The vacant lot would go in about five more minutes. He needed five to walk down to the real estate office and plant the device and another five to get up the street before ignition so he could watch. Engine Six, in the meantime, would be roaring to the other side of its district to the diversionary fire.

In the alley Aaron picked up an empty paper bag next to him and jammed several pieces of newspaper into it. Holding the device in his hand, he got out of the car and started walking. He rounded the corner and slowed his pace. Cautiously, he looked up and down the street. A few people were walking within the same block, but he knew they wouldn't be in the area when the fire started. Thus, potential witnesses would be gone so they just didn't concern him and there were very few cars were on the street. He nonchalantly brought the bag up from his side and slipped the now-lit cigarette into it, as he came abreast of the cypress tree, he shoved the bag into the thick branches. The outer green growth gave way to old dead branches on the interior of the lush three-foot diameter tree where he planted the device. Green as it was, the natural oils in the growth were highly flammable when ignited.

Several steps later he jammed his hand into his pocket, as if retrieving something, and looked into his empty palm. To an onlooker, a potential witness, it appeared that Aaron had forgotten something. He turned around, walked briskly toward his car and passed the cypress where he saw the paper bag nested well into the lower branches. "*About eight more minutes,*" he thought as saw smoke curling up through the foliage.

After reaching his car, he drove on side streets toward a viewing area two blocks north of the fire station, careful not to drive by the edifice again. When he rounded the corner, he heard Engine Six leaving its station. It was followed by a second siren wailing independently of the engine. *The ladder truck at Six's was going, too.* This was better than he planned. Usually only a single engine is sent to a small vacant lot fire. Apparently, the 911 calls reported more than just a grass fire. He knew that a ladder truck was also stationed at Six's, but that didn't matter to him. Ladder trucks don't carry water and the firefighters on the apparatus couldn't do shit to his office fire until an engine arrived to help, anyway. So, now they were gone, too! The next nearest engine was two miles away at Station One! Aaron knew the city and most fire departments in Southern California well.

He pulled up to the boulevard and saw the heavy diesel exhaust clouding Stocker Street where the two rigs were speeding toward the grass fire. Their rear yellow lights winked through the haze as they disappeared. Beyond, he saw a thick column of black smoke rising from the area near his vacant lot.

What the fuck is that? I only lit the grass on fire. Shit!

Ignoring everything, Aaron was drawn to the blossoming column of smoke a mile away. Down the street, the paper bag ignited prematurely. He continued toward his first fire, not seeing the cypress tree starting to burn. He was so enthralled with the column of black smoke he almost caught up with Station Six's rigs. He slowed and cut over just short of the vacant lot and approached a police car already blocking the street. Aaron's heart was racing, and his stomach was knotted so tightly he felt pain. He couldn't find a parking spot and only after driving by the front of the vacant lot did he see the now smoldering remains of several old tires that were hidden in the dry grass. The firefighters had the small fire almost out.

The burning tires caused all the fucking smoke. Gotta get back to the real estate office.

Traffic brought by the black smoke and sirens made it almost impossible to move. Aaron idled by the ladder truck and heard the rig's radio blare with a transmission, "Engine One's out on a small tree fire at the Fleming Realty Office. Substitute us on Engine Six's incident. No help needed here. Maybe we should contact an investigator for these two fires?"

Aaron gasped as the dispatcher answered, "Engine One, 10-4. Engine Six is canceling you anyhow. We'll let the on-call investigator know and advise. Engine One, confirming you're on Brand Boulevard across from Station Six?"

"Affirmative."

Aaron froze, bewildered by what he was hearing. His fire at the real estate office was already being extinguished. How could this be? He then realized Engine One had also been assigned to the reported "major fire" in the vacant lot and, its response pattern, took it right by the real estate office. Right by it as the fire started, prematurely again.

"I've gotta fucking change cigarette brands or something," he swore. Aaron drove angrily back toward the real estate office. Passing by, he saw the firefighters rolling up their hose and only a small portion of the tree damaged.

"Son of a bitch!" he said out loud. Not wanting to see an investigator, he drove aimlessly toward the center of town, away from the area of his fires. He slithered through alleys, finding comfort in the darkness but not finding anything worth burning. Passing a 7-11 store, he pulled in, now feeling hungry and depressed, too. Maybe food would ease the pain in his stomach.

As he parked, he looked into the store and saw a young looking blonde girl walk up to the counter. He watched her large breasts hanging loose under her T-shirt until she stepped out of his view, heading toward the door. He got out of his car and timed his arrival with her exit. Feeling cocky now, he held open the door. She approached and he saw she was only fifteen or sixteen years old.

"Nice shirt," he said as she passed.

"Fuck you!" she spat at him as she walked to a nearby car. Several other girls were in an old sedan and talked to her through the open window. Aaron stared from inside the store, oblivious to the other customers walking around him. She bent over to speak with the car's occupants. Her loose T-shirt fell away from her waist as she bent, showing one of her firm breasts from below. His body tingled and he wandered to the rear of the store, his anger smoldering. Passing a stack of Styrofoam coolers, his mind imagined them burning. He glanced around and saw a convex security mirror hanging from the ceiling. It was filthy and his image was distorted. He smiled and felt inside his T-shirt pocket and found a loose cigarette. Attached to it was a dried bead of glue, secured there earlier in the evening as his backup device. He usually had one ready in case he found an additional opportunity to set a fire after already placing a device. One was never enough. Series fires were his specialty.

Standing next to the paper napkin display, he picked up a package and stuffed it behind the coolers. His stomach knotted and he shivered uncontrollably as he walked toward the end of the aisle and picked up a package of potato chips to cover his activities, pretending to be a customer. He saw the girls from the car, including the blonde, walking back toward the front of the store. He lit the cigarette, passed the cooler pile, and stooped down. The device was placed at the base of the napkins.

When Aaron approached the check-out stand, the blonde was trying to talk an old man into buying her beer.

Edgy, Aaron decided not to wait in line. He put the potato chips back on the display and walked out, digging in his pocket as if reaching for a forgotten wallet. He glanced over his shoulder. No one was paying any attention to him.

Starting his car, Aaron saw the girls near the beer cooler talking to yet another older man. He eased his car out of the parking place and froze. Noticing for the first time, above the cash register area, a small red light attached to the base of a roving video security camera. His mind raced as he tried to make a decision. Go back and get the device or get the hell away. He had timed the device to go off in less than four minutes.

The blonde was now leaning against a corner with her two friends, only a few feet away from the napkins and the coolers. They couldn't quite see the coolers but were very close. A car honked behind Aaron, impatient for his parking space. The horn made the decision for him. He drove away.

Aaron turned around and doubled back, passing the front of the 7-11 and saw the video camera sweeping in a 180-degree arc, but he couldn't tell if the camera had captured him. If it swept the area of the device, it wouldn't record him since the displays were so high he couldn't be seen. It did appear to cover the cash register area where he had walked out and put the chips back. He drove on, wondering, his heart still racing.

4

The fact that Marta had paged Phil always meant one of two things. She wanted him, or she had an emergency and needed his help. The help was usually something as simple as locking her keys in her car or running out of gas. She seldom contacted him for any other reason. Never wanted to just talk or to ask him over for dinner. He missed Marta's three daughters, and the ready-made family they shared so briefly, but having her like this wasn't so bad after all. He'd at least be able to see his "daughters" for a while. He cared for them as if they were his own.

Phil drove toward Dodger Stadium on the way to Marta's house and thought of the conversation they had just minutes ago. He was glad he decided to answer her page from his room so Sean couldn't hear how she talked him into driving the five miles to her place. The drive wasn't so bad, it was just that Phil was exhausted and really needed to stay at home and rest after a particularly busy day.

The area near Dodger Stadium was severely depressed and one of the oldest sections of Los Angeles. Marta's parents had bought several properties in the residential area nearby because their business was also in the area. Marta rented a small wood-frame house from them and took care of the other tenants in return for a break on her rent. Phil found the area had a very warm, friendly air about it. The residents, mostly Hispanic, were always cordial. He had gotten to know them for the short period he had lived there with Marta and the kids. Even the local gang, Frog Town, had made peace with him and treated him simply as a resident.

The sun had just gone down and the residents of Frog Town were sitting on their front porches and lawns. Small groups of teenage girls stood on each corner, looking toward the park where the local gang members congregated, all staring at his narc-looking car as it approached. Even the five and six-year-olds could pick out the "official" car. Phil grinned at the body language. As he approached, shoulders tensed and their bodies automatically started to turn away as if preparing to run. A split second later, their heads would gently roll back toward him to evaluate the threat. The girls, too, knew the role they played and mimicked the men they worshipped. Phil felt bad that his presence would cause such an intrusion but also wouldn't give up free transportation the city gave him.

Less than half an hour later, the kids were in bed and Phil and Marta were alone on the living room sofa, waiting for the three girls to talk themselves to sleep in their tiny bedroom. As they cuddled, the beeper sounded, jarring them both.

"You set that off on purpose!" she shouted.

"I changed it to audible a couple of minutes ago. My hand wasn't near it, Marta!" Phil protested.

"Damn Phil, if you didn't want to stay, why the hell didn't you just say so?"

Phil walked to the phone and stretched the cord back to the sofa. She sulked as he dialed the dispatch center's number. He held the receiver near her ear. The dispatcher explained that there had been two small fires in Engine Six's district, only minutes apart. Engine One's Captain wanted the investigator notified. Phil looked into Marta's eyes.

"If there isn't any damage to property or good suspect info, just have the cops take a report," Phil said.

"O.K. Phil," the dispatcher said, "I'll check. Hang on a sec." Marta continued to sulk as Phil thought of the sudden increase in fire activity.

"Phil, Captain Austin says he doesn't have any good info at the vacant lot fire, and Captain Pierce at the real estate office just got dispatched to a heart attack call. He said that there wasn't anybody around when they arrived and nobody came forward, either." Phil told the dispatcher that he wasn't responding to either fire but would check them out in the morning. The dispatcher told him that she would be off at 6:30 the next morning and would try and get some more info for him if he'd take her to breakfast. Wanting to do just that, Phil tried to map out the breakfast meeting without alerting a still jealous Marta, but fumbled his words miserably. Marta's curious glance brought him back to more immediate needs and he mumbled his thanks to the dispatcher and said he would talk to her later. He wanted to spend the night with Marta and also be able to catch the dispatcher, Dani, before she went home. That meant either going home after making love to Marta or getting up at 5 a.m. and rushing home for a quick shower and shave to meet Dani briefly before he had to be at work. Fortunately, his work schedule was flexible, but Dani usually didn't settle for brief, but Marta was usually asleep shortly after their lovemaking anyway, so slipping away afterward wouldn't be too difficult. The way Phil was feeling right now, however, meant he'd also be asleep very shortly.

The pager going off may have initially caused her to be suspicious and distracted, but she was now content to just have him there.

Phil awoke at 5 a.m. and found the two of them still on the couch. Marta's head resting on his shoulder. He slipped away from her and found a blanket nearby to replace the warmth of his body.

It was already warming outside when he walked to his car, a slight Santa Ana wind blowing. He stood still briefly and smiled, knowing that the typical summer smog would be taken away by the increasing winds as the sun came up. The smile quickly dissipated as his mind thought about his workload for the day.

He called Dani when he got home and arranged to meet at a restaurant on Central Avenue at 6:45 after she got off work. He quietly showered and forced himself into a suit, knowing that he would be meeting with insurance people and his boss at some point during the day. He sometimes longed for a return to fire suppression so he could have as much time off as his co-workers, but wearing a uniform just wasn't something he wanted to do, either. Too regimented. He preferred the flexibility Chief Harris gave him to wear his Levi's and casual shirts for day-to-day operations, except for "public contacts". He had to laugh at that. All he did was talk to the public and most of them were transients, hookers, drug addicts and the assorted assholes that are typically the victims or witnesses of arson. They didn't give a damn whether he wore a suit or a dress.

The meeting with Dani was businesslike and informative. She had called the two fire captains after they returned to quarters and asked them for any information about the fires. Dani knew that they were obvious arsons and were probably related. The captains played down any significance of their being related, even though Captain Pierce had, at the time, requested an investigator. Pierce, like most fire captains, just wanted to avoid any extra paperwork. If an investigator was called out, he did the report, not the fire captain. Dani, being helpful, told the captains to document their fires "at the request of Investigator Langtry." She then told him that about an hour after the two small fires, the police department had received a 911 call asking for the fire department. The police dispatcher transferred the call and as Dani picked up the line, the caller at the 7-11 said that the fire was out and everything was all right. She asked if they wanted an engine to come by and he said that everything was okay. At about 6 a.m., she heard the police radio dispatch a car to the same 7-11 to take a malicious mischief call that was apparently a fire started inside the store. Dani said that she called the police and found that the 7-11 owner came in to work and the night clerk related that there had been a fire earlier. The owner then wanted a police report taken due to several hundred dollars' worth of damage. Phil was so pleased with Dani's intuition and follow-through that he couldn't bring himself to try a come-on over breakfast. They had dated briefly a year before, but he had also been involved with Marta again and an opportunity had never presented itself for him and Dani to further their relationship. Dani, being married at the time, didn't pursue it either.

They finished their breakfast and he walked her to her car at the rear of the restaurant. She opened her door and moved close to him, touching his hand, the door was between them. He thought about pursuing the contact, but she brought up the 7-11 fire again. Phil quickly moved his thoughts back to work.

5

Phil drove to his office and found Ash industriously cleaning their small office. Ash sometimes surprised Phil. It was only 7:40 and he had obviously been in the office for some time, judging by the obvious progress he had made on the littered cubicle they occupied. They kept the mini-blinds on the door closed. The investigators, although necessary, were like outcasts in the day-to-day routine of firefighters. They weren't quite firefighters and not totally police either, thus there was some suspicion about what they actually did. Phil, a loner, liked it that way. Phil poked his head into the cubicle, exchanged greetings with Ash and walked to the station's kitchen for a cup of coffee. While there, Battalion Chief Dartel walked in. Dartel was going off-duty and had been to the previous night's fires in the vacant lot and real estate office.

"Busy night, Chief?"

"Not really. Just those two calls up in Six's district. Did you get a chance to check them out yet?"

"No. I wanted to take Ash up with me and survey the neighborhood. Somebody might have seen something that the cops missed. They usually don't take very thorough reports on small fires, anyway. They seem to think it's a waste of time." Phil sighed.

"You think the two were related? They started just a couple minutes apart. If somebody set the vacant lot on fire they would have had to drive 100 miles an hour to get down to Brand Boulevard and set the tree off, too."

"That's why we're spending a little more time on these. The timing of the fires says a lot. They were probably set with time-delay devices. The first fire was at the far west end of Six's district. The real estate office may have actually been the target, and the first fire may have been a diversion to draw Engine Six away so the real estate office could get going."

The chief laughed. "That's pretty exotic isn't it?"

"Yeah, but our coin-tosser might be back." The Chief's smile quickly faded as he remembered the serial arsonist torching the city's hillsides earlier in the year.

"Are you serious, Phil? You think he's back?"

"Maybe, but only because we had an unreported fire in the 7-11 on Broadway last night, too."

"You still think the brush fire guy is the one burning the stores, too? I thought you gave up on that theory." Phil was the only investigator in Los Angeles who thought the coin-tosser might have also branched out to structure fires. At the same time as the coin-tosser's brush fires, neighboring communities suffered a series of small fires set in paper product displays inside stores. Phil's theory was based on the obvious time-delay devices used in the store fires. Some of the devices that were recovered consisted of the same components as the coin-tosser's fires, minus the coins. The cigarette brand was the same, and so was the model airplane glue he used. Phil felt that the coin-tosser obviously didn't need coins to weight down the devices in the stores since they were physically set down on the displays, not thrown for a distance as in the brush fires.

"Chief, I'm not quite ready to say for sure it's the coin-tosser, but there just can't be this many serial arsonists running around. The guy setting the store fires sets two or three in a short period of time. Hell, he's set one right across the street from one where the firemen were just arriving. One block away, he set another one ten minutes later. That's just like the coin-tosser we had. This guy just goes crazy!"

"I see what you mean. Well, good luck. See you next shift," the Chief said as he walked away.

Phil sat down in the deserted kitchen while he sipped his coffee. The Chief still seemed a bit doubtful of Phil's theory, and Phil wished he had offered the Cal's Hardware Store fire as further proof that the coin-tosser was his man. Three years earlier in nearby South Pasadena, Cal's had caught fire just before closing time. Three customers and two employees were trapped and killed. An hour before Cal's burned, a napkin fire started in Pasadena and did several hundred dollars' worth of damage. Cal's was only a 15-minute drive from Pasadena. While South Pasadena fire units were rolling to Cal's, a second fire at a Von's grocery store nearby erupted. Alhambra fire units responded to that fire and, in the meantime, the Cal's fire went to a fourth alarm and destroyed half of the two-building complex. The five fatalities included a three-year-old boy. Local investigators ignored the two grocery store fires and, in a hurry to recover bodies, called Cal's an accidental fire. The investigation was poorly organized, and Phil, being an outsider, could only watch as a skip loader was used to tear down the walls of Cal's. Any evidence of arson soon destroyed.

6

The hardware business prospered in the small community south of Pasadena. Many of the homes were built in the 1920's and were reaching the age where they required frequent maintenance. Hardware stores such as Cal's did well.

Madeline Paulson went to the cluster of stores at least twice a week to shop. She could have accomplished all her shopping in one trip a month, but since her husband died two years before, she needed a reason to get out of the house periodically. Tonight, she was babysitting with her three-year-old grandson, Terrence. She took him to the Baskin-Robbins ice cream store next to Cal's. While standing in the parking lot sharing a chocolate mint cone, she decided to entertain Terrence further by walking through Cal's. The vast displays of tools and bright colors would surely keep his attention and give her an excuse to stay out a little longer. Her daughter wasn't due to pick up Terrence until 9:30, so she had plenty of time.

Madeline and Terrence had less than six minutes to live.

She and Terrence walked to the main entrance and immediately saw a sign, "No food or drink inside store." She stopped for a second, then continued on when she saw no one looking her way. She held the ice cream cone by her side as she walked through the large door leading to the Cal's annex. Madeline paid no attention, thinking that their cone was almost gone and it wouldn't matter if they slipped into the near-deserted annex area to finish eating. As she rounded a corner she almost ran into a man walking with his hands in his pockets. Both were startled. She heard his breath suck in and he mumbled his apologies as he continued on and she continued toward the back of the store with Terrence.

Aaron glanced back over his shoulder and breathed a sigh of relief as he saw that the woman and kid were walking away from the area of his device. He pulled out his wallet and looked into it while he walked through an empty checkout line. Again his ploy worked. No one paid any attention to him. He got into his car and headed toward the Von's market five blocks away.

As Madeline showed Terrence the garden tools and plants, a nice young man told her that the store would be closing in about fifteen minutes. She thanked him and continued to the back aisle. Minutes later, she heard a shrill whistling noise. She looked down the aisle and saw the young man rush by. The displays were floor to ceiling, so she saw nothing unusual and continued to browse with Terrence. Another employee walked by the end of the aisle as the whistling noise persisted. She then heard excited talking and the word "fire." She started toward the sound, realizing now it was a smoke detector. She saw a slight haze at the ceiling level. Her heart raced, and as she rounded the corner she saw the smoke was now swirling around the ceiling like a whirlwind.

The fire, originating in polyurethane foam cushions, raced to the ceiling and within 45 seconds, 1000-degree temperatures were being pushed toward the annex door opening. The fire breathed, continuing to look for more oxygen, traveled to the nearest opening and available source of air. This venturi-like effect sucked at the flames and smoke, increasing the flames' intensity. The thick, black smoke quickly traveled toward the rest of the annex. Running into walls, the smoke banked down to the floor. The annex opening was protected by a metal-clad fire door, designed to close when a light-weight metal link melted from fire and allowed the door to roll down its tracks, closing and preventing fire spread into the main store. The design was meant for fires happening after hours when no one was inside, not for hours when the store was occupied. It would prove to be a fatal design.

Madeline held Terrence close to her and stopped briefly to look down the aisle where she saw the fire boiling out of the displays fifty feet away. She stared at the fire, fascinated, yet terrified. As she turned toward the annex door, the fusible link melted and the massive door slammed shut, cutting off her, Terrence's, a man and three employees' escape. She started back again, hoping someone would open it up. The fire burned through a light fixture and shorting out all the lights in the annex. The emergency lights flashed on but the huge amount of smoke blocked them completely, leaving them in complete darkness.

With the fire door closed, the rest of the employees fled the main store to escape the advancing fire there was no one left to open the fire door. The blaze, with its oxygen supply cut off, died down briefly and produced more smoke. Quickly, the tremendous heat breached the attic above the fire and found a ready source of oxygen. The smoke, just above head level when the lights went out, now pressed down onto the heads of Madeline and Terrence. Instinctively, they dropped to the floor when they heard a young employee shouting out to them. She screamed back at him and within seconds he was at their sides. The three crawled in total darkness, toxic smoke attacking their lungs. The employee shouted that he knew where the fire exit was at the back of the store. Crashing into a chainsaw display, he realized he wasn't where he thought he was. The smoke, chokingly thick, was stealing their oxygen quickly and causing disorientation. He held Madeline's hand as Terrence clung to her neck. She heard Terrence's sobs. She now felt heat and saw flames in front of them. She screamed at the employee as he squeezed her hand tightly, continuing down the aisle toward the fire. Terrence's grip also loosened from her neck and he slipped down her body as they crawled. Unable to go any further, she felt the employee's hand drop hers. He continued on. The last thing she heard was a tremendous roar as the fire burned through the roof and vented to the outside. The smoke momentarily lifted but then was replaced by a solid wall of fire as the entire contents of the annex exploded into flames. Their last breaths were of 800-degree heat that seared their throats closed.

Madeline's body was found with Terrence's clinging to her ankles. The employee leading them was found face down, five feet in front of Madeline, just twenty feet short of a fire escape door. The other dead employee and customer were also found within ten feet of Madeline. One other employee had managed to escape and collapsed outside. All traveled away from the advancing heat and were found as far away from the fire as possible. The survival instinct was there, but toxic smoke felled them before they could escape.

There was never a follow-up investigation. The fire was ineptly termed accidental. Aaron was so furious that he set a nearly identical fire two days later in Hollywood at another hardware store. The investigating agency termed the fire arson, but no correlation was made to the Cal's fire. Aaron wanted the Cal's fire to be arson. He loved the inadvertent attention he derived from the newspaper coverage and hated it when he wasn't properly recognized. The deaths were blotted out of his mind. It wasn't his fault. Just stupid people acting as stupid people do.

7

Phil and Ash drove in silence to the 7-11. Showing great interest in Phil's theory about the coin-tosser, Ash volunteered to do the follow-up reports on the juvenile cases from the day before. Phil was grateful for the help. It would allow him to spend more time on his case.

They drove into the 7-11 parking lot. An employee was picking up the garbage, trash and beer cans that filled the lot, from the previous night. Phil asked him for the manager. As they followed the employee inside, Phil saw the remains of a stack of partially-burned Styrofoam coolers next to the trash dumpster outside the store. He directed Ash to examine them while Phil went to see the manager. Inside, he smelled the acrid stench from the burned plastics. He also saw a black, oily smudge on the ceiling near the back of the store. As the manger approached, Phil looked at the security video camera probing the store. Phil unclipped his belt badge and held it out for the manager to see. Unimpressed, the manager asked, "Did the night man sell to minors again?"

"No. I'm with the fire department arson detail. I need some information on your fire last night. What happened?" Now showing a renewed interest in Phil, the manager related the details of the previous night.

"My nighttime employee said that he was busy and had a line of customers, and all of a sudden this girl screamed at the back of the store. He thought some transient was waving his dick at her or something, and he looked up and saw fire. He says he slammed the register shut and ran back and found the Styro coolers burning. He told everybody to get out and he grabbed the stack and tried to carry them outside. 'Got too hot and he dropped them. Some customer grabbed the extinguisher while he called 911. The guy had it out in a couple of seconds so the night man just cancelled the 911 call. He thought he didn't need the fire department

28

since the fire was out. Really pissed me off though and I reamed his ass this morning. Told him he should have had the cops out to try and find out who did it. He said he didn't see anybody other than a couple of young broads around the stack. He thought they just threw a cigarette into the coolers. That wouldn't start them burning, would it?"

"No, it wouldn't," said Phil.

"I didn't think so."

Ash walked in and said, "Fire started at the bottom of the stack on the outside, not inside of them." Phil smiled. He had already made that determination before he came inside. The manager took them to the area of the fire. It had already been cleaned up.

"Shit!" Phil said. "Where's the other stuff that burned?"

"The night man cleaned it up. 'Said it was a package of napkins that was burning next to the coolers."

"Where's the remains of the napkins?" Ash asked. The manager led them outside and pointed to the dumpster that now had several loads of trash from the lot piled on top. Phil and Ash looked in and saw a small pile of burned material toward the bottom, just out of reach. They looked at each other. Phil smiled as he pointed to his suit, then laughed, pointing to Ash's T-shirt. Ash leaped into the dumpster. His frown turned into a smile quickly as he shouted, "Got it!" He held up the burned napkin package by its edges. The remains of a cigarette and a small, hard bead were locked against the plastic wrapper, melted there by the flames. Phil again smiled and found a cardboard box for Ash to place the evidence in.

"What's the big deal, the fire was an accident. Right?" queried the manager.

"No, sir. Look a little closer at this bead secured to the cigarette. That makes a nice time-delay, and that also makes it arson." Phil gleamed.

"Fucking kids. They get pissed when we won't sell them beer so they do this to me!" Phil asked if the security camera was real or fake.

"Oh, yeah. That baby's real, and it works real good too." They went back into the store. He led Phil to a back room where a monitor sat on the manager's desk. "It works two ways. It sends me a picture back here and also takes like a photo every three or four seconds and records it. I change the tape every morning and keep them for a week or so. That way, if one of my employees rips me off, I can show him the tape and fire his ass!" He reached into a cabinet and handed Phil a tape as Ash rejoined them.

"I took a couple of pictures and packaged the evidence. What do you have here?" asked Ash.

"Maybe the key," replied Phil.

The manager hooked up the monitor to play back the tape. The time of day was shown in the lower right hand corner as well as the date. He fast-forwarded to near the end of the previous day. The video was like an old movie, jerking forward with stills as the film advanced. There was no sound, just video. The time of the fire approached and they saw the clerk and a line of three customers suddenly turn toward the back of the store, just out of the fish-eye lens view. Customers walked out as the clerk was seen heading back to the rear of the store. Three young teenage girls also were seen running away.

"It's one of those girls, I'll bet!" shouted the manager.

"No. Remember the fire was started with a time-delay so it was placed five or 10 minutes before the fire started," said Phil.

"There musta been ten people that came and went in that time!" said the manager.

"Yeah, but as long as he walked by the check-out, he's in here somewhere," said Phil. "The fish-eye catches the ends of all the aisles except a little bit of the one nearest the door when the camera sweeps back!"

"I'll rewind it to fifteen minutes before the fire," said the manager.

"Take it back thirty minutes," Ash said. "We might see our guy as he came in. He coulda' fooled around inside for a long time before he set the thing up." The film was rewound and started forward. There were about twenty people that came in and out of the camera's probing eye.

"This place does some volume. Is it always like this?" Ash asked.

"Yeah, sometimes more. On Friday and Saturday I run two clerks." The manager beamed.

"How much do you take in a week in this place?" Ash asked as Phil rolled his eyes at the question.

"This store takes care of my mortgage, my cars and my wife's Nordstrom's bill each month." The manager said as the film advanced.

Phil thought back to the previous fires. The fires credited to the coin-tosser, if he was their man, had happened during the daytime as well as at night. Several days would elapse with no fires that they knew of and then there would be a sudden rush. This suggested that the arsonist had a flexible work schedule and was obviously not a teenager attending school. His fires were sometimes widely scattered, thus he was old enough to drive. Since he set fires in a variety of jurisdictions, it was hard to accumulate information. Some agencies wouldn't even dispatch an investigator to a small vacant lot fire or a fire like the one in the 7-11 store. No one had could provide a description of the suspect since the time-delay ensured he was long gone when the fire ignited. Phil was sure that the arsonist was an adult male, probably unmarried, based on his frequent late nights out setting fires. He was probably a normal-appearing adult male, inconspicuous and obviously insecure, not a rolling-eyed lunatic who would draw attention. Of the serial arsonists that Phil arrested during his years as an investigator, they all fit into the profile of studies done on convicted arsonists that Phil had read. Insecurity and a need for attention was the common denominator. They weren't flamboyant individuals. They were weak and insecure people, uncomfortable with crowds, except during their fires, and the fires they set were their way of gathering attention. Arsonists gained a warped recognition they needed from the excitement of a fire. Phil knew that some serial arsonists, the true pyromaniacs, actually gained sexual excitement as they watched the fire and its related activities.

At six minutes before the time of the fire, they saw a teenage girl walk by the camera to the door.

"That's the same one that ran out when the fire started," said the manager.

"Right," said Ash. As she cleared the door, the legs of a male were seen entering and walking up the aisle. The camera couldn't quite pick him up. His pants were dark blue and he was wearing Nike shoes. The camera panned, and he was again picked up as he walked toward the check-out. Several other people were also in view, but Phil focused on this lone male. The wide angle of the camera distorted the face of the man but showed a plaid shirt and a jacket being worn by a 30-something-year-old male. His clothing was nondescript, with the exception of the shoes. As he walked away from the camera, Phil saw that the back of his right shoe showed an excessive amount of wear on the right side, possibly caused by many hours behind the wheel of a car. The thick rubber on the floor of a car scuffed and discolored the back of the shoe while the foot pressed the accelerator if a soft floor mat wasn't in place. This guy obviously spent a lot of time behind the wheel of a car. Probably while traveling, looking for places to set his fires. Phil's cheap car had no floor mats. He held this information and didn't say anything to the other two men. The male left the camera's view briefly, only to return and walk away a third time.

Phil swore, "Son of a bitch! He almost seems to know the camera's watching!"

"Who are you talking about?" Ash asked. Phil realized that he had said nothing to the other two men about his suspicions about the male. He filled them in and they all concentrated on the tape. It was quickly rewound to the point when the male entered. It rolled forward to the point when he picked up the potato chips. As soon as the man walked away, the teenage girl again entered.

"Here he comes again!" said Phil. The male put the chips back and put his hand into his pocket as he walked into view. His head turned down and away from the check-out as he passed, looking into his hands. His face was never clearly seen.

"Shit," said Phil. "Keep it rolling and let's see who else goes into that area between now and when everybody turns their heads to the back aisle." The film played and several people walked in and out of view, but none went near the Styro coolers.

"Most people go behind the camera toward the beer and wine section that time of night," the manager volunteered. Faster than they expected, heads turned as the clerk went to the fire. The glow could just be barely seen. The customers ran out and another man was seen rushing forward with an extinguisher.

"That does it. Unless the time delay was longer than thirty minutes, that's our guy!" Phil said, pleased with the progress.

"Nobody went into that area from the time the crook did until the fire started. Now all we gotta do is develop a suspect and check his shoes," laughed Ash. "Piece of cake."

Phil and Ash took the tape as evidence and tried to obtain more information about the teenage girl for an interview. The manager knew nothing about her other than that she frequented his store several nights each week. He called the night manager and arranged for Phil and Ash to meet with him that night when he came to work. The night manager was given the girl's description and he, too, could offer little information other than her name was Trish or Trisha.

Phil and Ash drove to the police lab and filled out the proper paperwork to have the plastic napkin wrapper checked for fingerprints. The Glendale Police Lab was renowned for its fingerprint work, and Phil was confident that if there were any prints, they would be able to lift them. The small police lab couldn't process the video to obtain still photos of the suspect but they recommended that Phil and Ash take the tape to the L.A. County Sheriff's Lab on Beverly Boulevard for the more extensive work they needed.

It was only 10 a.m. and already Phil was feeling the effects of his lack of sleep as they drove the ten miles to the Sheriff's Lab and had them run off a copy of the video for them. They still hadn't checked the vacant lot or tree fire next to the real estate office. The vacant lot was examined and they found nothing significant. The fire obviously started off the alley but that's where Engine Six chose to attack the fire from. Firefighter's boot prints and hose drag marks, destroyed any evidence of a device, but the real estate office had more to offer.

Phil found the remains of a paper bag and wadded newspaper still resting in the tree branches. Also intact was the same brand of cigarette with the glue bead still nested in the bottom of the bag. The fire had burned upward and the tightly wadded paper actually protected the device from burning completely out.

"Pisses me off that Fire Captains don't spend more time looking at their fires," Phil grumbled. "Pierce will probably list this as a lightning strike!"

"So you think this is the coin-tosser guy?" asked Ash.

"Just a gut feeling, but yeah," said Phil, glancing around the busy street. "This guy's got to be pretty ballsy to pull this shit off on a busy street and an open 7-11!"

8

Aaron got home from work at 8:15 a.m. on Saturday and he had the whole day to himself. He walked into the living room and read his mail from Friday. It was very warm inside. His small two-bedroom home was already feeling the effects of the heat from the rising sun. During the night, the hot Santa Ana winds raced down through the canyons of the San Gabriel Mountains from the Mojave Desert. The Los Angeles Basin usually was cooled by the air coming off the Pacific Ocean, but several times a year, the hot desert winds forced their way through the canyons, cleared the stagnant air and caused the temperatures to jump 10-15 degrees, and more. It was only 8:30 a.m., but the temperature was already near 80. Aaron could hear the rustling leaves in the eucalyptus tree outside his bedroom window. The winds were gusting to 50 miles per hour after several hours of early morning tranquility.

Aaron thought back over the 24-hour shift he just worked. The engine company he was assigned to responded to no emergency calls until late Friday afternoon. He and the other three firefighters assigned to the station spent most of the day cleaning the old fire station and inspecting small businesses for fire safety violations.

The Los Angeles Fire Department had over a hundred fire stations and Aaron, having over eight years on the job, could have picked any station he wanted and probably gotten assigned to it. This one, however, had character and was fairly busy. He liked the variety a mountain station offered. They fought brush fires as well as an occasional house fire in the exclusive neighborhood. They also responded down the mountain to the San Fernando Valley to assist Valley firefighters on major structure fires, and more frequently to Hollywood. Hollywood, aging rapidly, had many major fires in the redeveloping community.

Aaron reclined on his bed and back to Thursday night. He grimaced, clenching his teeth in frustration over his unsuccessful attempt at burning the real estate office. His mind wandered to the large-breasted girl at the 7-11 and how he had considered stalking her for more excitement than his fires provided, but quickly remembered how frightened he was when he discovered the video camera sweeping the store. How he drove away and parked at darkened health food store lot just across the street from the 7-11. As soon as he parked his car, he saw the stream of thin black smoke rising from the Styro coolers. He was amazed at how long it took people inside the store to finally notice the growing fire and how the smoke hit the ceiling and blossomed out. He remembered picking up his binoculars and focusing on the teenaged girl as she fled. Aaron began fondling his penis and unzipped his pants to relive the excitement he'd felt. He had almost totally ignored the fire as he watched the girl and her friends stand outside the store. One of the girls was so frightened that she was crying.

"Today will be a much better day", he thought. The Santa Anas were blowing and he had nothing but time on his hands.

He showered and dressed in a pair of shorts and a T-shirt. Walking into the kitchen, he sat and thought about where he could go to start his day's activities. He decided to focus on the north Valley area near Chatsworth.

Getting off the freeway in Burbank, he drove to a drive-through bank teller. He was almost out of cigarettes and had little cash with him. He also didn't like buying his supplies too near where he set his fires. As he drove out of the bank parking lot, he spotted a discarded mattress and box spring leaning against a wooden garage. His trained eye saw that the burning mattress would easily set fire to the old structure. He was already excited by the Santa Ana winds, and this fire would start off his day perfectly.

He drove around the block and parked near a restaurant. He saw that the restaurant dining area looked directly down the alley where the garage was. He set up his device and drove back to the bank, where he opened a paper bag, stuffing it with newspaper. He looked around and saw that there was no one in the alley. No windows from the surrounding apartments looked down on the area where he was to set his device. He lit the cigarette and slowly drove up to the mattress, lining his door up with the end of the stained bedding. He opened his door slightly and set the bag between the garage and the base of the mattress. Anyone seeing his actions would simply think that he was throwing away trash. He drove several blocks out of his way and entered the restaurant parking area from the back so no one inside could see his car. Aaron was always worried that an off-duty cop might observe his activities and later put two

35

and two together when the fire finally erupted. He took many precautions.

Entering the restaurant, he found a seat at the counter where no one was sitting on either side of him. One seat had a newspaper lying on it. He picked it up. After ordering, he allowed himself to look down the alley. He had set a substantial delay this time, almost the entire length of the cigarette. He peeked over the top of the paper and saw nothing. The garage was over 500 feet away. The yellow mattress was visible, but the device was set up on the end away from Aaron's view.

Within minutes, he saw smoke blowing up the alley. The wind was spreading the fire along the underside of the mattress and the smoke was coming out of the lean-to space like a chimney. Soon flames could be seen, but only by Aaron. He held the newspaper up so he could just barely see the fire. No one inside the restaurant noticed.

The erratic winds spread the fire around the end of the garage toward a trailer storage lot. Aaron's breakfast was served. As he raised his coffee to his lips, he heard a child discover the fire, pointing to it from a booth. The boy's mother sat staring. Aaron put down his cup and again picked up the paper, imagining how a normal customer would act, what the woman would decide to do. From past experience, Aaron knew that many people enjoyed a fire and would simply watch assuming someone else would call the fire department. He figured she would be no different. He was correct. She sat watching with her son as the entire side of the garage burst into flames, heat swelling from the burning foam rubber-stuffed mattress. Others began to notice, too, for the thick, black smoke was now blowing up the alley to the restaurant. A waitress serving coffee to people seated near the windows saw the flames and raced to the cashier asking her to call the fire department. There was still nobody in the alley; most residents in this area were still asleep. Aaron continued to eat and watch the fire openly as anyone would once they saw it. He relaxed, blending in with everyone else. His tension went away and was replaced with excitement. His metamorphosis from criminal to bystander was complete. No one noticed him. As the fire entered the garage, the contents began to burn and the flames subsided somewhat due to lack of oxygen. A sudden 40-mile-per-hour gust provided the air needed and the garage seemed to explode. Bright orange flames fanned, the burning side of the garage fell in, opening the contents of trash, boxes and an old car to the full assault of wind and fire. Aaron got a sudden rush from the increase in flames and yearned getting nearer to the fire. He fought the urge, but saw others in the restaurant eating faster while several others paid their bill quickly so they could rush toward the fire. He gulped down his food. The flames blew sideways by the fierce wind. A garage 30 feet away, licked by flames from the intense heat, began to smoke. It, too, ignited. Sirens sounded in the distance. The sirens did it for Aaron. He could no longer resist the temptation to get closer. Before quickly walking out the door, he left enough money on the counter to cover his bill and a large tip.

He debated going to his car, but decided to use the cover of the other customers to allow him to get closer. He usually felt much safer inside his car, but this fire had already involved a third garage and was now blowing into a storage lot containing several boats. Aaron had never seen a boat burn. Excitement overwhelming him, his cheeks tingled and shivered uncontrollably as he got closer. The wind had slowed slightly, and the column of thick black smoke was now rising straight up into the clear sky. He looked across the Valley and saw another column of smoke in the Topanga Canyon area 15 miles away. Aaron smiled. He knew that there were other arsonists who acted the same way on days when the Santa Anas blew. Sometimes it was as if they were competing, he thought, each trying to set a fire bigger than the other. He had seen as many as four separate columns of smoke from the Valley at the same time.

He forgot about the other smoke and focused on his fire. Two engines arrived simultaneously and began laying hose from nearby hydrants into the fire area. He could hear their radios blaring now as the Battalion Chief requested a second alarm for more help. A ladder truck swung down the alley and screeched to a halt. Confronted with a roadblock of fire and smoke, their progress crippled. The first garage was already collapsing, spilling its burning contents across the alley, against another building, onto several cars. As the ladder truck backed up, it blocked Aaron's view. Anxiously, he walked closer to the fire.

"Hey! Get the hell back outta' this alley!" screamed a cop appearing from nowhere. The crowd reluctantly started easing back. The ladder truck continued its retreat. Suddenly, Aaron heard screeching tires followed by a crash. He turned around and watched, horrified, as a small Toyota careened off the street into the rear of the ladder truck, crushing the ladders that extended out the back of the rig. The car had turned off the street to go down the alley, not expecting to find its path blocked. The wooden ladders splintered, piercing the windshield of the small car. Two men in the front seat threw their hands in front of their faces. The car came to a halt, the ladder end resting on the man's forehead. They were both covered by broken glass and shattered wood, and now Aaron saw blood. His instincts as a firefighter were to rush in and help, but this situation was different. He froze as firefighters and policeman rushed forward. The ladder truck's driver also rushed to the crash, abandoning the cab to help. Within seconds, the wind changed and again blew heat, flames and smoke toward the truck. Aaron, now frightened, began backing away as the crowd rushed in to look at the injured occupants of the car. He looked at the fire and felt the heat pulsate on his skin. The nearest boat burst into flames. He again started to back away as the ladder truck's captain shouted into his radio to send an ambulance. At that same moment, Aaron saw the plastic emergency light bar on top of the fire truck's cab begin to melt.

"Your truck's burning, Cap!" shouted Aaron, cursing himself for using firefighter's vocabulary.

"Shit! Muldown, get back in the rig, it's on fire!" the Captain pleaded. Muldown, the driver, saw the problem and quickly analyzed how to save his rig without having to back over the disabled car adhering itself to his truck. The Captain, also realizing their predicament shouted into his radio to the Battalion Chief to divert one engine to protect his rig and another to lay a supply line to it so they wouldn't lose everything. The fire briefly subsided and continued its trek in the opposite direction, but soon the wind again changed. The light bar finally caught fire and the rig's windshield cracked from the heat. The firefighters worked frantically to free the trapped occupants of the car, but the doors wouldn't open.

The second alarm companies were still minutes away, and the Captain decided to back up the ladder truck anyway. The Captain and Muldown hastily debated their plan and Muldown charged the cab as the other firefighters tried to lay the car seats flat to get the two men out of the jeopardy of broken, twisted ladders. The car seats wouldn't lie flat, and Muldown quickly found the heat too much. The front seats of the rig began to burn. Muldown ran back and advised the Captain. They opted to do what firefighters do first, save the lives; the burning ladder truck would have to wait. The burning cab was almost 50 feet away and actually protected the rescue efforts from the flames.

Aaron felt helpless but knew that there was nothing he could do. He started moving back toward the restaurant and noticed the fire's progress on the far side subside by hose streams dousing the boat. The firefighters quickly worked their way toward the burning ladder truck, drowning as much fire as they could, waiting for the assisting engines to arrive. Their hose lines, stretching over 300 feet from the other side of the fire line, stopped just short of an effective reach to the ladder truck. The exhausted firefighters couldn't pull any more of the heavy hose lines with the manpower they had.

Two engines suddenly appeared from the nearby freeway and were quickly followed by two Glendale engines and another ladder truck, brought in on the third alarm. The Glendale companies had already started rolling to adjacent Burbank when they heard a second alarm called. Routine called for them to fill the empty Burbank stations during a major fire to handle other emergencies. With the heavy winds and a rapidly progressing fire, they knew they were probably going to be needed at the fire. They guessed correctly. The two agencies worked smoothly and took advantage of the momentary lull in the winds to attack the fire with ferocity. The black smoke quickly turned to steam and the fire halted. Aaron glanced at the two badly injured crash victims as he walked back toward his car. The fire was out so he lost interest quickly. As soon as he got in his car, he decided to stay in the Burbank area a little longer. There were a lot of alleys nearby and he wanted more excitement like he had just experienced. He sat behind the wheel of his car and took a deep breath, hugging himself and shuddering.

"That was so fucking great!" he muttered.

He steered his car out of the parking lot, driving slowly. The residual smoke and steam from the fire blowing up the alley made it difficult to see very far. He continued north in the alley toward the nearby residential areas. People were still drifting toward the fire, walking by him without giving him a second glance. Aaron felt a chill go through his body, enjoying the ecstasy of his successful fire and the accompanying Santa Anas.

After driving two more blocks from the restaurant, he found an alley lined with apartment buildings. Each two-story building had carports off the alley, open for his easy access. He saw many with stored cardboard boxes, some with discarded furniture and several with trash containers stored inside. None of these usually attractive possibilities appealed to him. He had just scored a three-alarm fire and he wanted to at least equal it if he could.

In the next block, he found a wood-frame two-car garage similar to the one he had just burned. The old structure sat between two of the apartments, just off the alley. Behind the garage, facing the street side was a large two-story wood frame home. Aaron figured that an older person lived in the home and probably refused to sell out to developers as the street filled with condos and apartments over the years. He drew abreast of the garage and saw that the doors were closed and the yard next to it was overgrown with dry grass and weeds. The weeds were 10-12 inches high and actually climbed up the wall of the garage in several places. Aaron knew from experience that the grass was more than sufficient to ignite the wooden structure. At the next street, he turned into the flow of traffic, reached down beside him and put together several devices. He drove two blocks and turned down the street in front of the old home. As he passed, he saw that the house appeared abandoned. The front yard was as poorly kept as the back. He hummed to himself thinking that this meant that there would be no occupant to discover the fire early and probably no garden hoses or water for anybody to use to catch the fire before it got going. He continued driving and picked up a back-up device, the glue now dry, and placed it inside his T-shirt pocket.

Aaron was momentarily confused as he tried to find the entrance leading to the garage. He pulled into the next alley and found himself at the garage before he knew it. He jammed the cigarette device into his mouth and lit it with his lighter. As he rolled down the driver's side window to throw out the device, a young mother and child pulled out of a carport. They both glanced at Aaron but he kept looking straight ahead and continued to drive. His throwing the device out at that moment would have made the woman a witness. As he drove, he looked into his mirror and saw them continue walking. He saw that they were dressed in swimsuits and carried beach towels. "*Probably walking to the bus stop to go to the beach*," he thought. He drove through the street at the end and re-entered the alley in the next block. His device was still burning and appeared to have 8-10 minutes delay left. He glanced up the alley and saw a pile of discarded furniture and trash falling onto the ground. Loose papers were being blown around in a small whirlwind by the gusts. The pile was right next to a camper and close to the side of the apartment building. *Not much*, he thought, but dropped the device into the trash anyway. Quickly, he sped up and returned to the original target and lit his backup device. The two-car garage came up fast and this time he saw the brake lights of one of the cars in the carport suddenly shine.

"Fuck it!" he said and tossed the device toward the garage. The gusting wind picked it up and he saw it carried further into the yard than he wanted. He had no inclination to do anything about it and saw the car start to back out as he passed. He sped up again. His heart was pounding as he accelerated and tried to blend in with the traffic. He headed back toward the first fire near the restaurant and found that traffic was still heavy in the area and smoke was still coming up from the destroyed garages. Another ladder truck was parked parallel to the burned truck with the Toyota still imbedded in its rear. An ambulance was parked nearby, and he saw CPR being administered to one of the crash victims. *Really fucked the guy up*, he thought to himself. He gave it no further thought. The victim didn't concern him.

Aaron drove back to the restaurant and parked where he could see up the alley toward the pending fires. Within seconds he saw smoke blowing into the alley from the trash pile next to the furniture. The smoke was quickly blown out of his sight by the erratic winds. The garage started emitting bluish smoke from the grass fire blowing next to it. He chuckled to himself and turned his engine off so he could hear the radio on the engine parked next to the restaurant. He wanted to time how long it would take for the two fires to be reported.

The smoke increased in volume and both columns soon turned black. One from the furniture and the other from the garage. Aaron fought the urge to drive to the fires and watch, not wanting to be seen a second time by the firemen or the cop that yelled at him. He started his car anyway, and drove toward the engines, away from the fires. As he passed the Burbank engine, he heard the radio dispatch a single engine company to a grass fire. Being in Burbank, he wasn't familiar with the street name but knew that this was one of his fires. He saw the Chief and several other firemen running to their rigs. Aaron drove back toward his fires. Turning a corner, he saw two columns of thick, black smoke being dissipated by the strong winds. The bases of the columns were highlighted by fingers of orange flame shooting toward the sky. He heard sirens behind him and rushed on. Driving by the front of the abandoned house he saw several people watching the fire. One man was on the porch, pounding on the door. The garage, seen back up the driveway, was covered by a sheet of flame from one side to the other. Aaron heard breaking glass from the apartment nearest the fire and people screaming.

"This is great, so fucking great!" he muttered.

Driving past the burning garage, he saw that the other column of smoke was smaller and the fire was probably not going to get any bigger. He turned onto the next block and parked his car, ignoring his earlier thought of not wanting to be seen twice. The fire and excitement going on in that block were his and he wanted it. He wanted to be close to it.

It was almost 95 degrees outside now, so he took off his shirt as he got out of his car and walked toward the fire. He stuffed the shirt into the waistband of his shorts and hurried onto the street. Several fire engines arrived. Aaron joined the blossoming crowd. His excitement remained, and his concern about being discovered in the crowd went away. The firemen unraveled their hoses and dragged them down the driveway. They were weighed down by their protective gear and air bottles and many were soaked with water from fighting the earlier fire. Aaron sympathized with the firemen fighting fire in this heat with over 60 pounds of equipment dragging them down, but smiled, knowing that each of them was having the time of his life. He knew that firemen went to work every day hoping for disasters like this, even if there was destruction. *Enjoy yourselves*, thought Aaron as he moved in closer.

He saw a police car driving up the street and started moving back toward his car. A loud pop came from the garage as the firemen started putting water on the fire. The gusting wind suddenly pushed the flames and smoke down on top of them.

"Wires down!" came a shout from the alley. The wind now blew the loose wires along the top of a chain link fence in the yard, showering the firemen with sparks. The crowd collectively took in its breath as firemen scattered to get away from the 700 volts of electricity. Once the downed lines could be seen, the firemen recovered quickly and continued their attack on the flames, which were subsiding. Aaron looked up toward the other fire and saw that the smoke was still pushing skyward, but didn't appear to have been attacked by firemen yet. He got into his car, then decided against it, rather walking the short distance to see what was happening. In his excitement, he crossed the street without looking. A blue Chevy approached rapidly, causing him to dart across. His shirt dropped out of his waistband. The Chevy driver jammed on his brakes as Aaron reached back to retrieve the shirt. He waved at the driver of the car and nodded a thanks, an apologetic shrug and a sheepish smile as he continued on his way toward the fire. He heard more engines approaching and saw four suddenly roar onto the street heading to his third fire of the day. Again he joined others racing to the smoke and flames.

While walking, he looked closely at the blue Chevy again as it turned the corner nearest the fire. A police-type, four-door sedan. *Fucking arson cop*, he thought to himself, subtly reversing his direction and heading back to his car. He automatically reached into his pocket as if he had forgotten something. He didn't turn around until he was almost to his car. He checked the street for approaching cars, but also to look farther beyond to see where the blue Chevy was. It was out of sight so he crossed toward his car, noticing that other rubberneckers had parked in front of and behind it. He was grateful that they had; his own license plates were invisible from a passing car. He stood with the door open briefly then reached in and turned on the engine and air conditioner. The powerful engine of the old Chevy purred. Aaron's car was just like him; inconspicuous and blended in with just about any atmosphere. Although old, it was in good condition with a powerful V-8 engine. Painted a medium grey with stock rims, it looked just like a thousand other Chevy's on the street. Traffic had thinned so he decided to make a U-turn rather than drive back where the cop cars were. After the turn, he started to accelerate rapidly. He fought the urge to gun it, but felt too excited. He shifted into second gear with a slight chirp of the rear tires. He slowed heading back to the freeway. Heading west, he saw the column of smoke from the Topanga Canyon area above the treetops lining the street. He decided to drive to the West Valley and see what was happening.

Still miles away, he heard a radio report that the Topanga fire was under control. The smoke column was breaking up. He drove up Ventura Boulevard and headed toward the Van Nuys area. He was a little reluctant to do anything in Van Nuys since it was close to fire stations he worked alongside battling fires. An off-duty fireman seen at a single fire was not unusual, but if he were to be seen by the same person more than once, he could become a suspect. However, it did offer so many opportunities for a good fire, he didn't really care.

9

Phil tried to sleep late Saturday morning, but the incessant gusting winds troubled him. He was always fearful of a brush fire and the Santa Ana winds doubled that concern. He tossed and turned and finally smelled breakfast cooking. Sean had been up for several hours and had made coffee, fried chorizo and eggs.

Phil slipped on a pair of shorts and walked to the kitchen. Sean was just setting the table where Beth, Sean's wife, sat with a cup of coffee. Sean asked, "You going to Hollywood this morning to look at that burned carport for me?" Phil, still sleepy, had to think a minute before responding.

"Oh, yeah. Thanks for reminding me. I didn't even think about it until now. Anything special you want on this one?"

"No. The insurance company is sure it wasn't the owner who set the fire," Sean replied. "So they just want the usual pictures and report."

"I'll head out after breakfast and get it done before it gets too hot out." Sean added another place at the table for Phil without asking if he was hungry. Phil mumbled a thanks when the steaming plate of eggs, chorizo and tortillas was placed in front of him. Phil quickly turned his attention to the steaming plate of food. Sean returned with another plate and set it in front of Beth. He then sat down with a cup of coffee. Phil looked down into the canyon. It was a magnificently clear day for L.A., but the winds continued to howl through the trees in the yard, concerning him because of the fire danger. He had seen many brush fires and knew that days like today were the favored times for pyromaniacs.

Driving down the narrow, winding canyon road toward the city, he heard several emergency dispatches on the car radio. They were all wind-related. *"Wires down...Sign blown down onto a car"*. As he drove through the Los Feliz area on the edge of Hollywood, he heard dispatchers sending equipment to a garage fire in Burbank. The radio immediately was cluttered with responding companies reporting a large column of smoke from the area of the reported fire. As the firefighters arrived, Phil heard the call for the second alarm and report of a car crashing into a ladder truck, too. He debated heading for the fire, drawn like most firefighters by the sounds of the excitement. He was almost to his destination and decided to go ahead and hurriedly conduct his investigation instead.

The burned carport was easy to locate. Being early on a Saturday morning, no one was around. Fortunately, the fire didn't require him to dig in the debris. The point of origin of the fire was as easy to read as a doctor examining a patient with measles. The remains of an old couch were totally consumed and, judging by the remains, it was a cheaply constructed piece stuffed with polyurethane foam. The worst fire damage was done in the area of the couch and to a lesser degree as you moved away from the furniture. This indicated that the fire burned longest on the one end of the couch near the remains of several trashcans. He also found the bottoms of several cardboard boxes next to the couch. The fire had consumed their contents to the ground, but didn't have sufficient air to burn the bottoms. This gave him a clear pattern of the fire travel. It also told him that no competent arson investigator had examined this fire. Had there been an investigation, the debris would have been cleared as he had quickly done to reveal the fire travel. He knew that this fire was arson. Cigarettes discarded into trash could start a fire, but in a busy alley like this one in the early evening hours, the smoldering mass would be noticed quickly and extinguished. It took at least thirty minutes for a smoldering trash fire to break into an open flame, and this fire did not smolder. The five or six nearby fires which also occurred that night gave Phil a comfortable margin for error.

He took several photos and heard the third alarm equipment arriving at the Burbank fire 10 miles away. He thought that the Burbank fire could also be related to the fire in the carport. Phil wanted to get a better feel for this fire by examining the other fires in this series, but Burbank's fire was much more interesting.

Pulling onto Sunset Boulevard, he glanced across the street and saw a market parking lot. He then looked over his shoulder back up the alley toward the fire scene. The traffic cleared and Phil drove across the street and entered the parking lot, looking for a good observation post for an arsonist that would allow for an unobstructed view of the carport. It was easy to find. The alley was narrow, with a building on one side and several parked trucks on the other side. A telephone pole sitting slightly into the alley limited the view of the fire scene, with an exception of one or two parking spaces in the lot. Phil imagined himself the arsonist. He reached down and turned his radio off and sat, looking up the alley. He was fascinated as he realized how the arsonist probably worked his trade. The pyromaniac would most likely drive up the alley and quickly throw or place his time-delay device in the trash at the side of the alley. This fire would have required the device to be physically placed, since the point of origin of the fire was a good 10-12 feet off the alley. He might have walked up the alley, Phil thought, but a Caucasian male in this area might draw attention if he was on foot. A Mexican or a black man wouldn't. If this fire was done by the same guy from the 7-11 security camera, he was a white man.

After the device was placed, thought Phil, *the pyromaniac does what all pyromaniacs do: blend in with the crowd.* He probably drove around the other end of the alley and circled the block, coming back to the parking lot to watch his fire develop. *Damn,* Phil thought, *if firefighters could just train themselves to look at the crowd a little more often during a fire, we might catch these guys!* Phil realized that this was asking too much. Even he couldn't quite train himself to check out a crowd until the fire was out. The fire itself was such a spectacle that doing anything but watching it was difficult.

He glanced to the northwest and saw smoke over the Topanga Canyon area. He switched his radio back on and could still hear the chatter of firefighters in Burbank, joined now by units from neighboring cities. Phil pulled out of the parking lot and headed back toward Burbank. He activated the flashing yellow light in his rear window and used the gutter lanes to pass traffic and run red lights without actually going code three. He didn't like using red lights and siren in other jurisdictions. It just confused the local cops when they saw a police-type car going code three and they couldn't figure out who it was or why. When he did do it, he inevitably found the local cops following him, also code three, until he left their jurisdiction. It made him uncomfortable getting the other cops all excited, then having them realize that the response was by another agency.

As he dropped down through the Griffith Park area, he could see the black and gray smoke from the Burbank fire. The base of the smoke column was now turning white, indicating extinguishment. He slowed his pace slightly as he entered the northbound Interstate 5. When he was just two miles short of the off ramp nearest the fire, he saw two smaller columns of smoke sprout several blocks north of the now-dying original fire. Immediately he knew it was a serial arson. Two points of origin. The wind was blowing east and these fires were erupting directly north of the main fire. It could not have been blowing embers from the first fire, so it had to be an arsonist.

Phil tuned his radio to the primary dispatching frequency and heard a report of a single grass fire near the first fire, followed by a Battalion

Chief asking for a full first alarm assignment. The smoke turned black and thick as the garage ignited. Phil again raced toward the fire but found the freeway now congested and no way to get around it. Using a siren on a freeway was useless; there was no way for anyone to pull over along this stretch. A siren usually caused erratic reactions from commuters. He sat, crawling along until he came up on an off ramp, south of where he wanted to be. The first column of smoke was starting to turn white, but the other was still going strong when he got within one block of the burning garage. A shower of sparks from a falling high voltage line startled him as he stared at the smoke and flames, which could be seen above the rooftops surrounding his destination. Traffic was crawling here, too. He drove past the flames on the next street over and stared at the sight, his heart racing. *What am I doing?* He thought. *My guy is around here somewhere and I'm gawking at the fire!* He shook his head and turned his attention to the bystanders. None stood out to him. He followed the traffic flow and found a cop ushering everyone away from the direction of the fire, where he needed to go. He quickly flashed his badge and was allowed to turn on to the street. He heard another fire engine racing to the other fire burning nearby. Phil gunned the big Chevy. Suddenly a man ran in front of him, causing him to brake sharply. A shirt dropped out of the man's waistband to the street and, as Phil braked, the man grabbed it and continued toward the fire. Phil cursed out loud and barely noticed the man's apologetic shrug and smile.

He glanced into his rearview mirror as he started to turn onto the street where the fire was still building. The man had abruptly stopped and turned around in the same motion and was again crossing the street. Phil thought, *must have forgot his keys in his car or something.* The man appeared to look at Phil's car as he completed the turn, but Phil had now focused his attention on the spectacle in front of him. There were more people on this street than he imagined. The two previous fires had drawn many to the smoke and they continued to multiply.

Again he cursed aloud as he tried to thread his way through the mass. He found a driveway and pulled into it, looking for anybody suspicious in the crowd. Many people stared at him as he stepped out of his "official" car. He thought, *If my guy's here, he'll spot me instantly.* He hurried through the crowd, making his way to the fire scene. He waited to catch the attention of the Burbank investigator, then motioned him to a nearby carport.

"Hey, Phil." Phil extended his hand to Captain Tom Carey, Burbank's main investigator. Carey, almost 50 years old, had been working arson investigation for the small city for many years and it showed. His gnarled face exhibited countless frustrating hours trying to investigate fires while holding down numerous other jobs for the small department. The fire chief in Burbank preferred to let the police department handle follow-up arson cases and wouldn't allow Carey to spend too much time on investigations.

"You just get here, Phil, or were you down at the first one?"

"Just pulled in. What do ya got so far?"

"Nothing. The first fire started alongside a garage off Glenoaks Boulevard and nobody saw anything. The wind really caught it and it took off two more garages, a boat, and scorched a car and an apartment," related T.C. "I'm afraid the same guy's hittin' us but this time during the day. He usually favors nighttime."

"I think he hit us a couple of days ago, but he wasn't as successful as he was with you guys. He did a vacant lot and tried the front of a real estate office but neither one caught very well," Phil offered. "Then he tried a 7-11 store on the inside in a pile of Styro coolers!"

"No shit! We had an unreported fire in the 7-11 down on Glenoaks a week ago. We just got a police report that somebody set fire to a pile of napkins. They didn't call the fire department, just put it out and called the cops."

"Would you mind if I went by your 7-11 fire to see if they have a video security camera inside that might have caught something on film?"

"No. Go right ahead. I'm going to be tied up here for a while anyway," T.C. said as he viewed the now-dying fire. "Figuring out a cause on these fires won't be too tough, but I might spend a little time on interviewing."

"Well don't spend too much time. The guy's still using time delays and nobody can remember who drove by fifteen minutes before the fire started."

"I know, but I still think surveying and interviewing everybody is the way to solve this kind of shit. Not your wham-bam method," laughed Carey as he walked away. Phil preferred talking to as few people as possible and depended on gut feeling for filling in the gaps. Witnesses were notoriously inaccurate and undependable, and Phil preferred doing without many of them.

He drove to the 7-11 store nearby and found that the store security camera was a fake. It was the hull of a camera only, electricity running to it only to supply a little red light on its side and a motor to make it sweep back and forth. The clerk who was on duty the night of the fire was working this morning also. He answered Phil's questions in a straightforward and articulate manner. He even had an investigative mind.

"Do you remember anybody unusual that was in the store before the fire?" Phil asked.

"Yes. This man, about twenty five years old, came in, and as soon as he walked in he turned to the first aisle and headed to the back with a purpose. I assumed he knew exactly what he wanted, but he stayed along the back wall for several minutes. This usually tells me that someone is a shoplifter but he was a clean-cut man and didn't even pick up anything. I could see him plainly in the security mirror there," he said as he pointed to the standard convex mirror mounted near the ceiling. "He waited while another customer walked away and was at my register before he moved again. This time he stayed along the back wall by the coolers and walked across to the other side of the store where I couldn't see him. This made me relax a little bit since he now appeared to be a normal customer. The next time I see him, he's walking out the door, and reaching into his pocket. I think, he must not have enough money to buy, but then he has to stand by the door as three other people come in and I see him pull out a twenty-dollar bill! The man looked at me and then left. This man made me very nervous!"

"Did you see what kind of car he got into?"

"It was a gray car, maybe a Chevy. I saw him go onto the freeway there," the clerk said as he gestured toward the Interstate 5 on ramp. "It had loud exhaust pipes. Four or five minutes later I see smoke from the napkins near where this man was. I locked the cash register and pushed the robbery alarm to get the police here quickly. I knew I could put the fire out so I did not call the firemen."

"Okay, okay, slow down a minute," Phil said as the clerk continued rapidly relating the events of that night. "What happened next?" he asked.

"I pulled down the napkins and stomped them out and looked around to make sure the man did not sneak back in to try and steal from me. I thought for sure that was what he planned, but there was no one else in the store until the police came two minutes later, and they did not care anyway! I told them about the man, and all the police could say was that I should not push the robbery alarm except when someone steals from me with a gun or a knife! How can they be that way, Mr. Langtry? The robber can only get forty or fifty dollars, but the fire can destroy thousands! This is not reasonable! What can I ..."

"I'm on your side," Phil said. "I know what you're saying, but did the police finally take a report from you about the man?"

"Oh, yes. They took a report, but my boss got a copy two days later, and all it said was that someone probably dropped a cigarette in the napkin display and it started a fire. I gave them a good description of the man, and it never appeared in the report! What is wrong with the police anyway?" he said as he flailed his hands over his head. Phil shook his head sympathetically.

"Is there anything else you remember about this man?" Phil queried.

"Let me think…Oh, he was wearing a T-shirt. It was white with a little black cross printed over the left breast here," he said as he pointed to his own chest. "But it wasn't really a cross, it was more like an 'X' like you see on a treasure map, you know? The 'X' marks the spot? And it also had some letters around it like they stood for something. I think some of the letters were f's, maybe two of them." The clerk continued to complain about the police. Phil tuned him out and focused on what the man had just revealed. The 'X' he was describing was a Maltese cross, long the symbol of firefighters everywhere. The double f's could mean that the symbol was that of one of several firefighters' associations acronyms, such as UFFA, the United Firefighters Association. *The man could be a fireman*, Phil thought.

He continued questioning the Pakistani between customers and gained a good description of the potential arsonist. He was young, clean cut, with a good build, and the description fit only five or six thousand firefighters in Southern California. Phil didn't reveal the Maltese cross information to the clerk, but did ask him if he would recognize the design if he saw it again, as well as the potential arsonist. Yes on both counts.

He tried to buy a Budweiser to quench his thirst. The clerk wouldn't take his money, and Phil was forced to listen once again to the tirade against the police. He ultimately reached down to his side and told the clerk that he got paged and had to go. Phil smiled and begged off, walking out the door to a pay phone. He looked back over his shoulder and saw the clerk watching him, so he felt obliged to call someone. The call went through to Marta but the pay phone refused to open the line as Marta answered at the other end. She quickly hung up when there was no one on the line. Phil cursed.

He slipped inside his sweltering car and sat thinking about the possibilities of a psycho firefighter setting the fires. It was a well-known fact that firefighters and police officers had been caught setting fires before, but these problems were primarily in small communities with volunteer firemen and part-time cops. The small communities couldn't afford in-depth background and psychological exams of new-hires, and occasionally a bad one got through. Phil had heard of volunteers teaming up and taking turns setting small fires for the excitement of the fires and, in some cases, the money paid to volunteers on a per-call basis. These were the exceptions, but it had happened in the past. Most volunteers Phil knew were exceptionally devoted individuals. There was only one volunteer fire department in Los Angeles County, and Phil didn't even give a second thought to their ranks for a possible suspect. The fires were occurring all over the Metro Los Angeles area and in at least four different jurisdictions that he was aware of. This pyromaniac, if he was a firefighter, had to be a full-time smoke-eater. That would explain many things. The motive couldn't be money or the excitement of responding code three to a blaze like the convicted volunteers. He could only set the fires when he was off duty. It was simple pyromania; a compulsion to set a fire and watch things burn. He certainly couldn't be setting fires for any other reason.

Phil instantly recognized the potential clue that would convince him of the firefighter pyromaniac theory. All firefighters in the Los Angeles area worked the same type of three-shift schedule of 24 hours on and 24 hours off. The make up of the schedule provided that firefighters worked only 10 days per month. They were 24-hour days, but they still had almost 20 days off per month. Plenty of time to travel around and set fires in different areas. The three shifts were color-coded on a calendar that Phil carried with him. He finished his Bud and brought the calendar out to study it. There was 'A', 'B' and 'C' shift, red, blue and green, respectively, on the calendar. Phil thought back over the past week and remembered his real estate office and the 7-11 fires were on Thursday night. Friday was a quiet day and did not have any fires, nor did Burbank or Pasadena. He had gone over the computer read-out of those cities by calling in this morning and asking the dispatchers. This was Saturday and already there were several fires. Wednesday night, there was that string of fires in Hollywood, too. That meant that only one day this week, Friday, there weren't any fires locally. Friday was a 'B' shift day. 'B' shift had been off this week on a normal four days off cycle; Monday through Thursday. Friday they went back to work.

Phil analyzed the week further. The 7-11 he was sitting in front of had their fire on last Saturday night, another off-day for 'B' shift. It appeared that fires were only occurring on 'A' and 'C' shifts, thus only an off-duty 'B' shifter could be setting the fires, if there was indeed a firefighter involved. Phil knew that once a pattern was set, he would be better able to continue the investigation. He needed to check past fires and the days they started, as well as waiting for more fires to further his theory. Unfortunately, checking fires in other agencies might require a great deal of assistance from other investigators, and Phil wasn't prepared to allow anyone to know that he suspected a fellow firefighter. That type of information, should it be leaked, would certainly get passed around, if not publicized, and cause the pyro to stop. The only practical way to continue was to wait for more fires, and to check dates of past arson fires in the area. Phil felt that his brush fires earlier in the summer were possibly related to the garage and carport fires, so correlating their dates would help broaden the database for his theory. He pulled out of the 7-11 lot and headed back toward home, thinking, *what if he did the Cal's fire, too? A firefighter killed five people, just for the thrill of it?*

Arriving at his office, it took just a short while for him to check his computer to find the series of brush fires. There were seven over a two-week period and all were set on a day when 'B' shift was off-duty. Ironically, there was one oddball brush fire that didn't quite fit the pattern of the rest and was probably set by someone else. That fire started in an area away from a roadway at the rear of a park's baseball diamond. "Probably juveniles" Ash Nolan's report said. Ash handled three of the other fires, too, and all were termed arson and all had started within 10 feet of a street in the brush-covered foothill areas. Ash, his partner, had also found the remains of two of the time-delay devices with coins attached.

Phil was now convinced. It was just too much of a coincidence that this many fires could have happened on a 'B' shift off-day. The arsonist must be a 'B' shift firefighter.

He reluctantly took out his personal file on the Cal's fire. He had kept newspaper clippings and other documents relating to the fire for such an occasion as this: the development of a suspect. He had also obtained copies of some of the investigative reports from South Pasadena's police investigation. Phil looked at the date of the fire. It was three years ago, a weekday, but he did not have the firefighter shift calendar for that year in his office. He picked up the phone and called Chief Dartel, the on-duty Battalion Chief.

"Chief Dartel," was the curt reply to Phil's call.

"Morning, Chief. Phil Langtry here. How's it goin'?"

"Hi, Phil. Okay so far. Hell of a fire over in Burbank this morning. Hear about it?"

"Yeah, I was over there for awhile with Burbank's investigator. Did you get assigned to the fire?" Phil knew full well that he had. Nearby agencies automatically get assigned to a second alarm fire. A second Battalion Chief is frequently needed at major fires to take command of various support activities at the Command Post or to take over a portion of the fire.

"Yeah, they dispatched me, but by the time I got there, it was pretty well knocked down. What'd you find at the fire, a pile of nickels and dimes?" the Chief laughed.

"No, sir. I let Carey from Burbank handle the investigation. He really didn't need any help. He did tell me about a fire in a 7-11 store they had last week that matches the one I told you about over on Broadway Thursday."

"What burned?" asked the Chief.

"Just a pile of napkins. The clerk put it out and only the cops came. No fire response and their suspect matches ours perfectly."

"Good luck findin' him. He sounds real whacko. What can I do for you, Phil?" Phil was instantly sorry he had called the Chief, remembering that Dartel went to the Cal's fire and would recognize the date immediately.

"Uh, yeah, Chief…I was wondering, do you have old shift calendars around from the last couple of years?"

"Yeah, I can look in the old files. What date you interested in?"

"October 10, 1984," Phil reluctantly said.

"That was the Cal's fire. What are you on to?" the old Chief questioned. The Chief had worked arson many years ago, and he still had a sharp, suspicious mind.

"Oh, I was just checking some old files and needed to find a fire captain's name from Pasadena that I talked to during the fire. I'm not sure what shift he worked," Phil lied.

"Well, I went to that fire and I was working for Chief Becner while he was on vacation. The fire was on a 'C' shift day."

"Great. Thanks a lot, Chief. You saved me a lot of time," Phil said as they hung up. *B shift off again*, thought Phil. He picked up the thick file and took out a copy of the South Pasadena Police Department's interview of the employee that escaped the flames. The only one working in the area of the fire who got out alive. The interview was brief and did very little to enlighten Phil. The police, convinced that the fire was accidental, asked few questions pertaining to people in the store at the time of the fire, focusing mainly on the discovery of the fire. One statement did catch his eye. The employee said that he saw only one person in the area of the store where he first saw the fire. It was almost closing time so there were few people around. The description of the man was about 25 years old, clean-cut, and he was seen about ten minutes before the employee heard the smoke detector going off and saw the flames in the same aisle where he had seen the clean-cut man. Phil had written down the employee's name, phone number address and date of birth, intending to find him later for an interview. He decided to call the employee. He dialed the number and it was answered by a woman.

"Hello. This is Captain Langtry from the fire department, is Alton Williams there?"

"No. He lives with his girlfriend in Pasadena. Is this about his application with your department? I'm his mother."

"Yes, it is," Phil lied, "do you have his home number?"

"Yes, just a minute. He hasn't lived there very long." Phil also got the address and considered going by to see the man personally. At the same time, he also heard his fire radio pick up a dispatch of a brush fire in Sun Valley, just west of Burbank. Phil looked out his office window and saw a column of smoke 10 miles west. The Los Angeles Fire Department covered that area and Phil tuned into their firefighting frequency on the radio after the dispatch. He heard the dispatched units confirming their assignment and several stated they could see the smoke from their scattered positions. Phil also heard A-Unit 2 confirm their response. L.A.'s Valley Arson Investigators were going, too.

Phil picked up the phone and dialed Alton Williams's number. It was answered by a man on the second ring. Phil asked if they could meet and discuss the Cal's fire. Williams agreed to meet.

Williams lived in a quiet residential neighborhood of apartments off Lake Street in the southeast side of Pasadena. Williams invited him in. Phil shuddered slightly at Williams' obvious burn injuries. Alton had suffered second-degree burns on his back and the back of his head as he fled the exploding hardware store three years before. The scars bleached the skin on the back of his head almost pink, much of the hair still gone.

Phil found Williams very articulate and candid about the fire at his former employer. The young man's voice lowered as he explained the events leading up to the fire's discovery, his own terror of being unable to get out and his ultimate escape through the fire exit. Williams narrated his story as if he had repeated it a hundred times. There were a number of civil suits as a result of the fire and one still pending. Williams had been part of one of the suits and received several hundred thousand dollars and lifetime medical care for his burn injuries. He was an excellent witness.

Phil explained to the man that there were those who still felt that the fire may have been intentionally set and he wanted to get a few more specifics about the male that Williams had seen that night. Again Williams narrated the scenario and placed the man as the only other person in the part of the store where the fire was first seen for the last 15 minutes before the inferno. Langtry asked Williams if he had any idea how the fire might have started.

"I heard that it started in the attic or roof, but I don't see how!" Williams said.

"Why do you say that?"

"I'd been working in that area of the store off and on for a couple of hours and never smelled any smoke or ever saw any lights flicker. The way I see it, if that fire got started in the attic, it had to have been electrical or something. We shoulda heard something! There was nothing, man! We hated the elevator music that was always on the P.A. system so we had turned that shit off. It was totally silent in there. If the fire started in the attic, then there would have been noise as the roofing fell into the displays!" Williams continued without Phil asking. "It was just all of a sudden. I saw this ugly billow of black smoke along the

53

ceiling and at the same time I heard a smoke detector go off. From then on, everything went so fast! I shouted 'fire' and ran down to the aisle where the fire was and it was just blowing out of the patio furniture and the foam rubber display. I couldn't get anywhere near it so I started to run to the fire extinguisher by the back of the store but the lights went out before I got there. I barely remember anything else 'cuz I started to lose it with no air. The next thing I remember was feeling the paint cans and brushes on the back wall and knowing that the fire exit was along that wall, too. It got real hot and I just barely had enough strength to push open the door. As I pushed it, the fire just raced over my head and burned me as I crawled away." Williams sighed and shuddered as he finished his story, beads of perspiration showing on his upper lip and forehead.

Langtry continued the questioning in another area to get Williams' mind off the near tragedy. He asked Williams about what his mother had said about a firefighter job. Williams smiled and said that after the fire, he recovered pretty well psychologically and got real interested in firefighting. He didn't go back to work for months and spent many hours trying to learn more about fires and fire departments. He was even visited in the hospital by several firemen and paramedics who helped him that night. His interest continued and he began putting in applications at departments around the area when he reached 21.

Phil finally got to questioning about the man seen by the aisle where the fire started. Williams said that he noticed the guy walk near him as he stocked a lower shelf near the main aisle. He didn't think the man saw him, but Williams said that he smelled cigarette smoke as the guy passed.

"I don't smoke, so I notice cigarettes. We didn't allow smoking in the store, but back then, nobody really enforced that kind of stuff."

"Did you get a good look at the guy then?"

"Not really, but I did watch him as he turned into the patio furniture aisle. I guess I was looking for a cigarette, but he had already turned and I didn't see anything."

"When did you see him next?"

"Just a couple of seconds later, I got paged by the store operator to answer the phone in the hardware department. As I walked by the next aisle, I saw the guy facing sideways reaching into the foam rubber piles, about waist high. He didn't look at me and I went to the phone." Williams said that as he walked back after talking on the phone briefly, the guy was gone. He continued working for about eight or ten minutes and then the fire started. He also provided a description that closely matched the man seen at the 7-11. Williams said he probably wouldn't remember the guy if he ever saw him again. It had been too long.

Langtry thanked Williams for his time and explained that there was some new information that might indicate that the Cal's fire was arson. Williams was curious but didn't pursue questioning. Phil also asked that Williams not talk to anyone about their discussion.

"Talking about what we discussed today would jeopardize my investigation and make you subject to arrest," Phil told Williams. "It's that serious."

Williams agreed.

10

Phil Langtry studied the *L.A. Times* Sunday morning and analyzed the stories of the Burbank fires and the brush fire in Sun Valley. There were two more brush fires in the Valencia area, 20 miles north of Sun Valley that same afternoon. One burned 75 acres and damaged three homes. Judging by the times the fires were reported, the serial arsonist was moving north from Burbank and setting the fires within minutes after each preceding fire was being extinguished or knocked down. Langtry looked for any information about witnesses seeing anything suspicious but came across nothing but the usual "the fire is under routine investigation" statements.

Phil also saw a story about a small fire inside a toy store in the Valley. The fire, discovered in a pile of stuffed animals by a customer, did several hundred thousand dollars' damage before store employees and the fire department extinguished it. The fire was reported at 7:30 p.m. and was just off the Interstate 5 freeway. Phil theorized that this was the arsonist's route as he left on his day's activities Saturday, and he was probably on his way back home when he hit the toy store.

Looking at a map, Phil saw that the fires' locations lined up perfectly, time wise as well as geographically, with the arsonist traveling north until mid-afternoon, then returning southbound as the sun set. This meant that the arsonist probably lived in the San Fernando Valley area since his fires started fairly early. Phil contemplated the past fires as well and it seemed to him that the fires did radiate away from the East Valley and Glendale areas when the pyro worked a series of fires like Saturdays.

Phil set the paper aside, thinking about the cases. It was Sunday, a 'B' shift on-duty day, so he didn't expect any fires. The house was quiet except for Sean and Beth's mutt Romeo attacking a slipper in the dining room. Phil picked up the companion slipper from the couch next to him and tossed it at the snarling dog. The slipper missed its mark and slid along the tile floor past Romeo. The white mutt, as fluffy as the slipper, immediately leaped at the sliding shoe. His tiny feet slipped on the slick tiles and by the time he gained momentum he had already passed the now-stationary shoe. Romeo skidded past and slid into a trash can before he could stop. The dazed dog then stood up and staggered toward the slipper and fell upon it snarling as if nothing happened. Phil chuckled.

Sean and Beth were sleeping in late. Phil started cleaning up the scattered papers when the phone rang. He grabbed it on the first ring. It was Marta. In a low voice, she asked him if he'd like to come over. It was Sunday and the kids would be home. Her husky voice caused him to question her.

"Where are the kids?"

"They're with my brother and his wife's today. They went to the beach and won't be back until four of five."

There was silence. He debated between going to Marta's and working on the case.

"I'll be over in about an hour," Phil said.

"Hurry."

Phil hung up and began thinking how to accomplish so much in less than an hour. He shaved and showered then went down to Sean's bedroom. He knocked softly on the door after hearing the muted sound of their television.

"Come in," Beth called.

He peeked in and saw Sean still tangled up in the top sheet, asleep.

"I'm heading over to Marta's before work. I'll be home around dinner," Phil whispered. She scowled. She, too, distrusted Marta.

"See you tonight," she mumbled.

It was as hot as it had been for the past few days, but at last the Santa Anas had died down. He paused briefly and looked down the hill beside the house. The dry, yellowed grass was much too close to the house, and clusters of extremely flammable chaparral dotted the hillside. Phil pondered the problem, then remembered that Marta was waiting.

He drove down the winding canyon road to the city, noticing the dry grass growing down to the sidewalks everywhere. *If that pyro ever hits this canyon, we'll lose 20-30 homes*, Phil thought, *including ours*. He decided to cut down the grass when he got back from Marta's.

On the way, Phil thought back to when he and Marta were married. He had left their home several times after fights, just trying to get her attention. On one occasion, she wouldn't let him back in. She stood her ground. He found it easier to walk away from her. His first two marriages ended the same way. He walked away from the problem. "Ran away" was the way wife number two put it.

The streets in Marta's neighborhood were deserted. Most of the residents stayed up late on warm nights and slept in weekend mornings. He saw a small group at the park holding down a spot for a birthday party. Brightly colored balloons were being strung up between trees and a piñata hung from a low branch. Several Mexican blankets were spread out and a few children played with a ball.

Phil pulled into Marta's driveway behind her battered Mustang. He walked behind the house found her standing diagonally in the screened doorway. She smiled at him and said, "What kept you?" She looked so beautiful and innocent, he just stared. Her eyes were damp and her face flushed from the heat.

He stepped up to the door and she let him in. He took her hand and pressed her against the doorjamb. The back porch was secluded, covered by a large avocado tree and thick bushes, shielding them from others. The wind blew the leaves softly above them. He leaned down into her lips, his tall body pressing against hers.

"I hope you're hungry 'cause I just started laying out brunch," Marta said. Phil leaned down to her and kissed her again. He bent down and scooped her up in his arms. Walking into the kitchen he noticed that the oven was on, a mixing bowl on top of it with blueberry muffin mix inside. He reached over and turned off the oven, heading to the bedroom.

Phil relaxed as their lips met.

They lay in bed tangled in her sheets, her head resting on his chest.

"I've been seeing someone," Marta confessed.

Phil didn't respond.

"He's a cop. He gave an anti-drug program at the kids' school, and he really is a nice guy. The kids love him, and he appears genuine anyway," she explained.

"Is he married?" Phil queried.

"Yeah. But that's okay for me. You know that," Marta said.

Phil lay silently fuming. He hated cops and hated the thought of Marta with anyone.

"I trust him. I really do. He doesn't bullshit me," she continued.

The day was spent in her large bed with a small oscillating fan blowing on their sweaty bodies. Phil fought for the urge to leave several times but his passion for her kept him there.

11

Phil awoke refreshed Monday morning, the bright sun streaming in his windows. Although the day was hot outside, he left his windows open to enjoy the silence of early morning canyon. A ceiling fan kept him cool. It was only six and he didn't have to be at work for hours, so he just propped himself up in the bed and stared out the window. He saw his deer across the canyon, walking slowly up the grassy slopes after spending the night feeding on canyon residents' landscaping. During the day, they went high up onto the mountain to catch the afternoon breezes on the ridgeline and in the oak groves where they slept.

An hour later he got ready for work and drove to the 7-11. The owner was there along with the nighttime clerk who was on duty the night of their fire. Phil quizzed the night man about "Trish," the girl who was also in the store the night of the fire. He knew her and gave Phil several leads on where to locate her. She would definitely be around the store that night, according to the clerk. Her usual routine was to arrive at the store at about 8 p.m. and get a male customer to buy her something to eat and purchase beer for her. She would typically lead the customer to believe that they would then take the beer somewhere and drink it together. Sometimes she did, he said, but usually she just took the beer from him and walked away. This led to several verbal altercations in the store, and the police were called several times. Her plan was apparently to have someone buy her a few six-packs, then sell the beer to her friends that dropped by at twice the price. She made a few dollars each night. The night man also said that she might be selling herself to the more affluent customers.

Phil asked the night man if he remembered the man in the video tape that captured the action prior to the fire that night.

"I remember very little about him except that he tried to hit on Trish. She didn't even give the guy a look. That was unusual because he wasn't a bad-looking guy and she might have gotten him to buy for her."

"What drew your attention to her as she walked out?" Phil asked. "Was it him, or her? I mean, did he do or say anything as he came up to the door?"

"Well, it sure wasn't him! I see her every night, but you can't keep your eyes off her. I saw him because he was there, nothing unusual about him."

"Did the guy do anything that caught your attention as he was in the store?"

"No, I lost track of him. Felt a little sorry for him though. She cut him right off!"

"Would you recognize the guy if you saw him again?"

"Maybe, but I don't really remember his face. I was real busy at the time and when I looked at the video tape I was recognizing the clothes, not the guy."

"Was there anything about the clothes that caught your attention?" Phil asked hopefully.

"No, not really...but...ah...you know, I do remember one other thing. He lit up a cigarette while he was in the store. I didn't really see it, just saw the puff of smoke over by the coolers as he lit it up. I was going to say something to him about it 'cause we don't allow smoking in the store."

"Why didn't you?"

"Well...Trish came back inside and I couldn't think about much else..." the clerk smiled.

Phil left the store with very little good information about the arsonist, but he felt he could now locate Trish. Her latest confrontation with a customer took place last Tuesday and the police were called. He drove to the police department and walked to the front desk. The desk officer recognized him and pushed the buzzer to open the access gate to the Records Bureau. The supervisor gave him permission to use the computer and he quickly ran up the police response history to the address of the 7-11. The disturbance call last Tuesday came at 8:15 p.m. The computer gave the disposition of the call as "verbal altercation only. One F.I. card." Phil cursed. The name of the individual wasn't on the computer. Field Identification cards, when completed, were sent to the detectives for their review and ultimately put in a 3x5 card file under the individual's name. It had been almost one week since the incident and the card was probably already in the file under Trish's last name. The name he didn't have.

Phil called his office and told his partner, Ash, that he was out at the PD and would be in shortly. He also briefed Ash on the weekend's activities and asked him to get a hold of any of his snitches in the downtown area and try to I.D. Trish.

After further research of the 7-11 history proved futile, Phil walked to the detective bureau and looked up the newest assigned officer, fresh from the streets. He hoped that he would have some street knowledge of Trish through his contacts with her. The detective did remember Trish but couldn't remember her name. He did remember that she lived in an apartment building on Jackson Street. The address was one of the most notorious in the downtown area. Illegal aliens, drug dealers and users, as well as common criminals congregated at the building. The young detective was even familiar with her scam at the 7-11. He added that she also attended the local high school.

"She surprised me when she told me that," the detective said. "She's young, looks about 15-16, yet lives in that rathole by herself. I think her mom's in jail or dead. No father around either."

"Do you know which high school?" Phil asked.

"I think it's Hoover High. Is she a suspect in the little fire down at the 7-11 the other night?" he asked. Phil was surprised that the detective was aware of the fire. The report wouldn't be sent to the detectives, but routed directly to the fire department for follow-up.

"How'd you know about the fire?"

"I usually scan all the reports taken, 'specially in the downtown area. I've been off the streets for a couple of months and I like to keep track of what's happening around town," the detective replied. Phil was impressed. Over 50 reports were taken each day in his city. Most were routine thefts and traffic accidents, but anybody who would review that many reports was an excellent investigator. A great deal of information can be revealed about criminal activity by this kind of evaluation. Phil himself looked at the "Hot Board" weekly, but didn't examine all reports.

"That is great," Phil said admiringly. "There'll be an opening for an officer in arson in another year or so. Keep it in mind," Phil offered.

"I will." The cop smiled as they shook hands.

Phil drove back to his office, passing Trish's apartment building on the way. Several immigrants stood on the front steps, waiting for passing contractors to pick them up for a day's work at less than minimum wage. Phil couldn't imagine the young girl living in that squalor alone.

At his office, Phil found Chief Harris and Ash drinking coffee in the kitchen. Harris had been their supervisor for only a short while, and Phil hadn't quite figured him out yet. He was still suspicious. The man had been hired as the City's Fire Marshal from another jurisdiction, unheard of for a Battalion Chief's position. Fire departments traditionally promoted from within. Harris, however, had an excellent knowledge of fire prevention laws and evaluation of building plans for fire safety. He was also very young, with a baby face and quiet manner. His sparkly-eyed innocence caused the firefighters to quietly refer to him as "Sparky". You didn't go out for a beer after work with Chief Harris. You went out for a glass of milk. Despite the levity, Chief Harris was still a good supervisor, giving the arson investigators a great deal of flexibility in their operation.

"Morning, Chief," Phil said as he nodded at Ash. "What's up?"

"Not much. I was just meeting with Communications about some problems and thought I'd stop by and see why the weight of the world was on Ash's shoulders on Monday morning," he said, referring to Phil's tardiness. It was 8:35.

"I was at the 7-11 on Broadway talking to a witness and over at the PD on the computer for a while," Phil said flatly, resenting any implication that his unit would take advantage of the flexibility that they had been given.

"Take it easy, Phil," said Harris. "Ash filled me in. Got anything?"

"No. It was a pretty quiet weekend. Communications didn't call me for anything. I did go over to Burbank and help Carey for a while though. They actually had three fires in the same area in a span of about 30 minutes. All arson. Probably the same guy..."

"What's the story on the 7-11 fire?" Harris asked.

"Which one? Ours or theirs? Burbank had one, too."

"No shit? Theirs the same as ours?"

"Identical. We have the guy on video from ours, but it doesn't really show all of him, just misses his face." Phil related the similarities and the status of the investigation, looking at Ash during the updated information on Trish's identity and her home address.

"Interesting. Would it be worth it to let the media know so we can keep him from doing it again?" Harris asked.

"Rather not, Chief. He is dangerous, but we'd only be putting him on his guard for a while. He'd still set fires eventually and it would just let him know that we're building a case against him. The video's not fabulous, but it can still be beneficial if we find him and the clothing matches," Phil explained haphazardly, trying to cover all the facets of his strategy. "The media would pick up on it, especially with the video, but if the guy saw it, he'd probably have enough sense to destroy the clothes he was wearing, and since we can't I.D. a face, the clothes are the only solid evidence we have at the moment. The shoes are significant," Phil said.

"How so?" the Chief asked, admiring Phil's intuition for building a case.

"The guy drives around a lot, probably looking for places to burn. When you drive a lot, the back of your right shoe reflects how much, and some info about your car. Chief, let me see the back of your right shoe." The chief crossed his right leg over his left knee, exposing his shiny uniform shoes.

"See how the right side of the back part here is slightly discolored? The rest of your shoes are real shiny, but this part rests on the floorboard of your city car. It doesn't have floor mats does it?"

"No. It doesn't."

"Well, you don't drive a lot so your scuffing and discoloration doesn't do much damage, but you probably just shined your shoes or you haven't driven much since you shined them. Probably the latter?" Phil inquired.

"I shined them yesterday evening and just drove 30 miles to work this morning," the Chief said.

"OK, look at mine," Phil said, now feeling a little guilty wearing old sneakers and jeans to work again. "I drive a lot. The back of my shoe shows that I drive a lot. I drive the city car almost exclusively, or my truck, which doesn't have floor mats either. My shoe looks just like the crook's shoe. Now look at Ash's."

Ash rolled his right leg over to show the back of his brown loafer.

"Ash, I know your Z car has carpeting and it's been a long time since you shined these babies! Right?" Phil said as they looked at the dulled and discolored shoe.

"Yeah. I haven't shined them in a month and you know I don't drive but 10 miles to work and you always drive when we're here," Ash replied.

"Exactly my point. This isn't the kind of information that will convict somebody by itself. However, if I catch a suspect and his shoe matches and he doesn't have floormats in his vehicle, the jury will find me to be a very credible guy. Maybe incredible, in the good sense!" Phil beamed.

"I see your point. So if we publicized this thing and showed the video on TV, the guy might polish his shoes?" Harris asked.

"Well, yeah. We wouldn't say anything about the shoes, of course, but he would definitely try and get rid of anything he saw on the tape. He'd probably just can everything he was wearing. It's that simple."

"OK, Phil. These are kinda chickenshit fires, though, aren't they?" the Chief asked, chipping away at any credibility he was gaining with Phil.

"They're small, but all part of a pattern that I—we—feel are related to a serial arsonist. He's probably the one doing brush fires around the area, too," Phil said as he looked for confirmation from Ash. Ash nodded his head affirmatively.

"Do you have any suspects?" Harris quizzed.

"Not yet," Phil said matter-of-factly. "He's using a time-delay and we don't have much to go on. The areas he's hitting are so scattered that we've got a million possibilities. There's just not much to work with."

"Do you need any other resources or help that I can assist you with?" the Chief offered.

"Not yet. I am concerned, though. He's setting fires inside occupied buildings. He may have set a fire inside a toy store in Van Nuys on Saturday afternoon." Phil outlined Saturday's fires on a map on the wall of the kitchen. He finished off by showing the location of the toy store. "Setting a fire in an occupied building is just too bizarre, Chief. We gotta stop this dude!" Phil said strongly.

"I agree. Let me know what you need. If it's overtime, go ahead. Just keep me advised," the Chief said as he stood up to leave.

"Thanks, Chief," Phil said as he followed Harris into the hallway. The Chief left and Phil followed Ash back into the office.

"How'd you find Trish so fast, Phil?"

"Just good work. You know, we old detectives can still come through when it's needed!"

"Well, there aren't many older than you." Ash renewed their familiar old guy/young guy sparring.

Phil sat down and updated Ash on Trish and his conversation with the 7-11 clerk. They then mapped out their day. Trish was at the top of the list. They drove to Hoover High School and found that she was enrolled, but was absent today. The Vice Principal related that Trish was a good student, but had spotty attendance. She maintained a good grade-point average, but was prone to be a little caustic with her instructors. She was asked about parents, and the VP said she had never met either parent.

Phil and Ash drove to the Jackson Street building, and Phil saw the same four men standing out front. They started to drift away as the official-looking car parked. Phil told Ash to stay inside as he got out. Phil called out in Spanish to one, asking him to talk. The man looked at his friends, then back at Phil. Phil overheard the words "la migra" passed between the men. Although his Spanish was weak, Phil quickly related to the men that he was a fireman, not Immigration or the police. He added, in Spanish, "He's a cop," as he pointed at Ash, still seated in the car. The four men laughed as they walked toward Phil.

One of the men spoke some English, making the conversation easier. Phil asked if they knew a young girl who lived alone. All responded by vigorously nodding their heads up and down, one stating that she lived on the second floor of the three-story building, in the back. None of the men, it turned out, actually lived there themselves. They just met in front, daily, hoping for work. Phil thanked the men and asked if they had worked lately. Only one had done anything in the past five days. They all had families in Mexico they were trying to support. Phil told them he had a friend who owned the Mexican restaurant on Broadway nearby and his business was doing poorly. He handed one of them a 20-dollar bill and asked if they would have lunch at his friend's restaurant to help his business. The men graciously accepted, knowing full well that Phil was giving them the money, not as charity, but because he understood their plight.

Ash got out as the men departed and they both walked into the filthy building. The security gate covering the front door was wide open. Phil noticed a piece of duct tape covering the latching mechanism, rendering the lock useless until the tape was removed.

The mailboxes provided no clue as to her last name. Someone had, however, drawn two crude breasts on the mailbox next to the number 19. Ash nodded at Phil and they chose to walk up the stairs rather than use the dirty elevator. The stairwell smelled of urine and alcohol. Old beer cans were lying on the staircase as well as on the landing of the second floor. As they reached the top of the stairs, they both looked down the hallway. A figure was silhouetted against the open fire escape door at the other end. The bright sunlight made it difficult to determine whether the figure was male or female, but whoever it was, appeared to be working on a door lock. Phil and Ash stopped as both tried to figure out if it was a resident or a burglar. They automatically reached for their guns. Ash's small revolver was in an ankle holster that required him to bend down to retrieve it. As he slightly raised his left leg to reach for the .38 the flooring creaked. Instantly the figure looked up and sprinted for the fire escape. Phil and Ash ran down the hallway after the figure as it disappeared through the stairwell door. As they passed the door he was working on, Phil glanced at it. Ash continued on.

"Hold it, Ash! No pry marks."

Ash quickly stopped at the fire escape, looking down into the alley. He saw nothing.

"No crime, Ash, unless you want to chase him!"

"Naw, not me. He's gone anyway."

Several doors opened, including number 19. Phil flashed his badge at her.

"Some guy was trying to break into this apartment. Who lives here?" Phil asked.

"Some lady and a couple of kids. She works and the kids are probably in school. Was it a skinny Mexican guy?" Trish asked sleepily.

"Yeah, he was pretty skinny, wearing some kind of uniform. Dark blue, like a mechanic or something. You know him?" Ash asked.

"It sounds like her ex-husband. He comes by every couple of days, but he never broke in, though," Trish said as she opened the door wider, wearing only a very large T-shirt.

"Are you Trish?" Phil asked

"Yeah, are you the school cops?"

"No, we're arson investigators with the fire department," Phil said. "Can we come in and talk?"

"Sure," she said, as she opened the door to reveal an immaculate apartment. The room had bright curtains and smelled as if it had been recently painted. It was a small single, the bathroom off to one side and the kitchen in the corner, partitioned off by a bookcase.

Trish walked to a corner and picked up a pair of jeans from a chair.

"What can I do for you?" she said as went into the bathroom to slip the pants on. She threw her long hair back as she came back out.

The men looked at each other. Neither could speak for a few seconds. Phil asked about her parents.

She explained that her mother was arrested and sent to jail for failure to appear for her sentencing on an embezzlement charge. She had stolen several thousand dollars from the bank where she worked and was convicted two years before. They moved from San Diego to keep her from going to jail too quickly. Trish explained that her mother set up a joint checking account for her and they carried on normally until the inevitable. Her warrant was found when she was stopped for a minor traffic violation." Trish continued telling her history to Phil and Ash at very little urging from them. It seemed that she needed to talk to someone.

"My dad still sends child support to our checking account, and Mom sold her car before she went to jail. It was worth a few bucks since

66

her employer paid for most of it!" She smiled. "This place is cheap, and I do odd jobs sometimes," she quickly added.

"Trish, you seem real nervous. We're here only on fire business. Nothing else," Phil reassured her.

"Okay," she sighed. "I always worry about the school finding out about me living alone, ya know?"

"We understand," Phil told her. She was well mannered and seemed mature beyond her years.

"You guys want some coffee or something?" Trish asked.

"Sure, if it's no problem," Phil said.

"I slept in today 'cause I was up real late last night doing laundry and ironing for the insurance agent up the street," Trish said as she prepared the coffee.

"The lady insurance agent up the street," she quickly added. "I take in laundry and sometimes ironing to make a few bucks," she added with challenging eyes.

"Doesn't the school call and ask for 'Mom' when you're absent?" asked Ash.

"I don't have a phone, and I rarely take any time off from school. I get real good grades, and they usually don't call for verification when 'good' kids are absent." She hesitated. "Is this about the fire at the 7-11?"

"Yeah. What do you remember about the fire?" Phil queried.

"Not much. Somebody just dropped a cigarette, right?" she asked.

"No. It was arson, and you may have had contact with the guy just before the fire."

"Somebody actually set that fire while we were all inside? How can that be?" Trish asked, leaning against the kitchen counter.

"Tell me what you did the 15 minutes prior to the fire," Phil asked.

"Did somebody say I set the fire?" Trish inquired as she stared at Phil, not believing that the fire was arson.

"Not at all. The guy that set it was in the store while you were there, Trish. You talked to him."

"That fire scared the shit out of me," Trish said, "and my girlfriend Rosa is still staying home because it scared her so bad. What happened?"

"Like I said, what do you remember about the 15 minutes before the fire?" Phil said, intently staring at Trish.

Trish crossed her arms across her chest and looked at the ceiling.

"I'd tell you, but…okay." She paused. "One of the odd jobs I do is pulling off a beer scam at the 7-11. I usually con some guy to buy me a couple six-packs. Most of the time I pay him for it but sometimes I'm broke and I just scam him and he buys it for me. Anyway, I get a couple and stockpile them around the corner of the store by the dumpster. My friends at school come by and they pay me twice what it costs in the store so they don't have to hustle anybody themselves. I can make 50 to 60 bucks a night pullin' off this deal."

"What about that night?"

"I started hangin' out around 7:30 and had two or three packs by the time Rosa and a couple of her friends came by. They usually don't come by till later, but they were going to a party and wanted two or three cases. She gave me some shit about the price, and we went back inside and argued about it for a while. No big deal, just business, you know?"

"Yeah," Phil said, "go on."

"Well, I was dealin' with this older guy down inside the store and Rosa comes up and starts raggin' on me while I'm still talking to the guy. It pissed me off and the old guy said he wouldn't do it so I got into an argument with Rosa. I told her to come outside with me so we wouldn't piss off the clerk. We went outside and got the price settled with her friends in the car and Rosa came back inside with me." Phil analyzed what Trish was saying as he remembered the videotape of the store activities before the fire.

"Do you remember the guy that held the door open as you walked out with Rosa? He may have said something to you," Phil asked, trying not to put words into her mouth.

"Yeah, what about him?"

"What did he say to you?"

"Something about my breasts, I think. I don't really remember. I wasn't paying any attention to him 'cause I was pissed at Rosa. Was he the one?"

"We think so. Why didn't you pay any attention to him? Wasn't he a potential customer for you?" Phil asked.

"No. Not really," Trish replied. "He was pretty good-looking, and he was kinda young for my deal. Older guys work better. They're probably married and don't want to make a big scene when I don't agree to go someplace with them. It's just easier with middle-aged guys…like you," she smiled at Phil. "Like, I'd never hit on this guy…" she pointed at Ash with a smile.

"Would you recognize the guy if you saw him again?" Phil asked.

68

"Yeah. He was real clean-cut, like a cop. That might have made me leery, too. You know? I like the way he looked and what he said wasn't all that vulgar as I recall. It was just something kinda complimentary about my shirt, but obviously complimenting my breasts. If I saw him again, I might recognize him. You want me to call you?"

"Yes," Phil said, handing her his business card. Ash handed her his card, too.

"Why did this guy start the fire?" asked Trish.

"He's a pyromaniac," Phil said, "We don't really know for sure. He just gets his kicks watching people while the fire burns and gets excited about the action of the fire engines and stuff."

"You want me to believe that this guy…"

"It's sick, yes," Phil interrupted. "He stays close to the fire, watching the whole thing go down, just enjoying the excitement."

"But I don't think he was still inside when the fire started," Trish said. "I remember him leaving now." Phil saw Trish concentrating on the night of the fire. He saw that she was re-living the event and recalling more than she thought she could. "He kinda hovered around where we were while I was trying to talk to another old guy. I think I saw him light up a cigarette too…yeah, he did!" She smiled. "I remember now. He was cute enough for me to take a second look at him, and I remember thinking it was too bad he was a smoker. I don't go out with smokers, so I just watched him walk out the door a minute later."

Phil was ecstatic. He let her talk on.

"I think he got into a nice car, too. It was grey, but older, like an old Chevy or something, but restored." Trish stopped for a moment, thinking. "The old guy said he would buy me a case but he was uncomfortable. I looked at Rosa and motioned for her to walk away so the old guy could say what he wanted to say to me. I knew he wanted to come on to me." She said matter-of-factly.

"I turned him down real diplomatically, and he was still cool, so he went to get the case. Rosa came back up and we hung out for a couple of minutes, waiting for him so we could follow him out. I told him to meet me by the dumpster," she said.

"Did you smell or see anything while you waited?"

"No. We were watching him buy the beer when I felt heat behind me. It was real bizarre. I was only five or six feet from those coolers and when I looked around, they were burning. Rosa looked at me and saw my face and at the same time, somebody by the register yelled, 'Fire!' Rosa was really fixated on the fire and wouldn't move, so I jerked her arm and we hauled outta there. She just fell apart. I was scared, too, man."

Phil saw the look on Trish's face as she told her story. She was genuinely frightened by the experience. She may have thought little about it since it happened, but now, hearing that the fire was set intentionally caused her to change dramatically. "How did he do it?"

Phil explained how it was done without being specific about the device. She was fascinated and asked more about the arsonist. He explained what little he knew about the man and asked her to watch for him. She agreed. They enjoyed their coffee and conversation until she said she had to get to school. She didn't want to miss the whole day. They offered her a ride, but she declined, not wanting to be seen with cops.

Phil and Ash left the interview with Trish with a lot of information about her, but little more about the arsonist. So far, the witnesses seemed to agree on the suspect's description, and now the car played a more important role in the investigation. Two witnesses, Trish and the Burbank 7-11 clerk, had seen similar cars. Phil decided it was time to tell Ash of his theory.

"Ash, now that we've got the car description, that narrows our search down to about 200,000 possibilities. That's about how many 70s Chevy's are still on the street." Phil sighed. "I think I can cut that down by about another 190,000 possibilities."

"No shit…how?" Ash asked incredulously.

"I think our guy might be a fireman….."

Ash pulled the car over to the side of the street, leaving the motor running. For several seconds, the only sounds were of the fire and police radio chatter.

"You gotta be bullshittin' me. Why?"

Phil enlightened his partner about the fires over the weekend and of his research correlating the firefighter's shift schedule and the arsons, including the Cal's fire. As Phil spoke, Ash began nodding in agreement as each point was covered.

"What next?" Ash asked when Phil completed his story.

"The way I see it, we can't go poking around other agencies asking about which of their firefighters might be an arsonist. I don't even feel comfortable enough yet to tell anybody but you," Phil said, raising his eyebrows at Ash.

"No problem, man. It's the same story when a cop goes bad. They try to hide as much as they can, but word always gets out," Ash stated.

"I'm glad you agree on that point. If we nail him, great, but I don't want anyone to be brought on board with this yet," Phil said, staring directly at Ash. "I don't often pull rank on you, but it's absolutely imperative that we research this thing under the table as much as we can.

70

Like you said about word getting out at the police department, I don't want you to even hint at this thing yet."

"Come on, man." Ash straightened up. "You can trust me. I got no reason to talk to anybody. We should probably at least tell my sergeant, though, shouldn't we?" Ash said questioningly. Phil squinted, then rubbed his eyes, taking a deep breath.

"Ash, *nobody* can know this yet, not even the sergeant. I know your department's operations manual requires you to pass on potential internal affairs stuff involving city employees, but we can't do this. Besides, we're probably not dealing with an employee from here. I know almost all of our firemen and none of them have an old Chevy," Phil said. He enjoyed working with Ash and found him to be an excellent investigator, but he found that cops were generally prone to gossip. He had been burned before and wasn't about to let the cops jeopardize this investigation. "I'll take any heat that comes along. OK?"

"No problem, Phil. You want some coffee?"

"It's getting too damn hot already," Phil said sharply, not completely convinced that Ash could be trusted. "Let's go to the Lab and see if the fingerprints are ready from the 7-11 napkin wrapper."

As they drove, Phil mulled over what needed to be done to speed up the investigation. As he thought about the upcoming week, his memory was jarred.

"I've got that class I'm teaching in Fresno Wednesday," Phil said out loud. "Damn, I really don't want to go now that we've got something solid to look into."

"I'm on call this week, so just leave me a list of what you need done and I'll handle it," Ash offered.

"I'll only be gone from Tuesday to Friday," Phil said. He didn't want anything done on the case while he was gone.

The prints from the napkin wrapper were recovered, but were also in poor condition. Only one or two were good, but not clear enough to classify for identification. A good print should have 8-10 identification points and these had only six. Six points were enough to help point toward a possible suspect, but not enough for a court case. It was not even enough to enter into the Automated Fingerprint Identification System. The computer could positively identify the suspect with enough identification points, but they were shy several.

Frustrated, Phil called the Sheriff's Department Lab and asked if they had been successful in copying any still photos from their 7-11 video. The lab technician said that they had several and were attempting to enhance the photos as they blew them up to a larger size. They promised to call when the work was done.

12

Aaron sat at his dining room table putting together several devices. The morning sun was shining brightly, but the Santa Ana winds had died down. The temperature was expected to reach the 80s instead of over 100 degrees. A layer of smog covered the Valley as he drove home from work, and he could only see about a mile in the thickening haze. Not a good day for brush fires.

He put together three devices and allowed the glue to dry. He then put them in his shirt pocket as he walked to his bedroom. He lay on his bed and lit one of the devices, setting it in an ashtray on a nightstand. He glanced at the clock. It was 9:15. He lay on his side, fondling himself and thinking of the large-breasted girl in the 7-11. The smoke from the cigarette drifted upward in a straight line for several inches then was dissipated by the air currents in the room. He blew the smoke away from him and felt his heart racing as the smoldering tobacco worked its way to the glue. He stroked his erection faster as the inevitable flame approached. He slowed when he almost climaxed prematurely. His mind wandered to the large-breasted girl and he half closed his eyes, seeing her running from the flames.

At 9:24, the flame erupted, as did Aaron's climax. He continued to stroke himself long after the flame disappeared and the cigarette fell into the ashtray. He closed his eyes tightly, imagining the large-breasted girl beneath him as he came. In his mind, he had pinned her down controlling her. His mind retaliated against her for passing him by without even talking to him.

"I'll fucking show you, bitch!" he muttered as he finished, his chest heaving. He lay still for several minutes, almost falling asleep. Opening his eyes, he looked out the window and planned his day. He thought of the toy store fire he had set and how excited he got when the women and children in the store fled when the fire began to grow. He could see the glow and the smoke from the parking lot and stayed almost until the fire engines arrived. He then drove across the street to watched as others slowed to see the excitement, too.

Aaron found himself stroking his penis again as he thought about the toy store. He smiled to himself and went to the bathroom to clean up.

In ten minutes he was in his car heading north on Interstate 5 toward Fresno and the annual arson investigators' conference. He traded Tuesday with another firefighter and he didn't have to be back at work until next Sunday.

Although only a firefighter and not an arson investigator, Aaron attended the annual conference for years. He was fascinated by the topics at the meetings and learned much about his adversaries. He tried to mix in with the groups, occasionally seeing members of his own department's arson team among the 200 people that showed up. It was difficult to get accepted with the elite group, but he hoped that by showing interest he, too, could someday be accepted into the arson unit. Aaron totally blocked out his history when he attended the events, divorcing himself from the fact that he was an arsonist.

As he drove, he passed the areas that he burned on Saturday. Most of the fires he set were off the freeway and he could see the partially destroyed homes in Valencia and near the Magic Mountain amusement park as he passed. He laughed out loud and started looking at the fields of dry, dead grass that lined the freeway over the mountain to Bakersfield. He reached into his shirt and took out one of his two remaining devices. He hefted it in his hand and found it too light to be thrown out from his car going 70 miles per hour.

In a paper bag next to him was a tube of glue. He took it out and also reached into his pocket and found a handful of coins. He selected a quarter and put the rest into the bag. A small dollop of glue was squeezed onto the cigarette. He rested the coin against it and drove on, waiting for it to dry.

Before he realized it, he was headed down the Grapevine, a steep canyon the highway followed from the mountains down into the San Joaquin Valley and Bakersfield. Traffic was heavy and the dry grass was too far away from the roadway for him to throw out his device. He felt a heaviness in his chest and frustration caused him to accelerate to over 80 miles per hour, rushing to find something to burn. At the bottom of the canyon, he opened his window and felt a hot blast of air hit him. The valley temperature was at least 100 degrees and it exhilarated him. The air was crystal clear and he could see the foothills of the Sierra Nevada Mountains to the east. A small group of restaurants and gas stations were just ahead. On the left, he saw a Denny's Restaurant with a huge pile of discarded cardboard boxes stacked against the back of the building. Several large juniper trees and a field of grass were nearby.

Aaron got off the highway and drove to the restaurant. The pile of boxes was too visible to people inside the restaurant, so instead he parked in front. He felt in his pocket for the device, and as he got out he saw the backup device with the quarter attached sitting on the front seat in plain sight. His breath drew in sharply at his carelessness. He slipped the device into his pocket and walked into the restaurant and directly to the bathrooms at the rear. In the hallway leading to the bathrooms, there were more cardboard boxes. They lined the wide hall on one side. Entering the bathroom he found no one inside. He calculated the burning delay and which customers had seen him walk inside. If he set the device in the boxes, it would start them off readily, but also could be discovered quickly with people coming in and out of the bathrooms. There weren't many people in the restaurant since it was only 10:50, between breakfast and the lunch hour.

A man, possibly a truck driver, entered the bathroom, startling Aaron. He walked to the urinals as Aaron went to a stall, closed the door and sat down.

Too much time in here, he thought to himself.

The man quickly finished as Aaron's excitement increased. The challenge was there. He fumbled in his pocket, terror-stricken that someone else would enter as he lit it. He found the device with the quarter attached and decided to go with it instead of wasting time trying to get the other one out. He lit it and took a deep breath. As he walked out, he grabbed a paper towel from the rack over the sink and wrapped it around his device.

The instant he stepped out, he felt better. There was no one in the hallway and no customers could look down at the bathrooms from the dining area. Windows lined the hallway and looked out directly to the highway about 50 yards away. Across the highway, Aaron saw a gas station that would be an ideal location for his viewing. He bent down placing the device and paper towel inside the bottom cardboard box and walked away. His heart again began to race as he slowly walked across the edge of the dining area, trying not to look at anybody's face. Several people did look at him but he avoided direct eye contact. He debated ordering a cup of coffee to go, but decided that delaying his exit would allow too many people to notice him. He also noticed his erection beginning and feared it would be quick to show through his thin shorts.

He got into his car and quickly drove across the freeway overpass and pulled into the gas station. He went to the air hose and water station and positioned his car so he could look around his open hood and appear like he was checking his engine. It was over 100 yards to the restaurant, but he could clearly see the hallway and the bathroom entrance. He waited.

The device, wadded up in the paper towel, caused the soft material to smolder, creating smoke. A minute later, another trucker walked down the hallway. He instantly detected the odor of burning paper and saw the thin line of white smoke coming from the boxes. Aaron watched the man stop and look around, ultimately stooping down and discovering the incinerating paper towel. Aaron watched, his anger increasing as the man stood up with the smoking towel in his hands. He dropped the towel and stepped on it several times. Aaron closed his hood and drove off.

He clenched his teeth, breathing heavily through his nose. He drove with his window down and continued, his breath shallow and calculated, trying to control himself. Retaliation was his first thought, but he just wanted to get away from the restaurant. He couldn't wait around for the man to come out, and trying to burn the cardboard boxes outside was too risky. Aaron seldom went back when something went wrong as it had today. People would remember his returning to the restaurant and not sitting down to eat. They also might just remember his car if he pulled around to the back and placed something in the cardboard boxes outside and was seen a second time. In the city, it would be no problem. He would be in the next jurisdiction before the witness ever came forward after the fire was out. In a rural area like this, only one law enforcement agency covered most of the county and the information would likely be broadcast over the radios before he could move on. *There are other places*, he thought. There always were, but he was anxious.

He drove northbound and shortly entered the Bakersfield city limits. "Nashville of the West" the sign proclaimed about the former center of agriculture. Now, the population center of the San Joaquin Valley, country and western recording stars flocked to the area. Aaron had been here before and found it provided many potential areas for his fires.

He got off the freeway in the middle of town and checked his watch. It was only noon. He couldn't check into a motel for about two hours. He drove aimlessly, finally finding another restaurant near a shopping center. It was a small Mexican restaurant that was actually a converted wood-framed house. The front looked well kept, but the rear was littered with old car bodies, dry grass and a garage, only a few feet from the restaurant. A high fence covered the cluttered rear area from the customer's view, but Aaron wasn't looking for food and could not care less about the condition of the establishment. He saw the mess from a freeway overpass that looked directly down into the yard.

Aaron drove by the front of the restaurant and saw only three cars. In front of the old garage was a pile of cardboard boxes, forcing him to remember his earlier failure. On the other side of the pile of trash were the fence and the filthy yard. At the same time, Aaron saw that the wind was blowing toward the garage. A small cloud of swirling dust could be seen peppering the boxes as he drove. There was an alley just behind the garage. He made a U-turn and lit up a device while driving back toward the restaurant. As he turned into the parking lot, he checked his rearview mirror and maneuvered toward the garage. Passing it, he threw the device with his right hand so his exposed arm would not be seen outside the window as he drove. Smoothly he steered into the alley and away.

Aaron cruised the neighborhood made up of mostly manufacturing and warehouse buildings until he saw a large parking lot with a view of the restaurant a quarter mile down the road. He slipped into a parking spot marked "Visitor" and picked up an old newspaper lying on the seat beside him. He placed his binoculars in his lap and looked around. The business he parked in front of was close by, but had no windows in front, so no one could see him. He felt safe and lowered himself in his seat. Peering over the top of the open newspaper, he could barely see the garage. Cautiously, he raised the binoculars and saw the trash pile, partially covered by an old truck blocking his view. The wind was still gusting and the heat waves caused the garage to be somewhat distorted through the binoculars. Within a minute, Aaron could see a puff of smoke coming from the trash. The fire fed on the accumulation of windblown papers and dry grass at the base of the garage. The small amount of smoke quickly blended in with the blowing dust as the fire grew rapidly. Two men walked out of the restaurant, less than 50 feet away, but both were absorbed in their conversation and didn't see the flames. They got into their car and backed out. Still, the fire was not noticed.

Aaron put down the binoculars and again looked around the area. There was no one around. As he looked back toward the restaurant, he could see the flames and the heat waves emanating from the, now,- sizable fire. Smoke was still very light due to the complete combustion taking place in the lightweight papers and cardboard. Cars driving by didn't slow, either, giving the fire enough time to ignite the garage before it was finally noticed by a passing trucker. The trucker honked his air horn several times but dared not slow down too abruptly along the busy stretch of highway. Cars behind him slammed on their brakes as he braked briefly, so the trucker chose to continue driving on. The following cars, too busy watching the erratic trucker, didn't see the fire. Aaron smiled to himself and clenched his hands into fists, cheering the fire on. Only two minutes into the fire, Aaron saw a huge cloud of smoke suddenly erupt from the garage's door, sides and eaves. The fire had apparently entered the garage and ignited its contents. The exterior fire continued to build, feeding on the boxes and grass, setting the fence on fire. As soon as the smoke from the garage started, it drifted against the restaurant itself and across the highway. Passing cars and trucks began to slow immediately and, in no time, a traffic jam started. As flames exploded from the garage, the traffic had already backed up, almost to Aaron's position. Aaron sat up and started his car. Seeing the garage burst into flames, he wanted to be closer to his fire. He glanced at the traffic and decided to stay where he was so he could watch the inferno.

It was now five minutes after the fire began and Aaron still heard no sirens. He was unfamiliar with this section of Bakersfield and didn't know how near the closest fire station was. The smoke from the burning garage now turned grayish-black and had enveloped the restaurant. The customers and waitresses had run from the building and crossed the street, leaving their cars behind. Heat from the garage fire was already causing paint to blister on the customers' cars and the side of the restaurant was smoking. A utility pole only 30 feet away spat melting creosote tar toward the flames before the tar burst into flames, too. The flaming utility pole gave up its high voltage lines quickly as they snapped and dropped to the grass-covered field below it.

As Aaron admired his fire, thrilling at the sparking power lines, a white fire truck drove into his field of view without warning. The rotating red lights startled him as they mingled with the failed wires. The engine had not used its siren as it approached. As the wires dropped, they set the foot-high grass on fire, starting second and third fires some distance from the garage. The wind whipped the flames in the field and set it on a clear course away from the destroyed garage. There was nothing to stop the grass fire as it advanced as fast as the 40-mile-per-hour gust would take it. The first-arriving firemen sat watching the garage and grass fire burn, trying to decide which to attack. The garage was already collapsing. The side of the restaurant was now flaming, but could still be stopped. The grass fire was now inaccessible and had almost a half-mile before it would reach another road where it could be extinguished. The firemen stretched a hose line and began spraying the side of the restaurant. Shortly, several other fire engines roared by Aaron, causing his heart to race and his chest to puff out. The wind changed and blew smoke back toward Aaron, obliterating his view. In only minutes, the white steam could be seen rising from the restaurant as the firemen gained the upper hand. The garage was now just a bonfire, emitting very little smoke as the open fire blazed. Aaron began feeling deflated as the flames disappeared. He could not see the grass fire from his position. As he backed his car out of its parking place, he could see the huge column of brownish-gray smoke from the field beyond the restaurant. With renewed interest, Aaron raced away, trying to get ahead of the grass fire, wanting once again to be near his fire. He drove with his window down, smiling and feeling the hot air blowing against his face. Looking into his rear view mirror, he saw the smoke column clearly. A small paved side road came into view and he braked quickly and turned, now paralleling the spread of the fire over a mile away. He pressed his foot to the floor and heard the V-8 screaming as his speed approached 100 miles per hour. In the distance, he saw the winking red lights of a fire engine approaching the next intersection from the side. Aaron obediently slowed to give the engine the right of way.

13

Phil felt uncomfortable leaving town while he had a case with hot leads. While Ash was a competent enough investigator, Phil just didn't want his theories to leak about. Nevertheless, the semi-annual conferences in Fresno were always interesting, and he had promised to provide a two-hour lecture on fire-police relations. Ash could handle any other cases that came up in Phil's absence, and if any other fires occurred, Ash had been instructed to call Phil at his room in Fresno.

Monday produced few new leads in the investigation, but Phil still felt that he was accomplishing something in the complex case. The fireman/arsonist theory could be a completely bogus lead, but at this point it was all he had. As far as he knew, it was all anybody had. It was highly unlikely that any other L.A. area arson investigator was even aware of this particular serial arsonist.

As he drove north on Interstate 5 on Tuesday, on his way to the conference, Phil allowed his mind to wander to the Trish interview. He was genuinely concerned about her, wondering how he could help her in her situation. It seemed such a shame to have her living in those conditions and little that she could do to change them. He had checked on Trish's mother's case and found that she had two other arrests before the latest one. She was currently serving four years before she could be eligible for parole. It was a federal offense and there was little flexibility in her sentencing. She had one previous conviction for embezzlement from her employer.

Phil was driving down the Grapevine when he noticed a column of smoke in the distance, west of Bakersfield. He quickly forgot about Trish and found himself accelerating to nearly 80 in the direction of the fire. He was in Bakersfield before he knew it and could see the blackened trail the fire left behind. Judging by the number of acres he could see already burned, he judged that it had been burning for at least a day. The wind was now calm and the smoke he had seen appeared to be the last remnants of the fire. A few hand crews worked the blackened fields, cutting a trail around the perimeter to insure it didn't flare up again. Phil lost interest and didn't really want to leave the Interstate to see a day-old fire, although he naturally wanted to see where it came from. He got off the highway, finding it near lunchtime anyway. He drove into a nearby shopping center where he stopped at a McDonald's. As he left, he saw the charred fields and fire-scarred trees, brush and fencing showing the fire's point of origin to be in the direction he was traveling. Within a quarter of a mile, he found the damaged restaurant and destroyed garage. He drove slowly through the lot and saw the burned power pole, too, theorizing that maybe high winds blew wires down and started the fire. *Probably not*, he thought as he examined the scene closer. The damage to the power pole was on one side only, pointing toward the remains of the garage. Corresponding damage to the side of the restaurant also substantiated the fact that the fire started in or near the garage and spread from there. Phil could also see that several heavy timbers and part of the roof of the garage had collapsed, pointing toward some metal trash containers at the side of the garage. The side that had suffered the most damage indicated that the fire started, most likely, in the trash area. Phil smiled to himself and returned to the Interstate.

Two hours later, he arrived at Fresno and checked into the Holiday Inn, site of the conference. The temperature was over 100 degrees in the booming agriculture center. Winds were brisk and the Sierra Nevada Mountains could just barely be seen to the east. High rise buildings filled the skyline and gave credibility to the city's new status.

Phil's room was comfortable and had a view of the Convention Center across from the hotel. He would have preferred a room a little higher up in the 10-story structure, but he couldn't complain. He unpacked and went to the bar. The staff of the conference was in a meeting, and the conference itself didn't actually start until Wednesday morning. Phil bought a beer and went to his room to change into swim trunks. He walked to the pool and was recognized by several investigators from Northern California. Phil was a regular lecturer at the event and soon was involved in a lively conversation. The investigators had an active bar tab and the group quickly grew loud and boisterous.

Phil dove into the pool and floated in the fading sunlight, drifting into the shallow end which was partially sheltered by a patio cover. He found himself examining the investigators. *Is it really possible that a fellow fireman could be setting fires? It sounds just too bizarre.* Phil drifted back to the group and hung on the side of the pool.

"Didn't some Forest Service fireman get arrested for arson up your way last year?" he asked.

"I don't think so," one of the older of the group said. "But there was some guy in San Luis Obispo a couple of years ago. He was a seasonal worker or something." Beer continued to flow and the discussion took off on its own. Phil's original, pointed question was forgotten, and the group shared its own stories of firemen and arson. None had real solid information on specific instances of arsonist firefighters, and none offered any link to fires they were experiencing. The focus of the group changed when two thirty-something females strolled out of the hotel. Dressed in brightly-colored suits, they sat down nearby, silencing the group. Phil recognized the women from last year's arson conference, representing the insurance industry. One of the younger men offered to go to the bar to get them drinks. Phil met eyes with one of the women, who held up her drink, as if toasting him.

"To your lecture, Mister Langtry," one of the women, Anne, smiled. Phil reached for his beer to join in the toast. He now felt a little uncomfortable with the rowdy group, wanting to pursue talking to Anne. Feeling the sun blasting down on his back, Phil hoisted himself out of the pool. He now felt the extra 15 pounds he had gained eating his roommate's cooking. He quickly grabbed his towel and dried his body, allowing it to discreetly cover his midsection as he eyed the table next to the women.

Conversation came easily with Anne. Phil knew it would. She was about 35 and had short auburn hair. Her fresh, natural face had totally taken him. She was lightly freckled and had a beautiful smile and bright eyes. She looked directly into his eyes as she talked.

"Have we met before?" Phil asked.

"No. Not directly. I was at a meeting of the Southern California Fraud Investigators last year in Downey. You spoke about arson fraud fires."

"I don't know how I could have missed you," Phil offered, with a smile.

"I wanted to meet you but you left rather quickly," she said.

"Did I? I'm not all that comfortable with a crowd. I mean, when I'm talking my stuff, I'm okay, but afterward I usually prefer to take off."

"I understand," she said, her chin in her hand, resting her elbow on the table. Phil smiled and gazed into Anne's eyes. They continued to talk. The others made their way over and joined in the conversation. As the group talked, other investigators arrived at poolside, and both Anne and Phil were sidelined by necessary conversations. Phil found the contacts he made were far more important than the learning experience of the conference. Anne seemed to be well known in her industry and was involved with several other insurance types that showed up. Phil frequently glanced over at her and those captivating eyes. He found a lull in the conversations and maneuvered himself to Anne's side.

"Dinner?" he asked.

"I can't. I've got to meet a private investigator my company is considering hiring. It may be the only opportunity I have to check the guy out personally. He covers Northern California and is a real hermit, but he's been doing fire investigation for 25 years. Maybe you know him. Keith Tallon?" Anne asked.

"Tallon? Yeah, I know him. He's probably one of the few cops that has ever grasped the concept of fire investigation. I don't mind a bit that he's taking you to dinner."

"What do you mean you don't mind him taking me to dinner, Mister Langtry? Are you marking your territory?" She smiled. Phil flushed, thinking of his jealous behavior with his ex-wife.

"Sorry, never mind," Phil added nervously.

"Why don't you arrange to drop by the Fireside bar at about 9:30 tonight? Mister Tallon should be ready to leave by then. My boss met him here last year and feels he might drink a bit, but writes a good investigation report. We are getting a lot of fires in rural areas now and really need someone up here to represent our company. The small town arson investigators just don't seem to be well-trained and they lack the experience of you big city guys. We don't want any of our insureds getting away with anything."

"Keith knows fire causation and he also is very good at communicating."

"Thanks for the input. Why don't we have dinner Wednesday night?" Anne asked.

"I'm sorry. The organization has its installation of officers Wednesday night, and I'm supposed to have a small part in introductions. I just can't get out of it."

"Well, anyway, meet me at the Fireside bar at 9:30 tonight. Okay?"

"Alright, Anne."

"See you tonight, Phil," she said as she flashed another dazzling smile. Phil and Anne drifted apart to talk to other people, and ultimately Phil returned to his room, feeling a little light-headed from all the beer and the sun. After a short nap, he returned to the bar and found the majority of the conference staff seated in a booth. He singled out the lecture coordinator and found that he was to speak for three hours on Thursday morning from 8:30 to 11:30. This was one more hour than they had originally asked for, but Phil was prepared to fill in an additional hour. He would simply throw in some more slides and prepare a list of audience participation-type polls and questions that would generate more conversation from the students. This was a sure-fire way to keep the interest of the group as well as gather information about the audience itself.

Later that night, Phil joined the group from the pool, now continuing their party at the bar and spilling over to several nearby tables. Gina, the woman with Anne from the pool, was there, but Anne was missing. After having a beer with the rowdy group, Phil decided it was time to leave, giving up on Anne. On his way to the door, another group from the L.A. area stopped him and shoved still another beer in his hands. It appeared that it was going to be a long evening.

14

Aaron spent Monday evening circling the slum areas of Bakersfield, driving through alleys and walking in shopping malls. He found little opportunity to burn anything. Earlier, he had tried to get close to his fast-moving grass fire, but was stopped when the Highway Patrol shut down all roads leading into the area. He continued on into Bakersfield and checked into a Motel 6 near the highway.

Tuesday morning Aaron drove north toward Fresno and again had trouble locating anything to burn. He got off the highway and drove through the small towns that lined the Interstate. He attempted several times to set fires in alleys, but residents seemed very wary of him. It was still morning and there was little traffic for him to blend in with and he didn't feel comfortable at any viewing sights he scanned near his potential fires. At one point, he threw one of his devices into the open window of a truck parked in an alley, but a patrolling sheriff's car drove by as he emerged from the alley. The deputy didn't look directly at Aaron, but he felt uncomfortable so immediately drove back onto the highway and again headed north. He repeatedly looked into his rearview mirror to see if he saw smoke from the burning truck. He saw nothing.

After arriving in Fresno, Aaron checked into his room and left the hotel a short while later. He cruised the streets of Fresno, re-acquainting himself with the city and its suburbs, its slums and communities nearby. He took notes on a pad next to him, writing down the addresses of potential fires. Overflowing trash dumpsters next to buildings, vacant lots overgrown with weeds next to buildings and rundown stores in the downtown area all offered him fires. Only once did he get so excited that he couldn't wait. He saw a large pile of discarded furniture behind a discount furniture store. The parking lot next to it was almost filled with customers' cars offering plenty of cover for him to park and set up a device. He pulled into the lot and looked around briefly. The pile of furniture was next to the outside storage area of the store, also piled high with wooden pallets. He quickly reached under his seat, looking for a paper bag to put his device in. His hand felt his .45 automatic and he quickly withdrew, singed by the hot metal surface. The gun, lying on the floorboards, had heated up, making it almost too hot to touch. He re-wrapped it in a rag and brought it up to the seat to set it beside him. He again reached under the seat and found a package of brown paper bags. He lit his device and dropped it into a bag. Getting out of his idling car, he glanced around as he walked toward the pile. There was only an elderly woman in the parking lot, fumbling with her keys as she walked to her car. Aaron approached the old, discarded furniture, determining which way the slight breeze was coming from, calculating the placement of his device to ensure a fast-moving fire toward the huge pile of pallets. He bent down to the pile and picked up a cushion from a six-foot long sofa. He examined it as if he was interested in it, then placed his bag behind the sofa and put the cushion on top. The wind would not blow it away before it burned, and the cushion would explode with flame once the flaming paper bag ignited it. This placement would also allow the blossoming fire to go undetected for several minutes, hiding the flames behind the cushion.

Aaron walked back to his car and got in. As he clipped his seatbelt, he checked his mirror. Seeing no one watching him, he backed out and drove onto the wide boulevard. He looked into the furniture store as he passed and made a U-turn at the next intersection. Aaron pulled into a taco stand parking lot about a half-block away from the furniture store. He backed his car into a space at the rear of the lot and found the view to his liking. He then went to the stand and ordered a Coke. As he stood in line, he found himself getting an erection. He moved closer to the counter and looked at the reflection of the furniture store in the stand's front window. He didn't have to turn around to see that the parking lot was empty and the furniture pile could not be readily seen from any nearby businesses. He paid for his drink and walked back to his car. As he got in, he glanced at the furniture and saw nothing. He sat quietly in the hot car leaving the driver's door open while softly stroking his erection. Five minutes passed and Aaron felt that his device had failed. He dared not approach the furniture store for fear that the time delay was just a little longer. As he considered his options, he glanced at his watch. It was 3:10. Less than five seconds after looking at his watch, he saw thin black smoke and a small flame at the back of the old, brown sofa. In less than a minute, the sofa was blazing across the back, and adjoining chairs and cushions were bursting into brilliant orange flame. Thick black smoke billowed and was kept at ground level by the increasing wind. The smoke blew into the pallets, following the path of the flames. None of the passing cars on the street slowed. Aaron then saw a head pop up from behind a concrete block wall downwind from the furniture fire. The head dropped back down and he then saw two hands appear and the man's body again appeared for a better look at the source of the smoke. Hoisting himself up to the top of the six-foot wall, a young man jumped into the furniture storage area. He ran toward the store, only to find himself penned in. The gate was closed and locked. Aaron could barely hear him scream out the word "fire" several times. Again he looked at his watch and saw that only a minute had passed since he first saw the flames and the wooden pallets were already burning.

"It'll be at least six minutes for the first fire truck to arrive," Aaron muttered to himself. He wished he had bought a scanner to monitor the fire calls. It would be interesting to hear when the rigs were dispatched and how long it took them to get to his fires.

In the next two minutes, the fire doubled in size and the column of smoke started rising into the air. The thick black smoke stained the clear, blue sky, like an oil spill attacking the clear blue sea. The smoke was beautiful to Aaron, causing his heart rate to quicken, his breath to come in shallow gasps. He tried to control his outward appearance, to look normal to anyone around him. He glanced around and saw that the lot was empty. He relaxed and partially closed his door, pulling the zipper down on his shorts. He reached in, stroked his erection, watching the fire. He heard sirens in the distance, and within a minute there was an engine pulling into the lot. Aaron let go of himself and pulled his zipper back up. He heard no other sirens. The call must have come in as a trash fire and only one rig was sent. Aaron knew that others would now be requested with the pallet piles burning furiously. The engine backed out of the driveway and down the street, seeking a fire hydrant for a water supply. The 500 gallons on the engine would last only two minutes if the firefighters decided to use the large bore water cannon mounted on top of the engine as Aaron correctly predicted.

The engine found a hydrant, leaving one firefighter to hook up as the engine roared back to the furniture store, being careful not to block the way for other incoming engines. The engine parked where Aaron had parked when he set the fire, and sprayed the advancing fire with the water from their tank until the hydrant flow could reach them. The water shot out several hundred feet and was used to protect the side of the furniture store and was occasionally played back onto the stacked wood. The furniture pile had now burned down to almost nothing as other engines and a ladder truck arrived and began attacking the fire with 2 ½" diameter hand lines. Aaron saw the end of this fire approaching and finished his Coke. He got out of his car and walked to a trashcan and dropped in the cup. As he walked back to his car, he saw a police officer leading the handcuffed man who had jumped over the wall to his patrol car. Aaron laughed and drove off.

He drove to nearby Clovis and found little to his liking. The suburb of Fresno was clean and well kept, with few opportunities presenting themselves for a fire. Aaron did pass the time setting several grass fires before the evening rush hour started. With the increase in car and pedestrian traffic, Aaron knew that getting a good fire started would be difficult. He had to register for the conference at seven anyway, so he went back to the hotel. In his room, he relaxed, feeling excited by the five fires he had set that afternoon. A vision of the girl from the 7-11 crossed his mind and further inflamed him. He thought of going out to look for a prostitute, but couldn't contain his excitement and masturbated instead. Aaron fell asleep.

At 6:30 that night, he awoke and walked to the bar for a beer. There were a number of faces he recognized but he seldom talked with the investigators. He preferred to be alone and sat against the rear wall of the bar until seven, when the registration began. After waiting nervously for 30 minutes in the registration line, Aaron received his materials and walked back to his room. He sulked, feeling uncomfortable about not knowing anyone, but relieved that he didn't have to make small talk. Besides, he didn't want to just sit around a bar with a bunch of investigator types. He didn't have any war stories to tell and that's all the investigators seemed to do anyway, just share fire stories. Aaron smiled to himself, knowing that he had more fire stories to share than any of them. He felt better thinking about his fires.

He left the hotel and walked into the warm evening air with his list of 17 locations that were adequate for a fire. The sky was clear and there was no moon. Fresno, although heavily populated, had no smog problem. Being in the flatlands bordered by nearby mountains, there was a constant breeze to blow away any accumulation of smog.

Aaron found his car and drove toward the slum area near the hotel. He had found several alleys that were strewn with trash and a series of small trash fires was a common thing in slums. A series would likely be blamed on kids or transients and not bring any attention to the conference and him. If the trash fires spread to buildings, as he predicted, all the better. Aaron had thought about his fires occurring during the semi-annual conference, but he thought that the way he set them wouldn't be noticed. *I never leave evidence behind and, of course, no one ever sees me set the fires,* he thought.

Cruising the slum area, Aaron felt uncomfortable. Many people were outside enjoying the cool evening after the hot day. Far too many people to allow him to drive through the alleys. He thought about parking his car some distance away and walking into the area, but that would be too dangerous. He always carried his gun when he walked around setting devices, but this area might present him with unwanted attention. All he wanted to do was set his fires and get out. He did not want any kind of contact with anyone while he set his fires. He just wanted to be left alone.

Aaron drove back by the hotel and on to the north side of town. He had logged several places that offered possibilities and found himself at a Mexican restaurant. There was an outdoor patio area overlooking a shopping center across the street. He could see an outdoor storage area behind a K-Mart that was piled high with plastic trash containers and garden supplies. The trash area was next to yet another large pile of wooden pallets. Aaron prepared several devices and put them in his shirt pocket. He slipped his gun into his Levi's pocket and pulled down his shirt to cover it. Locking his car, he walked up the block and crossed the street to the shopping center. He walked behind a group of teenagers entering the store from the outside storage area and veered into the storage area itself. The area looked good so he calmly pulled out a device and lit it with a lighter. As he started to place it, an employee came out of nowhere and asked if he could help. Aaron mumbled and walked away, frightened by the encounter. He walked around to the front of the store and cupped the device in his hand. As he walked by the trash area, several cars passed, again frustrating his attempts. Not wanting to be seen in the same areas twice, Aaron walked away toward a nearby fabric store. As he approached, he looked into the store from the front windows. There were about ten female employees and customers inside. His device was still cupped in his hand and he didn't want to waste it. It had about eight minutes left before ignition. He was scared, but the fear excited him. The women in the store might notice a man in a fabric store, but he knew that they would never remember anything. He slipped in the front door and immediately turned left toward the nearest wall. He skirted the displays of rolled fabric and the women, intent on reaching the back of the store where he found piles of pillow stuffing and pieces of foam in various sizes. He reversed his direction briefly to make sure no one was watching and returned to the pillow stuffing. He reached to his left pocket and shoved the device into an upright display with several shelves holding the material. Without breaking stride, he headed back along the wall opposite his entry and reached into his rear pocket, taking out his wallet. He fumbled with the contents as he walked by the check-out, no one even giving him a glance.

What seemed like a blast of cold air hit him when he pushed open the glass doors to head across the parking lot. He was sweating. He looked across the street at the restaurant and began to breathe easier as he distanced himself from the fabric store blending in with shoppers heading across the street. A red light stopped him at the crosswalk as nervousness swept over. Several people around him made him extremely agitated. He hoped no one noticed him sweating so much. The broad boulevard was controlled by a long signal, and Aaron started to force himself to relax as he knew he could not control what was going on around him. He took a deep breath. No one on the corner paid any attention to him. He looked at his watch. Five minutes to go. As the signal changed, Aaron tried to stay with the group crossing the street, but he found himself outdistancing them. He cut across the parking lot, quickly walked through the restaurant lobby and into the men's room. He grabbed a paper towel to wipe off his face, looking at himself in the mirror. He felt worse than he looked. His outward appearance was normal, relaxing him a little more. The brief intensity of setting fires inside stores was exhilarating, but sheer terror at the same time.

He emerged from the bathroom and walked to the patio where he found a seat far from the nearest view of the fabric store. He wanted to distance himself from the fire until after it started. If it started. He was surprised that it had not yet taken off. A waitress took his order for a Margarita. Her uniform exposed her breasts and Aaron felt his erection beginning now that he settled.

As his eyes adjusted to the dimly lit patio, he could see the interior of the fabric store over 100 yards away. The open patio was partially covered with ivy growing on lattice-work. A full ten minutes had elapsed since he first lit the device at K-Mart, and still it had not taken off. Again Aaron felt the possibility of failure. As he thought of the reason for his lack of success, he saw flames licking the back of the store wall. His stare fixed on the flames as they spread. He was still amazed at the rapidity of the fires he set. It took only ten seconds for the flames to get big enough to reach the 12-foot ceilings. Billows of thick, black smoke raced across the ceiling, forced by the intense flames silently advancing. None of the employees or customers noticed the fire until the smoke hit a side wall and banked down toward the floor. Aaron saw a woman look up. Her hands drop to her side in surrender. The flames continued to build, feeding on the plastics and fabrics. The woman finally placed her hands on the side of her head, squeezing out an obvious scream. All the heads in the store simultaneously turned toward her, stopping in mid-turn to see the flames. The smoke had hit the nearest woman and began to drop, covering the flames as they advanced, fanning out in a V-shaped pattern from their origins on the shelf. In seconds, all the women in the store had run out the doors. Aaron saw the smoke push out behind them, as if gasping for more air. The fire billowed out, through the smoke, for more oxygen. The doors were held partially open by the internal air pressure displaced by the heat from the flames. The smoke column coming out of the door pulsed like shallow puffs of breath, and after only one minute of life, the fire started to die down from lack of oxygen. The store was now totally darkened by the immense blanket of smoke.

The women grouped in the parking lot, their chatter and sobs carried to the restaurant, causing several customers to look toward the shopping center. Aaron was given his drink and he pretended to read an appetizer menu as several of the other customers analyzed what they were seeing and hearing across the street. The store was dark and the people in front were excited, but the observers could not actually determine what was happening until the heat from inside the store caused one of its windows to break. The ten-foot high piece of glass weakened dropping in a loud crash, followed by a sheet of flame leaping out of the window. The interior of the store, preheated by the building fire inside, now exploded in flame, causing all the windows to crack and drop out, shattering on the sidewalk. All heads in the restaurant now turned toward the inferno. Several screams were heard from the parking lot nearest the fire.

"Oh my God!" several of the restaurant patrons shouted. Aaron started to relax again; however, inside, his excitement continued to build.

"Where are the firemen?" a nearby man said to no one in particular. Aaron shook his head, then felt that he shouldn't have. He straightened up, thinking, *the damn thing hasn't been burning more than two minutes and this idiot's already looking for the fire department?*

Most of the patio customers were moving toward the side nearest the fire. Aaron, not wanting to stand out, did the same. He looked up and saw the huge column of smoke, already hundreds of feet in the sky. He looked into the store and could see the displays igniting as the fire filled the entire storefront. Two Fresno police cars roared up to the front of the fabric store and quickly withdrew when they felt the heat generated by the fire. The officers busied themselves dispersing the crowd in front, including the customers and employees. Aaron smiled, knowing that many of the witnesses would be long gone by the time any arson investigators arrived.

Fire trucks began arriving. Aaron struck up a conversation with two women sitting at a table nearby. His conversation was cautious at first, but they began to pay attention to him as he volunteered that he was a firefighter. He felt comfortable now that the fire had advanced and he knew his device was consumed. Anybody who saw him inside the store would be so confused by what had just taken place that he would just be a blur in their mind and only an excellent investigator would ever bring out the fact that there was a man inside the store just before the fire. The women at the table downed their drinks quickly. They were fascinated, excited by the fire. So was everyone else. It was unusual excitement and Aaron was the only one who knew what had happened. He cherished this feeling and had to control himself from being too garrulous in his chatter with the women. It was he that had made their evening memorable, and for that, he felt fantastic.

15

Phil looked in the hotel's lounge and quickly found Anne and Tallon. They were in a remote corner, but Tallon's booming voice could be heard over the blaring music from the adjacent bar area. There were about fifty investigators in the main bar, renewing acquaintances and attempting new ones.

As Phil approached, he could see that Tallon was well on his way to getting drunk. Anne was just finishing a white wine.

"Phil! How the hell are you? Sit down. Miss, bring a couple of beers here, please!" Tallon shouted at the barmaid, his speech slightly slurred. Tallon's face was red as a beet. Small blood veins could be seen on his nose and between wrinkles on his cheeks and under his eyes.

"I'm just fine, old man," Phil said, "How've ya been?"

"Not bad. Anne here is just about to sign me up for a couple of cases for Mid-Century Insurance. You heard of them? Anne, this is Phil Langtry from down in L.A."

"We met this afternoon by the pool," Anne smiled as she extended her hand to Phil. Phil's hand nearly dwarfed hers. Tallon laughed as he gulped down about half of his Scotch and water.

"What kind of cases are you lining up?" Phil asked, picking up Tallon's next drink and sipping from it, waiting for his beer.

Anne replied, "A fire in a butcher shop in Stockton and a farmhouse fire about thirty miles from Fresno." Phil could tell by the quick assignment of the cases that Tallon had impressed Anne sufficiently to begin working immediately.

"How old are the fires?" Phil asked, knowing that the fires in rural areas and small towns usually went for several weeks before being assigned to a private investigator to examine.

"Both are fairly fresh. Stockton happened over the weekend and the farmhouse burned just Monday afternoon," Anne responded. "The farmhouse is quite literally on the ground. The nearest fire truck was seven miles away and by the time they got there, it was already a write-off."

"I don't know how you can tell much from a roast like that, Keith." Phil shook his head. "Everything's probably collapsed into the basement, including the cause."

"Yeah, but those farmhouses are pretty solidly built and the heavy timbers can tell a tale where the fire originated by the depth of the charring and collapse pattern," Tallon said, obviously embellishing his expertise for the business meeting. Phil saw the opening and continued to draw out Tallon's abilities as an investigator for Anne's benefit.

"I guess if you can at least establish the level the fire started on, you can narrow the search a lot."

"Most of the time, anyway. The time of day, day of the week and even the response time all help determine whether the fire was boosted with gasoline or burned a normal length of time compared to the damage," Tallon explained as he looked at Anne and Phil alternately.

"It seems there is a large variance in each investigator's reading of a fire. I'm used to adjusting personal injury claims. Broken bones are hard to fake!" Tallon nodded.

"Most investigators have a real limited experience and depend on what they've learned or heard when they try and read a fire. You just can't determine what causes a fire until you've actually examined a ton of them and, for my money, set a few and watched 'em burn!"

"Set your own fires?" Anne raised her eyebrows.

"Keith and I used to set fires in vacant buildings back in L.A. before he retired. With the city's approval, of course. By actually watching a fire develop and spread, you can learn so much more than what's available in investigation books today. So many hard-and-fast rules of investigation of fires in the '40s and '50s are now obsolete. The contents of homes and buildings nowadays are so much more volatile than the past. Plastics and vinyl make up the majority of the furniture and furnishings in your average house today. In 1950, cotton fabrics and wood were the most common materials. They burn slow and build up slow. Plastics go like gasoline."

"So how does that affect these small town investigators' abilities?" Anne asked, intrigued by the explanations.

"I think Keith would agree," Phil said looking at Tallon, "that your average arson investigator today learns from a series of classes, and young instructors are using old investigative textbooks that haven't been updated or are simply plagiarized and presented in a little different manner. It's not the investigators, necessarily. Not every jurisdiction will allow you to burn like we did. Even controlled burning like ours can get out of hand real quick."

"Can't you guys teach this updated stuff at this conference? It seems like everybody attends these things," Anne said as the next round of drinks arrived unexpectedly.

"Your drinks are from the three at the bar to the left of the TV," the waitress said as she set them down.

All three turned toward the bar to see Gina and two of their poolside friends toasting them. They all joined in the toast, laughing. Anne looked into Phil's eyes as she smiled.

"Well, I'm enjoying this, but I've got a 30-mile drive home," said Tallon. "I appreciate your business, Anne, and thank you for the dinner."

"My pleasure, Keith. How soon can you take a look at those fires?" Anne asked as she slid out of the booth to let Tallon leave.

"Well, since it's just Langtry speaking tomorrow morning, I can afford to miss his usual dry humor. Besides, I know what his views on fire and police relations are already! I can have a look at both tomorrow and probably get you my reports by the time you leave on Friday."

"That would be great," Anne said. "One more special favor? I'd really like Gina to get some more exposure to fire scene investigation for the company. Would you be able to allow her to accompany you? Tomorrow's lectures aren't related to her job, and she could benefit from some actual time at a fire scene."

"Absolutely. I was going to thank them for the drink, anyway, so I'll arrange it with her on my way out."

"Great. Thanks, Keith." Anne smiled. Tallon walked steadily away, despite his alcohol consumption.

"He's very impressive, Phil. You've known him a long time?"

"About twelve years. When I first got into fire investigation, he helped me out a lot. My predecessor and he had a unique relationship with my city. The L.A. Sheriff's Department helps out smaller cities when they have major fires in the L.A. area, and Keith was assigned to us. My former boss was a real egotist, but he was an excellent fire investigator. Keith and he respected each other and actually worked well together, but they clashed a lot. The love-hate thing, you know?" Anne nodded, resting her chin in her hand.

"Enough shop talk. Tell me about you," she said.

"What do you want to know? My work is my life!"

"I doubt that. You're quite different from most men."

"I don't really perceive myself as different, Anne. I truly am your typical male." Phil reached for his beer, hoping it would help smooth the conversation.

"Well, you don't come across that way," Anne said looking into Phil's eyes. He looked up at the ceiling.

"It's getting late. I need to prepare my notes," he said as he again placed his hand on hers. He was comfortable talking with Anne, yet a little unsure with the closeness.

"I have a feeling that you could give your lecture right here and right now and keep the whole bar fascinated."

"Thanks for the vote of confidence, but I've had a lot to drink today and I truly don't need anymore and this restaurant is a little stifling."

"I agree. Why don't we go back out by the pool?" she asked. Phil looked at her, feeling less threatened. They walked to the pool, taking their drinks with them. By the pool, they found two other couples and a table in one corner under a small palm tree. As they sat down, Phil immediately stiffened and sniffed the air. He looked out into the moonless sky and saw a patch of black where the stars had been blotted out by a large cloud of black smoke, several miles north of the hotel.

"Fire," Phil said.

"Is that what the smell is?" Anne asked.

"Yeah. You're smelling the roofing tar and plastics. The smell travels for miles then drops down like radioactive fallout from an atom bomb."

"Is it dangerous?" she asked.

"Not this far away. In a confined space, it'll kill you," Phil said, regretting this negative statement immediately. He hated to break the earlier mood. "Sorry," he said.

"Relax, you're off-duty, aren't you?"

"Yeah, but, like I said, my job is pretty much my life. I'm working a case right now and it's pretty involved. A serial arsonist." Anne raised her eyebrows.

"Like a serial murderer?" she asked. Phil fell back into an instructor-like mode.

"The serial murderer is much more aggressive, of course, and he has the capacity to relate to people better than a serial arsonist. The serial murderer has direct contact with people. The arsonist cannot relate well to people on most levels and prefers no regular human contact. Arsonists are typically loners and losers, like serial murderers, but the arsonist sneaks around behind people's backs to do his crimes. His thrill comes by the indirect attention and human contact he gets after the fire is set. He blends in with the crowd and basks in the activity he has created. The serial murderer gains his attention from actually touching the victim."

"Frightening," Anne said. "You ever catch one of these guys?"

"A couple. Two kids and two adults."

"Kids do it, too?"

"Yes. They usually start serial arson after they have experimented with fire when they're young, and just continues it if they aren't caught early. As they grow up, it takes on a sexual atmosphere. You know, they are too insecure to relate to people in a direct, person-to-person way and the fire becomes their friend, mentor and sometimes their lover. Actually, it's a sexual thing."

"No way," Anne said incredulously.

"I'm serious," Phil said stressed. "I've seen it in the guys I've arrested and I've read about it in studies that have been done. These people are warped, and really tough to catch."

"So you're working on one of these characters now?"

He stared at her for a long time and quickly went over his case to this point. He trusted her and felt comfortable sharing with her.

"Yeah. He's hit the L.A. area a lot. He likes brush fires and I think he's ventured into structure fires, too."

"So he's hitting more than your city?"

"Everywhere, I think. I can't be totally sure since a lot of his fires are caught before they get big and no one examines the fire scene. Like the L.A. Fire Department. They can't send an investigator to every little grass fire and check to see what started it. The fire captain just puts the thing out and goes back to the station, so if there is an incendiary device at the scene, it gets missed."

"He uses an incendiary device? What kind?" Anne asked as she leaned closer to Phil.

"He puts a small bead of glue on a cigarette and lets it dry. Then sometimes he'll put a coin against the glue so it has enough weight to throw out of his car as he drives by. He tosses it into the dry grass by a road and never even slows down. Eight or 10 minutes later, the cigarette burns down to the glue and ignites it, along with the grass. In the meantime, he's up the block buying a beer or something. Then he drifts back to the fire with everybody else that drives by."

"Phil." Anne squeezed his hand. "This guy set some fires here in Fresno last June." There was an awkward silence. Phil didn't know what to say. He just stared at Anne.

"What?" he finally breathed.

"I handle the mid-state areas as well as L.A. After I got back from the conference last August, we were notified that two stores burned in and around Fresno while we were in town. I think one of them was actually before the conference, but about the same time. Both of them were fabric stores in the same chain. Fabric Plus, I think. Anyway, the Friday the conference ended, there was another attempt to burn one in Bakersfield. There was a sprinkler system in that one and it just did minor damage."

"Why do you think it was my guy?" Phil said, already knowing that what she said was true.

"There were at least two other attempts at stores up and down the San Joaquin Valley. Two of your devices were found. I guess customers or employees caught the fires before they got too large and the investigators recovered the devices. Cigarettes with glue attached. They were put inside brown paper bags." Phil let out the long breath he held as she explained.

"That's too much. How'd you get into this, Anne?"

"Mid-Century insures the Fabric Plus chain and we lost two stores. That's where we got Keith Tallon. He did an investigation for us, and through him we learned about the devices and the other fires. The investigators up here thought it was union-related since the same type of stores were hit but they never got any leads. It's got to be the same guy you're talking about in L.A."

"You're probably right. I've got something else to tell you, but it can't go any further than here, OK?"

"No problem, Phil."

"The arsonist is probably a firefighter or an investigator." Phil said. She stared at him, contemplating the possibility.

"It stands to reason. If fires are happening here during the conference only, then that seems to be the only logical conclusion. Should we talk to the Fresno cops or something?" Anne asked, concerned.

"I think so, but I don't know them real well. If word gets out that it might be a fire guy, the press would eat it up. The crook would surely find out and no doubt stop setting fires. We really don't have any solid leads yet," Phil offered as he downed the last of his drink and sat back, looking at Anne. She leaned toward him.

"If we didn't talk tonight, you may never have found out about these Fresno fires," said Anne.

"You're right. I only spent one night up here last year and I don't remember watching the news and seeing any coverage on the fires. I wonder if the local investigator has any inclination toward my theory. I wonder what that fire is that we're smelling right now!"

Anne, too, was excited and grabbed Phil's hand in hers. She could see his mind racing, trying to analyze the information they just shared. She tried to remain calm.

"You want another drink, Phil?"

"Yes, I do," he said not really paying any attention. He said nothing as she got up and walked back to the bar. He stared at the black patch staining the sky and was tempted to jump into the investigation immediately. He looked around and saw one of the other couples staring at him. He appeared bewildered but quickly regained his composure when Anne returned.

"Thanks," he said as she set the drinks down. "I should have gotten these. I'm sorry."

"It's okay. Relax," Anne said as she moved behind him, not sitting down as he expected. She massaged his shoulders. He reached up and touched one of her hands.

"I think I saw one of the Fresno investigators just inside the door over there," Anne said as she pointed toward the hotel's side entrance. Phil could barely see the man talking on a pay phone just inside the glass door. The man stepped slowly back out of view.

"He's the lecture coordinator for the conference. The one that added an extra hour to my session for tomorrow. His name's Doug Stillwell."

"Maybe you should try and talk to him about this," Anne said, continuing to massage him.

"No. He'll probably be getting called out to that fire anytime now, anyway. Maybe tomorrow. I would like to go look at that fire myself, though. Want to join me?"

"Sure!"

Stillwell's eyes met Phil's as he approached and he slowly turned away. Phil thought this was a little peculiar since they knew each other fairly well. As they passed, Phil heard his conversation. It sounded like Stillwell was talking to his wife or girlfriend.

Phil and Anne walked to his car and drove toward the smoke on the north side of town. The patch of black still blotted out the stars and the column below it was no longer feeding it. Where the flickering flames could be seen illuminating the underside of the cloud earlier, only a small amount of steam was now rising, pushing the blackness away into the dark night.

In ten minutes they were there. Traffic was moving slowly along the broad boulevard and they could see the winking red and blue lights from blocks away. Powerful lights from the fire rigs brightened the sky surrounding the fire scene, highlighting the steam rising from the burned hulk. As they drove by, Phil tried to determine what kind of store was destroyed. The fire had been so intense that the flames melted and burned the store's sign mounted on its front exterior wall. A large pole on the roof also appeared to have been for a sign, but it, too, was melted and only a metal framework remained.

Phil jammed on his brakes as traffic stopped in front of him. He searched for a sign near the building.

"Sorry. I'm trying to find out what kind of store this was. Can you tell? I'd better watch the road."

"I can't see any signs and everything inside is gone," Anne said. Phil pulled into a hardware store's parking lot across from the now-cold fire. Spectators were getting into their cars and leaving, adding to the heavy traffic on the street. The shopping center across from them was littered with firefighters, engines and the piles of hose that looked like spaghetti thrown haphazardly around the parking lot. Two trucks still had their ladders thrusting up into the sky, one pouring water onto a small pocket of flames far to the rear of the store. The lights that flooded the scene caused the fine particles of water from the fire stream to sparkle like jewels as they dropped away from the main jet of fluid.

"This is so tragic, but still so beautiful with all these lights and colors!" Anne spoke quietly.

"You sound like an arsonist."

"I just meant, I can see how you could enjoy being a firefighter with all these visuals, the equipment and then you add the fire itself and it's almost overwhelming. It is exciting isn't it, Phil?"

"It is. It's the same type of feeling the arsonist gets but by now he's lost interest and is probably lining up something else to burn. The firemen start to wind down now, too, but they feel the warmth of being victorious over the fire without anybody getting hurt. If this guy's a firefighter, I don't know how he ever got through the interviews and psychological tests to become one," Phil said as he shook his head, continuing to look for a clue to the store's name. "There! On the marquee for the shopping center. This place was a fabric store! K-Mart's still standing and the drug store's over there on the right. This was Cloth City!" Phil almost shouted as he scanned the remaining stores listed on the sign next to the street. "Does your company insure these places too, Anne?"

"No. I don't think so, but can we walk across the street for a closer look?"

"I'd rather not. I mean, I could put my badge on and slip through the lines, but I'd be outta line taking you in the area. In my city, okay, but not here. Tell you what, take these," Phil said as he brought out a pair of binoculars from under his seat. "To focus them, you just…"

Anne spoke quickly, "I know how to focus binoculars, Mr. Langtry!" She smiled as he handed them to her. She scanned the fire scene, asking questions about the different types of equipment and tactics used to fight the fire. She abruptly took her attention from the fire and scanned the crowd behind them.

"You really think he's gone by now?" Anne asked, curious about the arsonist. "That's weird!" she said suddenly. Phil sat upright from his slouched position behind the wheel.

"What?" Phil turned in his seat. She handed the binoculars back to him.

"Duck down a little and look at the dark blue Ford in front of that closed bakery. It's about a hundred yards behind us to the left as you turn around," Anne whispered.

Phil focused the binoculars as he rested them on the back of his seat. As he picked up the Ford in the binoculars' field of view, Stillwell's face appeared inside, also looking through binoculars at Phil's car.

"He's looking right at us, Anne."

"Exactly. When I picked him up he was looking right over here. Is he still staring at us?"

"Yeah. It's almost like he can't see us looking back at him." Phil paused, "I think he's just watching the fire, but it's a little eerie running into him again like this."

Phil dropped the binoculars and looked at Anne. "I know. You're married and this guy's tailing us…" She managed a tight smile.

"No. I'm not married," she said as she turned to look back at the Ford. "Phil, he's moving!" The Ford slowly drove through the parking lot with its lights off, taking up a new position several hundred feet away.

"He is following us, Anne. Watch him when he stops, he'll be facing us directly, not the fire." The Ford did just that.

"Anne, move a little bit toward me so I can watch him through these things over your shoulder. I don't want him to know we're checking him out." She shifted slightly. Phil dropped the binoculars to the seat as he sat back up quickly.

"What happened?" Anne whispered.

"He is watching us. I wonder why."

"Phil, how did you know he was watching us before he moved?"

"He was trying to check us out through our rear window but he couldn't see in because the parking lot lights were reflecting off the glass. Look across the lot at that police car. See how the rear window is almost white from the light glancing off it. That's what he was probably seeing. It's happened to me a million times on surveillances. He moved to get around the reflection so he could see us, not the fire. Why the hell is he following us?"

"Maybe it's just a coincidence. He could have been dispatched to the fire and he's looking for the arsonist, right?" she asked.

"They probably don't even know if this thing's arson yet. It's too early and the arson guys by the fire scene haven't even gone inside yet. See them over there by that Chevy Suburban? That's the Battalion Chief. The investigators probably just got here and they're trying to find out what took place. The investigators are the ones with the clean jump suits. They aren't even dirty yet so I know they haven't gone inside!"

"Could it be that they are just assuming it was arson since the fabric stores burned last year?" Anne asked.

"Yeah, you're probably right. It is unusual to have a third arson guy around though. Stillwell's really acting weird. Maybe they are onto the fireman arsonist theory and they think we set the fire!" Phil laughed as he said it. "It's easy enough to check. If they're following us, or me actually, there will be at last two other guys involved. You can't do a one-man surveillance. In the movies you can, but not in real life." Phil slouched down in the seat again as he scanned the area surrounding the fire and the parking lot they were in. After looking over the area, Phil sighed. "It looks like maybe one other guy's with us. He's in a black Nissan over by that Mexican restaurant. He's got a girl with him for cover. No binoculars, but Stillwell's probably got the 'eye,' as we call it, and he calls the shots until someone else has a better view. That way you don't have everybody with their binoculars out."

"So, if we pull out and Stillwell and the Nissan do, too, we're being followed," Anne said matter-of-factly.

"That's right, but no big deal. If they thought you or I were involved and they've been on us all evening, we haven't been anywhere near this place so we're home free."

"True. But it also proves you're on track with your firefighter theory, right?" Anne said.

"Right again. Let's take a drive and see what happens."

Traffic was still heavy, and pulling into the long line was difficult. No one wanted to let them into the flow. Finally one of the rubberneckers stared too long at the fire and Phil quickly jumped in. As he drove slowly forward, he glanced sideways and saw a small puff of exhaust from the Ford's tailpipe.

"The Ford just started. Move over next to me and rest your head on my shoulder, then look back at the Nissan, Anne."

She slipped over to him, sneaking a look back. "The Nissan's gone!"

"Not completely. He's doing what I call paralleling. On the right," Phil said as he nodded toward the large parking area they just came from. She saw the Nissan driving quickly along the access road fronting the darkened stores several hundred feet to their right. It pulled slightly ahead of them and turned quickly into a parking slot next to the driveway to the boulevard. Its lights darkened and the heads of the two occupants could not be seen as they drove by.

"They ducked down out of sight," Phil smiled. "They must be shorthanded and this Nissan guy's new at this. Experienced guys would be at least a couple of hundred feet behind us or to the side. New troops always want to be within inches of their subject. I shouldn't play with them, but I want to be sure we're right. Is the Ford still back there, Anne?"

"Yes. He used his red lights to get a break in traffic. How come he's using an official-looking car like that on a surveillance? I mean it's not marked, but it's a four-door sedan like yours," Anne inquired.

"Like I said, they're probably shorthanded and didn't expect me to leave the hotel or something since it was getting so late. Then the fire happened and we left, so they had to make do with what they had."

"The Nissan's moving again, too, Phil. He just cut in ahead of the Ford."

"Perfect," Phil said. They pulled up to an intersection as the light turned yellow. At the last second, Phil roared across the intersection, the cars behind him effectively blocking the Ford and Nissan's forward progress. "This doesn't prove anything, but I just don't like being followed. Let's go back to the hotel and wait for them."

"Don't you think they saw us watching them with binoculars, too?"

"No. I don't think so. When you saw Stillwell that light was blocking out our rear window and he couldn't see you looking at him.

Since Stillwell had the 'eye', the Nissan guy probably wasn't using his binoculars and didn't see us." They drove back to the hotel and pulled into a darkened space near the side of the building by the pool. The warm evening air was cooled by a slight breeze.

After relaxing for several minutes, they heard a car slowly driving by. Phil looked into his rearview mirror and saw the Nissan pass, its brake lights winking briefly when the driver saw Phil's car. It continued on.

"It's them. Let's go," he said. As they walked toward the front of the hotel, the blue Ford parked in a corner of the lot and the Nissan continued on to the street and drove away. Phil asked Anne to wait at the entrance to the lobby.

He walked directly to the Ford. Stillwell rolled down his window.

"Hey, Doug, how's it goin'?" Phil asked, hoping for a straightforward answer. He didn't get it.

"Hi, Phil. Just waiting for Dick Bernal. We're going out for a couple of beers."

Miffed, Phil said, "Doug, why the hell were you following us?"

"I wasn't following you. Why, were you over at the fire? I didn't see you."

"Come on, man. I saw you with my binoculars while you were trying to check us out. What is this?" Phil knew he was getting nowhere. His face turned red as he spoke, his anger obvious to Stillwell. He abruptly turned to walk away.

"Phil, wait a second. Maybe you should talk to my boss. We're on to something about that fire and I just can't talk about it. My ass would be hung out to dry if I said anything. You know what I mean?"

"Yeah, I suppose so," Phil said, softening. "You think it's somebody at the conference, don't you?" Stillwell's shoulders rose slightly as Phil said it, betraying his response.

"No. We just, uh…you know, are just checking out leads."

Phil shook his head. "I know you can't talk about it, man. Can you tell me this? Am I the only one being watched?"

"No. At least three others, maybe more. I'm not told everything either. Just don't tell my boss I'm talking to you like this. He would really flip out. So would everybody else. I been on you since you got here today, and the only time I wasn't watching you was when you went to your room at about four. You couldn't have set this fire. You're eliminated as far as I'm concerned. Look, I gotta get going. I've said too much already."

"OK, Doug. No problem. Thanks for the info," Phil said, "By the way, the same guy's hitting down in L.A. too."

Phil walked Anne to her room. They embraced for a long time.

"What's next?" Anne asked.

"I'll look up Stillwell's boss tomorrow and find out what they've got so far. I imagine they're going to be as quiet about this as I am. It may be tough." Phil sighed, and held her closer.

Stumbling for words, he said, "Have breakfast with me tomorrow?"

"Sure, pick me up here at my room at about seven?" she smiled.

"How about seven-thirty? I'm really drained."

"Alright. Goodnight," she said and embraced him again.

16

Despite his turmoil, Phil slept soundly, waking only once when he heard a siren go by the hotel. Even then, he dropped back off quickly, his mind just too overloaded with facts and situations.

The wake-up call came much too early, but he found himself humming, anxious to see Anne again. He walked to Anne's room where he found her not quite ready. She let him in. Gina was already off exploring fire scenes with Tallon.

As she closed the door to the room, he slipped his arm around her waist and looked into her eyes.

"Thanks for helping out last night. I enjoyed your partnership."

"It was my pleasure," she said, "and I learned a lot, too, although nothing about you..."

"I don't talk a lot about myself. My work, yes, but me..." She shook her head at him, smiling.

She was wearing a light silk robe that came to the top of her thighs. They embraced for a long minute. He could hear a radio playing in the bathroom and a slight rushing sound from the air conditioning vent above them.

"I'll be ready in a minute," she said as she parted. She walked into the bathroom, leaving the door slightly ajar.

He heard the news broadcast of local traffic conditions, as well as a brief statement about an upcoming story on last night's fabric store fire.

She appeared in minutes, wearing a very business-like outfit. A white voile blouse and a pair of light-gray wool slacks set her off in a way that he knew would make her stand out in the primarily male audience they were headed for.

They entered the hotel's restaurant. She initiated conversation readily and totally ignored the surrounding men glancing over at her. It seemed that she knew Phil was a little apprehensive about the lecture he was giving in less than an hour in front of over 200 people. Anne's questions and dialogue relaxed him and he marveled at her. He didn't feel uncomfortable at all, and actually looked forward to having her in the audience.

They parted at the door to the conference room. He met with Stillwell to ensure that the slide projector and handouts were organized and ready to go. He watched Anne walk to a crowd of investigators chatting with one of the other speakers. The investigators, dressed in everything from jeans and cowboy boots to three-piece suits, mixed well with each other, and pockets of laughter mingled with more hushed conversations. One group, in particular, gathered near the front of the room. The group consisted of three Fresno investigators and two other faces that Phil didn't recognize. One of them was obviously an undercover cop of some kind. He was disheveled, bearded and didn't quite fit in with this crowd. Occasionally, an undercover investigator would attend the conferences, but this one seemed to be the focus of the conversation and familiar to the Fresno cops.

Stillwell excused himself from Phil and walked to the group. Phil watched cautiously as the group stopped their conversation at Stillwell's approach. The narc-looking cop then re-started the conversation with a young man in the group. Phil thought he recognized the younger man as the Nissan driver from the surveillance last night. The narc then jabbed his finger at the younger man as the novice dropped his head.

There was a third party to the surveillance last night, and he's chewing out the new guy for his tactics, thought Phil. The observation was confirmed when the Nissan driver glanced at Phil and quickly turned away when he saw him watching. The narc, too, saw the exchange and threw his hands up while clenching his teeth, and walked away shaking his head. The narc, a true professional, thought Phil, never looked directly at him, but caught a sideways glance at Phil as he walked to the rear of the room. As the narc drew a cup of coffee, he looked into the mirrored wall behind the coffee pot to look at Phil. Phil smiled and waved. The narc raised his shoulders slightly at the exchange and immediately walked over.

"Hi. Orv Priest, Fresno PD. You're speaking this morning," the narc said as he shook Langtry's hand firmly.

"Yeah, appropriately enough on fire and police relations. You work with the Fresno arson guys occasionally?" Phil asked. Priest was about 40 and weathered from his years of outdoor cop work in the Fresno area. His pupils were the size of pins, but he opened up quickly when their idle conversation became more focused. The man was nervous. Phil's years as an investigator enabled him to read almost anyone from their eyes alone.

"Not only have I worked with them, I was a Fresno fireman once. Switched over to the PD after a couple of years of putting out grass fires. Not enough excitement, I guess."

"I suppose this town has really grown in the 15 or 20 years you've been on the job?"

"Yeah. It's unbelievable how the place has grown."

A silence followed as the two sipped coffee. It was obvious to Phil that the man forced himself to come over only after being discovered looking in the mirror. Phil decided to lay everything on the table.

"Look, Orv. I know you code-fived me last night," Phil said, using cop vocabulary for a surveillance. "It's no big deal. I know the case you guys are working because the same guy's hitting in the L.A. area. I didn't know he was hitting up here until last night. He's using the same device in my town..." Phil let the statement drift off, hoping for a positive response from the narc. Priest looked around, over his shoulders and finally to the floor before responding.

"It's a bitch, man. These arson guys don't do this shit very often, and the new kid blew it! He hasn't had any training," Priest said, obviously frustrated. "We're really short-handed now."

"No sweat, Orv. It was just a fluke that we spotted you. The real arsonist was probably gone by the time we got there, anyway. You are aware that I couldn't have set that fire aren't you?"

"I dunno," Priest replied defiantly, thrusting up his chin at Phil. "I know of three or four ways to set up a time delay that'll give you a couple of hours before it sets something off." Phil felt uncomfortable at Priest's accusations but understood the need for the suspicions.

"OK, I can relate, man. But I checked in and never left the hotel. Stillwell can attest to that," Phil said heatedly.

"Alright, Langtry," Priest narrowed his eyes, flaring quickly. He started to jab his finger for emphasis but saw Phil ready for it with a clench of his fists. Priest's eyes continued to narrow; frustrated that he could neither conclusively win the encounter nor distort it into a win as only cops can do. He took one step back instead, and turned and walked over to the coffee pot.

Phil noticed several men nearby watching the confrontation escalate. Phil did not expect Priest to return, but he did.

"Look, I'm sorry," Priest said as he took a deep breath and let it out. He cocked his head slightly, looking up at Phil. "We've been working on this case for about two years now and the only real leads developed during the conference. That means we wait a whole year to see if more fires happen. Then, and only then, can we examine what we have. As far as we can see, these fires have been going on for at least five years. Our arson unit didn't really get organized until five years ago and the fires then were just grass and brush fires. These structure fires didn't get noticed until we found a couple of devices that didn't go off or were recovered from small fire scenes."

"That's the same as my case, Orv." Phil softened. "If I can get you guys to share your info, maybe we can work on it."

"Won't happen, Phil. The boss says that this thing's too controversial to let anything out yet." Phil held back a laugh at the same statement made by Stillwell the night before. He fought the urge to enlighten Priest at the case "security" thus far.

"Who's in charge of this thing, anyway? I'd like to talk to them."

"Name's Jeremiah Plank. He's the senior investigator at the fire department. I don't get along particularly well with him. Nobody does, for that matter," laughed Priest. "There he is over there." Priest pointed to the group he earlier abandoned. The man, a new face in the group, was dressed in uniform pants and the traditional firefighter's dress white shirt and a gold badge pinned on his chest.

"Gold badge. He's a Battalion Chief?" Phil inquired.

"Yeah. Fire Marshal, actually. He's been on the department for about 30 years or so. Very well entrenched in politics in this town."

"That's typical in a town that's grown like this one," Phil said, reflecting on a similar situation in his own city. "A fire marshal makes million-dollar decisions on proposed buildings."

"We've had our share of those, and this guy knows his way around the media, too. Uses them like he does everybody else. Not a bad philosophy, actually, but he's just too aggressive for my taste."

"You had a run-in with him?" Phil asked.

"Yeah. He was the training officer when I came on the fire department and we just didn't hit it off. He knew my dad. We lived on neighboring farms about 20 miles east of town. I was a friend of his son, and I guess I got him into a few binds when we were in high school. It was a little crazy here in the '60s, just like everywhere else."

Phil didn't respond immediately to ask the inevitable question about the Chief's son. Too many sons during that era weren't around now. Priest, almost the same age as Phil, knew the question would come and answered for him.

"His son died in Germany, not Nam. He went into the Air Force and got orders to Europe instead of to the war. He was a military cop and got run over at the base's main gate in a truck accident," Priest said. "You went to 'Nam', didn't you?"

"Yeah."

Stillwell walked up to them and told Phil to get ready for his session and advised him that Plank would do a welcoming speech first. Phil expected that and moved to the seat next to Anne to sit through the opening.

Phil sailed through his lecture, appealing for cooperation between police and fire agencies in all facets of their endeavors. Fire and police relations were generally poor everywhere with a great deal of petty jealousies apparent at everything from accident scenes to major homicide-arsons. Although the jobs differed widely, the basic type of individual was attracted to both. Psychological entrance exams for police stressed the need for aggressive individuals while fire psychological exams looked for the more passive compassionate person. Phil outlined the same basic "needs" for each professional in these groups and stressed the need to set aside competition that sometimes arose in an incident. He also took the liberty of discussing the recent surveillance incident as an example of how an aggressive experienced cop can harm a working relationship between agencies with a lesser degree of training. Priest smiled during the example and even ventured a question to Phil on how to resolve such conflicts. The session went well, although many seats were empty after the 10:30 break. Phil knew from experience that the nearby hotel bar would be filled with older investigators, renewing acquaintances despite the early hour.

At the lunch break, Phil saw Plank walking out with several of the locals. He joined them in hopes of connecting with Plank and discussing the on-going investigation. Plank obviously avoided him. They all walked to a meeting room where a buffet lunch was being served. Phil saw Anne mingling with the insurance industry-types and waved at her from across the room.

After lunch, Phil moved toward Plank and again saw that he was being avoided. Plank repeatedly looked away when Phil met his eyes. A meeting now would only result in a confrontation, so Phil walked into the parking lot and located Plank's white, four-door Chevy sedan. The unit was clearly marked 'FIRE MARSHAL' on its side. Phil waited in the shade of a nearby palm tree, hoping that Plank would emerge quickly after his free lunch.

He did, and as Plank strode toward the car, Phil intercepted him in the middle of the lot.

"Hey, Chief. How was lunch?" Phil nearly shouted over the din of a passing jet.

"Uh, fine, Langtry. Nice lecture…"

"Chief, we need to talk for a minute," Phil said as he stepped between two cars to block Plank's path.

"OK, what is it?"

"I was followed last night as I went over to your fabric store fire. I made out Stillwell and a younger guy in a Nissan shadowing me. What gives?"

"Must've been a coincidence, Langtry. If they were tailing you, I'd know about it. Why would they be following you, anyway?"

"Come on, Chief. I'm working the same case as you and I want to share what I have. You might have the key to this thing," Phil urged.

"I don't know what you're talking about. I always instruct my men not to discuss cases, anyway. Nobody was following you," Plank said, taking off his sunglasses for emphasis. He was tough and Phil knew that he wouldn't get anywhere with the man and could possibly create conflict if he pursued the matter. They stared at each other.

"I don't know how I can impress upon you the importance in that we share our information, Chief," Phil carefully chose his words, his cheeks flushing with anger.

"Look, I'm late, Langtry. You're talking in riddles and I don't have time for it. Talk to one of the conference people if you have a problem...." The Chief said as he bulldozed past Phil.

"Asshole," Phil muttered under his breath as the Chief walked away. Phil stood in the hot sun and he stared down the old Chief. The Chief picked up his cellular phone when he stopped at the driveway before entering the street. He looked back at Phil, surprised to find him still staring. He put the phone in his lap as he drove away, hoping it hadn't been seen.

The bar was full when Phil returned to the conference. He found Anne and motioned her over a booth.

Phil was still upset at his encounter with Plank, but Anne spoke and her voice immediately softened him.

"I enjoyed your lecture, but you were a little hard on the cops weren't you?"

"I usually am but I try to make up for it by praising their investigative abilities. That's something that not many fire department investigators ever get good at." Phil smiled. "Did it still come off as harsh?"

"Uh-huh," she said, sliding closer to him. He quickly relaxed and ordered a beer.

"I just talked to the local Fire Marshall about our little tail last night and he denied that we were being followed."

"You really didn't expect anything less, did you?" Anne asked.

"Not really. I also talked to a narc that also was involved in the surveillance. We didn't ever see him."

"Was that the narc that you talked to before your lecture?"

"Yeah, that was him. He copped to the surveillance and the investigation but wouldn't provide any specifics. It was a good contact, though, and I might get some info from him and Stillwell if I play it straight," Phil replied.

"How about Keith Tallon? Do you think that he can help?"

"Don't know. He's only been in Fresno a couple of years and may not have developed any good local contacts but we can ask. Have you seen Stillwell, Anne?" Phil asked, looking around the bar.

"He got paged to the phone just before you came into the bar. He left with the narc a minute ago. Should we try and catch them?"

"Nah. Stillwell has to be in the afternoon session to monitor the classroom, so I'll get him then," Phil said, slightly irritated. "How are you, by the way?"

"I'm just fine. Enjoying the contacts I'm making and fascinated with you and your investigation." She rested her elbow on the table and her chin in her palm as she smiled at him. He stared back affectionately, grinning.

"I have to make a few calls. Come up to my room with me?"

"OK," she replied.

Phil was slightly embarrassed by the condition of his room. Although housekeeping had cleaned up, his clothes were lying around on chairs, his notes still littered a table. His .45 peeked out from inside a three-ring binder on the table.

"High security notebook?" she asked.

"I put it there last night when we got in, and I forgot to stow it this morning. Damn, I'm usually more careful."

"I didn't know you carried a gun. You weren't wearing it last night."

"Yeah, I had it in an ankle holster."

She walked over to him and hooked her thumbs in the belt loops at his side. She pulled him to her. They kissed lightly at first, and then fell onto the bed. Phil broke the kiss, cupping her face in his hands as he looked at her. He pushed her up the bed to the pillows. She looked at him quizzically as he placed an extra pillow under her head.

"I've gotta make a call, Anne."

Phil reluctantly broke the mood, not wanting to rush things with Anne. He picked up the phone and called his office.

Ash was out, so he left a message for him to contact Chief Dartel to get hold of him at the conference. Dartel knew many of the Fire Marshals around the state and Phil hoped that his contacts could smooth over the current situation. When he was finished, he found Anne staring at him with a contented look on her face.

"Sorry. I really needed to make that call. Are you still open for dinner tonight, Anne?"

"Yes, but I thought you had other dinner plans…"

"I did have to say a few words at the installation dinner tonight, but I'm not real happy with these locals right now so I'm gonna cancel."

"Of course. How about 6:30?"

"Sounds good to me. By the way, can you contact your office and get copies of the fabric store fire reports? I'd like to see what I can learn from them."

"Sure, I can have them faxed to the hotel if you'd like. Anything else?"

"That's it for now. What's the one o'clock class about?" Phil asked.

"A discussion on Satanic Cults, and another dealing with vehicle fire investigation. You going?"

"Yeah. If I'm not mistaken, Priest, the narc, is the speaker on the cults. Interested?" They agreed to meet in the classroom later and went their separate ways.

Across the hotel, Aaron leaned on the banister of the open hallway looking down into the atrium. He saw Anne and watched as she entered her room. He then took the elevator to the lobby and walked to the conference room. Groups of investigators mingled at the entrance, waiting for the one o'clock class to begin. Made nervous by all the people, Aaron stepped outside into the hot August sun. A man called out to him.

"Hi. Aren't you with the Forest Service?" he asked, blowing cigarette smoke and alcohol breath at Aaron.

"Uh… no, I'm with L.A.," Aaron said reluctantly, glad that he hadn't put on his nametag. The tag was required to enter the classroom, but Aaron wanted to remain as anonymous as possible and frequently removed it.

"Oh, sorry, you look a lot like a Forest Service guy I talked with at the bar last night. Are you sure we didn't have a beer together last night?"

"Yeah," Aaron said, his mind racing. "I was in my room by about seven watching TV," he replied, making up the story as he went along.

"Well, I talked to a lot of people last night," the stranger laughed, "and I probably couldn't tell you who any of them were."

Aaron managed a weak smile, fearful that he might have been seen elsewhere by someone at the conference. He was worried that one of the investigators might have seen him in the crowd at the fabric store fire.

"I'm Hal Milford, Linley Fire Department." The man extended his hand to Aaron. They shook hands as the man continued, "You come up here often?"

"No. I'm on vacation and just thought I'd drop by and see what the conference was all about." Aaron continued to lie, "I was at one once before, too," he said, trying to divorce himself from his annual visits to Fresno. Aaron had actually attended every conference for the past six years, but had only registered at the last two. Prior to that, it was easy to sneak into the classes and watch. Two years ago, the name tag entry was enforced, compelling him to register to gain entry.

"I see they opened the doors. Devil Worshipping or something's next, isn't it?" the man said as they went inside.

"Yeah, I think so. Gotta go to my room first. See ya later," Aaron said as he walked away from the man.

Aaron was uncomfortable now and didn't want to meet up with the man, or anyone for that matter. He went outside and straight to his car. As he drove, he nervously put two devices together, the glue hot to his touch from sitting in the sun all day. In minutes, he was driving through alleys in the slums southeast of the hotel. His excitement began building as he found a stand of dry grass next to a dilapidated garage and shed. Children played nearby and he had to circle the block and drive by a second time to give him time to light up.

He rolled down his window and lit the cigarette, quickly throwing it out as he passed the grass. The cigarette struck the side of the garage, knocking most of the glowing ember off before it fell into the dried weeds. Aaron drove on, expecting the usual 5-10 minute delay. He pulled into a 7-11 parking lot a half block away and went in to get a beer, not knowing of the defective device.

He returned to his car, he nearly finished his beer and glanced at his watch, seeing that 12 minutes had elapsed. The cigarette, after nearly going out, was fanned by a slight breeze, bringing it back to life after a retarded period of smoldering. Feeling that his device had failed, Aaron took a discreet look at the grass through his binoculars. The children had moved on, and he decided to try a second device. The garage looked too inviting to give up on. As he entered the alley, he lit his second device and prepared to throw it. Just before he came abreast of the grass, the first device ignited, sending two-foot flames up quickly. Startled, Aaron accelerated and, before he could catch himself, the powerful V8 spun the rear tires in the dirt alleyway.

"Shit!" Aaron breathed as he checked his rearview mirror, seeing the flames spreading quickly as he neared the alley's exit onto the street. An elderly man appeared on his right and continued, blocking Aaron's path. Aaron slammed on his brakes, the old man jumping slightly but tottering on. Fearing the man might see the fire up the alley, Aaron gunned the car slightly, drawing the man's attention. As he turned onto the street, he again glanced at the fire and saw a delivery truck approaching his fire from the other end of the alley. As he accelerated away, he looked around and saw no one else watching, the old man now hidden behind a telephone pole. The truck suddenly appeared from the alley and turned onto the street, going in the opposite direction. Aaron assumed that the truck driver, too, wanted out of the area for fear of being blamed for the fire. Aaron relaxed and then realized that he still had his second device still lit and in his hand. He steered into another alley and drove through it slowly. The device still had 5-6 minutes left on it. A pile of trash and discarded furniture loomed on his left and he threw the device out as he passed. At the end of this alley, he slowed before getting to the sidewalk. Buildings on each side blocked his view as he eased up to the street, his engine rumbling between the structures.

As his view cleared, he looked to his right and was startled to see a Fresno cop writing a parking ticket. Aaron's engine noise caught the cop's attention, and she looked at him briefly. Aaron froze, but his years of experience enabled him to maintain his composure. He drove on, increasing his speed as he headed back to the hotel. Looking off to his right, he saw a column of grayish-black smoke coming from his first fire. Although drawn to it, he fought the urge to see it, needing to distance himself from the pending fire near the female cop.

When he got back to the hotel, he cautiously walked back to his room, constantly checking over his shoulder for anyone following him. He held his backpack close, feeling the weight of his gun. In his room, he pulled back the curtains to see the two smoke columns less than a mile away. Frightened that his car's description might be remembered by the cop, Aaron left the hotel and headed back to L.A. The farther away he got, the more relaxed he became.

17

After driving for 20 minutes, Aaron slowed down and pulled off into a small town that was intersected by the highway. Now that Fresno was miles behind, he felt more relaxed and he was hungry. Pulling into a coffee shop, he entered and sat down in a booth to the rear of the small dining area. There were only two other men inside and they were content to sit and talk about farming, giving Aaron no attention at all.

Aaron ordered his lunch and ate quietly. He picked up an abandoned newspaper from an adjacent booth and saw a picture of his fabric store fire from the night before. The headlines gave no indication of the fire's cause, simply reading, FIRE DESTROYS CLOTH CITY. Aaron scanned the articles, seeing no indication of anyone reporting a man in the store before the fire. There were several interviews with customers and clerks and only one ventured a guess at the fire's origin. The store manager said she saw the lights flicker and theorized that the fire was caused by an electrical short. Aaron snickered to himself, then remembered where he was. He quickly looked around and then re-read the article. The final statement in the article declared that the fire was under investigation. He thought back to the other two fabric stores he had burned. He shook his head, assuming that no one was aware of the pattern he had set by burning them during the conferences. This made him feel better, and he looked out the window next to him, scanning the small town. He missed driving through this community on his way north Tuesday, and decided to explore it for fire potential. From his vantage point he saw nothing that attracted him. The temperature was reaching over 100 degrees outside and most of the townspeople had retreated inside, leaving him deserted alleys and streets to prowl. He paid for his food and walked out. Glancing back toward Fresno, Aaron saw the telltale black smudges of his fires layered just above the horizon. He smiled.

Three devices were constructed as he drove and he quickly found a long alley behind the businesses on the main street running through the sleepy town. Rundown residences provided several patches of dried grass and trash. Aaron lit the devices one after the other as he idled along, tossing them into the piles. Cruising back into the business district, he saw an American flag flying above a large white building. Correctly guessing it was the civic center, he drove by, looking for the fire department. As he turned off the main drag, he saw the closed doors of the station. The sign in front indicated it was a volunteer fire department. Aaron laughed under his breath, knowing that his fires would grow considerably before the town's fire siren ever went off. Several more minutes would probably lapse before the volunteers got to the fire station to pick up their apparatus and finally respond to the blazes. He had seen it happen several times before. Only the larger towns with volunteers had at least a driver on duty all the time to respond immediately. This town was far too small for that luxury.

He slowly headed back up to the business district and saw a small puff of bluish smoke drifting over the top of the local newspaper office. One of the grass fires was already going. Aaron sped up slightly and drove four blocks beyond where he set the devices. He turned right and, as he passed the alley, he looked down to see three men stomping out two of the blazes. A delivery truck was parked nearby.

"Shit!" spat Aaron, as he headed back to the highway and south out of town. He checked his mirror once and saw no more smoke. They had put out his fires. He watched his speed as he passed the town of Tulare. A Highway Patrol cop had stopped him there last year, and he didn't want contact with anybody right now. He was fuming. Tulare did provide him with several fires two years before, but all he wanted to do was get back to L.A. where he was familiar with everything.

It was close to seven when Aaron dropped back into the L.A. Metro area, still on Interstate 5. He could see a thin layer of smog over the San Fernando Valley as he drove through Pacoima. The San Gabriel Mountains loomed on his left and he took the 210 Freeway cutoff. He skirted the Valley, looking for a new area. The sun was still high, but shadows from the Santa Susanna's chased him as he got off the freeway at Olive View. The sun would be setting soon and Aaron debated whether he wanted a brush fire or was going to prowl alleys in the slums of the northeast Valley area.

After his first three devices had been discovered by the delivery-men, Aaron tried three more as he traveled south. All failed to ignite. He took shallow breaths as he drove, finding himself drawn up Lopez

Canyon. The canyon was already in the shadows and its steep sides were covered with dry grass and shrubs. Small, trash-strewn businesses marked the entrance to the canyon and rundown residences dotted the canyon for several miles. Aaron knew he would have no problem finding a good location to start a fire as he drove and simply lit a device before finding what he wanted. A coin was already attached and he felt a rush as he came out of a gentle curve to see a field of grass leading up to a stable. The field was over 30 feet off the road, but the quarter had enough weight to carry it well into the grass. Suddenly, a car loomed on his left and was traveling slow enough to interfere with his throwing the device out the window. The cigarette's glow ash would be seen in the darkening canyon and he had to wait as the car passed. It didn't pass quickly enough and Aaron drove on. The cigarette was smoldering its way toward the glue and he wasn't finding anything, so he made a U-turn and headed back down the canyon. As soon as he hit the gentle curve again, he saw no other traffic and simply crossed the double center line and slowed down in the first dirt turn out. Still rolling, he glanced at the device.

"Four or five minutes left," he said to himself, feeling quite comfortable alongside the now-deserted road.

The stable contained at least two horses that Aaron could see, and the grass blossomed at the base of the wooden structure. He looked up and down the road again, seeing and hearing nothing approaching through his open window. He tossed the device out the window, watching it as it hit the upper stems of the wheat-like grass. There was a quick shower of sparks as the ash shattered at contact with the grass. The device then tumbled down the stems to nestle in the tangled mass of straw. He normally would be apprehensive at staying in one place too long, but Aaron reveled at the quiet area that would be roaring with activity in less than five minutes. Again he smiled as he saw a thin line of smoke curling up from the device's resting place. Still no cars drove by.

He pulled his car up to the pavement and stopped as he felt the front right tire creep up the small incline from the turnout to the road. He looked over his right shoulder and then pulled forward when he saw no cars approaching. Looking into his mirror, he accelerated down the canyon. As he approached the mouth of the canyon, two pickup trucks roared by Aaron as he was stopped at a stop sign in the dilapidated business area. He watched them weaving up the road in his rearview mirror. They were driving fast enough to pass his device before it went off, guaranteeing a good start before it was reported. He thought briefly about the two horses, but figured they would be able to run into their corral to escape the flames. He drove on to Foothill Boulevard and pulled into the parking lot of a mini-mall with a liquor store.

After buying two beers, he returned to his car and put the key into the lock of his Chevy. He placed the bag with the beer in it on the roof of his car as he looked at Lopez Canyon, a mile away. The sun had dropped well below the horizon to his west and behind him, and the canyon should have been dark, but it was not. The fire, now three minutes old, had raped the field of grass and the thick, burning mass sucked in oxygen from the atmosphere, looking for more air to continue its path of destruction. Its pursuit for air created its own wind and fanned the flames across the tops of the grass and created a huge front of flame. The front crashed into the wooden stable, heating it to its ignition in seconds. Aaron could tell from the smoke columns that the stable was already involved. One column was a whitish color and was pushed by the burning grass and brush. A darker column below it was the stable fire, fighting for its survival. The flames from the fire could not yet be seen by Aaron, covered by the steep canyon sides, but the light flickered across the bottom of the clouds of smoke.

Sirens overcame the traffic noises on Foothill Boulevard. Aaron got into his car and pulled to a dark side of the parking lot. Two engines raced by, followed by a ladder truck. The men on the ladder truck would augment the engine crews in advancing hose lines up the steep slopes, their ladders useless for a brush fire. The mini-mall's parking lot was dark and gave him an ideal location to watch his fire.

More engines sped by and Aaron's excitement increased. Aaron took a long swallow from his beer and sat back to watch the fire. His arousal quickly overcame him as he finally saw the tips of flames reach the top of the canyon. He finished the first beer and threw the empty can to the passenger floorboard. His hands now free, he rubbed his erection and closed his legs tightly together. He found his tight pants too confining and reached down to lower his zipper. Still not providing enough release, he unbuckled his belt and reached down to slide his seat back. He sighed as he spread his legs apart and reached inside his underwear to grasp himself. Seeing a sheet of flame explode from another slope in the canyon, he began to stroke himself wildly while glancing around the lot. More sirens approached and added to his excitement.

Suddenly, a low-rider '63 Chevy drove into the parking lot. The windows were rolled down and Aaron could hear its radio blaring. The car blacked out its lights before it rolled to a stop and shut off its motor and radio. The obviously underage occupants hardly noticed Aaron as they pooled their change for a beer purchase. Aaron released himself and cautiously slid up the seat. The low-rider was just ten feet away, and Aaron could no longer continue. He started his engine and froze as the adjacent Chevy's occupants glanced at him. They quickly returned to their own pursuits as Aaron pulled out of the lot, his jeans still open, his erection fading.

Flashing a look over his shoulder, he saw the flames waning as they reached the tops of the slopes. Winking red lights on the mountaintop indicated that the firefighters were already getting a handle on his fire. Approaching helicopters also signified that this fire would soon be contained. Aaron closed his pants and drove east into Sunland, tired from driving, but hungry for more excitement.

As he drove along Foothill Boulevard into Sunland, he checked his rearview mirror and could still see the clouds of smoke from his earlier fire. The top of the cloud was being blown in his direction, indicating an early evening breeze that would help along any other fires he set tonight. The Angeles National Forest was to his left as he drove, but he didn't care for fires in the forest areas. There was only one entrance and exit into the area, and that made it too easy for his adversaries to jot down license numbers as he watched his fires. Fewer cars traveled into the forest, and he knew from experience that the U.S. Forest Service had an excellent reputation for capturing arsonists that worked their territory. He learned Forest Service investigation tactics from his trips to the conference in Fresno.

Aaron continued stroking himself as he drove through Sunland. There were few opportunities for him here since the suburb of Los Angeles was mostly single family homes. Some apartments and small businesses lined Foothill Boulevard, but, in the back of his mind, Aaron knew where he was going. His excitement was still strong from his earlier fire in Lopez Canyon, and his mind frequently returned to the 7-11 girl. He was only a 15-minute drive from where he last saw her and his frustration grew as he drove. Turning off Foothill, he drove through an area with small businesses and two-story apartment buildings lining the quiet street. Teenagers wandered around the area, and Aaron felt comfortable mixing with the residents. He pulled into a parking space on a stretch of street that had several street lights out. No one noticed him. He looked around for several minutes. On his left was a row of small businesses, their interiors darkened. The closest, a travel agency, had a glass door that was recessed into the building. Aaron noticed that the entry door had a small slot in it for mail. The slot was on the right and several cardboard cutouts were pushed up near the door. The display showed a Hawaiian scene, and held a large number of brochures. Behind the display were a small sofa and more displays. Aaron's breath drew in as he analyzed the scene. He wasted no time and reached to his right pocket. Without looking down to the seat, he found the small paper bag and picked it up, too. He checked his mirror and saw no pedestrians and only a few sets of headlights approaching. Getting out of his car, he walked directly across the street and passed the travel agency. As he reached the sidewalk in front, he hopped up on the curb and brought out his device and a lighter. Passing the agency, he lit the cigarette and looked in front of him. No one approached. He abruptly turned around and walked back toward his target. Again, no one approached and he slipped the device into the bag. By now, even the traffic had cleared from the area and he could only hear sounds from Foothill Boulevard, two blocks away. Slowing slightly, he stepped into the travel agency entrance and forced open the mail slot. He folded the paper bag slightly to fit through the opening. It dropped to the floor below the display. Stepping again to the sidewalk, Aaron looked up and down the street and felt excited, but very relaxed. There were no open businesses or pedestrians around. He crossed the street to his car and got inside. There could be no one around to see his actions or be suspicious of him for any reason. His only fear was of a passing police car, but he knew that this area was patrolled infrequently and most cops in the area would gravitate toward his Lopez Canyon fire, anyway.

He passed the minutes by making two more devices. He looked down at the three cigarettes he laid out on the seat beside him. He placed a dollop of glue on each and briefly misplaced the cap to the glue. He searched for, and found it on the floor board of his side of the car. As he replaced it on the tube, he glanced at the travel agency. He drew in his breath sharply at what he saw. The flames had already consumed the bag and were racing up the front of the display. Flaming brochures dropped to the floor and illuminated the front of the sofa.

Aaron reached for his key looking and down the street. Stalling for a moment, he smiled as the front of the sofa began to burn. Slowly, he drove down the thoroughfare. A car approached and passed him, but didn't even slow as it went by the travel agency. Aaron caught a red light at Foothill, and as he waited, he adjusted his outside mirror. Smoke could be seen curling out of the recessed entrance and hugging the side of the building. The signal was long and Aaron began to get anxious. Seconds later, the smoke began pushing out much quicker and the flames illuminated the sidewalk in front of the agency. Aaron ventured one more look in his mirror and suddenly he heard the windows break from the immense buildup of heat inside. As the windows fell out in huge sheets, the flames lapped out, spitting the smoke toward the street. Aaron, fascinated, reluctantly allowed his car to idle forward onto Foothill and he completed a left turn.

Two cars drove onto the street Aaron just came from, and he knew his fire would be reported quickly. Even so, the local fire station had probably emptied at the report of Lopez Canyon burning and move-up companies may not yet have arrived. It didn't matter. His fire was already advancing. He could see the smoke cloud as he circled the area. Reversing his direction, he drove by the fire station and saw that it was dark and no engines were inside. Again circling the block, he turned back toward his fire and reached down with his right hand to again stroke himself. Behind him, he could hear sirens of the approaching fire companies, most likely moving to the vacant quarters he had passed. His fire could not have been reported yet but would be soon. Possibly even before they reached the abandoned station.

Foothill Boulevard stretched out for a mile behind him and the line of approaching emergency lights indicated at least three and possibly four pieces of fire apparatus coming. He pulled to the side of the street and opened his other beer. Taking a long drink, he let the cold liquid slide down his throat. Again he adjusted his outside mirror and quickly looked toward his smoke column and then to the fire station. The engines approached and he heard the large, turbo-charged diesels downshift as they slowed at the station entrance. He didn't expect them to stay long.

Traffic waited for the engines as they blocked the broad boulevard. In seconds, their diesels roared to life again and sirens pierced the air. Still two blocks ahead of them, Aaron accelerated in the direction of the fire. He cut to his left and took side streets back to the fire. Pulling up to a stop sign, he looked to his right and saw that the travel agency was now in flames. Pieces of debris rained down onto the sidewalk and into the street, pushed by the belching fire from inside. Aaron sat watching the spectacle. The engines roared off Foothill and onto the side street, their sirens and air horns blaring. Several cars had stopped nearby and small groups of people congregated across from the inferno. Occasionally, a loud pop came from the fire and the groups quickly retreated several steps, only to press in farther as the firefighters stretched their hoses toward the fire. Aaron idled through the intersection and drove on through a darkened street lined with apartments. Small groups of people left the buildings and gravitated toward the fire. Aaron saw a lone teenaged girl standing on a balcony, debating whether she should follow the crowds. He pulled over quickly. She was wearing a tight T-shirt and looked about 15 or 16, and had long blonde hair.

He shut off his engine and lights as he parked, almost crashing into a small wall where a sidewalk should have been. His mind raced as he saw the girl glance toward a sliding glass door with a small child leaning against it, looking out.

She's babysitting, thought Aaron. *No adults around.* Without thinking, he slipped out of his car and walked to the apartment stairs leading to the balcony. He glanced down the street and saw that the onlookers had congregated at the corner. He checked the teenager out and was aroused by her vulnerability. His fire had excited him almost to the point of orgasm. He debated forcing his way into the apartment and was astonished at himself when he found that he had his pistol in his pocket. He decided to go through with it.

He casually strolled up the stairs and she met his eyes as he approached.

"What's burning?" she said to him.

"Uh, I think it's a store down on Commerce Street. Are you going down to watch?" Aaron ventured.

"No. I gotta watch my sister." She smiled and looked over her shoulder.

Aaron searched for the right words, hoping she wouldn't worry.

"It looked like it might be small. They'll probably get it out quick," he said as he eased toward her, looking back, checking the street.

"Oh, good. My mom's on her way home and has to drive by there. Is the street blocked off?"

"Yeah, but she can probably come around like I did," Aaron said as he reached into his pocket. "See ya later." He retreated back down the stairs to his car, pretending to search for something in his pocket. He quickly drove off, frustrated and flaming with desire. As he drove on, his hand cupped his crotch and slowly moved up and down. His mind wandered back to the fire and he imagined the large-breasted girl at the 7-11.

In 15 minutes, he found himself across the street from the 7-11, sitting low behind the wheel with his binoculars focused on the store. She wasn't around. His remaining beer was warm but he dared not return to the store, its camera probing. The 7-11 was on a busy street and traffic flowed back and forth, slightly bothering Aaron. He did not want to have a cruising patrol car come by and check him out. As he glanced around to assess his situation, he saw a figure in an apartment building lobby less than a block away. Even without his binoculars, he could tell it was her. Roughly jamming the optics to his eyes, he saw her open her mailbox and retrieve several letters. She stood there briefly, then walked back into the dark hallway. He debated running to the building and following her to her apartment, but decided that it would be too risky. He didn't have any idea who might be inside. He saw a light come on and again her silhouette appeared in a window on the third floor. The binoculars, already focused to the distance, picked her up readily and he saw her close the door. As he watched, he ran his hand over his chest, shuddering at his touch. His mind raced, debating how to get to her. Turning slightly, he rested his arms on the driver's side window, re-focusing on the girl as she leaned against the door, reading her mail. He instantly saw that she had not locked the chain running from the jamb to the door. The room's light switch was right next to it. He smiled, and held his breath when he saw her toss the remaining mail onto a countertop with a frustrated look on her face.

121

She was alone.

Aaron decided he must act now. Quickly he started his car and drove to the next block, finding a parking space in a nearby retirement home parking lot. He turned off his car and lights, silently slipping out and walking away. He kept his right hand in his pocket, wrapped around the small gun. As he walked, he felt the cool steel of the automatic. His breath came in short gulps, his mouth open as he approached the lobby of the apartment. He stayed on the sidewalk opposite the building and looked upward as he past her window. She was leaning on the window sill, staring into the night. Before she could see him, he turned around, but not before he measured her location. She was in the second window from the rear of the building. As he walked up the front steps, he looked at the mailboxes and immediately saw the hand-drawn breasts on the label. Emboldened by the discovery, he walked up the stairs. He was relieved to run into no one and relieved at finding few lights working on her floor. A radio was blaring behind one of the doors. Mariachi music filled the hall. Its racket comforted him as he reached up to knock. He knew he must act quickly and not think about what he was doing. A too soft knock would cause her to be wary, but one too loud might get attention from neighbors. He hit the door slightly with his open hand, causing an authoritative thud.

Trumpets blared in the background. He felt the vibrations of her footsteps as she walked to the door. He brought out the pistol and held it to his side as his breath froze in his throat.

"Police. Did you call?" he heard himself say aloud.

As the door opened, he heard himself continue, "We had a complaint about this music….." Her face appeared briefly and seeing the clean-cut face in the hallway, she stepped back from the door's arc. He took the opportunity to immediately bring the gun up for her to see. He reached across with the back of his left hand to turn off the light.

"Shut up or I'll fucking blow you away!" he said as his right hand found her mouth, the gun still in it. They were close enough to each other that she didn't have time to scream as he shoved the door toward her, the pistol pressing against her cheek. Her legs gave out and she collapsed to the floor, followed by Aaron. He kicked the door shut.

"Don't say a fucking word. Nobody'll hear this gun with all that music, anyway," he spat into her ear.

She was stunned and said nothing. Aaron kept the pistol against her face, shoving her mouth to the floor as he looked over his shoulder at the door, listening. Only the music and her muffled sobs were heard. The gun's barrel was resting against her left eye as he debated his next move.

"Don't fucking move and you won't get messed up. Just fucking do what I say, exactly. You understand?" She nodded her head as he rolled her onto her stomach. Quickly he straddled her while still holding the gun close to her face. He placed his mouth next to her ear, "I will fucking put a bullet in your head if you say anything."

Aaron felt her tense body beneath him as he set his gun down on the floor, close by. He looked at the back of her head and then glanced around the room. He placed his hands around the collar of her T-shirt and ripped it down, pinning her arms with the cloth as it bound up at her elbows. Seeing a bathrobe in the dim light of the room, he reached for it and removed the tie. He wrapped the tie around her wrists and forced them behind her back. He tightened it, then sat back to look at her on the floor. Reaching for his zipper, he lowered himself. His erection hardened as he pulled down his pants. He ripped her light shorts from her body as she softly sobbed. Aaron roughly pulled apart her legs as she lay face down, causing her to gasp.

"Shut up!" he spat at her. She froze as he moved over her.

As he lowered himself onto her, his erection softened causing him to sit back in disbelief at what was happening. He stroked himself but it didn't help. He became more aware of his surroundings and looked at the door. He got up and locked it, quickly returning to her on the floor. He gagged her with a towel. As he sat beside her, he heard footsteps walking down the hallway. His penis remained flaccid. Outraged, he slapped the back of her head.

"You bitch!" he hissed at her. Feeling trapped, Aaron pulled up his pants and looked around the small apartment. He then pulled up the tattered remains of the T-shirt to cover her face as he rolled her onto her back. He roughly grabbed her breasts and tried again to mount her. He remained soft. Frustrated, he walked into the small bathroom, all the while watching her on the floor. Finding a robe, he returned to her and trussed her arms further as he dragged her to the kitchen. He stretched the robe's tie around her neck, but not drawn taut. The slack end was secured around the drain pipe beneath the sink and her head was pulled into the tiny space, her cheek touching the gleaming metal. Aaron forced her legs up into the base of the sink and tied them in place with a length kitchen towel he found. He stepped back and looked at her, hearing her soft sobs but paying no attention, except to tighten her gag. Reaching into his pocket, he brought out a device. Silently, he lit it as he searched the room. He picked up his pistol and slipped it into his pant's pocket. As he walked around, he bent down to the edge of a tattered sofa, covered by a knitted blanket. The blanket was lifted and he pulled some of it down from the seat. He nested the smoldering device into the folds at the bottom edge of the sofa, noticing his erection returning. Gauging the remaining time on the device, he debated.

"Six minutes," he said out loud as he felt his excitement build. He knelt down to her and lowered his zipper, looking back over his shoulder at the device as his erection returned. As he ripped open his belt, he couldn't control himself as the jeans rubbed against his penis. Before he could enter her, he ejaculated, staining the carpet and his clothes.

"Shit!" he said as he fumbled at re-securing his pants. He stood up before he was even finished, kicking the bewildered girl in his frustration.

Walking to the door, he finished straightening himself up and listened. Opening it slightly, he peeked out. Hearing nothing, he glided into the hallway and down the stairs. Without looking back, he walked briskly to his car, feeling the wetness spreading around his crotch. He smiled and felt relief as he reached his car. Entering it, he cranked the engine over and drove up the street to the intersection by the 7-11. Not wanting to stop, he circled the block several times until he saw a glow and a thin wisp of smoke from the third floor window. Satisfied his device functioned, he headed to the freeway, invigorated by the warm evening air blowing in his face.

18

Anne and Phil sat together throughout the afternoon training sessions, paying particular attention to Priest's lecture on Satanic Cults. Phil not only wanted to learn about the bizarre groups, but also to analyze Priest himself. Despite the volatile discussion they shared earlier in the day, Phil felt he had established a rapport with the man, even if he was a cop.

Priest finished his lecture and Phil tried to get him off to one side of the room, but others swarmed around. Their eyes did meet briefly and Priest saw that Phil wanted to talk. Others continued querying Priest through the break, and Phil was relieved to see Priest sit down near him as the next lecturer began. Phil passed a note to Priest, asking him to step outside to the lobby. Priest nodded at him, and Phil nodded to Anne as they got up and left. She followed behind.

"What's up, Langtry?" Priest asked.

"Orv," Phil said, "this is Anne. She's with Mid-Century Insurance." Anne extended her hand and Priest took it, shaking it firmly.

"I enjoyed your talk, Mr. Priest," she said warmly.

"I talked with Plank and he seems to be a real jerk," Phil sighed.

"I told you. You won't get anywhere with him," Priest said, shaking his head back and forth.

"I thought maybe he would have realized by now that I couldn't have had anything to do with last night's fire, thus eliminating me from this case."

"That's true, but it was pretty embarrassing for him to have you see his surveillance like you did."

"Yeah, I can deal with that, but damn, it seems that by now he would be willing to share a little info. Obviously he's onto the same thing as I am and the best lead is who's attending the seminars when these fires are occurring," Phil ventured, "And to take it a step further, who lives down in the southern part of the state who's attending regularly."

"What do you mean, Langtry?"

"Plank's onto the correlation between the conference and his major fires. He has looked into who has attended the damn things during the periods when his city burns down, and he has at least come up with my name or he wouldn't have set you guys on my tail last night. Right?"

"Yeah, but he's looking at several guys and a couple of them are from Northern California. You say you're having the same kind of fires in L.A., too, right?"

"Yes. Here's where Anne comes in. Last year, the guy burned a couple of stores up here, and he also hit towns south of here as far as Bakersfield. He's traveling south after the conference and probably lives at least in L.A. or further south from there. If Plank knew this, he might stop wasting his time screwing around with the Nor Cal suspects and concentrate on anyone from the L.A. area. Anne has cases that confirm the same kind of devices used in Bakersfield and, of course, from my area."

Priest let out a breath, his cheeks puffing out. "Plank is supposed to go to meetings where all the mid-state investigators share this kind of information, but I hear he doesn't really attend. 'Could care less what's happening elsewhere. Damn, intelligence information is where it's at."

"That's right, but if he won't open up, where do we go?"

"I'll go to my boss at the PD and let him know where this thing's at. Like I said, Plank's pretty well-heeled politically, but if he's jeopardizing an investigation like this, I think we might be able to work around him."

"Great. That's all I need. If he would just open up and provide me with the suspects that he's lined up from the conference roster, I might be able to narrow this thing down. I've even got it down to what shift the asshole's working." Phil added.

"No shit? How's that work?" Priest asked.

"Most of my serial fires—almost all of them—are occurring on days when 'B' shift is off-duty in the L.A. area. Your fire guys up here work the same kind of schedule, don't they?" Phil asked.

"Basically the same."

"OK. Well, I don't experience fires on 'B' shift days and the neighboring towns I've been checking don't have any either. That means that this guy's on-duty at some firehouse and can't set any fires. If Plank would give me the names, we could find out which ones are 'B' shifters and maybe narrow it down to just a couple."

"It sounds easy," Priest sighed. "I'll see what I can do. Where are you going to be tonight, Phil?" Phil looked at Anne.

"Here."

"What room are you in?" Priest asked.

"I'm in room 419, but we'll probably be at the Fireside until 6:30 or 7:00. It's almost 4:00 now. Do you have enough time to get to your boss and bend his ear before he gets off?" Phil queried, anxious to continue his investigation.

"Yeah. If I don't catch him, I know where to find him after work anyway. He always stops at Lucy's on his way home."

"By the way," Phil pursed his lips, "who are you following tonight?"

"I'm supposed to tail some volunteer from the Columbia area, but I can't find Stillwell anywhere. He's organizing this thing, but he just disappeared. He's supposed to be here during this afternoon session...he can page me if he needs me anyway. The volunteer is sitting in on this class, and it won't be over for another hour or so," Priest said.

"If he's from the north, he's not your man, anyway," Phil added.

"I'm inclined to agree with you now. One way or the other, I'll catch up with you at the Fireside or your room about 6:30. OK?"

"Great. Thanks, Orv." Phil shook Priest's hand firmly.

"What now, Phil?" Anne asked.

"Well, I don't much feel like going back to class. You wanna hit the pool for a while?" Phil asked.

"Sounds good, but let me check with the desk and see if my faxes are in first. I'll meet you at the pool." Phil walked briskly to his room.

A small red light was blinking on his phone, indicating a message. He dialed the operator and found that Ash had returned his call. The message said that Dartel had no pull with Jeremiah Plank or any of the Fresno fire officials.

Phil cursed. "Priest, you're my in..."

He quickly changed and headed for the pool. As he walked through the lobby, he saw several of the conference staff watching him from the atrium bar. He suddenly wondered how many of them still considered him a suspect. He wanted to go over to them and shout out his innocence, but shied away, knowing that some of them, being from other agencies, might not even know of the investigation.

As he walked into the blazing sun, Phil saw Gina and Keith Tallon sitting together at a nearby table. Anne wasn't there yet. Phil sat with them and asked about their morning investigations.

"We didn't even get our hands dirty. They were both accidental fires," Tallon answered.

"Well, easy money. You might have been fooled...." Phil let his voice trail off, laughing.

"Nah, really," Tallon chuckled, "the butcher shop's point of origin was at a folded-over power cord on an air conditioner, and the farmhouse turned out to be a three-year-old playing with a lighter."

"Sounds reasonable enough. Was he enlightening, Gina?"

"Fabulous. I never imagined that it could be so simple to find out how a fire started," Gina said, lifting her glass of wine.

"What are you learnin' in there, Phil?"

"Same old, but something's up." Tallon's face turned solemn.

"Yeah," he said as he got up to get himself and Phil another round.

Over their beers, Phil advised Tallon on what had happened since their meeting the night before. Tallon's eyes narrowed as he listened, nodding his head occasionally.

"Plank's a real idiot. Since I moved up here, he hasn't given me any slack when I did fires in Fresno, and I've always had to go around him to get anywhere," Tallon said, shaking his head.

"Well, a local narc named Priest is helping me out. You heard of him?" Phil asked.

"The name rings a bell, but I've never met him. If he's undercover, I probably haven't. Isn't he lecturing here?"

"Yeah, that's the guy. He's one of the tails I had last night. I guess he's a narc primarily but does surveillances when they need somebody. I never even saw him. Not even when I jumped Stillwell's shit when we got back here to the hotel," Phil said.

"Stands to reason. He's a pro," Tallon said approvingly. Just then, Anne walked out of the hotel, a beer in each hand and a handful of papers tucked under her arm. She wore a two-piece suit under a light cover-up. She handed one beer to Phil, stepping to his side, her hand lingering on his upper arm.

"You guys have an interesting day?" Anne said to Gina.

"Very," Gina said. "Keith showed me so much."

Keith briefed Anne on his findings at the two fire scenes as he finished his third beer. Phil looked on, anxious to discuss his case with Tallon.

"The mother of the three-year-old really resisted me for a while, but I could tell by the kid's actions that he realized that we were talking about his fire. He didn't warm up to me at all, and I usually get along well with kids. Mom and the kid stayed well back as Dad filled me in. He said he was in the barn and his wife came screaming out of the house that there was a fire," Tallon told his small audience. "I could already tell by the burn damage that the fire started on the north side of the house. It looked like a bedroom and the worst damage was in a closet. Closet fires scream that a kid started it. They look for a secluded place to play with fire and usually end up torching clothes by mistake. I just told the old man what I thought, and he copped to it. He called the wife up, and she and the kid just confirmed it by their actions," Keith continued. "She told me the kid ran up to her while she was in the kitchen and clung to her side. Couple of seconds later she smelled smoke and ran into the bedroom. The closet was blazing so she ran out to the barn, and she called the fire department while the old man tried to put it out."

"Great, Keith. Thanks a lot," Anne said. "Gina, would you like to join me in the bar? I'll buy you a Tequila Sunrise," she added as she looked at Phil. Anne knew that Phil would want to share more with Keith, and she would create the opening by taking Gina away for a few minutes.

Phil took advantage of the break and filled Tallon in. As Phil concluded, both men lay back, basking in the hot afternoon sun, each lost in his own thoughts of how to further Phil's investigation. Long silences were ended by Tallon's abrupt questioning, using his years of experience to insure Phil was covering all possibilities. Phil's responses reassured him that all that could be done, was being done.

Anne and Gina returned shortly, and all quietly reclined by the pool. After 30 minutes in the blasting sun, Tallon said, "Class is almost over inside, and I need to rub a few elbows. I think I'll shower and hit the bar. Can I use your room, Phil?"

"Sure," Phil replied as he threw his room key to Tallon. Within minutes of Keith's departure, Phil felt restless, unable to nap or otherwise relax, something nagging him.

"Anne, are those the reports from last year's fires?" Phil asked as he sat up, pointing to the folded papers.

"Yes, they are. I'm sorry…" He quickly moved to the shaded table where the assorted reports lay. Phil scanned each page of the insurance company's reports, picking up only the highlights regarding the origin of the fire and witness interviews. The reports she had received covered only the private investigator's examination of the fire scenes and his interviews with the store management people. A couple of fire department reports were also included. Phil had never heard of the private investigator Anne's company had hired.

"Who's this P.I., Henry Gerloch?" Phil asked without looking up from the paper.

"He was a long-time Kern County Fire Department investigator. He retired five or six years ago and started freelancing up and down the San Joaquin Valley. I met him up here last year and once down in L.A.," Anne replied.

"He's in British Columbia now," Gina said, tilting up her sunglasses. "We got a letter from him about six months ago, remember?"

"Yes, that's right." Anne answered. "We dug up Tallon about that time to fill in the gap."

Phil returned to his reading, grateful for the P.I.'s use of plain English instead of the more-common police report style. He could readily tell that the man was a good investigator by his including only the highlights of the investigative facts and no speculation. Phil liked his style.

The concluding report on the two Fabric Plus fires the year before ended with reference to two other attempts to burn stores in the Valley, south of Fresno. In both cases, a paper bag containing the remains of a cigarette was found at the seat of the two small blazes. Although Gerloch did not find any evidence of the cigarette and paper bag device in his fires, he included the information on their discovery by other investigators. The two small fires occurred, one in Tulare and one in a roadside restaurant off the Interstate, just hours before the final fire in Bakersfield. Gerloch indicated that the fires were part of a series originating in Fresno with the Fabric Plus fire during the days preceding the Fresno conference. Although the fires along the Interstate were hours apart, more than enough driving time for the distances, Gerloch theorized that the arsonist had to take time to find the locations for his fires. This was Gerloch's only speculation. As far as Phil was concerned, the man was correct.

"Mid-Century seems to have a habit of hiring only the best. This guy Gerloch is a true professional," Phil said.

Anne laughed heartily, "If you met the guy on the street, you'd swear that he was a farmer. His speech is cowboy, but he is quite capable of presenting himself and his abilities. His wife does his reports for him, thank God!" Phil smiled, remembering many of the old-timer arson investigators from around the rural sections of the state. Even some of the

Fresno investigators still wore cowboy boots and hats while pursuing arsonists in the city of almost a half million people.

"Apparently," Phil said, "Gerloch picked up the information about the two smaller fires at a monthly meeting of the arson group based down by Bakersfield."

"What kind of group?"

"Same kind as we have in the L.A. area. Arson-types, both fire and police, and the P.I.s, get together and share information. Part of the concept is to help the smaller jurisdictions when they have a major fire investigation and limited resources. You know, like the fire department mutual-aid setup," Phil continued. "Say Podunk has a major fire and the surrounding towns all send fire trucks to help out. Same thing applies to the investigation process. The various arson groups send an investigator to help with sifting through the ruins to find out what started it."

"I see. But you mean cops actually attend these things and share information?" Anne asked, lifting an eyebrow.

"They do…sometimes. The only problem we encounter is the cops sharing criminal intelligence info when the P.I.s are present. Just because they are 'privates', and not law enforcement, the cops will sandbag information and not give it up except to the agencies they think might need it. By doing that, the cops really miss the boat. P.I.s work every jurisdiction and probably have a broader sense of what arsonists are working and where than any single agency." Phil stopped himself. "Sorry. When I get started on cops, I can get carried away."

"No apology needed," Anne replied. "It's getting too hot for me and I'd like to shower before we go to dinner. I'm going back in."

"You mind if I keep these reports for a while, Anne?"

"They're yours, Phil. I have my files back in L.A.," she said gathering her things.

Phil returned to his room as Tallon left. Lying on the bed, Phil re-read the P.I.'s reports to pick up any more information he could. It was uncanny how closely the fires resembled each other and matched those that Phil was aware of in L.A. The arsonist might have been setting fires for years and was just now being noticed.

Kicking off his flip-flops, Phil reached for a beer in his room's refrigerator and opened it. His stomach growled audibly. Glancing at the clock, he saw that his dinner appointment with Anne was only 35 minutes away.

Phil reached for the TV remote control, turned up the volume and saw the lead-in showing the store fire on a monitor behind the announcer's head. In seconds, the background music dropped, followed by a brief silence as the blazing fabric store filled the screen, the only sounds were sirens in the background as two firefighters dragged a large hose toward the flames. Phil's heart raced, as it always did at the sight and sounds of a fire. The cameraman was obviously at the fire scene early, evidenced by only one engine in front of the blazing store as his lens swept the scene. The announcer then broke in as the camera picked up a ladder truck turning into the parking lot, its siren and air horn piercing the air.

"A possible arson fire destroyed the Fabric City store on the north side last night, almost trapping two employees working in a rear storeroom," the broadcaster continued. Phil scanned the crowds as the camera focused on two sobbing employees, hastily interviewed by the cameraman before a reporter ever arrived on the scene. One of the crying women had greasy soot marks shadowing her entire face, obviously one of the last people out of the store. The coverage continued with a brief mention of last year's local fabric store fire, speculating on this fire's cause as arson, too. No investigators or fire authorities were interviewed. Phil chuckled when he heard the TV stations' volume drop as the cameraman moved in too close to the working firefighters. The Fire Captain's lips were read by Phil, readily, "Get the fuck outa here," the perturbed smoke-eater said. The screen soon filled with world news and Phil flipped it off, frustrated.

"This guy's right here in this hotel and there's nothing I can do..." Phil headed for the shower.

Leaving his room, he checked his phone for messages, the red light dark. He walked into the hall and looked down onto the atrium bar, scanning the crowd for Priest. He was nowhere.

Their dinner went quickly. The conversation was almost formal, as if they had just met, Anne sensing Phil's anxiety.

"We've spent almost 48 hours together," Phil said, "and I don't even know where you live or work, Anne."

She smiled, "I work on Wilshire, almost into Beverly Hills near La Cienega, and I live in West Hollywood, right off Sunset. And you?"

"Glendale, just north of the Ventura Freeway," Phil replied. "I'd like to meet with you after we get back in town."

"I'd like that," she answered with a smile.

It was well after 7:30 when they finished. Priest still hadn't come by. They walked to the atrium bar where they could watch both the restaurant entrance and Phil's room. Frustrated, they walked to Phil's room. The message light blinked as they entered. Phil almost ran to retrieve the message, dialing the hotel operator. He listened and then hung up.

"It was Priest. He couldn't find his boss right away so he had him paged and he didn't respond. That was about 30 minutes ago..." Phil said to Anne as she moved next to him, standing by his side. The phone rang, startling both of them, its volume on high.

Phil breathed out, picking it up.

"Hello?" Anne listened as Phil asked several questions of the caller, obviously distraught by the news. He hung up, looking up at Anne from his seat on the bed. "That was Ash, my partner. I don't know if I told you about my 7-11 witness, Trish?" he asked.

"No, you didn't."

"She was a witness to one of the fires in a 7-11. Actually saw the guy that set it. Well, somebody just tried to kill her. Tied her up and set her apartment on fire. She's in the hospital in Glendale. They don't know if she's going to make it," Phil said, hanging his head. Anne moved in closer to him.

Phil stood up, "I gotta get back to L.A. This doesn't make any sense. It's too much of a coincidence that somebody tried to kill her and burn her out. It has to be our guy or I'm way off base. How could he be in both places at once?" Anne let him talk on as she picked up the phone, dialing the hotel operator.

"This is Anne Kilmary, room 432, would you please call the airport and see if there is a flight leaving Fresno tonight for..." She looked at Phil, "Burbank Airport?" she said as he nodded his approval of the airport nearest to his home.

"9:45?" She again looked at Phil, getting his nod to go ahead. "Yes, please, for one...Phil Langtry, and charge it to my credit card number under my room number...432, yes," she said as she hung up. He was already throwing his things together. Anne opened her purse and took out a small planner, picked up the phone and dialed an outside number. "I'm going to page Tallon and see if he's still in the hotel."

"Yeah, thanks. I can't think straight right now, anyway," he replied, looking around in a daze.

As she entered Tallon's pager number into the phone, she looked over her shoulder and said, "Just pack what you'll need tonight and I'll bring the rest with me when I drive back Friday."

"OK," Phil replied as she hung up.

"We can fill Keith in and maybe he can dig up Priest later tonight?" Anne asked. "I think Priest would be more willing to deal with an ex-cop than me."

"You're probably right. Can you also let Stillwell know if you run into him? I need all the help I can get from this end while I'm back in L.A."

"Sure. Maybe Keith can spend the night in your room so he can be here when Priest shows," Anne added as the phone rang. "Hello...Yes, this is Phil's room, Keith. Just come up here right away, please," and she hung up.

She walked over and kissed his cheek.

Tallon arrived and agreed to stay in Phil's room for the evening in hopes of Priest calling or coming by.

As they drove to the airport, Anne reassured Phil that she would continue to coordinate with Tallon, Priest and the Fresno investigators. She dropped him at the front of the airport. He had 45 minutes before departure.

"Thanks for everything, Anne," Phil said as he leaned across the seat to kiss her.

"My pleasure. I'll have one of the L.A. area guys bring your car back and drop it off at the address on your business card. But I will need your keys," she said.

Phil took it off the ring. "You could even have Gina drive it back if you want. The tank's full."

"I'll call you Friday night or sooner. Better yet, I'll page you when I get anything up here," Anne stated as Phil got out of the car, closing the door. "Bye."

Phil checked in and had a double bourbon and water as he waited for the plane's departure call. He was in the air by 9:50, wondering if he would be able to find someone to pick him up at Burbank or have to take a cab. He cursed himself for being so rattled. Work never affected him like this.

As the jet leveled off at 20,000 feet, Phil looked out the window into the blackness of the summer evening. Thousands of stars winked at him. Small dots of light from farmhouses and towns were the only illumination from below. To his left he could barely make out the silhouette of the majestic Sierra Nevada Mountains, their peaks lightly snowcapped, even this late in the year. He stared at the mountains, trying to recognize a familiar place he had hunted in past years. He searched until his neck began to ache from the uncomfortable view out the window. He turned back facing front, closing his eyes and keeping the beautiful sight of the mountains in his mind. The only sounds came from the aircraft, racing along at 500 miles per hour. In less than 30 minutes, Phil was startled awake from his surprisingly comfortable rest by the pilot announcing their pending arrival at Burbank Airport. Phil again looked out the window to see Interstate 5 below winding its way down to Castaic, just 25 miles north of the San Fernando Valley. In minutes, the plane had dropped over Sun Valley, north of the Burbank Airport, and the ground came up quickly, meeting the plane with a dull thud as they landed. The pilot came on again stating the temperature was 85 degrees at 10:45 P.M.

Phil walked past the pick-up area and immediately saw Ash Nolan parked in the red zone nearby.

"Hey, Ace. How the hell did you know I was flying in?" Phil shook Nolan's hand as if they'd been separated for months.

"The dispatch center paged me. They said that a lady in Fresno called and asked to have me pick you up."

Phil knew before Ash said it, "Anne. She's an insurance investigator I met up there. Really amazing lady...." Phil said as his voice trailed off. "How's Trish?" As he drove, Ash brought Phil up to date on the fire at Trish's apartment.

"They got a 911 call from the 7-11 payphone saying that an apartment building was on fire down the block. I guess you could see the flames from the front of the store before anybody in the apartment knew it was burning. Anyway, when Engine One got there, they confirmed the fire and asked for a second alarm for evac help. That building's loaded with people." Phil listened, wanting every detail. "The fire was confined to just Trish's room and as Engine One's crew forced entry they knocked the fire down real quick and found her pushed up under the kitchen sink. You remember how the sink was mounted on the wall and no cabinets or anything under it?" Ash asked.

"She had some curtains rigged up and a couple of homemade shelves under it, I think," Phil remembered.

"Right...Well, anyway, she was fucking tied up with towels and a bathrobe tie....and...,"Ash stalled, trying to soften the statement, "one was tied around her neck and secured to the sink drain pipe. Not tight enough to strangle her, but it held her in place. I guess he set the fire as he left."

"How bad is she, Ash?"

"She's alive and doing surprisingly good. Some second degree burns on her feet and legs, and she took a lot of smoke," Ash continued. "The only thing that saved her was the fact that he set the sofa on fire and it's an old piece of shit and had little foam stuffing, and her windows were wide open because of the heat wave. The fire pretty much vented itself out the open windows, but she still took a lot of smoke."

"What hospital is she in?" Phil asked.

"She should be at Sherman Oaks Burn Center by now. They took her to Glendale Adventist E.R. first to keep her breathing, then they said they were going to transfer her," Ash continued. "You want to go to Sherman Oaks?"

"You got anybody there to take her statement if she comes around?" Phil asked.

"Yeah, one of the homicide detectives showed up at the Adventist E.R. and was going to stay with her," Ash confirmed.

"Let's go by the fire scene, Ash."

They arrived there in minutes. Small groups of itinerants mingled in front near a Red Cross van and a police-type-four-door sedan behind it.

"Homicide's still here, Ash. Do they know anything about her yet?"

"You mean about your fireman theory thing?"

"Yeah. I mean do they know she's our witness?"

"Well yeah, they do…" Ash let his voice trail off, expecting the worst from Phil.

Phil took a deep breath while Ash parked the car, "How much do they know?"

"Well, I let it slip that she was a witness in an arson case, but I played it down. I told the homicide guys that she gave us some info on the 7-11 fire, and I didn't say anything about the rest of the investigation. I wouldn't have said anything, but when I got here, they were still trying to ID her and I told them her name. They, of course, wanted to know how I knew her," Ash explained.

"You did good, partner," Phil said. "Let's go up the back stairs. I don't want to run into the homicide guys just yet."

They walked around to the alley at the rear of the building and to Trish's apartment, the wet smell of a recent fire filling the air. A group of teenagers crowded around the still-open apartment door, chattering in Spanish, ignoring the bright yellow tape stretched across the entryway that proclaimed 'CRIME SCENE—DO NOT CROSS'. Two of the youths were just inside the doorway.

Phil approached and, in Spanish, asked the two to step out of the room, checking their hands as they left. The group explained that they were residents and were trying to figure out how to secure her room from thieves. Phil smiled at the group and asked that they leave, saying he would arrange to have the door secured. Phil recognized one of the two who had been inside the room and grabbed him by the back of his shirt, pulling him back into the blackened apartment. The 15-year-old had terror in his eyes.

"Tony! It's been a long time," Phil said through his teeth. "I didn't realize you were such a caring person, looking out for your fellow residents. When did you move into this building?"

"I don't really live here, man. We were just checking out the fire and these other kids came by, so we...."

Phil cut him off as Ash checked up and down the hall. "Tony, I am personally putting you in charge of security in this apartment. If anything gets stolen, I'll come looking for you. Understand?" Phil said as his grip on the young man's shirt tightened.

"Si, señor Langtry. I always did right with you before. I don't steal anymore! You took care of me good before." To Ash, Phil said, "I caught him trying to steal a helmet off of Engine One about a year ago while the guys were doing CPR in an office over on Brand Boulevard. Ash, go find the landlord and call Budget Board-Up's 24-hour number and tell them you're the owner of the building and you want the windows and door secured on this place tonight." Ash nodded, remembering Phil's propensity for cutting corners in order to accomplish a reasonable end. "I'm going to check the fire scene. Come on back here and avoid the guys downstairs if you can. Also, get a fire road lock out of your trunk and give it to the manager. Tell 'em to give it to the board-up guy to put on this door so we can get back in if we need to."

Ash left and Phil examined the burned apartment, noting the damaged sofa as the point of origin. The fire's pattern showed the developing flames lapping up the wall behind the sofa and striking the ceiling. The stark, white trail caused by the intense heat contrasted with the rest of the blackened room. The flames burned off the years' accumulation of paint and left just a pattern of white, durable plaster as evidence of the fire's path. He could see where the flames raced toward the ready source of oxygen, the open windows. The lace curtains were burned off as the fire touched the rod, dropping them in a smoldering mass on the floor and starting a second small fire there in a trash can and an adjacent chair. This secondary fire may have saved her life, Phil theorized. The growing flames from the curtains and trash created another thermal of hot air; it, too, reaching for the air from the open windows. The flames from above the window and those below created a venturi-like effect, sucking the flames and much of the smoke out into the night. Unfortunately, the increasing flames created a larger amount of heat that exposed Trish's feet and legs to their assault. Phil shuddered at the thought of the helpless girl tied up against the drainpipe. Mercifully, she probably had passed out from breathing the smoke and the lack of oxygen before the fire ever built sufficiently to burn her.

Ash returned and Phil asked several questions about Trish's injuries to validate his findings.

"She was up under the sink, over there, right?" Phil queried. "And she was on her left side, about here, with her legs pulled up tight?" Phil continued as Ash nodded affirmatively.

"Where were you on the night of the crime?" Ash asked skeptically at Phil's accurate knowledge of the crime scene.

"From what you told me about the locations of her burns, and the clean area near the sink, it seems that her body had to be on its left side to be exposed to the fire coming from over on this side of the room," Phil said pointing to the sofa, "and this clean area was where her body kept the smoke and soot from falling on the floor. She also had some cuts and abrasions on her wrists and, most likely, a couple of burns on her shins about here," Phil pointed to the area below his right knee.

"Yeah, it looked like she struggled when she smelled the smoke since she couldn't actually see the fire, and her bindings gave her some pretty nasty friction burns on her wrists. How'd you know about the burns on the front of her shins?"

"Well, her natural reaction would be to curl up into a ball as she felt the flames. That would have left her right knee and shins exposed to this secondary fire next to her, here," Phil stated as he pointed at the burned pile of curtain materials and the remains of a plastic trash container. As he looked up, he saw a small figure in the doorway.

"Interesting, Langtry," the figure said as he stepped into the room.

"Hi, Jim," Phil said as he recognized the homicide detective. The man stood five-seven, but he had a reputation that was bigger than both of them. "This your case?"

"No, it's probably going to be assigned to you since you seem to have so much information about the young victim. Information that Ash here has so conveniently sandbagged on us." He said as he nodded toward Nolan.

"Sergeant Berry, I'm not holding anything back from you. I just told you that the 7-11 arson was Phil's case and he knew more than I did about it," Ash said, trying to defend himself.

Jim Berry looked at Ash and said, "Nolan, you are a fucking police officer. When cops talk about cases, we gossip like old women. You didn't even go into the type of fire at the 7-11 and who the suspect was," the middle-aged cop shouted. "Are you still going to tell me you weren't sandbagging me?" Phil had to admire the older cop. The man knew his business and had correctly figured Nolan's attempt at trying to hide the facts.

"How about we co-investigate, Jim?" Phil said, trying to defuse the issue at hand, quickly pointing back to the sink. "She was drawn up into the drain pipe here?" he said as he bent down. "Look at this." Phil pointed at the pipe.

Both Ash and Berry bent down to see a piece of the bathrobe tie hanging under the sink's drain pipe, partially hidden by blackened, stained curtains strung around the sink base.

"Are you finished processing this scene, Jim?" Phil asked, knowing that the oversight was just now being caught, but hoping to leave Berry an out.

"Ash, go down to apartment D and ask that asshole Martinez to get back up here, now!" Berry said as Phil shook his head. "Martinez did the scene and I probably hurried him too much. We did get some prints from here on the sink and off the lock on the front door. See, here," Berry pointed at several barely discernible fingerprints in the soot covering the blackened porcelain. "We think the guy might have held onto the sink while he bent down to tie her up. See how it would be natural to hold yourself up here as you bent down like I'm doing," Berry added.

"Great," Phil said, "and the top of the lock where he would have had to hold the top of the mechanism as he twisted that knob?"

"Right. But missing this end of the tie is unforgivable," the old cop said. "What kind of knot is it, Phil?"

Phil examined the knot closer, not caring that his clothes were brushing against the sooty surfaces under the sink. He allowed his knees to drop to the floor as he saw the colored material wrapped around the silvery drain pipe, goose-necked below the sink. He moved closer, seeing the end hanging neatly at the base of the knot itself, not askew as with most haphazardly tied bonds. It took several seconds before he realized what he saw. The knot was a bowline. The firefighter's friend! Phil remembered it from his training days and the times he had used the knot in his day-to-day life. There was no mistaking it.

"Can't quite tell, Jim. It's all covered with soot. Doesn't look real significant," Phil responded, trying to sound disinterested at its obvious implications. "How do you want to take it, Jim? Or you want me to book it in to the property room? We gotta go by the PD anyway?" Phil said hoping the detective would downplay the significance of the item.

"Nah, I'll let Martinez get a wrench and take the drain pipe, too. The whole thing'll look good in court if we get the guy." Phil cursed to himself. If the knot was examined by anybody and identified, Berry would immediately become suspicious and Phil's evasion would be discovered.

Minutes later, Ash returned with Dennis Martinez, the newest detective assigned to the robbery/homicide division. Martinez, like Jim

Berry, was immaculately dressed in a suit and tie. The young cop was almost the same height as his sergeant. They looked like Mutt and Mutt.

Berry took Martinez to the sink and pointed at the find. As the new detective bent down to look at the evidence, Ash joined him. Phil stiffened, hoping that Ash would overlook the type of knot he was observing, if he even knew what kind it was. As Martinez and Nolan examined ways to remove the drain, Berry motioned Phil into the hallway.

"Martinez is a pretty good detective, but I gave him a little shit about overlooking that knot. It was probably as much my fault as it was his, though," Berry said, "but I did learn something from him I didn't know."

"What was that, Jim?" Phil queried.

"When we looked around the sink for evidence, he saw the handprint. It looked like the oils from the guy's fingers actually drew the soot particles as the fire was burning. Martinez told me that he had heard that from one of the classes you taught. 'Says that soot particles are almost like the graphite that the lab technicians use?"

"That's right. But I can see that your lab tech didn't lift the prints with tape like normal latents, right?"

"No, the lab tech said that, and he learned this from you, the soot is thicker than graphite and the print will be destroyed if it has tape placed on top of it like a regular print. So, they photo'd it instead. How come I don't know this shit, Langtry?" the older cop said, shaking his head with a smile.

"Because you're old, Sergeant. You could still learn something if you went to a class once in a while," Phil said, slapping the sergeant on the back.

Ash called out, "Phil, I just got paged. I think the phone number is from the burn center where they took Trish. You wanna go now?"

Phil thought briefly, concerned about the knot, then replied, "Yeah, go on down to the manager's office and call and I'll be down in a minute.....Berry, you think you'll be alright here?" Phil said sarcastically as he smiled again.

"No problem but let me ask you one question before you go." Berry stood up with his hands resting on his hips. "Do you want to fill me in on what might've happened to this girl, why or maybe who did it?"

"That's three questions, Jim," Phil said, "and I'll let you know as soon as I come up with any answers," he shouted out as he ducked into the hallway.

"Langtry! You better fucking call me if you got anything!"

Phil felt obligated to enlighten Berry about the suspect, but there was nothing they could do tonight. He wanted to see Trish.

Finding the manager's apartment, Phil was met at the door by a middle-aged Hispanic woman, and Ash.

"Phil, Trish is awake and asked for you, so I told them that we were on our way out. The manager here is going up to Trish's apartment and stay there until the board-up company arrives."

"OK. *Gracias señora,*" Phil nodded at the woman as they left.

Phil got into the passenger's side of the car as Ash jumped into the driver's. They headed quickly toward the freeway on-ramp, turning on the police radio as they drove. In minutes they were headed to the Valley at over 80 miles per hour, the only sound from the drone of the police dispatchers.

Suddenly, a familiar voice was heard on the radio, "58 Sam, station, can you dispatch a fire company to our location."

The dispatcher responded, "10-4, 58 the reason?"

"We have to secure some evidence from a sink drainpipe and we don't have any tools available," Berry replied.

"Damn!" Phil muttered.

"What's wrong Phil?" Ash queried.

"By any chance did you notice what kind of knot was used on that drainpipe?"

"No. I couldn't tell. Was there something significant about it? I really couldn't figure why you and Berry were so hot about it as evidence."

"The main reason is the way a knot, any knot, is tied. You can usually tell if the guy that tied it is left or right-handed by the way the binding twists. That's just a small piece of circumstantial evidence. Fortunately, Berry didn't look at the knot but I'm sure he'll take a closer look at it when they remove it. I was hoping that Martinez would get it off and just book it in, but now a fireman's going to remove it and may recognize it for what it is…a bowline knot…"

It took a moment for the statement to register with Nolan. "Oh, shit…the guy that tried to kill her was our guy….a fireman…"

"Exactly. I just hope the fire guys that remove the thing don't pay too much attention to the knot and say something to Berry. With the way we avoided his questions back there, he'll be on to us in a second," Phil said.

"That wouldn't be all that bad, would it?" Ash asked. "We probably could use more help. Did you come up with any good leads in Fresno?"

"I trust Berry and he is an excellent investigator. As for the Fresno leads, the key lies with a certain Fresno Fire Marshal." Phil updated Ash on his findings in Fresno, Anne's fires, and the fact that he was considered a suspect at one point.

"So they are onto the same theory as we are and they won't give it up?"

"It seems so, but they're not covering anything up, just conducting a good investigation and surveillance by keeping a lid on it. After we interview Trish, we might be able to convince them that this case should be shared. We are really close to identifying this guy and we've got prints now, too!"

"We've got those partial prints from the 7-11 napkin wrapper, too," Ash remarked. "They aren't real good, but it could help tighten this up."

"Right, we'll talk to Berry in the morning and have him work with the lab on comparing the sink prints with the napkin wrapper. Now if we could get a few names from the Fresno conference attendance list, we'd be in the money. Firemen have to give prints when they're hired, so the Department of Justice and the guy's own agency should have the print cards available for comparison," Phil sighed.

"But that means we have to get another fire agency involved,"

"Can't be helped at this point, but we can get the crook's prints without going to his agency. It just requires a little creativity..." Phil raised his eyebrows at Ash. They pulled into the burn center parking lot.

They entered the waiting room and met with a nurse who was in charge of the ward. They were told that Trish was listed in critical condition, but she was young and was responding well, now that she was on oxygen and her lungs were clearing. Overall, the doctors felt that with the small amount of carbon monoxide level and minimal burns on her body, she hadn't been exposed too long to the fire.

Phil explained the fire scene to the inquisitive nurse. He confirmed the reason for the small CO levels in her blood from the fire and smoke venting itself out the windows, and the burns were from fire exposure, not direct flame contact. The nurse quickly left and walked to the intensive care unit where Phil and Ash could see Trish being treated. She returned and told Phil and Ash to slip into hospital garb.

The nurse spoke, "She's a little groggy, but says she has to talk with you about who did this to her. You should also know that she may have been raped. When the Adventist doctors were treating her before she was transferred here, they found what appeared to be semen on her backside and upper thigh. She did not look like she had been penetrated, but they took swabs anyway. They are quite positive that the liquid was semen and they're going to test the other swab and let you know."

"Thank you," Phil looking at Ash. "DNA matching. One more piece of evidence…"

Phil had been in the burn unit before, but knew Ash had not, so he watched him closely as they walked past several patients. There was no burned flesh smell. Various ointments and salves, as well as alcohol were very evident.

The nurse nodded them in. Phil leaned toward Trish's smoke-stained face. Her eyelids, ears and nostrils still showed signs of the soot from the near-fatal fire. Her hair was singed and was also covered with soot, a clear oxygen mask covered her mouth and nose.

Phil quietly called her name. She opened her eyes, squinting slightly at the bright lights above her.

"Trish, I'm Phil Langtry from the fire department. You talked with me and Ash last week in your apartment," Phil said softly, hoping she'd recognize them through the paper mask covering their faces.

She nodded in recognition and managed a slight smile, mumbling something under her own mask.

"Nurse, can we take her mask off so we can hear what she's saying?" Phil asked with a pleading look in his eyes. The nurse reached over and pulled the mask up and off as she raised her head slightly Phil shuddered at her reddened face.

"I think it was him, Mister Langtry," she whispered, coughing harshly. The nurse rushed to her side as her body shook, causing her burns to twinge with pain, her face contorting. Phil and Ash stepped back quickly, but returned when the nurse motioned them back to her.

She continued without any questions asked, "He knocked on the door and said he was a cop, so I opened it right up…Really stupid, I know," she shook her head back and forth. "I only saw him for a second, but I'm sure it was the same guy I saw in the 7-11 that night. He had a gun and slapped it against my cheek and then he turned off the light…" she said as she took a deep breath.

"Take your time," Phil said glancing down at her legs. The burns were covered with white gauze and they were stained with an antiseptic that looked like blood.

"He told me to keep quiet…Then he ripped my shirt and shorts," she continued, saving Phil the need to query her. She knew what they wanted to hear. "He fumbled around for a while and then he tied me up with my clothes…I don't know why, but then he dragged me over to the sink and shoved my face under it and tied something around my neck." She breathed heavily several times as the small group listened.

143

"Did he say anything to you while he was doing this?' Phil asked, giving her a moment to catch her breath.

"Just to keep my mouth shut…and he mumbled to himself a couple of times…once he slapped me in the back of the head." Trish closed her eyes for a moment.

"When he tied my neck up to the pipe, I couldn't hold myself up and I had to let the rope thing hold me…then I smelled a cigarette… and then I think he was going to rape me. He pulled my legs apart…" she stalled, looking around. "You need to hear all of this don't you?"

Phil nodded, "But stop if you get tired or in pain."

"My legs hurt a lot…a whole lot." she asked, biting her lip as she said it. "Sorry…"

"Don't worry," Phil said, "Can you go on?"

"Yeah…after I smelled the cigarette, I felt him pull my legs apart and I could feel his knees against my thigh…and right away I felt his…" She looked around again. "I guess he came on the back of my legs….and then he got up real quick and sounded real pissed….then he kicked me."

Phil asked, "What did he do then, Trish?"

She thought for a moment, reluctant to go. She rolled her head to one side, "I don't think he did anything else but leave…." She stopped, thinking. "Then I smelled smoke. It wasn't the cigarette and I got so scared…and I saw a glow in the drainpipe. It was right next to my face and I could see that the couch was on fire….That's when I really remembered who this guy was."

"You mean you weren't sure who he was at first?" Ash asked.

"No, it happened too fast, but when he left, I started thinking and saw the flames and it came together. I got so scared and tried to pull my hands out of the thing on my wrists, but they wouldn't come out. I tried to scream, but the lady next door had her stereo on so loud nobody could hear me anyway," she said as she took another breath, letting it out slowly. "In a couple of minutes the flames died down and I really couldn't feel the heat, but then the smoke came up into my face and I panicked….I kicked my feet and then just blacked out. I came back a couple of seconds later and felt the heat, but I was out again right away…." Trish let herself relax as she finished. "Who saved me, the firemen?"

It took Phil several seconds to answer, saddened by her frightening story. "Yes. They broke down the door and found you before the fire got very big. I'm glad you're OK. You rest now and we'll come back tomorrow," Phil said, patting her hand. "I'll let your mom know you're OK, too."

Trish nodded agreement.

The nurse accompanied them as they returned to waiting area.

"Who is this guy that tried to kill her?" she asked.

"We aren't sure, but we're getting close. If Trish asks for me, or us again, please have the on-duty nurse page me and I'll come immediately," Phil said as he handed her his card.

The petite woman nodded with a serious look on her face. She walked away.

Phil pulled his pager off his belt, looking at the tiny, lighted window on top. "I got paged while we were in there. It's Sergeant Berry's number...damn. I'm not really in the mood for this right now..."

The waiting room was empty, the clock reading just after one a.m. Phil reluctantly picked up the phone and dialed the police detective bureau number.

"Berry here. That you, Langtry?" was the abrupt greeting to Phil's call.

"Yeah, what's up, Jim?" Phil said nonchalantly. There was a brief pause as Berry fumbled with his words.

"You've been around a long time, Langtry, almost as long as me...But this attempted murder you've info...cough it up, now." Phil was still frustrated with Berry, but understood the sergeant's need to know.

"Berry, I'm not in the most understanding mood right now, so I'll say this once. Yes, we have some info, but there is literally no suspect at this point and we can't do a thing tonight. We just interviewed the girl, and she's been through a hell of an experience. She did not solidify anything....nothing. How about we meet tomorrow morning at El Serape for breakfast and I'll bring you on board."

There was silence, then, "You know about the knot, then?" Berry asked.

"Yeah, we might be looking at a fireman, but we don't even know what agency he works for. Did one of the firemen recognize the knot?" Phil asked.

"Yeah. The captain had the rookie get under the sink and loosen the pipe and he recognized it as a bowline right away. He even called it the fireman's friend. You asshole, Langtry, why didn't you say anything while you were here?" the old sergeant bellowed.

"Hey, I'm sorry, Jim. It'll all make sense to you in the morning. I'm buying, OK?"

"OK, you want me to bring Martinez, too? It's his case."

"No. We need to keep this under wraps as much as possible. Discreetly tell him you're taking it over. I don't want to blow this one. It's too big," Phil replied.

"See you at eight, El Serape."

He hung up and sighed.

"Ash, drive me home. I'm beat."

19

Phil awoke early, still exhausted. The sun had not yet peeked over Mt. Thom, but enough light filtered into his room to see the clock on his nightstand. It was 5:30 a.m. A slight wind gusted and Phil watched the window screen puff inward like a sail as he felt the warm air ripple the sheet covering his body, then hit his face. Looking up the slope across the canyon, he saw a large cloud of dust lift off the bare firebreak cutting down the mountainside. In a few seconds, the same gust of wind hit Phil's window screen, causing small particles of dust to rain down on his bed. *Santa Ana's again*, he thought.

He thought of the previous day; of his visit to Trish at the burn center.

The wind was getting steadier now, and Phil reached up and partially closed the bedroom window. He searched through a small pile on his nightstand, finding the scrap of paper with the Holiday Inn's phone number. A cheery operator answered.

"Room 432, please." Anne answered quickly.

"Good morning. You're up early."

"Good morning, Phil. How's Trish?"

"Exceptionally well considering what she went through," Phil replied.

"And how are you, Phil?" she asked with concern in her voice.

Phil updated Anne on the previous night's occurrences. She in turn told him that nothing new came up after he left Fresno.

"So you think the guy who tried to kill Trish is the same one that burned the fabric store up here Tuesday night?"

"I suppose he could be the same guy, but why did he leave Fresno and come back to L.A.? It doesn't make any sense, and I just can't believe there are two different guys doing this."

"A pair would be more likely than two different guys operating with the same M.O. Like I was telling you the other night about serial murderers and serial arsonists sharing some characteristics. There have been a number of serial murderers that worked together, but I've never heard of two arsonists pulling the same capers."

"Phil, if it's just one guy, and he was up here on Tuesday and is now back in L.A., he probably registered for the conference Tuesday evening. If he left Fresno Wednesday, isn't there some way we could determine who on the registration list is now missing up here?" Anne ventured. There was a brief silence as Phil thought.

"Yeah," he pondered, "you're right, but we aren't sure if he registered, number one, and I don't think there would be any way to have a roll call of all 230 participants to see who left early.....but, hell it's one way of pinning down a name. The only problem would be getting co-operation from the conference staff."

"Let me try the hotel first. The registration desk probably has a master list of all the conference participants since they usually block off a special floor and give special room rates for these things. If they'll open up to me, or maybe Orv Priest, we can see if anyone has checked out."

"That wouldn't even have to involve the conference staff and Priest's being a cop should get us in immediately. But we have no guarantee that the guy was staying at our hotel, either," Phil sighed. "Anyway, good idea, Anne. Thanks for all your help."

"No problem. I'll get Keith Tallon to hook up with Priest today and see what other angles we can work. Maybe the bad guy got called back to his city because of a fire or a death in the family. There's got to be some reason he just left like that," Anne said.

"Or maybe he thought he was seen at the fabric store fire and got scared, although that's not likely. Do whatever you can and page me if you find anything."

"OK. Bye, Phil."

Phil pulled on a pair of shorts and walked to the kitchen to start a pot of coffee. He sat at the kitchen table with a steaming mug and watched the Santa Ana winds blowing below him in Chase Canyon. He could see the wind racing through the treetops and causing waves to ripple in the dried, dead grasses.

Phil showered, shaved and walked to his truck, parked in front of the house. He headed down the canyon, towards the waking city.

Aaron's home in Arcadia was located in the flatlands off Santa Anita Avenue, near the famed Santa Anita Racetrack. By 5:30 a.m., the sun had already risen, waking him with a blast of light. He stirred reluctantly, still feeling the effects of the seven beers he had consumed the night before. Rolling over onto his back, he listened to the winds gusting outside. Leaves and dirt splattered against his windows and the side of the house. He smiled, remembering his fires from the night before and quickly forgot his hangover. Shuddering, he recalled the moment he lit his device in the young girl's apartment and thrilled at recalling the power of his orgasm.

Aaron reached over and turned on the radio, hoping for any word on his fires in Lopez Canyon, Tujunga or in the girl's apartment. He gave little thought to the girl herself, wanting only to hear about his fires. He was not due at work until Sunday, still three days away. Black ink marked the conference dates on his calendar. He remembered he had not checked out of the hotel. He had fled at 2 p.m., already past the normal 11 a.m. checkout time. He would already be charged for the extra day, so he simply went to his car and left without checking out. Grabbing a small notepad on his nightstand, he wrote a reminder to himself to call the hotel and advise them to cancel the remaining two nights of his reservation. He also added, "Check girl's apartment on Jackson," referring to Trish's.

Aaron spent the next hour unpacking and listening to the news, hearing nothing on his fires. The lack of coverage recognition for his successes enraged him. As he hurled his suitcase into a closet with frustration, he froze, thinking about the girl.

"Shit, maybe she's still fucking alive," he mumbled. *She saw my face for a second before I turned out the light*, he thought, looking down and cocking his head to the side.

A gust of wind broke his trance and he turned to look out his bedroom window. The sun was washing the mountainsides, causing deep black shadows in the ragged granite-walled canyons. A wall of flame entered Aaron's mind as he looked, chasing away all thoughts of the young girl. He knew he would be setting brush fires today.

As excited as he was already, it seemed too early to be setting brush fires. He reclined on his sofa, thumbing through a magazine briefly and listening to the radio. Still hearing nothing of his fire, he tossed the magazine aside and got dressed. As he made breakfast, he put together six devices, attaching coins by adding another small dollop of glue.

At 7:35, he was in his car heading west on the Foothill Freeway. Traffic was already thick as he got on and traveled through Pasadena, the rush thinning as the freeway turned north toward exclusive La Canada. Most of the traffic flowed into Glendale at the Ventura Freeway cutoff, heading toward the Valley and downtown L.A.

The morning air was still cool but the rising sun's glare off his right shoulder gave evidence of the potential 100-degree temperature he predicted. He got off the freeway at the Angeles Crest Highway turnoff and headed into the National Forest bordering the expensive hillside homes. Traffic funneling down the winding mountain road was thick, commuters coming over the pass from the Antelope Valley 40 miles away. He remembered that several of his co-workers might be headed back over the mountain after getting off duty from their firefighting jobs in the L.A. area. His car was too easily recognized so he made a U-turn before getting into the forest itself. Driving back into La Canada, he headed west on back streets, climbing around the winding, narrow arteries, constantly looking for something to burn. The roads he traveled were still in deep shadows. The huge San Gabriel Mountains sheltered this area from the hot, dry winds that were forcing their way down from the desert. The winds would rip this area later in the day as the blasts from Tujunga Canyon raced across the front country.

Aaron, still hungry, found a small restaurant on Foothill Boulevard. He sat in a booth at the back of the restaurant, watching the flow of traffic and the few customers drifting in and out. The winds outside increased as he ate.

Phil drove to the El Serape restaurant, arriving before his 8 a.m. meeting time with Berry. The old sergeant was already in a booth, sipping coffee and reading a *Daily News*.

"Morning, Jim," Phil said cautiously, unsure of Berry's demeanor after their confrontation the night before.

"Hi," was all he said as he cleared the scattered papers from the table, continuing to read as Phil sat.

Phil flagged down a waiter and was pleased to see the man had automatically brought a cup and a pot of coffee as he dropped menus on the table. Berry's cup was filled too as the waiter disappeared.

"How'd your victim look?" Berry asked, without looking up from his paper.

"Surprisingly good, considering how bad it could have been," Phil replied.

"Was she still listed critical when you left?"

"Judging by the little bit of progress we saw in her as we talked, I'd say she probably was downgraded to serious, but stable. She was responding to the oxygen, but she was still in a lot of pain from her burns," Phil said, shuddering slightly at the memory of the injuries. Berry looked up and stared intently at Phil.

"I understand you aren't particularly fond of cops and you work independently, but I've got some explaining to do today and I need some answers." He droned on, "I think you have an excellent investigative mind and know what you're doing when you work a case, but we will work this one together, and that's all there is to it."

Phil started to flame, but caught himself.

"Okay," was all he said as the waiter arrived and took their orders.

As the waiter left, Phil explained the case, beginning with the brush fires earlier in the year. Berry set his paper down, listening attentively to Phil's explanation. No questions were asked. Berry learned everything from the story unfolding across from him. Phil ended with his findings in Fresno and what needed to be done there to further the case here in the L.A. area.

"Truly fucking amazing...." was all Berry could say. He sipped his coffee, looking over the cup's rim at Phil. "Langtry, how much of this do you want to sit on for the moment? I'm going to have two or three reporters asking questions when I get to the office this morning. The Captain and the Chief will want info, too."

"Do you trust the chief and the captain?" Phil asked.

"Both can keep the lid on it if I give them a good enough reason,"

"Give the chief and your boss the scoop, but I'd rather the reporters be kept in the dark. Do they have any idea about what happened last night?"

"I'm sure they're aware of a victim in the fire, but I don't think they have any knowledge about how the fire started. Unless they got it from your firemen, we haven't released anything yet. How about we just say that the cause of the fire is under routine investigation and leave it at that?" Berry said.

Phil nodded in agreement. "As for anybody else, like Martinez, I wouldn't go any further with it. Can you let me and Ash work it for now until we get this guy ID'd? Until the Fresno information comes through, we have absolutely nothing."

"You can't go to other agencies and see who might have a schedule that matches your guy and narrow it down?" Berry asked.

"No. There's over 50 fire departments in the area and if we started nosing around, word would get out. The only real lead we have is that he works 'B' shift, and we're talking 700-800 suspects," Phil said as he shook his head.

"What I meant was the fact that your guy was off-duty on Tuesday and probably in Fresno. You said he must've traded a day off so he could attend the conference up there. Out of 700 guys working 'B' shift in the

L.A. area, there could only be 20-30 that had this past Tuesday off. Right?" the cop said smugly.

"Not bad, but it would still mean making direct contact with all those agencies involved to narrow it down. We're talking creating a task force to be able to continue."

"I'm just not ready to do that yet. Let's give Fresno one more day to come across," Phil offered.

"Okay. Sounds good. I'll let my captain know about the possibility of getting a task force going if we can't get Fresno organized. Here comes breakfast."

Phil felt his pager vibrating on his side. At the same time, several sirens could be heard in the distance, coming from downtown. The telephone number on his pager was from the dispatch center of the fire department. "Fire. I gotta go," Phil said as he stood up. As he searched for cash in his pocket, Phil saw the battalion chief race by, followed by two engines, one a brush fire rig. "Sounds like a brush fire, Jim, you wanna go? It might be our guy."

"No, go ahead. I'll follow when I'm through here."

Phil rushed to the street to see the engines turning north. He cursed, realizing he didn't have a radio to contact the dispatchers. His city car was still in Fresno. He turned to go back into the restaurant for a phone, when another battalion chief approached. The chief's car rounded the corner, headed toward Phil. He stepped into the street and flagged down Chief Dartel. Dartel slammed on his brakes and Phil jumped in.

The chief raced away from the curb as Phil asked, "What's burning, Chief?"

"Brush fire. Lots of calls. On the north side above Foothill Boulevard. Engine 9 says he has lots of smoke showing and forty-mile-per hour winds. Where's your car?" Dartel asked.

"I left it in Fresno and flew back to help Ash with that fire on Jackson Street last night," Phil said as they raced north, still not seeing smoke yet. The radio blared Engine 9's arrival, reporting two homes with roof fires and about one acre of brush burning, with high winds. The report was quickly followed by the first battalion chief asking for a second alarm, starting five more engines toward the fire. Hitting the freeway, the two men could see the flames almost four miles away. Smoke lay close to the ground, chased by the powerful Santa Ana's. The car's radio picked up the Los Angeles County Fire Department also dispatching five engines to the growing fire, fearing it would ultimately blow into the La Canada area.

"We'll need those extra engines," the Chief said. In minutes, they got off the freeway and raced past traffic on the surface streets, siren screaming.

"It's blowing back into Dead Horse Canyon, away from the homes. If we can keep it there, it'll be the Forest Service's fire," the chief commented. As they approached the scene, Phil looked around at passing cars, looking for the only way he could think of to identify a firefighter in a civilian car. Almost all firefighters placed a small red and yellow decal on their rear window, signifying their membership in the state firefighter's association. Phil didn't see any and soon found himself dragging a hose line from a nearby engine to extinguish a small fire on a wood roof near the command post. Phil worked for several minutes and was soon relieved by a firefighter from the L.A. County Fire Department. The wind had subsided briefly, and the quick response by both agencies flooded the narrow streets with fire engines. Phil took a drink from a garden hose nearby when Chief Dartel raced up to him.

"Phil, we got another one," he said pointing across the broad valley to the Verdugo Mountains. Phil followed the chief's finger, instantly spotting a small column of smoke at the base of the 3,000-foot mountains rising from a residential area. The chief reported the fire to the dispatch center as they ran to the car.

"We're just dispatching the call now, Chief," came the reply from his report, "Do you have any equipment available from your fire that we can send?" Dartel looked at the command post and cupped his hands, shouting at other battalion chief for an answer. Both quickly sized up their fire and saw that they were getting a handle on the flames.

The Chief at the command post spoke into his radio. "Divert any engine not yet on-scene from our second alarm to the new fire. We have enough County assistance here to handle, but advise the Forest Service that the fire is heading into Dead Horse Canyon."

Phil and Dartel jumped into the car and headed to the new fire. They could suddenly see flames as well as smoke. They traveled less than a mile when the new smoke column lay flat as the winds crashed into the growing fire. The flames began leaping up a steep slope, feeding on dry grass and small bushes.

Chief Dartel again contacted the dispatcher, "I'm going to need at least ten more engines assigned to the new fire. The wind has increased and the fire has now started up the slope and is running for the top. Also order at least two helicopters and advise the Chief."

"10-4, Chief Dartel. County already has two copters en route."

Police were arriving and blocked the main street leading to the fire, where a large amount of traffic already clogged the small hillside streets. Two engines arrived with Dartel and Phil, further clearing their path. They pulled into the circular driveway of a large home and Dartel went about sizing up the fire for its potential. The fire had only exposed two homes to its flames before the fire swept up and away from them into the thick brush-covered slopes. The first two engines attacked the burning houses as Phil walked over to the obvious point of origin of the fire. There were no sidewalks on the narrow street, and the dry grass and brush grew right down to the street. A 30-foot long stretch of the growth ran between the two burning homes. The patch was totally blackened and only the gnarled black skeletal remains of two chaparral bushes clung to the slope. Phil could see that the fire had attacked the large bushes from an angle that pointed right back to a large patch of now-burned grass. The smoldering grass looked like a black carpet with just a few highlights of white ash. The ash was the remains of twigs fallen from the chaparral. Several scorched beer cans and bottles showed discoloration on their sides, attacked as the fire advanced from its origin. The opposite sides were untouched, protected as the flames raced by.

Quickly Phil found an area where the fire appeared to be coming from several different locations inside a two-foot circle. He dropped to a squatting position, then stood up quickly, recoiling from the still hot ground. Peering through the smoke, he saw it. The glitter of a dime, still clinging to the ash of a cigarette.

He's been here.

Phil stood up and looked around; hoping to spot the gray Chevy seen by Trish and the clerk at Burbank's 7-11 fire. Smoke blocked his view.

He picked up a beer bottle and broke the neck off on the curb. Carefully, he slid the fragile remains of the device into the bottle, carrying it to the Battalion Chief's car. Before he had a chance to pop the trunk, Ash drove up, honking to get Phil's attention.

"Little early for a Bud, isn't it?" Ash shouted over the noise of the pumping engines.

"Not necessarily. Open your trunk, Ash!" Ash complied and watched as Phil found an evidence jar in the trunk. Phil transferred the device to the more secure container.

"It's him, huh?" Ash shook his head.

"Yeah. Get on the PD radio and broadcast the guy's description and his mid-70's gray Chevy. Maybe a patrol unit can get lucky and spot him if he's using the same car."

Phil ran to Chief Dartel and thanked him for the ride, wishing him luck as he left. He knew that only Mother Nature would stop this fire before it reached the top of the Verdugo Mountains. Fortunately, only two homes were threatened at the moment. The fire burned into thick brush where no homes were built.

Climbing into the passenger side of Ash's car, Phil rolled the window up to keep out the choking smoke. Ash carefully drove over the fire hoses and down the street to the intersection. Phil asked the cops handling the intersection to watch for the Chevy since they were unable to hear the earlier radio broadcast.

Phil and Ash drove around aimlessly, watching for the arsonist's car. Seeing nothing, they drove to a nearby McDonald's and bought coffee, drinking it in their car as they watched the fire climbing the mountain. Sirens continued to pierce the air as units from neighboring cities finally arrived to assist. The winds had again subsided as the water-dropping helicopters dove at the hottest flanks of the fire, unleashing over 350 gallons of water each time they swooped down. From their position a mile away, they looked like dragonflies in slow motion, skittering over a pool of fire.

"Looks like their getting a pretty good handle on the first one," Phil said, looking over his shoulder at the earlier fire.

"Did you find a device at that one?" Ash asked.

"No. Hardly had a chance to look when the second one came in. Why don't we head up there and see what we can find?"

As soon as Ash started the big Chevy's engine, another dispatch for a brush fire came in, this time on the opposite side of the mountain in Burbank.

"Shit! This guy's going nuts today. Let's go on down to Burbank," Phil ordered.

Ash flicked on the red lights and siren as they drove along Foothill Boulevard to the Glendale Freeway on-ramp. Phil clung to his seatbelt harness as Ash raced down the broad street skidding onto the freeway, heading south. Accelerating to 115 mph, the big police sedan hummed down the three-mile stretch of freeway, the downtown L.A. skyline visible directly ahead. Only a small amount of dust in the distance marred the view. Slowing to 70, Ash took the westbound transition to the Ventura Freeway, screaming through a short tunnel that led to the freeway itself. A column of smoke loomed to their right, several miles ahead.

"I still haven't heard anybody report on-scene of that fire yet, Phil."

"I know. The first engine dispatch was Engine 14 and they're way out on Burbank Boulevard. Those two fires on the other side were really depleting the companies down here," Phil said as he saw the huge column from the second fire, peeking over the top of the mountain. "It's about a four-mile run for 14's. They should be there soon. It doesn't look too bad from here, though."

"Maybe we should cruise the flatlands first. The idiot's probably watching from down here," Ash commented.

"Yeah. Just go to an area you think offers the best view of the fire. Think like the asshole would. He wants to be just far enough away not to be noticed but still in a good location to watch," Phil added.

They ended up in a parking lot near the center of Burbank with a view of the fire in the hills, two miles away.

"This seems a little far away, but it's the only place he can see the fires. Phil shook his head. "There's no doubt he's sexually motivated, based on what Trish said last night, but does that mean he's near the fire or away from it? Hell, he might even be pulling off another rape in the confusion around the fire scene. Let's head over there, Ash!" Phil said pointing toward the column of smoke.

Just ten blocks away, Aaron drove slowly along Victory Boulevard, periodically looking at his latest brush fire in the hills above Burbank. The fire remained small compared to the two previous fires he set on the other side of the mountain. He passed a fabric store, just opening. A line of customers filtered in. Aaron quickly braked and pulled into the parking lot. His latest fabric store fire in Fresno was spectacular and he debated setting another one so soon. *Fresno is a long way away*, he thought. He stepped out of his car and lit a device as he walked through the lot toward the store. Slipping in the door, he followed the same path he did before in Fresno; alongside a wall to the back, and then along the back wall until he found a display of curtain material. At the base of the curtains on display was a cardboard box containing scraps of cloth. He walked past it and slowly turned around, seeing no one nearby. At the box, Aaron bent down and set the device inside and covered it with several pieces of loose matter. Standing back up, he returned to the wall aisle and headed back to the front of the store. He reached into his pocket, brought out a wad of money and counted it as he stepped out the door. Sitting while the Chevy idled, Aaron evaluated the area at the back of the store. He had set the device directly below the frilly curtains, under a large sign proclaiming a sale. A shelf above the curtains held dozens of boxes that would ignite seconds after the curtains were destroyed. He smiled and lowered himself down in his seat, picking up the old newspaper he always kept handy. Spreading it out over the steering wheel, he rubbed his growing erection and soon saw the fingers of flame racing up the curtain display. As predicted, the boxes too began to burn as well as the sale sign. The sale sign dropped on one side as one of its support strings burned through. None of the people inside saw the fire yet. The flaming sign lost its final grip on the remaining string and fell in flames to another display. The slight whooshing sound it created drew the attention of one of the shoppers. Aaron chuckled as she ran, her scream unheard from Aaron's position outside the store. He put his car in gear and idled forward to the street. He drove across the boulevard into another parking lot, losing sight of the fabric store briefly. Through the huge plate glass windows, he saw one of the women inside trying to get near the fire with an extinguisher. By now the flames were racing across the ceiling and the smoke was banking down. The woman couldn't get close enough, and joined the rest of the fleeing customers and employees. In less than a minute, the smoke totally filled the store's interior as the women lingered around the entrance. One ran to a nearby store, apparently to call the fire department. The fire appeared to die down. Aaron fidgeted in his seat, waiting for the heat inside to break the windows out and the store to explode in flame as he had seen in Fresno. It only smoldered.

The call came in to the dispatch center on a 911 line. The caller from a liquor store said a hysterical woman came in and said there was a fire inside the fabric store. The liquor store clerk said that the woman ran back to the store, and that he couldn't see any smoke or fire so he was hanging up because he had customers to take care of.

With three fires burning at once and outside agencies moving in to fill up vacant fire stations, the dispatchers were overburdened. With only one call reporting the fire at the fabric store, they dispatched a single engine company to the call. The engine was from the Monrovia Fire Department and was already on its move-up, but still five miles away on a crowded freeway.

The fire in the fabric store found readily combustible items at first, but after consuming the lightweight cloth and cardboard nearby, the flames spread much slower. Smoke filled the 3,000 square foot structure, displacing most of the oxygen inside. The fire died down but still sent its smoldering heat to the ceiling. The heat accumulated, then moved off like a deadly snake, using the smoke to cover its stalk. The heat was over 800 degrees and blistered the ceiling's paint and melted the light fixtures as it contacted them. Hitting the sides and front wall of the store, the 6-inch thick layer of heat began to bank down, slowly dropping as it fed on the smoldering mass of cloth and cardboard at the rear of the store. Five minutes after the fire ignited, and still six minutes from the fire engine's arrival time, smoke began seeping out the front doors and roof vents. Passing motorist and neighboring businesses finally became aware something was amiss. The gusting winds quickly dissipated the smoke as the heat level now dropped to one foot below the ceiling. The store manager saw that the fire was not developing rapidly and opened the door to see inside. She bent down on one knee and held the door open wide, letting the wind blow the smoke away from her. A gust found its way inside and instantly the air was sucked into the store. The gust blew directly to the smoldering mass of cloth and boxes as the manager suddenly heard a loud whoosh. The glowing embers received the air they needed and exploded into flames, also igniting the layer of heat accumulated at the ceiling. The flashover at the ceiling pushed the huge cloud of smoke out the open door, grabbing for more air. The gust knocked the manager back forcing her to release the door as she fell. The self-closer on the door wasn't quite strong enough to totally seal the opening, the hungry monster inside more powerful and now voracious. A 40 mile-per-hour gust of wind pushed the door shut, overcoming the forces from within the store.

While Ash wheeled the car through a narrow canyon, rushing to the latest brush fire, Phil heard a dispatch to a fire in a store in Burbank. The narrow canyon blocked much of the radio transmission, but he heard the words "fabric store".

"Ash, turn left here and get up to the top of this street. They just dispatched a fire in a fabric store, I think."

As they reached the ridge, still three blocks from the small brush fire, Phil looked down onto Burbank and saw the grayish smoke drifting near the area they had just left. It almost appeared to be blowing dust, until he confirmed with the dispatchers that there was a report of a fire at a fabric store on Victory. The smoke dissipated as Phil advised the dispatcher to send a full assignment of fire equipment in addition to the single engine already responding.

"Ash, let's get the hell back to Victory," Phil shouted as they roared down the hill.

The store manager screamed as she was blown back, seeing the sheet of flame race across the ceiling as if chasing her. The loud whoosh and large gust of smoke caused the small crowd to run farther back into the parking lot as they could now hear the engine's siren in the distance.

Aaron, still in the parking lot across the street, was uncomfortable with the erratic behavior of his fire and drove around the corner of a large building and onto a side street. He then pulled in behind a large truck, with just a small portion of his Chevy showing. With its mechanical siren growling, the Monrovia engine flashed by Aaron's position and into the parking lot. With only four firefighters on board, the captain instantly dropped one man off to hook up a supply line to the nearby hydrant. Accelerating into the lot, the engine coughed up a cloud of diesel smoke adding to the ugly gray tide emitted by the burning building. A pipeline of limp four-inch hose fed out the back of the rig while the firemen connected their water supply. Stopping only fifty feet from the store entrance, the remaining crew split up to ready the engine for the coming water supply and pulled lengths of 2½-inch attack line. None of the twenty bystanders offered to help. Mesmerized by the smoking beast only yards away it seemed as though in their silent vigil, they encouraged the blaze to grow.

The captain radioed the dispatchers asking for a second alarm and advising of his size-up of the situation. The store manager confirmed all her employees accounted for, releasing the crew from the burden of rescue worries. He evaluated the lessening smoke production and decided the fire hadn't advanced enough to preclude an interior attack. The smoke dissipated from the front but continued billowing out the back through door cracks, loading dock entryway and various vents. Constant Santa Ana gusts kept the grayish-black clouds hugging the ground, out of the fire crew's sight. The mass looked like a thunderhead rolling in waves away from the building.

Inside, a storeroom piled high with boxed cloth and flammable merchandise fed the spreading flames, adding to the heat layer above. Another stratum of superheated air reached into the attic space and enveloped wooden components, cooking pine pitch from the 30-year-old beams. Bubbles of flammable liquid oozed from the frying timbers. The invisible heat searched for oxygen to complete the combustion triangle of heat, fuel and air. Below, in the display area of the store, the heat layer reached the tops of the huge windows lining the front of the building like a dam holding back a flaming tide. The thick glass weakened when the heat etched tiny half-moon-shaped bite marks on its surface.

The empty four-inch hose line sprang to life as it filled with water from the hydrant. The firefighter raced toward his captain. The meager two-man force dragged the smaller attack line to the front of the building and wedged the door open slightly with a trashcan. Donning their air masks, they crept into the seething floor-level smoke cloud. The engineer stood by the engine and watched as the building ate his companions. The remaining fireman fed loose hose through the door.

"I'll let you know when to charge the line, Ben," the Captain shouted into his radio while the team dragged the line through unseen aisles and over a turnstile. The hose tangled pulling over displays as they advanced, silently covering their only physical trail to safety. The captain heard no sirens in the distance, only a muted rushing sound like a distant freeway. Confident the fire had dropped to a smoldering condition, they inched forward, unaware that the mass of embers fifty feet ahead suckled fresh air from the partially open door behind. Tentatively testing the new supply before passing it on to the superheated layers above the fire, small banks of flame danced on the smoldering piles.

The empty hose snagged at the moment the Captain decided he should have water handy at the nozzle. A hose coupling grabbed a counter edge and held like it was bolted down. Now feeling heat from the front as well as from above, the captain turned to his companion. Smoke prevented him from seeing the man only 18 inches away. They yanked the recalcitrant hose line and heard a thump from above. Fire-weakened ceiling material dropped and flames successfully breeched the underside of the roof. Thinking other fire crews arrived and were cutting holes to release pent up smoke and gases, the captain saw the grayish shroud of smoke raise off the floor about three feet. His helmet now felt like an oven. The new hole in the roof acted like a chimney allowing some smoke and heat to escape to the outside. The veteran Captain had been in few major fires in his 20-year career working the small town fire department but his training shouted at him now. Smoldering pieces of ceiling material rained down around the team and the captain quickly realized that the ventilation was being created by the fire itself, not other firefighters opening up the roof. He froze. Grabbing the lead man's coattail he brought him to an abrupt halt. At the same time, the heat at the ceiling crashed down onto their heads, pulsing as it lowered and singeing their only exposed skin; their ears.

"Out! Out! Out!" He screamed as they tried to reverse their direction. Their path was blocked by fallen displays and cloth as the captain searched for the hose-line, their only path to freedom in the smoky store. It, too, was covered with debris. Hugging the floor, they quickly became disoriented, but finally found the hose and began working their way back as the heat kept increasing. The young firefighter dipped lower to the floor and lost track of his captain as the windows in front cracked from the heat. As the heat layer fell, the entire contents of the store began to bake their way toward ignition temperature. The breaking windows allowed the oxygen to be sucked in, the fire reaching out to grasp it in one explosive movement. The store flashed as the interior belched outward, throwing glass and the force pushing the front wall outward ten inches. The roof supports lost their grip, and portions of the heavy covering dropped down into the store, showering the firemen.

Ash and Phil careened onto Victory Boulevard as the roof dropped, pushing the smoke out from its sides. Phil saw the Monrovia engine in front and the single hose-line going into the store, now covered by flaming debris.

Ash raced into the driveway and screeched to a stop. Phil shouted, "Ash, call it in and have an ambulance dispatched," Phil was out the door running while he counted the number of firefighters he saw. The driver and one fireman were helping a third man out of the debris. The crawling man had on a melted orange helmet. He was quickly recognized as the captain. Phil breathed a little easier, hoping that Monrovia had three-man companies and not four. Before he could reach them, the driver had opened another outlet for a second hose-line lying nearby. The firefighter sprayed the Captain's smoldering coat as he ripped off the damaged helmet.

Phil shouted to the men, "I'm a fireman. We got an ambulance rolling...."

"One more inside!" the driver interrupted as he jumped on top of the engine and swiveled around the large water cannon mounted in the center of the rig.

The Captain lay moaning as the firefighter ripped off the burned protective clothing, alternately cooling the injured man with the hose line.

Phil took over, shouting at the disjointed crew, "I'm a captain! You stay here with this man and treat him until the paramedics get here. You have one fireman still inside. What area was he in when you last saw him?"

The driver opened up the water cannon as the young fireman answered, "They went in the front doors with the line and when the roof dropped, the cap was blown out through the front doors. I never saw Willis come out. I think they went straight in about 20 or 30 feet," the dazed man screamed as he retrieved a first-aid kit from the engine's compartment. Ash joined Phil and they watched helplessly. The roof had dropped from the front supporting wall and now lay down at an angle, covering the fire burning under it. The water cannon's spray splashed harmlessly against the ramp-like shield, the fire blowing out the sides. Phil looked at Ash and they grabbed the hose line and dragged it to one of the sides of the structure. The engines pumping pressure made the line difficult for the two men to handle, the nozzle wanting to kick them back like a giant snake's head.

"Driver, shut the deck gun down, it's doing no good anyway, and drop our pressure down 50 pounds to this line!" Phil shouted as he heard sirens approaching from the west. A line of engines from nearby Los Angeles City Fire Department rolled into position as Phil and Ash moved back from the growing fire.

"Shit, man. There's no way we can get to him with that roof down!" Ash shouted as they pulled back.

"Yeah. He's been gone for a couple of minutes anyway, Ash. The temperature under that roof's over 1000 degrees."

As yellow-coated firemen moved in, Phil and Ash walked back to their car, anger building. They scanned the area, looking for the elusive gray Chevy, but it was long gone, moving on to the north San Fernando Valley and the next fire.

20

The young firefighter's body was recovered by the L.A. City firefighters as Phil and Ash met with the Burbank and Monrovia detectives that gathered. They were joined by Berry and Martinez. Phil quickly took Berry off to the side and asked that they try and organize their task force now while they had the manpower at their disposal. Berry agreed. To keep control of the large number of cops gathering, it was decided to call the Chiefs of all three small agencies to appoint an investigator to be a representative before any investigation began. Berry left for a phone, taking one detective from each agency with him.

Tom Carey, Burbank's arson investigator, also showed up and Phil briefed him on the progress of the case. Rumors had already started, and Phil was interrupted several times by detectives and uniformed cops asking why they were on-scene so quickly and was it true they had a suspect. Phil cut them all off, referring them to their chief, asking that they not speak to any media people until the Chiefs had a chance to gather the facts. Phil did not want the suspect's description and car to be released at this point because it would certainly be seen by the arsonist.

During his discussion with Carey, Phil received a page from Fresno. It was an hour before he could return the call to Anne. She had paged him two more times during the hour, indicating some urgency. He called Anne's room.

"Hi, it's Phil. Sorry I took so long to get back to you."

"You sound down, what's going on?" she asked.

"Nothing, Anne. I'll fill you in shortly. You have anything?"

"Two things, actually." Anne said. "Keith Tallon met with Priest and they are approaching the police chief and mayor this afternoon at lunch to try and get Plank to give up the information. Actually,

Stillwell's the one who has access to the seminar lists, but he's disappeared. The staff says that he was called out to work a case by Plank himself. Secondly, I read in the paper this morning about two fires set in alleys south of the hotel yesterday afternoon. They burned up a couple of garages and a house in a slum area. One article says that a police officer writing a parking ticket saw a car in the area being driven by a young, clean-cut looking guy."

"Did it give any further descriptions or the car type?" Phil asked.

"No, but I went by the police station a little while ago and told them my insurance company covers one of the garages and I asked for a report. The officer that took the arson report was there and we talked."

"Go on..." Phil urged.

"The guy she saw pulled out of the alley where the second fire was and he was driving a gray '74 Chevy two-door with loud exhaust pipes. She said he was 30-35 years old and good-looking. Less than a minute or two later, she walked across the mouth of the alley to write another ticket and she saw the fire eating up the side of a garage. No one else came out of or went into that alley after the guy," Anne finished.

Phil reflected on her story briefly. "That's him. Have Fresno check the scene for the coin device at both fires and let Priest and Keith know that our guy hit down here today, big time. He just killed a fireman in a fabric store fire. The place had a back draft and the building fell down on the poor guy."

"Oh, no! I'm sorry, Phil. Did you know him?"

"No. He was from Monrovia. The crook set three brushfires in a row and all the local fire trucks were up in the hills when he set the fabric store off. The closest engine was from Monrovia and by the time they got into Burbank where the fire was, it had progressed too much. I guess the Fire Captain guessed wrong and they went in before the backup forces got there."

"Phil, I think the reason he left Fresno was because he thought he was seen by the Fresno cop when he came out the alley. The fires went down around two p.m. yesterday and if he took off right after, he could have been down in L.A. in time to attack Trish, couldn't he?"

"You're right. I wonder if he was staying at the hotel. Did you have a chance to see if anybody has checked out from the conference rooms?"

"Yes I did. Three have left since registration Tuesday. One San Francisco cop, a volunteer from the Eureka area, and one of the lecturers, besides you," Anne explained.

"The lecturer probably was the guy that spoke late yesterday and the other two are from Northern California, and we can probably count them out."

"If our guy thought he was seen, he may have just split south and not bothered to check out. I've asked the day manager to contact me if anybody else checks out today. I left him a fifty-dollar bill, so I think he'll follow through."

"Great. Call Keith and have him investigate up there. We need some leads down here so we can follow this guy."

"OK. Good luck."

"Thanks." Phil hung up, turning around to look at the smoldering bulk of the fabric store across the parking lot from him. He glanced to the north and saw a column of smoke coming from the Valley area fifteen miles away. He walked back to Carey and Ash. Berry, too, had returned.

"The Chiefs are notified and we're getting this thing organized already," Berry said, taking charge. "You're Carey?" he asked, extending his hand.

"Yes, Burbank Fire Department," Carey said. Phil looked at the command post area and saw several elder detectives ushering the cops away from the scene and congregating in the area. Phil squinted at Berry and nodded in the direction of the activity.

"What's this?" Berry looked.

"The Burbank Police Chief has spoken." He smiled. "That tall guy in the tan suit is the Burbank Assistant Chief. He's dragging everybody away from this scene and letting them know that Carey and one detective are handling things and everybody else is going back to work. He's also going to advise that none of them talk to any media."

Phil nodded approvingly as he also saw the two Monrovia detectives walking to a phone, one holding his pager, checking the return number.

"Word's already gotten to Monrovia, too," Phil said, pointing to the nearby phone booth.

"Great. They'll be joining us after they talk to their boss. I think we better find a place to meet and get rolling. Any more info from Fresno?" Berry asked.

"Yeah, some good. Some not so good."

"OK, you can fill us in later. By the way, the two prints from the sink at Trish's apartment come very close to matching the lifts from the napkin wrapper you took from the 7-11 fire last week." Berry smiled.

"The napkin prints weren't real great, though," Phil ventured.

"No, they weren't, but several points did match up. Not quite good enough for court, but, as an investigating lead, the tech says he's sure they're from the same person. They both appear to have been from a left hand," the detective continued. "When he stooped down to the sink, he put his left hand on the rim. When he peeked out the door before he walked into the hallway, he rested his left hand on the top of the lock housing."

"Alright. Why don't we meet at two o'clock at my office at Station One. That might give me enough time to get a few names from Fresno and provide us with something to work with."

"OK. I'll talk to the Monrovia guys as soon as they're off the phone. See you at two," Berry said as he walked away.

Phil and Ash slowly returned to the first brush fire of the day, but failed to find any evidence of the coin device. Fire crews mopping up the area had blasted the area of the fire's origin with hose lines, obliterating any remains.

They skipped lunch, returning to their office to get ready for the 2 o'clock meeting. Frustration overtook Phil. The meeting would only provide a history of the fires and possibly end up without a name to the suspect. He was further disappointed that his caution in the investigation may have led to the fire in the fabric store. He verbalized these feelings to Ash. Both finally agreed that the investigation could have only proceeded in the direction it went.

At 1:15, Anne paged Phil. He returned the call immediately. She told him that Jeremiah Plank was confronted at the lunch meeting by both the mayor and the police chief. She and Tallon were allowed to sit in on the session. Plank balked at their inclusion, but the Fire Chief and Mayor insisted on their input after they were told of the fireman's death.

"Plank told us that they weren't really aware of any pattern until last year at the January seminar. The fabric stores were the key and Plank did catch on to the information from Bakersfield. He just wanted to pursue the investigation under the table, much as you did, Phil," Anne explained.

"Was he investigating the thing alone or was Stillwell helping him?"

"Stillwell was the only other help he had until he decided to set up the surveillances this year. He ignored some of the obvious evidence like the Bakersfield fires and the direction the series took after the conferences. He said that he still had gut feelings about who the most likely suspects were, but he wouldn't listen to Stillwell. Now Stillwell had the right idea, but he couldn't stand up to Plank."

"That figures." Phil said, shutting her off. "How many names do we have, Anne?"

"Keith is still working with Priest on that in your room. They have the list and Plank's with them trying to narrow it down. When I left, they had the hotel security helping out and they were eliminating some of them because the suspects were still here in the morning seminar. Stillwell showed up mid-morning and was back working as a staff member. Apparently quite a few guys show up for only part of the seminar and have legitimate reasons to go back home early. Some have subpoenas and some get called back because they have fires," Anne explained.

"What about the others that were being followed while they tailed us Tuesday?"

"I've got those but none of them are from your area. Just a guy from San Diego. The only reason they followed these was because they were at the three seminars where fires occurred. Steve Holquin's his name. He works for the San Diego Fire Department, but he's still here!"

"Well, we're back to square one until they ferret something out," Phil sighed.

"Wait a minute, here's Keith….." Anne said.

"Phil, here's a couple of names for you. First, this is how we came up with them" Tallon explained. "There have been two seminars per year over the past five years. One early and one in July or August. They first noticed the pattern and didn't really put anything together until early this year when they decided that it was too much of a coincidence that their major fires started similarly, and always happened during the conference. The worst part of it is the fact that they didn't keep real good control on registration until last year. Anybody could come up and check into the hotel and attend the lectures and training sessions. They didn't have to register since nobody checked the people coming into the lecture hall."

"I wondered about that. The last couple of years it seemed like the registration list never truly reflected who was actually attending," Phil added. "Then they started issuing the name tags and made it impossible to sneak in."

"Right," Keith continued. "So if our guy just slipped in occasionally and didn't register for the conference, we won't have him positively, except for the past couple of conferences. The only thing that does is give us a couple of extra names because we don't have a real broad base to draw from. Some of the older registration lists have been discarded too."

"Figures," Phil sighed.

Tallon gave Phil seven names as well as the agencies they worked for. Some were in the L.A. area, and a few were from surrounding areas such as Orange County and Riverside, all within easy driving distance of L.A.

"I can eliminate a couple already, since the guys work regular Monday through Friday weeks; not shift work like our guy," Phil commented, recognizing his counterparts from the other nearby jurisdictions.

"If we get more, I'll call you back. You in your office now?"

"Yeah. I've got a task force forming and we're meeting here at two. Call me, Keith. Give me Anne for a moment." He waited a moment. "Anne, any luck from your desk clerk yet?"

"No. Nothing new yet. We'll call." Phil hung up and walked into the training room down the hall from his office. He wheeled in a TV set with a video player to show the 7-11 video of the suspect. Ash took two of the suspects' names and made cold calls to their agencies, posing as a Sears credit representative. Phil smiled at Ash's ability to scam the fire department administrators into giving him information on their employees. Ash's final question was what shift the firemen worked on.

"One's a 'B' shifter, but he's 49 years old and black," Ash said. "Two down. You want me to call on the others?"

"Yeah. You do good, partner," Phil said, handing him the other two names.

At 2 p.m., Berry showed up with the two Monrovia detectives, Martinez, Carey and the Burbank detective. Carey and the cop still wore stained, dirty jumpsuits, smelling of the fabric store fire.

"What'd you find, Tom?" Phil asked.

"Fire started against a back wall. Probably in a cardboard box. No electrical or anything else around to cause it accidentally. There was an emergency light above it, but the burn patterns put the fire down low, near the floor. The bottom of the cardboard box was intact, since the fire burned up and away from it..." he stalled, looking at the others. "I found this in the debris of the box," he said, holding up a small glass jar. He handed it to Phil. Inside was a dime with a small dollop of glue still adhering to the smoke stained coin.

"Good work," Phil said, passing the coin around.

Berry introduced everyone, finished up by saying, "Phil is in charge of this investigation and will tell us what his needs are. Phil, all three Chiefs agreed to provide whatever we want."

Phil briefed the audience, stopping several times when firefighters stepped into the small office to listen in. Phil's stare caused them to withdraw quickly. After 15 minutes of discussion, the phone rang. Ash picked it up, handing it immediately to Phil.

"It's Tallon, in Fresno."

"What have you got, Keith?" Phil jotted down six more names of conference attendees present during the past and current fires. Phil hung up the phone, handing the list to Ash.

"Ash, do the same for me, please. I should be finished by the time you get back. Use the Battalion Chief's phone. I saw him leave a couple of minutes ago." Ash walked out.

Phil related the Fresno investigation and what remained to be discovered there. Few questions were asked.

"He's killed one firefighter, tried to kill my witness and he may even be responsible for the fire at Cal's Hardware in South Pasadena several years ago. That's six dead and one attempt. Questions?" He waited. "Unless we get a positive match on fingerprints from Trish's place, there isn't enough to nail this guy," Phil continued. "So the first thing we need to do is to get fingerprints from the suspects we develop..." he paused. "And we can't go to their agencies to get them just yet." One detective from Monrovia offered that the Department of Justice catalogues fingerprints sent to it by fire and police agencies, and that would save having to go directly to the agency. The process, in his experience, took several days, even in hot cases such as this one.

"Great! Can you make the requests as soon as we get the names?" Phil asked. The detective agreed.

Phil's explanation was thorough and it was obvious that the only remaining thing to do was to follow the suspects from the list Ash was perusing. Although there was a tremendous amount of circumstantial evidence, none was all convincing yet.

"In the meantime we're going to probably need more manpower than we've got here if we do surveillances. I'd like to see at least four vehicles on each suspect," Phil said matter-of-factly, "and helicopter assistance if we narrow it down to one."

"I'll line up the 'copter," Berry offered.

"OK," Phil answered. "Each of you go to your surveillance specialists, narc guys or whoever has the most experience and vehicles available." He looked around. "I guess we can't do anything until Ash gets back with the names. What he's doing is cold calling all the agencies where our suspects work and scamming them into giving the guy's employment, assignment and, most important, what shift he works."

They took a short break and Phil peeked in on Ash. Ash held up two fingers, mouthing the words, "Two more." Phil brought the meeting back together.

In minutes, Ash returned, "Got 'em. Only four," he said as he recited the names and where they worked.

Phil spoke, "Only three, Harrison was at the seminar last night at the time I was leaving. I saw him in the bar talking to a couple of locals. He couldn't be here at Trish's and in Fresno at the same time."

Burbank was given one name, Monrovia another and Phil took the one named Aaron Stiles, because he worked closer to his city than the rest.

"The first thing is to run the guy's driver's license and find out where he lives and then see what kind of car he has registered to him. If any of them comes up with a mid-70s Chevy, call me right away. In fact, Jim, why don't you head over to the PD now and we'll just continue this meeting over there where we've got a couple of computers handy. We'll meet in your conference room."

Phil and Ash walked into the conference room 15 minutes later, everyone but Berry present. Martinez, too, headed for an exit as Phil entered. "Jim wants me to order driver's license photos of these three guys. He's running their licenses now downstairs. He should be here in a couple of minutes," Martinez said as he walked out.

Seconds later, Berry walked in holding a handful of computer paper, frowning. "No solid hits on the car. One guy lives in Arcadia, one in Valencia and the last guy in Palos Verdes Estates," Barry said. "None has a 70s Chevy registered to him."

"Maybe it's a girlfriend's car, or a friend's," Carey offered.

"Yeah, or we could even have the wrong car," said one of the Monrovia detectives. "Witnesses are notoriously bad about that shit. Now where exactly is the car description from?"

"The first witness was the clerk from the Burbank 7-11 and is a very good witness; really observant. The second time we got the description it was from Trish, the attempted murder victim from last night. She saw the guy in the 7-11 before the fire there and watched him get into a gray, mid-70s Chevy. She also commented that it looked restored and was in good condition," Phil continued, trying to sound convincing. "And yesterday, a female cop in Fresno saw the same kind of car come out of an alley where an arson fire started only a couple of minutes later. Two blocks away, and just five minutes before, the same kind of fire kicked up and burned a garage and a house. The cop described the Chevy as having loud exhaust pipes, just like the clerk told me. I think the car info is good," Phil concluded. All the cops agreed. The teams split up after receiving last minute instructions from Phil. He directed them to do everything behind the scenes and make no contacts with neighbors, employers or relatives. All operations were to be cleared through Phil and Ash first. Pager numbers were exchanged to enable all of them to keep in close contact. A secretary from the police Chief was assigned to type up their reports and was also sworn to secrecy.

The group split up and Phil told them to work up their suspects and check in between 5:00 and 5:30.

Phil and Ash sat in their hot car, sweating and talking as the air conditioner worked to overcome the heat inside. Before leaving the police station, they used the law enforcement computer to extract any information they could get on their suspect, finding nothing of interest.

Being a firefighter, of course, he had no criminal history or even any traffic accidents with other police agencies. Phil was tempted to call some of his arson friends with Aaron's agency, but all were at the Fresno conference and even so, he didn't want to violate the orders he had given the other detectives.

They drove to Aaron's home and saw no cars in the driveway and the neighboring houses very close by. It appeared to be a close-knit neighborhood of mostly elderly residents, prone to gossip. Phil told Ash to drive away, their supposedly unmarked four-door Chevy loaner standing out.

As they returned, Phil was again paged by the hotel's number in Fresno. They pulled off the freeway to a phone booth at a 7-11 in Pasadena. Phil dialed the hotel's front desk and asked for Anne's room. He was told Anne was unavailable.

"Did she leave a message?"

"Just a moment please," Phil waited on hold.

"Mr. Langtry, this is Wiltern Holden. I'm the day manager. Anne told me to give you a message. It says, she's returning to L.A. with your car and should be in the area by six this evening. She says she'll page you when she arrives."

"Anything else Mr. Holden?"

"Yes, she asked me to tell you about Mr. Stiles," Holden paused.

"Stiles? I don't know any..." Phil paused, suddenly realizing Aaron's last name was Stiles. "What about him?"

"Well, Mr. Aaron Stiles called in about an hour ago and said he was checking out of his room. Anne had me watching the conference check-outs for her."

"Yeah, I know. Did you handle the call?" Phil asked.

"No, but he offered no explanation to the operator. He had reservations until Friday morning but left his key in his room and the maids found it on the dresser this morning at 8:30 when they went to clean his room. They weren't sure if they should take the key since the room log showed that he'd be there until Friday. The maid supervisor brought the key to the desk since we don't like to leave them lying around."

"Is there any way to tell exactly when he left the hotel?" Phil asked.

"Not really. His room was cleaned yesterday morning at 9:00 a.m. He could have gone at any time and we wouldn't know it until this morning. All his things were gone at 8:30 this morning," Holden replied.

"One more thing. Do you know if the maids found his bed slept in when they cleaned this morning?" Phil asked.

"Just a minute, Sir. The maid supervisor is just clocking out. I'll ask."

Phil waited impatiently, the sun blasting his unprotected position.

"Sir, she says that his bed was still freshly made. The mint we leave on the pillow was still in place as if he wasn't even in the room last night. I'd say that he left sometime yesterday after 9 a.m. and called just this morning to check himself out," the manager stated.

"Mr. Holden, Anne extended a gratuity to you, did she not?" Phil ventured.

"Yes, sir. She was very kind," he replied.

"I'm still registered in Room 419. My friend Mr. Tallon is staying there. Please leave a message for him to sign me out when he's through with the room. Also, is there a way you can add a matching gratuity to my room bill and have it funneled back to you, Sir?"

"That can be arranged, Sir, and thank you very much," Holden replied. Phil hung up and returned to Ash, appearing very fresh in the cooled car.

"Stiles is our man, I'll fucking bet my job on it!" Phil beamed as they hit the freeway.

21

Ash dropped Phil off at his truck, still parked outside the El Serape. Three parking tickets fluttered beneath his windshield wipers. The lack of sleep crept up on him as he slowly drove home, his window rolled down. The temperature had dropped considerably, and the winds had died down, making it a perfectly clear L.A. summer evening. The clean air and progress of the case renewed Phil as he maneuvered through the narrow streets to his home. Just before he turned off his engine, his pager alerted. He didn't recognize the number.

He quickly dialed the number, remembering that Anne was due back in town with his car. She picked up immediately.

"Hi, Phil. I'm at the Sunland Boulevard exit at Interstate 5. Where are you?"

"I just got home. Can you come here or do you want me to meet you?"

"I'll come by your place. Do you need anything?"

"Just the drink I'm mixing as we speak," Phil said and he gave her directions to his hillside home.

"I'll see you in 15 minutes," she replied.

"You don't need to use the siren, Anne. I'll be here. It's not easy finding this street…"

She cut him off teasingly. "I'm perfectly capable of reading a map, Langtry," she said as she hung up.

He hung up and stared across the canyon. He took three long swallows from his glass, feeling the cold liquid descend into his stomach. The drink was very strong. He was pleased with the case nearing a conclusion, his new friend Anne, and to be at home. His thoughts drifted to the death of the fireman. He pictured the trapped fireman tearing off his air mask in his last desperate moments, thinking that his comrades could locate him by his screams. The plastic face piece was found in the fireman's death grip of his left hand. Phil knew the arsonist had simply moved on from the Burbank fire to set another one, not even concerned that a firefighter had died.

Phil shuddered, then quickly thought of Anne and more pleasant things. He took another long drink, finishing it. He made another.

Sitting at the dining room table, he looked down onto Chase Drive, watching for his car. He saw his sedan turn off Chase onto Golf Club Drive. Phil cracked a smile and walked out to meet her, the setting sun blasting him in the face from the west. His car turned around the corner, racing up a short straight stretch below his house. As Anne rounded the corner, she was startled to see Phil standing there laughing. She rolled down the window as she pulled up to him.

"Hi! Where do you want me to park?"

"Just turn around and park it by the ivy there," he said pointing to an area in front of his truck. The big Chevy's rear tires chirping as she pulled forward. She handled the car well, smoothly wheeling into the small parking space. Phil felt very warmly toward her. He watched as she opened the car door, setting one bare foot on the street. She glanced up at him and flashed a broad smile. She held his stare as she reached outside the car door and slipped a high-heeled shoe onto the foot.

Phil stepped back into his driveway as Anne approached and she moved into his arms. They held their embrace and separated only at the sounds of another car. He took her hand and led her into the front door, neither speaking.

He walked her into the kitchen. "Drink?"

"Please. Do you have a beer?"

"Yeah. How was your trip down?"

"Quick. That car of yours knows only one speed...supersonic!" He chuckled.

"It's an old police car geared for leaping tall buildings in a single bound. By the way, your hotel manager called and solidified our guy for us."

"Fantastic. Who is it?"

"A guy named Aaron Stiles. The whole profile fits him, right down to his home address being in the center of all the fires down this way. But there is one small problem."

"What's that, Phil"

"He doesn't have the old Chevy registered to him. Actually, he doesn't have any cars registered to him. That in itself in L.A. makes this guy suspicious."

"Yes, that would be an odd situation." Anne said. "Does he live with someone; his parents?" Anne asked.

"We don't know yet, but that's a good angle to pursue. I wonder who owns the house."

"If you have an address, I can find out for you in about five minutes." Anne offered. "I have a friend in real estate and he has a computer program that can access all property owners in the state, right from his home. I'll call him."

"Perfect. I was afraid we'd have to bang on Stiles' neighbors' doors to find out anything tonight. I really didn't want to do that."

Phil gave her Aaron's address and she called immediately. Her conversation was animated and indicated to Phil a close relationship.

"The house is listed to a Glenn Stiles," Anne said. "Apparently a relative that's dead and the house is still in probate. Maybe his father," Anne said.

"Great. I'll have PD records run on this guy Glenn and find out what they can, then we can drive out to Arcadia on my way to drop you off at home," Phil hurriedly said as he dialed the police department. Anne looked on, somewhat dismayed at the thought of ending the evening so quickly.

"Jenny Takeshita, please," Phil said into the phone. After a short pause, he began, "Jenny, Phil Langtry here. I need a complete run on a Glenn Stiles, unknown age, but an address of 1233 West Sycamore Road, Arcadia. I need vehicles, rap sheet, guns and anything else you can get. Page me when you get it. Have any of the other teams called in?" Phil listened for several minutes, nodding occasionally as if the girl could hear his head rattle. Anne smiled. Phil hung up the phone abruptly.

"Jenny...she's the secretary assigned to us for the surveillances. Says that both of the other surveillance teams have called in running names, vehicle licenses and other information for the past two hours. One of the teams just determined that their subject was injured in a car accident and in the hospital on the day of the series of Burbank fires last week. That eliminates him..." Phil was interrupted by his pager sounding.

"That's probably them calling me now," Phil said as he reached for the phone.

"How did they learn that so quickly?" Anne asked as Phil dialed.

"The driver's license run on their suspect showed a recent entry for involvement in an injury accident. They just called the reporting agency, the Highway Patrol, I think, and checked the report. It showed him transported to a hospital in..." Phil stopped as his party answered. "Yeah, I heard. Have you lined up any assistance for the surveillance yet?" He paused. "OK, then why don't you guys just call Sergeant Blakley from Monrovia and get into his surveillance on the Valencia guy. My guy lives right next door to you in Arcadia so I don't want to take any chances of his recognizing you." Phil said, pausing, again. "Yeah. I think they were just going to drive out there after the meeting and sit on the guy's pad until he got home tonight. If you help them out, they may not need to bring in anybody else. There's not much we can do tonight, anyway. The crook may still be out capering," Phil listened again as he finalized the plan. He hung up and continued talking to Anne. "Anyway, the Palos Verdes suspect was treated at a hospital and held for two days before being released. So, he couldn't possibly have been our guy. The hospital confirmed him being there."

"Then now you only have two suspects but neither has a '74 Chevy?" Anne asked.

"That's right," Phil replied as he pulled the top off a beer and handed it to her.

"Things are moving fast. Sit down, Anne," Phil motioned toward the table overlooking the canyon.

"You have a beautiful view here. Is this your house?"

"No. I just rent a room from an old friend and his wife."

Phil sighed and looked at Anne, who continued to admire the view. The grassy slopes caught the last of the sun's rays as they sat silently. Without braking her stare, Anne reached over and placed her hand on Phil's, squeezing slightly. She sipped her beer, then set it down on the table and turned to face him. She pulled his hand to her. Anne leaned to him and kissed him passionately, her arms pulling him tightly to her. His eyes closed and he fumbled to put down his glass without looking. The half-filled tumbler missed the table edge and fell to the carpeted floor heavily, bouncing away.

Phil ignored the spill, reaching with his free hand to embrace her, his eyes still closed. His hand brushed her breast as he reached around her. He broke the kiss to apologize and she quickly moved her lips back to hers. They held the kiss for more than a minute, the intensity softening, then their foreheads and noses finally the only things touching. With a final sigh, Anne broke away, looking into his eyes only inches away. "This is really bad timing, but I need to use your bathroom!" she smiled, "It was a long drive."

"Back by the front door, straight ahead," he replied as she got up. Phil smirked as she walked away. Shortly after she left the room, he received a page. It was Jenny. Anne returned as Phil took notes on the conversation.

"Thanks, Jenny. How late will you be working?" He paused as she answered. "OK," he said, and hung up. "You want to go with me to the Arcadia address Anne, or should I run you home?"

"I'm not due back at work until Monday, Phil. Do you have room here for me...." She let her voice trail off.

"Absolutely," he replied, smiling.

"What did Jenny get for you," Anne said, nodding toward his notes.

"Oh, yeah. Glenn Stiles must be a relative of our suspect. He died in March of this year and he's about 10 years older than the crook. They might have been brothers. Glenn Stiles has a 1969 Chevy still registered to him. His driving history shows him deceased. Glenn Stiles also has several arrests, one for a mental hold for observation at a V.A. Hospital last year. He's probably a Nam vet."

"So, Aaron Stiles has apparently moved into this Glenn Stiles' home and is also driving his car?"

"Yeah. That really indicates that they were probably pretty close. Tomorrow we can firm up the scenario, but the main thing is to follow Aaron Stiles and hope he sets something off."

"Can't you just arrest him before he hurts someone else?"

"No. The law's pretty restrictive, and until we get a positive ID from either Trish or a solid fingerprint match, we are just shy of good probable cause. If we make the arrest now, any confession or evidence we get from here on could be ruled inadmissible later."

"You mean that even if he admits guilt after you arrest him, the confession would be thrown out as evidence against him?"

"Only if we didn't have enough probable cause in the first place, and we don't, yet. One of the things we need to do is get a sample of his fingerprints. We could do that by getting a search warrant for his house and car and obtain a set that way, or maybe steal his trash and get some off the junk in his cans."

"You could get a search warrant, but you can't arrest him yet?"

"That's right. A real Catch-22 situation, so our best tactic is to follow him and hope for the best."

"Bizarre..." was all Anne said.

"Shall we go for a drive?" Phil asked.

They took Phil's truck and drove the short distance to Aaron's home in Arcadia. It was getting dark as they drove by the small dwelling. The lights were out and there was no car in the driveway. They parked about one block away and sat next to each other, blending in with the block they were parked in. There were several apartment buildings nearby and the street was filled with cars, unlike Aaron's block of single family homes. Phil occasionally raised his binoculars, focusing on Aaron's home. By 9:30, there was no activity and Phil had to fight to keep from falling asleep. A vibrating page startled him and they drove to a phone booth. The call was from Ash. He had secured a total of six police officers for Friday's surveillance of Aaron. Since the fires of Thursday started as early as 9 a.m., Phil and Ash agreed that they should meet at 6:30 and brief the assisting officers. All were from the Narcotics Special Enforcement Unit and well-trained in mobile surveillance.

Phil drove home with Anne, finding Sean and Beth just finishing dinner. They exchanged greetings and chatted as Phil updated Sean on the investigation. Beth and Sean shortly retired, leaving Phil and Anne on a couch in the darkened living room. In minutes, Phil fell asleep.

He awoke to the sound of a strange alarm clock chirping in his ear. Before he could reach for it, Anne silenced it and turned to face him, snuggling his shoulder. He was immediately aroused by her closeness until he saw the clock across the room from him. It was 5:30 a.m. He was to meet the surveillance team in an hour. She glanced up into his eyes as she ran her hand over his chest. He drew back slightly, putting distance between their bodies as he smiled at her.

"Do you want to use the bathroom before I shower?" Phil asked abruptly, still smiling.

"No, I'm fine, go ahead."

Phil quickly trotted to the bathroom.

He stepped out of the shower to smell fresh coffee through the steam. He opened the bathroom door slightly and shaved. Several minutes later, Anne knocked softly and entered wearing one of Phil's T-shirts with an obscene acronym across the front of it. Anne handed him a cup of coffee as he winced at the sexist shirt.

"It was a gift..." he said.

"I'm sure it was. Through with the shower?" she asked.

"Yes, go ahead."

He watched in the mirror her small naked body disappeared behind the curtain. He finished shaving and quickly left.

Twenty minutes later he held open the door to his truck as she slid in. He looked at her fresh face, beautiful with very little makeup, admiring her. He knew the surveillance team would question her need to join them, but Phil was convinced that her presence would be essential to helping cover their operation. One or two men in a car always appeared suspicious. A couple seemed to always have legitimacy in any atmosphere.

Everyone was punctual and Phil started off introducing himself and Anne, asking the others to introduce themselves. Phil briefed the newcomers on the background of the case, asking Anne to give her input and findings from Fresno. The group seemed relaxed together, almost somber at the task ahead. The hardened narcotics group gave little credibility to Phil normally, since he was an outsider, but had adjusted to the situation and laid aside their professional jealousies for this event. The fireman's death made their task valid, despite Phil's past experience with the officers.

Sergeant Berry and the narcotics lieutenant assigned the cars for the surveillance, Phil protesting slightly when he was given a compact station wagon, wanting to use his own truck instead. He withdrew his objection when he remembered a cardinal rule of surveillance: a vehicle has to be absolutely inconspicuous. No bumper stickers, body damage or unusual color schemes. Even a dealer license plate holder would make a vehicle stand out.

Phil outlined the fire situation that killed the fireman in Burbank and ran down how fast a fire can engulf a store. The men listened intently, occasionally asking questions about fire spread and how they would handle Aaron should he enter a store.

"Do we actually let him burn the sucker down?" asked the Lieutenant.

"Well, we'll try not to. If possible, if we see him casing a good location, one of us will try and get inside the place he's checking out and watch him from inside. Maybe get a store manager aside first thing and see if they have a shoplifter one-way observation post we can use or whatever. Be flexible," Phil continued. "Does anyone have a camera along?"

"Yeah," the unshaved lieutenant spoke, "Edison's got a 35mm with a telephoto and I'll have a 8mm video cam along."

"Perfect. Be sure and get as much footage as you..." Phil paused, "Sorry, I'm sure you've done this more times than I have."

Edison, a bearded hulk, spoke, "Yeah, this group has been together seven months and we'll handle your logistics for you. You concentrate on this guy and let us know whatever you need while we're out there. You know him better than we do. Alright L.T?" he nodded toward the unkempt lieutenant. Phil smiled at Edison's use of the Nam term, L.T. for lieutenant, feeling a closeness to the man already.

"Ok, if there aren't any questions, let's get set up. By the way, what are the chances for a helicopter?" Phil asked.

"They are on alert at the heliport and will be monitoring our frequency. The winds are expected to kick up and they can't fly if the gusts are more than 50 miles per hour. The prediction is for 40-50 mile per hour by 8 a.m.," Berry added.

"Let's do it then," Phil said with finality.

The group met in an underground parking area beneath the civic center's parking structure. The Santa Ana's were already howling through the cavernous structure as they found their assigned cars. Phil and Anne had no trouble finding their white station wagon. It was the only wagon in the lot. The radio, hidden in the glove box, was turned on and immediately was a mass of clicks and static as everyone verified the frequency they were using. Phil stepped in and organized the six cars by initiating a roll call of all the units. All answered readily, signifying the official start of their task.

Traffic going east to Arcadia on the Ventura Freeway was sparse, but the westbound side was already beginning to jam up as commuters headed to Los Angeles and the San Fernando Valley.

As they got off the freeway at Santa Anita Drive in Arcadia, Phil advised the others that he was going to slip into place one block away from Aaron's after doing a run by the house. The rest of the group was to meet, as planned, at a nearby Winchell's Donut Shop. A series of clicks was heard on the radio; the affirmative signal for receipt of the message. Anne moved across the seat and snuggled into Phil's shoulder now that they had separated from the rest. As they drove by Aaron's, Anne glanced up the driveway as Phil continued to look straight ahead.

"No car," Anne whispered, "but there's a light on above the driveway and the porch that wasn't on last night when we were here." Phil drove on and turned the corner at the end of Aaron's street, then over one block. As he circled Aaron's, the rising sun met them, causing both to look down. Two more turns found them sliding into the same parking space they found the night before. Phil checked his mirrors and looked around and over his shoulders, seeing no one as he spoke into his radio. "This is One," Phil whispered, dropping normal radio protocol for the Narc Unit's favored, abbreviated talk. "House appears occupied, no car in the driveway or out front. Two exterior lights are on that weren't on last night so he's probably home. The house sits mid-block with a 70-foot palm tree on the west side of the driveway. The tree can be seen from east and west, as well as from the major on the north," Phil droned, knowing the other units would appreciate the little locators provided. Phil knew that the other units were professional and would not drive down Aaron's street, but would circle the area and settle in like a pack of coyotes waiting for fresh meat to flush toward them. Phil guessed correctly and, within minutes, he saw activity two blocks in front of him as well as two of the other cars strung out behind his position. Phil felt more comfortable as the others shut off their lights and the radio chatter ceased. Phil was now the "eye" for the others and only he would speak, keeping down unnecessary conversation. As they waited, an occasional car came out of a driveway or subterranean garage and headed to the major street north of their position. The sun rose slowly once it got above the San Gabriel Mountains to the east. The heat could already be felt.

Phil immediately felt drowsy, drained by the previous weeks' events. Anne's hand unbuckling his seatbelt startled him.

"You were snoring!" she said.

"What? Oh shit! How long was I out?"

"Two or three minutes. I was watching so I thought I'd let you sleep but I was afraid you'd wake the neighborhood."

Phil sat up slightly, reaching under his seat for a jug of coffee he'd brought along. "You want some, Anne?" he said as he searched for a second cup in the bag.

"I'll just sip some of yours."

The outflow of traffic continued. Phil keyed his microphone every 10-15 minutes and made small talk to individual units to help keep them all awake as the surveillance stretched into two hours. The sun was now high enough to reach their roofline, protecting Phil and Anne somewhat from its assault, but the warmth further caused them all to lull into a relaxed state. Phil's eyes started to close slowly. He fought the urge, but too much was working against him. He surrendered to sleep.

"He's out!" Anne whispered, jabbing Phil in his side, again jarring him awake.

He turned to look at her, his eyes clouded, and found her looking through binoculars. He quickly rubbed his eyes, finding a blurred figure running in the opposite direction toward Unit Three, Berry and Martinez. Phil fumbled for his radio, surprised that the other units had not yet spotted the figure.

"One to Three," Phil whispered into the radio. "He's out, running eastbound toward you. He's in jogging shorts, no shirt," Phil continued, the warning coming almost too late. Phil picked up his own binoculars, the focus already locked on the proper distance earlier.

Aaron, obviously out for a morning run, quickly covered the distance to the end of his block as Phil focused on Berry's old gray

Mustang parked in the second block beyond Aaron's. His focus came as both Martinez and Berry dropped to the center console area. Phil could see one head pop back up. It was Martinez, on the driver's side, rubbing his forehead after the obvious collision. Martinez immediately feigned sleep as Berry's head stayed down.

"He's turned northbound," Phil heard Berry say as he saw the sergeant's head begin to rise back up above the dashboard level. He, too, was rubbing his head.

Phil spoke quickly, "Three, stay where you are. Any unit on the major to cover him coming north on S street." Phil took control, using letters only for the street names and landmarks.

Hearing no response, Phil repeated, "Any unit on major to pick up the eye..."

"Four. We're three blocks west on the major. I think he just ran across, continuing northbound...We'll check." In seconds, Phil heard the high winding motor of unit four's 300 SX screaming eastbound on the major street.

"Four, slow it down, I can hear your engine racing all the way over here on the eye location...."

"10-4, One," was followed by the engine noise dropping instantly.

Phil swore. "We must've all been napping."

"One from Four, we just passed S and north bound's clear north of the major. Anybody else around see him yet?"

"Two's got him. He just jogged past us westbound on K street toward M. He's just one block north of the major still. We've got the eye for another two or three blocks. He's well past us and still on the south side of the street."

"Four's now at the major and F street if he comes this far."

Phil listened intently, relieved that the team was now adapting quickly to the crisis as he spoke into the mic. "Three, can you pick up four blocks behind me and parallel the suspect?"

"10-4," came Martinez' voice as Phil saw the Mustang pull out and drive quickly by him.

"This is Four, he's now southbound down an alley. I've lost the eye." Silence followed.

"Anybody got him?" Phil said quietly, debating abandoning his position to assist. He elected to stay put.

"Four here, he's apparently run through a park over here at..." The sound of Four's engine was heard until, "I've got him at the park entrance at the major and E Street. He's stopped and taking a breather....now he's walking west on the major and into the Winchell's. Stand by."

"I got him, too," Phil heard the unidentified unit say.

"Four, he's now inside the donut shop buying a drink of some kind."

Phil came back on, "Three, return to your original location. Four, you have a good eye?"

"Yeah, I'm two blocks west of him and I've got a good eye and I haven't been spotted."

"Five, where are you?" Phil asked, not getting an answer. "Five, where are you?" he repeated, followed by a series of quick clicks on the radio, followed by silence.

"One, this is Two. We just drove by the Winchell's. Five's in the parking lot about 25 feet from the suspect." This transmission, too, was followed by the consecutive clicks. Obviously Five was giving the signal that he couldn't talk. Phil analyzed the positions, remembering that he hadn't heard from Six, the oldest veteran from the group.

"Six from One, where are you?"

"Six is on the major, in the second story of a vacant business. I've got an eye on the crook's backyard, the major all the way to the Winchell's and I can see you, too, One..." Phil quickly scanned the area, barely making out the second story roofline of the building, but unable to locate Six.

"10-4, Six. Good location."

For several minutes, there was no conversation. Phil looked at Anne, now leaning against the passenger door watching Phil work. He reached over and held her hand as he felt the pulsing of his heart winding down slightly.

"Six, all units, I've got a small column of smoke rising from the northwest near the park. Somebody check it out."

"Four's got the eye, I can't take it with Five tied up..."

"Two can handle...Six, you say it's near the park?"

"Yeah, I can see some fire burning up a palm tree now. It's really ripping. One, you want me to go to another frequency and report it?"

Phil responded quickly, "No. It's a populated area. Somebody will report it. I don't want to chance exposing our presence here. We didn't notify Arcadia PD that we'd be here. Four, what's the crook doin?"

"One, I'm videotaping him right now. His seat inside gives him a straight visual toward the fire. He's just peeking over the top of a newspaper. If he set this thing, how come we missed it?"

"Four, you lost sight of him down an alley before he hit the park, right?" Phil queried.

"Yeah, the alley's right about where the smoke's coming from. Two, are you there yet?"

"Two, yeah. We're driving by the alley now. It's a large pile of furniture and trash. The palm tree's right next to it and it's starting to burn a garage, too. I'm going to snap a few pictures then back out."

Sirens could be heard in the distance as Phil pondered his next move.

"All units from One. Did anybody see anything in his hands as he was running?" Silence.

"OK. We know it was him, but nobody saw him by the trash in the alley. That's how the rest of the day's going to go. Four, you and Five stay on him and the rest of you return to your original locations. That was a pretty good perimeter we had. Watch his hands from now on."

"He must have lit the device up before he left the house and carried it with him into the alley," Phil said to Anne. "I wonder how many times he's done that around this neighborhood."

"Probably not too many. It would be noticed wouldn't it?"

"Yeah. If there was a series of fires in the neighborhood, the locals would most likely be on to it. Hang on," Phil said as he reached for the radio. "Two, before you get set up again, drive around the neighborhood and the alleys and see if you can spot any old fires or damage that indicates he's done this before."

"10-4, One."

Phil turned to Anne, "You know how to work this radio?"

"Yeah, I think so," she replied.

Phil handed it to her as he reached under his seat to a small canvas bag he brought along. He pulled out two beer bottles and a small towel. He wiped the outside of the bottles and got out of the car, leaning back into the window, "Pop the horn once if Four comes on the air and says the crook's starting back, OK?"

"Sure, but what..." she said as Phil walked across the street and toward Aaron's. She watched him through her binoculars. He carried the bottles with his fingers jammed down inside the mouth, holding them to his side. He looked back over his shoulder once, crossed the intersection, then slowed slightly as he walked to Aaron's. Phil confidently turned up the walkway leading to Aaron's front porch. As he took the first step to the front door, he bent down and set the bottles on their sides, on the ground next to the steps. He feigned knocking on the front door, in case neighbors watched, then strode confidently back to Anne.

He slipped into the wagon as he heard the radio crackling, "Four, he's moving again."

Phil looked over his shoulder to see the column of smoke had broken up and was turning to steam as Arcadia's fire crews extinguished the small fire. Apparently it hadn't spread to the garage.

"He's southbound on F street crossing major."

Phil turned to Anne, "He's probably going to come back in behind us and right by. If he does, we'll both drop our seats back and stay low as he passes," Phil said as he spoke into the radio. "Three from One, if he comes back down my way, we'll drop out of sight and let you take the eye from us. After he's back at the intersection before his house, give us a couple of clicks on the mic."

"Three, copy."

Seconds later, Aaron turned east and Phil saw him in his rearview mirror two blocks back, "Drop back Anne." They both reclined. Thirty seconds later, they heard the soft footfalls of Aaron's running shoes as he ran past on the opposite side of the street. Shortly, they heard the radio click three times.

Phil raised his head slowly, seeing Aaron running across the intersection. He quickly brought up his binoculars and re-focused as Aaron slowed to a walk in front of the house.

As Aaron walked back and forth, winding down from his run, Phil locked in on Aaron's right running shoe, "Anne, check out his right shoe, it's smudged like the one in the video from 7-11!"

"I see it...but tell me what the bottles are for."

"Watch. Hopefully he'll pick them up, and maybe throw them in his trash can that's by the side of the house."

"And then what?"

"Then we'll have fingerprints, maybe two sets." he said as he watched.

Aaron walked up to the steps and stopped, then reached down and picked up the two bottles, one in each hand.

"All right, all right," Phil whispered. Aaron walked over to his driveway, then out of sight for several seconds. He returned, then fished in the pocket of his shorts and found a key and opened his door. He disappeared inside.

"How the hell did you know he'd do that?"

"I didn't really, but you'll notice he keeps the yard neat and trim; no trash. It just stood to reason that he'd see the bottles and throw them in the nearest trash can," he said proudly. "I put them back out of sight where he probably wouldn't have seen them on his way out. He probably just thinks some kids stuffed them there, at least I hope so."

"One from Three, nice goin...." Berry whispered at Phil's small success.

"Three from One. When he leaves, can you move in and retrieve the beer bottles from the trash? The can's on the west side, just up the driveway under the bushes."

"10-4, One."

Only 15 minutes had passed since Aaron had left the house for his run. Again the group settled in and waited. Thirty minutes passed when the stillness was broken.

"Six here. The crook's come out his back door and he's walking to the garage. He's carrying a small paper bag with him and what looks like a red mechanics rag." The mic stayed opened as Six gave a description of Aaron's actions, "And it looks like...yeah, he's got a small automatic wrapped in the rag," Six said. There was another silence.

"One to all units, be advised; the suspect has a weapon. It's wrapped in a red rag," Phil announced as he did a quick roll call to ensure everyone was aware of the new twist. He was relieved to hear Five was now back on the air.

In seconds, Phil saw the gray Chevy backing into the street. "He's on the street and he'll be heading westbound. We're dropping down. Four, take the eye," Phil said as he and Anne again dropped out of sight.

"He's northbound to the major. Northbound to the major, who's gonna pick him up?" Four said as Phil started up his car.

"Six has him. He's turning west on the major. I've got the eye. Looks like he's headed to the freeway..."

"Three from One, you got the goods from his house?" Phil asked.

"Yeah, One. We got 'em both."

"10-4," Phil responded.

"He's in the left turn bay at the freeway for westbound. Six is going on by him. Somebody pick up the eye."

"Two has him. Two has him. We've got Two cover in front of us at a fresh red," Phil heard as he approached Unit Two at the line of cars waiting at a red light to get onto the freeway. Six drove nonchalantly straight ahead, only to make a quick U-turn two blocks away as Phil followed the others onto the freeway.

"These guys are real pros," Anne said as they accelerated onto the still-congested freeway.

"They work well together," Phil said as they moved westbound at only 35 miles per hour. "Three from One, if we keep going west after the Foothill Freeway transition, pass the rest of us and head for Central Avenue off ramp. I'll call ahead and have a PD unit meet you there and you can give them the bottles. They can race them down to the lab and have the prints matched and you can still be close enough to join back up with us. Copy, Three?"

"We copy. How about if we just go ahead now? Even if he goes the Foothill Freeway, we can still catch up by going up Interstate Two..."

"OK, go ahead. Can you make contact with your dispatchers and arrange the meet with the unit?"

"10-4. You just stay with the caravan and we'll handle it and meet you back on this frequency in about 10 minutes. I'll let you know if we have any problems."

"One, copy. Two, you still have the eye?"

"Two has him, westbound in the number two lane, about six cover."

"How quickly can they match up the prints?" Anne asked.

"If Berry's on top of things, he'll request a priority through his dispatchers and have them within thirty minutes or so. It depends on the availability of the lab technicians. I'd say that the Chief is probably monitoring our transmissions right now and has already made the arrangements."

"If the prints match, do you have the probable cause you need to arrest him before he sets another fire?"

"Definitely. The prints tie him to Trish and marginally to the 7-11 fire where she saw him. It's more than enough, but we'll probably follow him, anyway. A videotape of him casing a store or throwing a device out his window into the brush will really impress a jury, though."

"Phil," she interrupted, "I'd hate to see him hurt somebody else, or you. He's got a gun."

"That puts a different slant on things, but if we're going to get him in the act, we've go to..."

"You said yourself that you would have probable cause with the match on the prints. Don't be Mister Macho. You're in charge here. You can do whatever you want."

Phil didn't answer. He reached down and pulled up his left pant leg to expose his .45 Auto in its bulky ankle holster. The heat didn't allow him to wear a belt holster since that would require a jacket or shirt to cover it. A jacket in this heat would scream that he was a cop. He pulled the cut-down version of the military standby out of its resting place and quickly pressed the small button that dropped the 6-shot clip out. It fell into his lap. He steered with one hand and examined the clip and gun as he alternately looked at the road in front of him and the gun. He said nothing, hoping Anne would see how serious the situation was becoming.

Phil put the clip back in its place and made sure it was seated by banging it on the bottom of the steering wheel. He then stretched his right arm forward and saw that soot and old fire debris from a week ago obliterated part of the three-dot sight system. He wiped the sights across his pants then crammed the weapon back into the holster. He fumbled with the snap and pulled down his pant leg. After a few seconds, he reached across the seat and placed his hand on top of Anne's, resting on her lap. She continued looking forward, but rolled her hand over and his palm now rested against hers. She squeezed it firmly.

"He's now in the number one lane, still westbound at about 50. I need somebody up here to take the eye. I've been here too long and I've only got one cover now."

"Four has the eye. Go ahead and drop back, Two."

Phil looked into his rearview mirror and couldn't see any of the caravan. They blended very well and he, too, decided to drop back somewhat and let the other units move in. They passed the Foothill Freeway transition and Aaron continued westbound. The traffic lightened and they accelerated to 60 miles per hour. The view westward from the freeway was spectacular. The downtown Los Angeles skyline was clearly visible as well as the beach areas beyond. A half dozen jetliners could be seen descending and taking off at L.A. International Airport near the horizon. The Pacific Ocean appeared dark; almost black. The air was crystal clear, the Santa Ana's gusts not yet strong enough to cloud the view with dust.

Two miles later, Aaron took the Glendale Freeway south into Los Angeles. Traffic again slowed as they approached the end of the freeway at Alvarado Street.

"One from Three," Berry suddenly broke in, barely audible.

"One, go ahead."

"We're southbound on the Glendale Freeway crossing San Fernando Road, stuck in traffic. You copy?"

"10-4. Looks like we're headed into Silverlake or maybe Hollywood. We're just off at Alvarado."

"OK, we should be with you in a couple."

Phil knew that with the amount of traffic they were encountering, the surveillance would become difficult. Heavy traffic and traffic lights would no doubt soon separate them.

"Five now has the eye. I've got two cover. We're at a fresh red at Sunset Boulevard...we're now westbound Sunset. Westbound Sunset...He's pulling over mid-block. I have to drive by him. Somebody pick him up."

"Six has him. I'm in front of him. Five, keep going," Phil heard and smiled. Somewhere along the line, the lieutenant had predicted Aaron's path and slipped in front of him, a tactic that only sometimes worked on surveillances. The L.T. was a true vet. The rest of them were left strung out on Alvarado with no parking lanes due to the early morning traffic restrictions. All now had to turn west onto Sunset and drive past Aaron's position, exposing themselves. There was no alternative. Phil was first after Five and both traveled a half-block and pulled to the curb, quickly reaching up to adjust their mirrors to watch as Aaron got out and walked into a liquor store. The other units continued on and turned onto side streets. Aaron returned and got into his car and sat for several minutes.

"He's still sitting in his car playing with something on the seat," Six said. "He's moving, he's moving now. Westbound Sunset." Phil ducked down as Aaron approached, telling Anne to remain upright.

"He's by," she said as Phil moved into traffic.

"One has the eye, still westbound Sunset," he called into the mic. Traffic was lighter on Sunset as it moved through the rundown business districts nearing Hollywood. Phil noticed the winds had died down, but didn't yet feel the need to order the helicopter out. With six units tailing Aaron, coverage was good.

Phil watched as the units fell in behind the gray Chevy. Then he, too, joined the caravan.

"Three, how close are you? We're now westbound on Sunset from Alvarado," Phil quickly broke in.

"One, we're just passing Rampart Boulevard. Should be with you in a couple."

Phil sped up, passing two of the units, since he still had the eye.

"Two from One, can you go ahead and take the eye?"

"Yeah, we got him coming up on Vermont Avenue. He's got a fresh red. We have three cover."

The traffic again got heavy as they approached Western Avenue, the east edge of Hollywood.

"OK, OK. He's signaling left onto Western. I've lost my cover. Two's going on by. Somebody pick him up. He's on a stale green. It's changing....Two's by him..."

188

Phil strained to see the Chevy and sped up. He couldn't see around traffic but suddenly the gray Chevy was seen completing a left turn, the light changing red. No other units got through the light to follow.

"One to units. He's completed his turn southbound on Western. Southbound on Western. Four, can you cut down short of Western and parallel?"

"Yeah, we're doin' it now. Five's with us."

Phil pulled up to the fresh red light and saw Two making a U-turn one block ahead. He couldn't pull up into the crosswalk to see Aaron's car making its southward run. A crowd of transients and alcoholics wandered across in front of Phil.

"We've got a dead end street here. One, Four and Five are delayed."

Phil swore as the light finally changed. Slipping forward, Phil bore into the oncoming lane inch by inch until an old woman in a red Dodge slammed on her brakes. Phil elbowed his way through the lane and edged into the second opposing lane as horns blared at him. Seeing an opening, he sped through as the radio crackled.

"Six has the eye. Two cover. We're still southbound Western, passing Santa Monica Boulevard," the voice calmly monotoned.

Phil looked at Anne, "How the hell did he get up there?" he said as he shook his head and smiled. Looking in his rearview mirror, none of the other units were visible.

"Four and Five where are you?"

"One from Five. We're still trying to get through traffic back here east of Western. Four's on the main frequency trying to raise the dispatcher and get the helicopter airborne."

"10-4, Five. Get up here as quick as you can. Two, you coming?"

"I've caught two reds and am about half-mile behind you. Three just pulled up beside me."

"OK. Six, you still got him?"

"Yeah, Phil. Still got two cover and he's now in the number two lane and slowing down just past Olympic....Shit...."

Silence followed. "Six, you OK?" Silence.

"This is Six. He just turned into a lumberyard or something. I couldn't follow him. It's just south of Olympic. It's not a lumberyard; it's a large hardware store or something with a nursery. I'm parking about a half block south of the location, and I'll be on foot and off the air."

Phil floored the accelerator and the small wagon shot forward. "Phil, we just passed Olympic. He's in this block somewhere," Anne shouted. Phil looked around and the store's driveway suddenly cut to the right.

"That's it. Shit." Phil breathed as be braked and coasted into the crowded parking lot, picking up the radio at the same time. Before he brought it up to his mouth, he checked around for Aaron's car. Not seeing it, he spoke. "One to all units. Address is 511 Western, Drake and Sons Hardware. The suspect's car is...." Phil scanned the lot, "parked on the southeast side, right off the street. I see the L.T. going into the store. No sight of the suspect yet. He may still be in his car. Somebody stay north of the store on Western and the rest of you hang in the area. One's going inside, too, but Anne will be on the air as the eye for now."

Phil pulled into a tight space on the north side of the lot next to a sedan and a small construction truck. Anne brought up her binoculars and scanned the lot for Aaron. "There he is," she said as Phil shut off the car. Whirling around, Phil squinted and barely saw Aaron's car door open over the roofs of several other construction trucks.

"I just saw his head peek up for a second and he got back in, but he left the door open," Anne said. Several seconds passed and Phil saw a small puff of smoke drift out of the car door, curling along and over the roof. He focused his binoculars then spoke.

"Did you see the smoke, Anne?"

He caught sight of her out of his left eye without lowering his binoculars. "Uh-huh," was all she said. Suddenly, Aaron stood up and looked around, closing his car door behind him.

"One to all units, he just lit a cigarette and he's now walking toward the store. One and Six are inside," Phil said as he slipped out the door, glancing at Anne. She raised her hand, fingers out-stretched as he departed.

Walking cautiously, Phil held back as Aaron briskly headed to the main entrance to the huge structure. The main building appeared to be very old with several smaller additions on two sides; one an open-air nursery area, the other held large piles of stacked lumber. Phil spotted a security guard in a uniform at the entrance. He swore, thinking that Aaron surely wouldn't walk past the guard with a device in his hand. A large "NO SMOKING" sign hung beside the entrance. Phil slowed his pace. Aaron continued his brisk walk and cupped his right hand close to his side, turning slightly away from the guard and actually smiling at him as he passed. Phil shook his head and followed Aaron inside, staying back over 50 feet.

As soon as Phil entered, he wished he had asked some of the others to come inside, too. The front part of the main store was a maze of aisles littered with high piles of displayed merchandise. The check-out lines snaked around the piles to his right even at this early hour, contractors and carpenters lined up to pay for their selections. Phil instantly lost sight of Aaron. The lieutenant was nowhere to be seen. He debated going back outside and asking for assistance from the rest of the group, but he then saw Aaron across an aisle mid-store, 40 feet in front of him. Phil moved quickly, running down an empty aisle of nut and bolt displays. As he reached the end, he faced the display, bending down as he peeked around the corner. Aaron was not seen. Phil started to stand up when he caught movement one aisle away, only 10 feet from his stooped position. There was a flash of a white running shoe seen through an open pile of plastic tool boxes. The right shoe was smudged.

The shoes moved away and Phil stepped across the aisle seeing the figure walk toward an open door leading to a cavernous building supply area. Phil sniffed and instantly detected the cigarette. He scanned the displays and saw nothing that would ignite readily. As he walked behind Aaron, he saw tons of other displays with lawn furniture, paper products and even paints waiting to ignite. As he traveled deeper into the structure, Phil felt a chill run down through the sweat on his back. He turned around, hoping to see the lieutenant nearby. As he looked back, Aaron was gone again. Phil sped up and stopped at the door to the huge room. On his left were lattice-work and fencing materials as well as spools of chain links. On his right were pallets covered with plastic trash containers. Beyond that a small sign read BULK PAINT ORDER DESK with an arrow pointing left. Several other aisles ran beyond the paint sign. Displays reached 15' to the ceiling. The height of the displays allowed little light to illuminate the interior aisles of the building. As Phil approached the paint sign, he saw the smaller letters read OPEN 10 A.M. to 4 P. M. Phil cut short of the aisle Aaron entered, finding it deserted like most of the others in this area. Phil glanced at his watch. It was 9:45.

Again he smelled the cigarette smoke, causing him to stop, not wanting to continue to the end of the aisle and risk running into Aaron.

A metallic sound caused Phil to freeze, holding his breath. It sounded a second time before Phil recognized it—the sound of a one gallon metal can being picked up by its side instead of its handle on top. The second sound was of it being released, the slack returning to the metal. In seconds, Phil heard soft footsteps in the next aisle. He stooped down and looked to his right through the bottom row of a stack of cardboard boxes. A figure moved off to the left as another sound was heard. Phil strained to listen and then he saw the glistening liquid dripping off a shelf in the next aisle. He also saw the one gallon can it was coming from. The can, nestled just two feet off the ground, was in the middle of a shelf with fifty or more cans marked PAINT THINNER.

Phil reached down and slid up his pant leg and, in a quick motion, felt the .45 fill his right hand. At the same time he looked to his left and saw Aaron staring at him. Before Phil could say a word, Aaron ran and was out of sight.

"L.T.! Now! Grab him!" Phil shouted, hoping the lieutenant was near enough to hear him. Running around to the next aisle, Phil debated trying to find the device or chasing Aaron. The liquid had already pooled on the floor and there were hundreds of crevices and cracks that the device could have been concealed in.

"Damn. He may not have even set the device down yet," Phil mumbled.

"Phil, where are you?" the familiar officer's voice broke the silence from near the entrance Phil just walked through.

"It's set. He's still in here, stay by the door, L.T.," Phil screamed. Seconds later, Phil heard a huge crash several aisles away.

"I got him. Running back toward you, Phil!"

Wanting to get away from the paint thinner, Phil moved cautiously, his gun extended at a 45-degree angle from his body. He pulled back the hammer on the old military gun, the click echoing through the store.

"What the fuck's goin' on here?" Phil heard a voice say.

"Beat it. Police! Move it and call the cops!" the lieutenant said.

"Let me see some ID or somethin' man," Phil heard the voice respond, answered by the L.T.

"See this fucking gun? Is that enough ID? Move outta here!"

"Call the fire department, too," Phil shouted as he saw Aaron run across the aisle in front of him. He quickly closed the gap and saw that the aisle led to a storeroom along the back wall of the building. A sign above its door said EMPLOYEES ONLY. Phil hesitated, remembering Aaron had been seen with a gun earlier. Aaron's jeans and untucked shirt were enough to cover the small weapon. Phil slipped quickly by the door opening, checking both sides. The room appeared to be an employee lounge area with still another warehouse beyond.

"Shit," Phil breathed. "L.T., I've got him in another storage area back here. He's spilled a bunch of paint thinner and the shit's liable to go off any second. Are you still by the door?"

Phil heard the L.T. curse. "Yeah, I'm still here. What do you need, Phil?"

"Hang on a second." Phil changed sides on the door again. "Stiles, come on outta there. If this thing blows up, you're trapped, too. How about it? Come on out. We got people outside, too."

No response was heard. Phil scanned what little he could see in the warehouse beyond and glanced at his watch. Over 11 minutes had passed

192

since Aaron left his car. The device gives up to 15 minutes before it ignites, Phil theorized.

"L.T., I'm going into this storeroom for a minute. Sound out if you see any fire, OK?"

"Don't be stupid, man. Come on out here by me. He probably can't get out that way, anyhow!"

"It looks like there might be a rear exit or loading dock back here. I don't want this fucker getting away. I'm going in. Stay put," Phil shouted as he slipped into the dingy coffee room. His back slammed against the wall. He worked his way to the door on the opposite end of the tiny room. He stiffened as he saw a light come on in the right side of the warehouse. The piles of storage, here, too, reached the ceiling, prohibiting him from seeing more than a few feet.

Feeling his grip tighten on the .45, Phil leaned into the warehouse and heard movement to his right.

"Stiles...." Phil started to speak as he heard a low whooshing sound behind him.

As he turned, Phil heard the lieutenant scream. "It blew! Come on man."

Turning to his escape route, oily thick black smoke poured into the room. Phil, panic stricken, stepped away from the advancing smoke to the only place he could go; the warehouse where Aaron was hiding. His fear of fire was more than the fear of Aaron's gun.

Keeping his back against the wall, Phil shouted again. "Stiles, it's burning, man!"

"There's no exit here. Everything's locked!" Aaron shouted, startling Phil. Phil froze as he stepped into the aisle with his gun raised. Aaron was only ten feet ahead with his gun pointing too. At the same moment, Phil could see tears streaming down Aaron's face as the smoke and now-tremendous heat slapped against his side near the door. They stood for a second, Aaron's gun dipping slightly, the smoke hiding it briefly. In the next split second, Phil saw Aaron's face change and the gun barrel rising to point at him. Two quick shots exploded from Phil's .45 before he even knew it. Aaron's body dropped to the ground in a pile. Phil turned to his escape route. He dropped to the floor, finding little relief from the ugly black death swirling around him. The heat was unbearable; more than three feet off the ground. Phil crawled across the small room to the door leading into the inferno beyond. Only a minute had passed since the blaze exploded and Phil could now hear other paint thinner cans rupturing from the flames. Phil knew that in seconds, the cans would begin exploding, not just rupturing as the intensity of the fire began to build. The oily death was already entering his lungs, causing him to sway, but Phil knew his only way out was the way he came in. By staying low, he could make out an aisle just four feet outside the door.

Above the sound of the fire, he heard the lieutenant shouting directions to him, in hopes that the noise would lead him to safety. Phil laid his head on the cold cement floor, his gun dropping from his grasp. A blast of heat brought him back from the brink of surrender and the ease with which he found himself giving up. The smoke was stealing his oxygen, causing erratic thoughts. He slipped his feet under his sagging body and looked again at the aisle in front of him. Peering above, he saw silent arms of flame reaching across the opening, spitting their deadly smoke.

The lieutenant and several employees stood in awe of the brilliant orange flames at the rear of the warehouse. The smoke swirled above them and finally dropped to their heads. All were ready to leave when they heard the two gunshots above the sounds of the fire. Two men ran away and one stayed with the Lieutenant as both shouted Phil's name.

They turned to flee when Phil staggered through the clouds of smoke. His hair and clothes were smoldering. He crashed into a tool display, opening a large gash on his head. The men staggered forward, grabbing Phil's arms and dragging him out. The Lieutenant dropped to the floor, pulling them down at the sound of small muffled explosions. They turned to look. A fireball belched from the corner where the fire had started, sending its heat rolling across the ceiling and exploding above them. Embers rained down on their backs, etching small black scars on their clothes. The heat gave the men the incentive they needed to stumble on, Phil's weight almost too much for them. Finally they were met by others. The voracious fire chased them from the store into the parking lot and the bright sun.

Phil was barely able to discern his surroundings. His body tried to suck in the fresh air, but the scum and mucous in his throat, in his lungs caused him to choke and cough. Only after he threw up was he able to finally enjoy the feeling that he was alive. His eyes were swollen shut.

Still groggy, Phil felt smoke again attacking him as he heard voices, "Let's get them back outta here. The whole place is going up." He felt hands all over his body as he was lifted up, again nauseating him. The blasting sun suddenly went out of view as the men laid him against a building in the cool shade. He heard Anne's voice, but didn't have the strength to respond.

22

Phil felt a damp cloth wiping his face and mouth. His mind focused on its trail as it moved around his head. Only then did he begin to feel the pain of his burned ears. At once he winced and said, "What the are you doing?" His head cleared as he heard more sirens and people talking around him. His eyes were still swollen. He felt another, heavier pain on the top of his skull. Another wet cloth was being held there.

"Phil, can you hear me?" He heard Anne's voice. He still couldn't respond, intent on evaluating his injuries and oblivious to what was happening around him. He could smell the acrid smoke, even through his ravaged nostrils and throat. Its stench caused him to cough, again bringing up blackened mucus. He felt hands turning him on his side as the cloth wiped away the soot.

"Phil!" he again heard her say. He opened his eyes slightly and, through the slits, he could see her with her arms extended, wiping his face. It seemed like he hadn't seen her in weeks. His mind was still fogged. He turned his head to his right and could see the flames and feel the heat from the burning store. Heat-weakened plate glass dropped from the windows, startling him. His contracting muscles caused the arms cradling him to tighten their grip. Only then did he realize someone was holding him.

Phil's eyes began to focus and he saw the scraggly face of the Lieutenant inches from his own.

"Get a shave, L.T.," Phil mumbled. The Lieutenant squeezed Phil slightly, patting his arm where his hands joined to hold him. Turning again, he saw several fire units in the process of laying hose lines to attack the fire.

"I shot him." They looked at him solemnly.

"Twice, or did he get a round off at you?" the Lieutenant asked softly.

"Twice. He's dead." Phil mumbled. Anne cupped his cheek.

"One way or the other," she said as she turned to look at the flaming building. They all three looked at it, smoke and flames belching out the front display windows.

"It's burned through the roof toward the back, Phil," a voice was heard from behind. Ash Nolan leaned forward and Phil nodded in recognition. Ash reached his hand to Phil's, squeezing it gently. "You always told me that the fire burns through the roof above the points of origin didn't you?"

"Yeah, I can see it in back," Phil wheezed, looking at a separate column of smoke being pushed skyward beyond the front of the store nearest them. "Watch. The smoke in front'll die down in a second," he paused. "The fire in the warehouse is gonna suck everything back toward the origin..." he again went through a fit of coughing, again spitting up phlegm.

"Take it easy, man" the lieutenant soothed. All eyes were on the growing fire.

"Let's back up some more," Anne volunteered.

A line of gleaming red trucks arrived, along with an ambulance. Phil was half carried and half dragged to the street, near the parked station wagon. The ambulance was directed to Phil just as two firefighters arrived with oxygen from a nearby engine. They slipped the oxygen mask was over Phil's face. One of the young firefighters patted Phil's shoulder before he raced back with the other to resume their fight.

"Smoke's dropping down in front," Ash said as the paramedics leaped from their ambulance. His head was pounding from the movement. He continued to suck oxygen from the mask covering his mouth.

"What's wrong with my head?" Phil mumbled through the mask, reaching for the wet cloth being held by Anne.

"You got a pretty good knock from something as we were bringing you out," the Lieutenant said. "I think you mighta' banged into something just before you ran into us. This guy here stayed with me until the last second and helped me drag your dead butt out!" he said pointing to a burly employee nearby.

Phil lifted his fist up toward the smiling man. "Thanks," Phil said.

A young paramedic evaluated Phil's injuries, and worked to stop the bleeding head. Everyone stayed quiet while they labored. A blood pressure cuff was strapped on his arm, and leads were attached to his chest as they fed Phil's vital signs into a monitor to a base station hospital. "Male adult, 45 years, victim of smoke inhalation and a 4-inch laceration on the head. Respiration's shallow; 26. Patient has rales bilaterally and both lower lobes. Pulse rapid, 108," she spoke into her radio. "BP 140 over 80, no other signs of trauma and pupils are equal and reactive." She glanced at her partner. His eyes were wide as he stared at the Lieutenant's side and Ash beside him. "You guys cops?" he asked.

"Yeah. Work on him. Make him better," The Lieutenant said in a low growl.

"He's in pretty good shape despite his outward appearance. How long was he in the smoke?" the female paramedic asked.

"Only about three or four minutes, but he was right near where it started and the shit was really thick. He crashed into something trying to get out," the lieutenant said.

"His color's returning and his respiration is coming around nicely, but he'll need some stitches on his scalp. Anybody want to ride in with us?" she said, looking around.

"I will," Anne said as a gurney was wheeled over to them.

Phil reached up and pulled the oxygen mask down, "Can't you just patch me up here? I wanna examine the body before it's pulled out."

"What? There's somebody still in there?" the female paramedic said.

The Lieutenant spoke. "Yeah, but he was shot twice. He's gone for sure by now," he said, looking at the inferno. A large amount of steam emitted from the front windows. A line of L.A. firefighters disappeared into the building, fighting the beast and knocking it down aggressively as they advanced. The column of smoke blasted out of the rear part of the store through the openings in the roof, still thick and black, being pushed aloft by the flames in the warehouse area. "It'll be a while before you can get into there anyway, Phil. I'll be the guy in charge here now, and we'll try and wait until you get back. Berry and Martinez are searching Stiles' car right now so you just go and get patched up."

Phil nodded.

As he was being loaded into the ambulance, Phil heard Ash's radio crackle. "Any unit, Hollywood, come in."

Ash keyed his radio, "This is Two, go ahead."

"Give us an update, please. We've been trying to raise you since you said the store was on fire!"

Ash responded, highlighting what happened in the past fifteen minutes, ending with Phil's being transported and the fact that the suspect was dead and still in the store.

Phil tried to take a deep breath at the end of Ash's transmission, but launched into a fit of coughing that fouled his oxygen mask, himself and the young, wide-eyed paramedic tending his head wound.

As the ambulance pulled back onto Western Avenue, Phil raised his head slightly and looked at the burning building behind. Steam was rising from the hole in the roof at the rear of the warehouse. A new column rose on the south side of the store as firefighters succeeded in cutting more ventilation holes in the maze of roofs covering the huge building.

"It'll be hours before they get that thing knocked down," Phil said as he lay back down.

The ride to the hospital took only minutes. A doctor met them at the emergency room entrance and talked with him and Anne as he was wheeled into a gleaming cubicle. An IV that he'd had in his arm on the ride was removed and re-inserted as soon as he was transferred to a table, causing him more pain than the burned ears and laceration combined.

Anne was ushered out of the treatment room immediately and slipped back in after twenty minutes when the doctors left him. She peeked in at first, checking the room, then rushed to his side while his eyes were still closed.

"Hey, how're you doing?" she whispered, testing his level of consciousness. He stirred, opening his still-swollen eyelids, smiling slightly.

"Not too bad. You still here?"

She squeezed his hand. "Where do you think I'd be?"

"I figured you'd be back at the hardware store trying to adjust the loss or something," he whispered.

She ignored the jab. "The Lieutenant came by. He said that the fingerprints on the beer bottle from Stile's house matched the prints from Trish's apartment. There's no doubt he's the one."

"Yeah, but we can't clear the fire cases yet; only the attempted murder. What'd they find in his car?" Phil asked.

"Not much. It was pretty clean. Whatever he used to make the devices was probably with him when he walked into the store and..." she stopped.

"How long have I been here? I want to go back and check the body."

"Just relax, Phil. You've only been here a half hour." She brought her face close to his, kissing his cheek. "Sergeant Berry and Martinez are getting a telephonic search warrant for Stile's house, and the Lieutenant and the others are working with the L.A. arson detectives on preserving the fire scene. They'd like you to be there, but the doctor says he doesn't recommend it."

"I'm feeling pretty good. Get him in here."

Anne disappeared for several minutes, returning with the medic.

"I understand you're adamant about leaving, Captain," the Doctor said.

"Yeah, I don't feel too bad and this is a major case."

"I understand. Give me your supervisor's name and number. You are a worker's comp. case, now, and I have to have some higher authority to release you."

Phil gave him Chief Harris' name and work number. As the doctor walked out of the treatment room, Phil pulled off the paper blanket covering him and swung himself to a sitting position. A nurse stood in the doorway watching him. "The doctor thought you might try that. Here, let me help you," she said as she moved to pull the IV from his arm.

"Thanks," Phil smiled at her.

"The call's a formality. You can leave whenever you want, Officer…"

"Officer? Who told you I was a cop?"

"Well, you had a holster on your ankle…."

"Oh, yeah. I'm with the fire department," he replied as he tested his legs. His strength had returned, and only his head and ears throbbed. His chest still rattled as he breathed, but the nausea had left him.

"Okay. Let's go, Anne. Do we have a ride?"

"Yes. The L.T. sent one of the surveillance units down to stand by."

They drove the short distance to the fire and were delayed by the heavy traffic being routed around the area. A motor cop delayed them even longer trying to get a supervisor to approve their entry.

Phil, exasperated, waited until the cop walked away to a parked police car. "Just drive on through, Anne, this jerk-off can't do anything, anyway. Damn cops."

Anne smiled and accelerated forward on Western Avenue, the voice of the large cop bellowing behind them.

The broad boulevard was devoid of traffic. Only police and fire vehicles were seen. A few engines were backed into the curb opposite the fire and several command vehicles were in the middle of the street. The surveillance team huddled in the shade of a ladder truck, sipping cold drinks from Styrofoam cups. Phil slowly brought himself out of the tiny 300SX, his joints aching and his head throbbing. Shirtless after having the doctor cut it off for his treatment, he looked around for his station wagon. "Anne, where's the wagon? I need that small canvas bag that's in there."

"I'll get it, Cap," one of the young narcs said as he ran across the street. The front of the store emitted very little smoke and only steam could be seen rising from the back.

An L.A. Deputy Chief walked over to Phil. "Fred Ramón," he said extending his hand to Phil and shaking it warmly. "How ya feelin'?"

"I understand you were involved with this. Your men here," he said gesturing toward the group, "said we should wait for you for an explanation. I've got my arson guys here and their boss, Chief Miles, is also on his way. Can you brief me a little since it'll be a while before everyone's here? I understand there's a body inside, also."

"Yes, there is. He's an arson suspect we tailed here from Arcadia. He set the fire then we both got trapped as it flashed over." Phil stopped as an L.A.P.D. Captain walked up. The Deputy Chief guided the Captain to the side and filled him in before walking back to Phil and Anne.

"Captain Devane, this is Langtry, right?" the Chief queried as they shook hands.

Phil repeated the brief scenario to the Captain and added the fact that the suspect had been shot.

"Shot? The fire didn't kill him?" The cop asked, his mouth hanging open.

"That's right. I was getting ready to get outta the place when the crook showed himself. He was pointing a small auto at me. Didn't say a thing and started to lower it when a cloud of smoke blew around us. When I could make him out again, the gun was pointed at my face," Phil paused. "Then I fired twice. One hit his chest and the other smacked him about here as he fell." He pointed to his left cheek. Phil turned to his team. "Do they know anything else, guys?" he asked.

"Nothing else, Phil," the L.T. spoke.

Looking back at the Captain and Chief, Phil spoke slowly, "The dead guy, the arsonist, is a fireman..."

"Shit," the two men said in unison.

"Yours, Chief," Phil said solemnly, holding the man's gaze. The Chief walked back to his command post, picking up a cellular phone.

"Langtry, I'm going to contact our Officer Involved Shooting Team to come out here, but first, I've got to have your weapon. It's our shooting policy," the Captain said.

"Where's my gun, L.T.?" Phil said.

"I don't know. I don't think you had it when we dragged you out. It must still be inside..."

"How about your business card or some ID for now. Have you contacted your department yet?"

Phil handed the cop a sweat-soaked business card from his pocket as the narc returned and dropped the canvas bag at his feet. Phil reached in and brought out a shirt, slipping it on as the Captain pondered his next question.

After waiting for twenty minutes in the shade, several other fire and police officials arrived, each walking over to Phil to ask questions. Annoyed, he asked them to wait until everyone got together so he didn't have to repeat his story. He was tired and irritable. He rested his canvas bag in his lap and tried to think of something else.

Two L.A. arson investigators dressed in dark blue jump suits wandered over to Phil, quietly sitting next to him so as not to be seen by the fire officers at the command post.

Phil recognized both and followed them to the rear of the ladder truck, away from the others.

"How ya feeling, man? Can we talk?" the older of the two, Marty McGuire, asked.

Phil smiled and shook their hands. "Yeah. Let's make it quick."

McGuire spoke first. "We were just inside in the back half of the building. One of your team said we had a body inside and said you'd been tailing this guy…"

"Right, he's one of your firemen; a guy named Aaron Stiles." The two L.A. guys looked at each other in amazement.

"I don't know him, but there's over four thousand guys in our department."

Phil interrupted before they could ask anything else. "We had a shootout as the fire broke out, and he's down in the back in what looked like a loading area and warehouse. I know this is your turf, but I want to help you locate the body…."

"I got no problem with that, Phil. My boss just got here and I'll just run it by him and we can start. The crews have pretty well knocked down the fire in the back and they're just clearing the smoke out now. Some of the roof's still intact. Have you got any turnouts or a helmet with you?"

"No. Nothing. Can I borrow some?" Phil asked.

"Wait here for a minute and I'll clear it with the Chief. I'm sure they want to clean this up as soon as possible."

Less than a minute later, the Lieutenant and Anne joined Phil.

"Big problem brewing over at the CP, Phil," the Lieutenant said shaking his head. Before he could finish, he heard voices rising above the sounds of the engines pumping nearby. McGuire reappeared, slightly red-faced.

"Phil, the Brass wants a briefing before we do anything. I tried to get 'em to let us get started first, but they want to start covering their bases, I guess."

"Let's do it and get it over with, Mac. If they start leaning toward keeping me out of there, will you get me in the back after I slip away?"

"Yeah. If it gets too heavy, just stride off back here and we'll somehow sneak you around."

"Thanks, pal," Phil said as they approached the big Chevy Suburban serving as the command post. The earlier crowd of fifteen people milling around the CP was now whittled down to the police Captain, a lieutenant and two deputy chiefs. The Arson Battalion Chief lingered nearby.

Phil gave a very brief overview of the facts of the case leading up to the surveillance as everyone listened. As Phil talked, the radio chatter on the fire ground settled down, allowing him to speed to the final aspects of the case. He finally told them of the selection of Aaron as a suspect and the events that occurred in the store just over two hours before. As Phil's explanation ended, McGuire immediately stepped in and told the group that it was now imperative that the body be located and evidence seized before it was destroyed by the firefighters during their overhaul.

One chief and the police Captain tried to speak at once, the Cop winning out. "Langtry, I'll need to have one of our shooting team with you as you process your scene. We need those two guns recovered." Phil nodded and the shooting team representative was waved over from a nearby unmarked police car. The man, about 40, was dressed in a tan suit and wore a solid brown tie, his shoes immaculate.

"Mac. You got another set of..." Phil coughed uncontrollably for several seconds, spattering the ground with the black phlegm. His head throbbed as his lungs tried to expel every piece of sooty gunk lining their walls. The pain brought him to his knees as McGuire supported him.

"I'm okay Mac," Phil said. He wheezed as he got to his feet.

"You got some more turnouts for this guy?"

"Yeah. We can borrow some boots and a helmet from one of the rigs."

Staggering to the surveillance team, Phil laughed, finding the cops sucking down doughnuts from a nearby Winchell's. He stepped beside Anne and asked them all to join him at the rear of the store while he located Aaron's body.

The warehouse and loading dock showed few signs of the intense fire. Heat and smoke had blistered paint above the two huge roll-up aluminum doors, but it was obvious that the doors were closed during the fire, blocking any escape. Early in the fire, the majority of the fire, heat

202

and smoke had followed the easiest vent, the hole that burned through the roof above the paint thinner storage area.

The firefighters had cut triangular-shaped breeches in each of the two roll-up doors, their charged hose lines snaking through the openings. Several exhausted firefighters reclined against a parked trailer, their water-laden coats lying nearby.

McGuire, his partner, Phil, and the quiet cop donned helmets, gloves and heavy boots before climbing through the triangular openings. There was still some heat inside, but, surprisingly, little fire damage near the doors. Their flashlights speared the darkness of the cavernous structure, the beams occasionally brightening as small smoldering masses of material released smoke, the light reflecting in the haze. As they advanced deeper into the structure, the ventilation holes, cut by the firefighters, allowed beams of light to filter down onto them.

McGuire spoke into his radio, asking for a ladder truck crew to bring in lights to assist them in their search. The truck crew brought along blowers to vent the smoke and heat. As they waited, they felt a welcome breeze coming from the loading dock.

With the lights in place, Phil surveyed the warehouse. He could barely make out the small doorway leading into the employee lounge directly in front of him. He started moving toward it, then stopped, remembering that Aaron had fallen between him and the doorway. As they neared, he could see where the fire had blasted through the lounge and the flames had etched a V-shaped char pattern around the upper half of the doorway. The fire, slamming through the opening, had started down the aisle and burned through the sides of the stored cardboard boxes. The boxes, stacked fifteen feet to the ceiling, had dropped much of their contents as the flames stripped away their sides. Melted plastic, charred pallets and roof beams littered the aisle. Small wisps of smoke snaked upward through the tangle.

"Let's move around to the next aisle and come in from the doorway. That's where I shot it out with him. I don't want to step on the remains," Phil muttered to the others. They picked their way over an even larger pile of debris in the next aisle. More shelving had weakened from the fire and dropped a huge pile of roofing materials onto the floor. The stinking mess was three feet deep. Suddenly the weight of McGuire's boot gave way and sunk into a stack of deep, smoldering asphalt shingles.

He cursed and quickly withdrew his heavy rubber boot, followed by a flash of flame as the mess found oxygen through the breech. "Engine 35, bring in a small hand line! We've got several areas that need to be overhauled!" he shouted into his radio.

"Thirty-five copy," it crackled back at him. In seconds, several more flashlight beams pierced the darkness near the loading dock as four firefighters leapt at the chance to be near the discovery of the body. They brought forward the small hose line as the flames began to spring through the pile and the smoke became almost too thick to breath. Several seconds of an open nozzle knocked the flames and smoke down. They again moved forward.

Running into the lounge's wall, they turned right, again stepping over twisted steel shelving material and melted plastic.

"Okay, let's start pulling some of this outta here, Mac" Phil coughed and wheezed.

"Phil, why don't you just step over there and let us pull the shit out. You shouldn't even be in here without a breathing apparatus."

Phil complied and stepped forward to stand in the doorway with his back to the fire's origin, as he had done when he faced Aaron.

Looking forward, he tried to remember how far away he was from the barrel of Aaron's gun. He looked down at where Aaron's body should be. There was over two feet of debris covering the area.

A flash of light startled Phil as McGuire's partner snapped a picture of the area. In minutes, the other two investigators had cleared a path to the doorway. McGuire looked at Phil. "You okay?"

"Yeah. Right there where that yellow pile starts is where he should be." Phil said pointing. "And on the other side of this employee lounge, and to the left about twenty feet is where the paint thinner storage area was. It shouldn't be too hard to pinpoint the origin." Phil stepped forward and helped them as they passed back pieces of debris. One final pile of plastic had to be pried up with a shovel, its melted mass gripping the cement floor. A greenish liquid dribbled as the mass was picked up.

"Looks like anti-freeze. Yeah, see there. One of the yellow jugs is still intact there." McGuire said. "But no body yet, Phil"

They worked their way forward scattering debris and stopping only so a photo could be taken occasionally.

"I don't fucking understand. We shoulda' found him by now, Mac."

They were now a full ten feet beyond where he should have been located when Mac shouted, "Here, look!" He stepped aside. "Blood maybe?"

A deep red stain trailed trough the wet blackness of the water pooled on the floor. "Look back here, too, where the anti-freeze was."

"The guy must've still been alive after you dumped him, Phil!"

They moved slowly forward, the debris now only about a foot deep. "Here, a shoe. I think it's him," McGuire said as he dropped to his knees. "Yeah, here's the ankle bone…" His voice trailed off as he stood back up. "Take some pictures, Eddie."

The flash washed the narrow aisle in light as Phil moved forward and assisted in carefully pulling debris off the body. No one spoke as the charred flesh was exposed from the back of Aaron's feet and calves. Blood had stained the area around the still form, trailing behind, its color darkened from the heat.

"He's laying face down as if he was crawling away from the flames. His jeans are still intact near the floor. Looks like the bulk of his body and the dampness of the blood kept the cloth from burning," Phil said as he, too, got down on his knees.

The heat had attacked the body's dorsal side. The jeans burned away, leaving the skin exposed to the full heat. Skin sizzled then shrank from the flames, ultimately popping open like a sausage to lay open the muscle, tendons and finally the bones.

McGuire and Phil carefully removed melted matter and ash, moving up the body, moving around the remains of Aaron's wallet, lying against his backside. They worked like archaeologists brushing away layers of matter to expose their find.

Looking above and around, Phil theorized that the flames never actually touched the body. The storage at the floor level showed only mild burning, indicating that the massive wave of heat blowing out of the lounge and adjacent warehouse attacked the body, not the fire itself. "He was literally cooked by radiant heat!" Phil offered.

"Yeah, look at this stuff," Mac said pointing to the pallets of boxed materials. "They're hardly touched down this low."

After the body had been cleaned of its ashy covering, they stepped back and allowed more pictures to be taken. The body was on its stomach, the arms drawn up under it as if about to start a push-up. The legs were slightly askew, locked in place with the final effort to push itself forward and away from the flames. Aaron's head was lying on its left side. The right was a blackish-red gelatinous mass, where the bullet had exited. The 230-grain hollow point had not struck a vital zone. The mass of blood was from the chest wound, the heart pumping its last of the vital liquid before it stopped or the smoke anesthetized Aaron into surrender.

Phil saw a small yellow dollop of melted plastic cling to the remains of Aaron's jeans, just under his left side. "What's this?" he said as he bent down. "Mac, can you lift him up a little so I can get this? Hold on. Take a picture, Eddie."

The flash blinded Phil for a second. He looked back to find McGuire raising Aaron's left side with his bare hands, his grip slipping slightly when remaining skin separated from the muscle. Phil pulled on the small piece of yellow plastic, the material clinging to the jeans.

"It's the remains of a cigarette lighter," Phil said as he saw the tiny striking wheel of the mechanism. He pulled a little more and the white cotton-like material of the pocket came with it, exposing the edge of a hard box of cigarettes, wet and darkened with blood and sooty water.

The flash went off before Phil even asked for it. He turned his face away to avoid the flash and smell of singed flesh trapped beneath the body. McGuire handed Phil a small plastic bag and the lighter and cigarettes were slipped inside. Phil handed the bag back to him.

"It's your case, Phil."

"Not really. It's your jurisdiction. Besides, when I get outta here, I'm going straight home to crash for a couple of days. I sure won't feel like booking evidence," Phil responded.

"'Suppose you're right. You holding up okay?"

"Yeah. Just getting real tired. The last couple of days have been pretty wild."

"I can imagine. I still can't believe this guy's a fireman. What went wrong with him?" McGuire asked.

"I don't have any idea. We just discovered who he was yesterday and haven't had time to go into his background. I imagine you and your department will handle that."

"Yeah. It's gonna be tough. I've never heard of anything like this. Cops go bad all the time, but not firemen."

"Mac, let's roll him over the other way and check his other pockets," Phil said as his eyes met the shooting team Cop, standing several feet away with a nauseated look on his face.

"You're really supposed to wait for the coroner before you search the body like that, guys," the cop said.

Phil took a deep breath and looked at McGuire. "He's right, Mac, but, Officer, his gun's not here with him. He probably dropped it back there when I shot him. Why don't you see if you can find it?"

"Okay," was all the cop said as he walked back to the doorway and began moving debris around.

"Thanks," Phil called in the cop's direction.

"I'll pick him up, Mac. You check his front pocket."

Phil grunted as he lifted the now stiff body, staying frozen in its position as he shifted it.

"What the hell is this doing here?" McGuire said as he reached toward the chest area instead of the jean pocket." Phil watched as McGuire picked up a small gooey mass and lifted it up, several trails of spider web-like strings stretching out behind it.

"It's a tube of glue, Phil. It was in his shirt pocket!"

"He used the glue to make his devices. The cig would burn down to it and ignite whatever was around. Sometimes he'd glue coins to it, too. The coins would give it enough weight to be tossed out a car window while he was driving." Phil said.

"Wait a minute. We've had several major brush fires with that kind of device over the past couple of years. It was one of our own firemen?"

"No doubt it was him, Mac. Let's turn him over again so I can check his other shirt pocket. Why don't you package that glue first? We might be able to match it up to other devices and solidify this caper."

McGuire quickly whipped out another plastic bag, slipping the glue into it as more photos were taken.

The burned body was again lifted, exposing the unburned front of Aaron's shirt. Phil reached down and tried to enter the soggy pocket, finally pulling the entire shirt away from the singed flesh so McGuire could lower the heavy stiff.

Phil leaned back against a metal support for a shelf behind him. He felt two small lumps in the pocket of Aaron's shirt. Peeling the pocket open, he peered inside, then looked up at McGuire, smiling.

"What?" Mac asked.

Phil reached in, then withdrew his hand as he looked up at Eddie, poised with his camera. The camera flashed as Phil held the pocket open for the camera's lens. Afterward, he again reached in and delicately brought out two of the soggy, yet intact, devices. Phil sighed.

"That's it. It's him, Mac. This clears a whole bunch of cases and maybe a couple of fatalities. I'd like to keep two devices and take them out to show my guys. Okay?"

"You got it. Me and Eddie'll stay here and wait for the coroner and help the cop find the guns."

"Okay. If I dropped my gun, it's probably about fifteen feet back, into the lounge there, near the doorway leading into that other display area where the fire started. I just can't really remember." Phil dropped his head slightly, his eyes beginning to dampen as the day's events began to catch up with his emotions. He stood abruptly and walked back out to the loading dock.

As he emerged, he looked to the west, his eyes adjusting to the bright sun. The sky was crystal clear. A small amount of smog to the south was chased away by the slight mid-morning breeze. He located Anne among the surveillance team reclining in the shade of the trailer. Their discussion stopped and all heads turned toward Phil, framed by the triangular shaped cut in the loading dock door.

He held up the small bag containing the two devices. At the same time, he brought up his right hand and made a fist, the thumb pointed skyward as he shook his head up and down, signaling the end of their task.

As he stood, he looked beyond the low trees lining the store property and saw a brownish-white column of smoke pushing above the distant Santa Monica Mountains and his slight smile faded. His shoulders dropped and he simply shook his head and smirked as Anne walked to his side, slipping her arm around his waist.

THE END

A Final Word from the Author

Subsequent to my arrest in 1991, I spent months in various jails awaiting trials. To fill my time, I started to write a sequel to Points of Origin. Using the same characters of Phil, Anne, Ash, and others, I picked up the story a month after the fatal Hollywood hardware store fire encounter in chapter 22.

Fully expecting exoneration in the first trial, I still thought I could get published. Convicted in July 1992, I was devastated and lay down my pen to work on the next arson trial in Los Angeles.

Financially forced into a bad decision to accept a plea bargain to avoid the second trial, I caved in and that resolution opened the door to a final indictment for arson/murder in 1998. Again the three sentences excerpted from Points, and highlighted in trial, convicted me wrongfully. The second paragraph of chapter six refers to an ice cream cone bought for a three-year-old who perishes in a fire. I based this scenario on a real fire, but the ice cream reference was pure fiction. A prosecutor later manipulated an interview to fit this "evidence" from my manuscript. As a father, I took my toddlers to stores and markets many times. I bought my fidgety kids ice cream to distract them while shopping frequently. I put this in my manuscript. Imagine a jury's reaction to a 72-year-old witness mimicking my manuscript and "confirming" the prosecutor's theory I was actually next to the child and his grandparents as they discussed buying a treat just minutes before they perished in a very real fire.

The other "evidentiary" sentence is the final statement in chapter six. Again, the look the jury gave me when this passage was read to them convinced me the death penalty was definitely in play. In reality, the sixth chapter's last sentence was based on my writing instructor's lessons: "Make your antagonist, the bad guy in your novel, as mean, deceitful, and sociopathic as possible; make your readers hate him..." So I did. The jury, by then, believed I was the arsonist who killed the little boy and that final sentence was my own contemptible uttering.

These issues and the entire case story is revealed in my autobiography, Points of Truth... Revelations of "...The Most Prolific Serial Arsonist of the 20th Century", available from Infinity Publishing.

John L. Orr P-13502
POB 5007 D5-219
Calipatria, CA 92233-5007
August 2007

CPSIA information can be obtained at www.ICGtesting.com
Printed in the USA
LVOW10s2053090516

487361LV00028B/715/P